BETTING ON HOPE

Also by Kay Keppler

Loving Lucy

Zero Gravity Outcasts

Christmas in Caterwaul Creek

Reading Gregory

On a Wing and a Prayer

The FBI series

No Margin for Error

No Time to Spare

Kay Keppler

BETTING ON HOPE

ISBN: 978-0-9848211-1-2

Special thanks to Beth Barany, Patricia Simpson, and Laura McClure—the best beta readers a person could ever have

Chapter 1

Hope McNaughton stood in her family's shabby kitchen and fingered the heavy, embossed envelope that she'd found in their mailbox on her way home from work. The envelope bore the return address of a local law firm, and in her experience, good news did not arrive in envelopes from law firms. So as Hope looked out the window at the sandy soil and scrubby grass that stretched across the Nevada high plain, she saw instead a dark and slippery slope plunging into an abyss.

Maybe if I throw it away, nothing will happen, Hope thought. *No one has to know.*

But of course she wasn't that childish. She was an intelligent, responsible adult, the chief financial officer of a software company. For crying out loud, *she was an MBA*.

Hope dropped the letter on the table like the hot potato it was and went to change out of her suit, nylons, and pumps into jeans, tee-shirt, and boots. Then she grabbed a few pampered but imperfect organic carrots that her younger sister Faith had grown in her greenhouse and, tucking the letter into her pocket, headed out to the barn where her mother would be mucking out the horses' stalls.

The doors to the barn were wide open, letting in fresh air and sunshine. As Hope entered, smelling the sweet hay and earthy aroma of the horses, she could see Suzanne at work. In the soft light of the state-of-the-art barn, her mother didn't look much older than the eighteen-year-old Vegas showgirl she'd been when she'd caught Derek McNaughton's eye thirty-two years before. Time had etched a few laugh lines around her eyes and slightly thickened the body that had brought Derek to his knees, but she still had the grace and flair of a girl. *Mom hasn't lost it*, Hope thought. *And I never had it.* Hope looked like her father. Not that she'd ever see him again.

Suzanne straightened up when she saw Hope and smiled at her older daughter. "Hi, Sweetie. How was your day?"

Hope smiled and grabbed a pitchfork. "Just the usual. You got a scary letter in the mail, though."

"I got a scary letter? What did it say?"

"Sheesh, Mom, I didn't read it," Hope said, handing her mother the envelope. "I brought it out with me, though. Just in case some long-lost Irish uncle died and left you his string of thoroughbreds."

"Oh, right. My long-lost Irish uncle. That must be it."

Hope grinned, breaking apart a hay bale and tossing a flake into each stall.

"I'll bring in the horses while you find out about Uncle Sean's spread," she said as her mother tore open the envelope.

Hope went out to the pasture and climbed the white board fence. Three horses stood idly under the trees, dozing and twitching their tails. Banjo, her favorite, ambled over to say hello. He put his nose on her shoulder and exhaled, blasting her neck with a gust of warm air and leaving a mucousy drool on her shirt.

"Hey there," Hope said, stroking his neck. She'd owned the gelding for five years, and he'd always been friendly and well-mannered, which was more than she could say about any of her boyfriends in the last five years.

"Mom got a letter from a law firm," she told the horse. "It'll be bad."

Banjo's ears pricked forward.

"Eviction notices, divorce papers, bankruptcies—that stuff means letters from law firms. Trust me, Banjo, you don't want to get a letter from a law firm."

Banjo shook his head, shooing a fly that had bothered him.

"Now, if I were a horse, somebody would give me a carrot," Hope continued. She reached into her pocket and took out the carrot that he knew was there but was too polite to demand. Banjo took the carrot delicately from her hand, tossing his head to show his approval. She patted him on the neck.

"Somebody would give me a carrot and pet me, and everything would be good."

Banjo turned his head into her hand.

"If I were a horse, I'd marry you," Hope said, the letter weighing heavily on her. "You've got everything going for you. You're good looking but not flashy, and you're loyal to the bone. And you don't seem to be crazy about sports. Well, maybe the Kentucky Derby. But that's only once a year, so I could deal with that."

Banjo shifted his weight, swishing his tail.

"But as it is, our love is doomed."

I must be nuts, talking to a horse. Hope stroked Banjo, feeling the sun heat her back. But at least it's cheap therapy.

The other two horses, sensing treats, started over to the fence. Hope dug out the other two carrots and gave one each to Blondie, the shy, elderly Palomino mare they'd had since Hope was thirteen, and Ralph, their goofy gelding. Blondie took her carrot and turned away to eat it in privacy, and Ralph took his with a little two-step sideways dance. Hope felt a rush of affection for the animals. When she'd left the office today, she'd wanted to ride Banjo out through the canyon, up into the hills. She wanted to hear the creak of the saddle and smell the mesquite and horse, breathe the warm, dry air. See the distance.

Now that the letter had come, though, she needed to

stick around to do damage control. If controlling the damage was possible.

She jumped off the fence and opened the gate to the barn.

"Time for supper, guys," she said as she led Banjo inside. "If the letter's really bad, I'll give you a little extra grain tonight. We all have to keep our strength up."

Ralph and Blondie followed them into the barn and turned into their stalls. Hope gave each horse a small measure of oats, then closed and latched the stall doors. Everybody slurped their water and munched their hay, settling down.

Then Hope looked for her mother.

Suzanne sat on a hay bale, leaning back against an empty stall. Her face was ashen. The letter had slipped through her fingers and lay on the floor.

Hope went over and sat next to her. Picked up the letter. Read it. And felt her world collapse beneath her feet.

Back from the barn, Suzanne went upstairs to shower and Hope called the lawyer. The letter was signed by Joseph Sharp, and when he answered the phone, his voice was reedy and thin. Not a good sign, Hope thought, not sure what a good sign would be.

"We got your letter today, Mr. Sharp," she said, "and we don't understand it."

"I have the documents right here, Ms. McNaughton." Papers rustled on the other end of the phone. "Indeed, Mr. McNaughton told me that he thought you would call."

"Yes, well, people who are cheated and lied to tend to get curious," Hope said, anger spiking against her father. He couldn't talk to her, but he could talk about her to the lawyer? "People who are forced off their land might complain. No wonder he thought I'd call."

"Yessss. Well. I assure you everything is in order."

"How could my father lose the ranch?" Hope asked.

"My parents bought it outright twenty-two years ago. There's no mortgage. Just tell me what happened, Mr. Sharp. That's what we'd like to know. Because you've told us to get out in a month, and after twenty-two years, that's just a little sudden."

Joseph Sharp cleared his throat. "Mr. McNaughton lost the property in a card game."

Hope closed her eyes. Of course that's how Derek lost it. She should have guessed. Her father wasn't the worst card player in the world, but he never knew when to quit. When his chips were gone, he'd bet anything—the car, the house, his kids' college educations. He just kept playing, expecting his luck to turn.

And now he'd made his family's luck turn, as well.

"The title was transferred in my office two days ago," Joseph Sharp said now.

"Who was the winner?"

"I don't know with whom Mr. McNaughton played. The owner on the transfer agreement is a Delaware corporation, Passaic Holdings."

"Can we make an offer on the place?"

Joseph Sharp sighed. "I don't think the ranch is in your price range."

"My parents paid a hundred thousand for it," Hope said. "Although it must be worth more now."

"A lot more." The lawyer's voice was ripe with satisfaction. "At least two million."

Two *million*? Hope glanced around the funky, old-fashioned kitchen, the battered kitchen cabinets and worn linoleum. For this, well, okay, not *dump*, exactly—the barn was a luxury hotel with room for eighteen horses—but they'd let the house go to pay for the barn, and the land itself was one hundred fifty acres of shrub.

"Two million," Hope said. They could never afford that. They just barely met their expenses on the ranch as it was.

"Passaic Holdings has a potential buyer, a global

corporation that specializes in destination entertainment," Joseph Sharp said.

Destination entertainment? The buyer wants to build a Disneyland in the middle of the Nevada high plain?

"Of course, you are welcome to make a counter offer. Mr. McNaughton insisted that you have first right of refusal."

Hope felt sick. The bad news was coming too fast and hard, flattening her. "Well, thank you, Mr. Sharp. I'll just have my lawyer draw up those purchase papers."

"Let me know if I can help. I also know an excellent moving service."

They talked about it over supper. Faith had come in from the greenhouse and fixed the meal—a big carrot salad, made with carrots not perfect enough to sell—and a comforting chicken casserole. Amber, Faith's daughter, who would turn eleven in a few days, sat silently, her food untouched on her plate, watching them.

"I don't understand this, Mom," Faith said now. "I thought you owned the ranch."

"Well, no." Suzanne still looked pale. Amber had a glass of milk in front of her, but the rest of them were drinking beer. Suzanne took a long swallow of hers.

A little extra grain for the humans, too, Hope thought.

"When we divorced, Derek got the ranch and I got what cash there was. I needed the money to support you girls until I could get on my feet. At the time, the value was about the same. Your father said we could stay here for as long as we wanted, or he'd give us a chance to buy him out. He's been more than generous. The rent has been very reasonable over the years."

Dad welshed on the deal, like always, Hope thought.

"He wasn't more than generous," she said flatly. "We paid rent. We paid utilities. We paid upkeep and repairs. We've done a ton of improvements. The greenhouse. The barn." She knew all about the expenses they'd paid. She'd written the checks herself.

"Well, we live here, Hope, Sweetie. We should be paying for those things."

Hope didn't want to argue with her mother. It wasn't Suzanne's fault that Derek, king of the losing hand, hadn't kept his end of the deal.

"But why is he forcing us off now?" Faith asked.

Simple, Hope thought. Derek had gambled and lost. Now the land, the house, the horses, the greenhouse—everything would have to be sold, their home would be sold.

The McNaughtons were welcome to buy it all back, of course. The McNaughtons, who couldn't afford to put a new roof on their old house, were offered first refusal on a two-million property—their own.

That was the kind of luck the McNaughtons had.

"It's not your father who's forcing us off," Suzanne said. "The letter mentions a corporation. Passaic Holdings."

"Yes," Hope conceded, nodding to Faith. "Technically, that's true. Passaic Holdings—or the person who runs it, the guy Derek lost the card game to—does not want to own one hundred fifty acres of land in southern Nevada. So he's selling. Dad, once again, gets away scot free while the rest of us get wiped out."

"That's not really fair, Hope," Suzanne said. "Your father is basically a good person. I'm sure he didn't mean to hurt us."

"And yet, here we are. Hurt and forced off, just the same."

And that was the issue. Where would they go? They probably couldn't afford even to rent a place big enough to pasture three horses and have a greenhouse. They might have to move to a house—even an apartment—in town somewhere.

Damn Derek. Damn her father.

Amber's anxious eyes followed her grandmother, her aunt, and her mother as the conversation bounced around the table.

"There must be something we can do," Faith said, seeing her daughter's distress. "Can we pay rent to the corporation? Or make a down payment to buy? I know you're paying the lion's share here, Hope, but I could increase the size of the greenhouse, get more customers. What do you think?"

The fortunes of the McNaughtons had never been robust. While Suzanne worked at the local diner, earning minimum wage, Faith had stayed at home with Amber and tried to make a living from the ranch. They were still paying off the loans for her failed hot-air balloon business and the bankrupt children's riding school, loans that had been secured by Hope's salary and stock options at the software startup where she worked.

Faith's latest effort was an organic farm. She'd built a greenhouse at enormous expense, and she served forty residential customers and one commercial account, who received a delivery of organic vegetables twice a week. So far, the venture barely broke even.

"I don't know, Faith," Hope said, a catch in her voice. "It's a good long-term plan, but I don't think we can increase the vegetable business fast enough to buy the place in a month."

"I wish organic vegetables were addictive, like nicotine," Faith said. "We could run a flashy ad campaign directed at teenagers, and with all the discretionary spending kids have, they'd get hooked early and stay hooked for life. You'd need one of those stick-on patches to kick the habit. A stick-on cabbage patch."

Hope had to smile.

"Wouldn't that be fantastic?" she said.

Faith's face crumpled and she looked like she was going to cry. Hope thought she probably looked the same.

"How much time do we have?" Suzanne asked.

"We have to be out in a month." Hope knew she sounded grim.

"I suppose we need to start looking now," Faith said.

"But we don't know when it will sell, right?" Suzanne asked. "Who knows how long it will be before they find a buyer."

Joseph Sharp had said the winner had a potential buyer. And it made sense. Their land had water and a hot springs. The commute to Las Vegas was fairly easy. The place wasn't fancy, but it had everything, and the area was booming. It could be sold in a week. Or less.

"Who's 'Dad?'" Amber asked. "Do I know him?"

Hope's heart broke all over again. Derek had never seen his only granddaughter. Probably didn't even know she existed. Faith had had some bad luck in the bed of a Chevy two-ton truck one weekend about eleven years ago, and when Amber's father learned that he had a child coming, he took off before Amber was born. Derek was long gone by then.

It's not just money, Hope thought. The McNaughton women don't have much luck with men sticking, either.

She looked around the table at her family and saw the mingled fear, hopelessness, and confusion. The way her family felt way too often.

They'd look to her, because she was the reliable one. The problem solver.

Their problem right now was that they needed two million dollars. And that was a problem she didn't see how she could solve.

Chapter 2

After they'd eaten supper and cleaned up the kitchen, Hope went to her room. She threw open the big patio doors and breathed deeply of the sage-scented air, and as she looked out into the dark Nevada night, she thought about what the ranch meant to them all. Her decision made, she walked over to her desk, unlocked the bottom drawer, took out a metal file box, and unlocked that, as well.

The box contained a small stash of papers—her will, some certificates of deposit, her passport. And a small black book.

She didn't know why she still had the black book. She hadn't opened it in seventeen years, and she didn't want to open it now. She hated what the book represented.

But the black book was her last chance. Her only chance. It might have the key that could save the ranch. Save their futures.

The black address book contained the phone numbers of her father's old friends, acquaintances, enemies, and gambling buddies—people on the right or wrong side of the law who made their living by risking everything on cards, dice, slots, ponies, dogs, cars, or sports. A few of the people in this book, the special ones, had always been more than friends. She'd called them her honorary uncles—people she'd known as well as her own family, people she'd enjoyed and respected.

People she'd loved.

Whenever Derek had taken her along with him to the casino, the track, the cardroom, the private parties—they were there. They bought her ice cream and sodas and treated her like a mascot. They sent her to bed when it was late and protected her from the darkness that hovered just beyond the bright lights. They taught her everything they knew, and she'd been awed by their knowledge, the vast sums of money that passed through their hands, their generosity when they won, their graciousness when they lost. When school sucked and her mother struggled and her father disappeared, the honorary uncles made her life bearable. Fun. Even cool.

On her fifteenth birthday—the day she realized Derek was gone and never coming back—she'd phoned Marty the Sneak. She'd been afraid Derek had been killed by somebody he'd cheated or by a jealous husband, something. At fifteen, Hope knew all the ways her father could meet his end. Marty had stumbled around, making excuses for Derek. And that's how she found out that her father wasn't coming for her birthday because he would rather play cards, or throw dice, or run numbers than see her. Marty had felt so sorry for her that he'd offered to drive out for her party. The toughest poker player on the circuit, a guy who'd once bluffed an unsuited ten-seven against a full house, had gone sentimental.

Hope said no. She didn't want Marty's pity. She was done, finished, with all of it. She'd never played another hand of poker, never bet another nickel. And she'd never seen or heard from her father again. She'd never talked to Marty the Sneak again, and she'd never called the other honorary uncles, either, although they'd tried off and on for months, even years, to call her.

Derek was addicted to gambling. She understood that now. And she understood that if she went back to that world, she could become an addict, too. Seventeen years

18

ago, she'd liked the life too much.

She was terrified of what she would become if she picked up the phone and made those calls, setting those wheels in motion. But what choice did she have? Today things had changed. Today she needed to save the ranch. Today she would do what she had to do to save her family.

And she realized that now that she wanted to ask for Marty's forgiveness and help, she didn't have much right to either.

The information in the book wasn't current. She might not reach the uncles. But she had to try.

Taking a deep breath and easing it out slowly, she picked up the phone and dialed the number. The voice that answered on the second ring hadn't changed a bit.

"Marty," she said, clearing her throat. "It's me, Hope. Hope McNaughton."

Marty the Sneak was from Brooklyn, a slight man with a sprinkling of acne scars and thinning hair who would by now be in his late fifties. In the old days, he'd always worn a dark jacket and pants that were too big on him. He'd been more crooked than straight and lacked a formal education. But he'd always had a tremendous memory, which helped him at cards, and he'd known every player, crook, and cop on the east coast and many on the west. A long time ago, he'd been very kind to one little girl. Hope prayed that none of that had changed.

"Hope?" Marty said. "It's you? Little Hope? No kidding?" He raised his voice and called out to someone in the room. "Eddie, put down that hand and get on the extension right now! It's Little Hope I have here!"

Hope rolled her eyes, feeling seventeen-year-old exasperation and, now, a brand-new affection for her former nickname. She and her sister had been named after the two qualities Derek had said every gambler needed—Hope and Faith—and the honorary uncles had liked to tease her about her name. She heard a second phone lift. Sharp

Eddie Toombs, another honorary uncle.

"Hope?" Sharp Eddie said. "Is that really you? How are you, kiddo? It's been too long. We've missed you. I've lost fifteen pounds since I stopped buying you ice cream."

A sudden stab of longing and regret caught her unawares. She'd missed them, too. Sharp Eddie had always had a huge girth and a kind heart. He loved silly jokes, and now she remembered all the treats he'd showered on her over the years.

"Don't believe him, Hope," Marty the Sneak said. "He's gained fifteen pounds. He's been eating his ice cream and yours, too. We're thinking of changing his name to Sherman. Sherman the Tank."

Hope blinked back tears and smiled, as memories— good ones—flooded back. Whatever her father had done to her, the uncles weren't to blame.

"Marty—" she began. "Eddie. It has been too long, and I'm sorry. It's all my fault. I—"

"Don't, Hope," Sharp Eddie said. "It's all right. We missed you is all. And now, here you are."

"Thank you for saying that," Hope said, clutching the phone, feeling a rush of relief so strong it left her dizzy. "Back then—I was so hurt. And angry. I couldn't handle it. But still, I shouldn't have cut you out."

"Hope," Marty interrupted her. "Stop. Enough. We understand how it was. Derek—well, we told him he was a horse's ass, not that it did any good. We didn't know what to do. Except let you know we were there for you. But you knew that, right? Because here you are."

Hope cleared her throat. "I—I did. I do."

"It's good to hear from you, Little Hope," Sharp Eddie said. "Now, tell us what's wrong and how we can help you."

Hope laughed, sniffing a little. You couldn't fool an old card player.

"I do need some help," she said. "What do you know about Passaic Holdings?"

There was a moment of silence on the other end of the line. Hope listened to the connection hiss. *Can't be good*, she thought.

"Why do you want to know about Passaic Holdings, Hope?" Marty asked.

"You must have heard that Derek lost our ranch in a poker game. I want to get it back. It's a long shot, but I thought maybe I could play the winner for it. What have I got to lose, right? So I need to know who Derek played. The name on the deed is a New Jersey corporation called Passaic Holdings. And, you're from Jersey. I figured you'd know who that is."

"I did hear about that damn card game, yes," Marty said.

Then he stopped. Eddie said nothing.

"And?" Hope asked. "What's the rest of it?"

"Passaic Holdings is a big conglomerate," Marty said. "They got the contracts for trash, recycling, paper waste, chemical cleanup and disposal, I don't know what, all over Jersey. I heard that Derek played Big Julie Saladino in that game. He'd be the CEO."

"Big Julie Saladino? The Jersey crime boss?" Hope's mood took a nosedive. No way could she negotiate a card game with a Mafia don. Yikes. One false step and instead of the ranch, she'd be staking out property six feet long and six feet under.

"Hope, please." Marty's voice was strained. "Big Julie has no documented ties to organized crime. Big Julie Saladino is a respected Jersey entrepreneur whose business interests just happen to fall in the construction, waste collection, and laundry sectors."

"Oh, right," Hope said, remembering that Marty's phone might be bugged. She was out of practice in dealing with her extended, unrelated-by-biology family.

"So—Big Julie moved his operation to Vegas?" she asked. "Or if not, is he still out here?"

"Jackpot, Hope," confirmed Sharp Eddie. "Bing-bing-

bing!"

"Big Julie is in Vegas for the foreseeable future," Marty agreed. "He wants to be with his girlfriend and away from his wife."

"It's a safety issue," Sharp Eddie said. "She says she's gonna kill him. The wife, I mean. Her and the Russian mob is both after Big Julie, so he took off for Vegas."

"Big Julie likes the action better in Vegas than Atlantic City right now, and he also likes the weather better," said Marty. "Who wouldn't, right? Better for your health."

"Do you know where he's staying?"

"He's got a suite at the Desert Dunes Casino and Resort," said Sharp Eddie. "From what I heard, he's got a big-stakes card game in his room every Saturday night. He's cleaning up."

"Yes, from my family, among others, probably," Hope said, her voice sharper than she'd intended.

Marty and Sharp Eddie were both silent.

"I'm sorry, you guys. I didn't mean to take it out on you. But Derek went too far. He lost the ranch in a card game. I am seriously mad."

"You can't stay mad if you want to get the ranch back," Marty warned. "You've got to be clear. Focused. Tell me what you need."

Hope realized that Marty had just said he'd help her. That meant that all the uncles, if asked, would help her. Her spirits soared.

"Thank you, Marty. I owe you big time. I need to see Big Julie this week—tomorrow if I can. I want to ask him to play me for the ranch. No limit Texas Hold'em. Winner takes all. Can you get me an introduction?"

"I'll call Big Julie," Marty said. "He'll see you if I ask him. What else?"

Hope took a deep breath. "If Big Julie agrees to play, I need to get my game back. I haven't played cards in seventeen years. I've forgotten everything I ever knew. It's a lot to ask, especially after all this time, but—can you help me? Can you come to Vegas?"

Marty didn't hesitate.

"On my way," he said. "I'll be staying at the Golden Palace. I always liked the card room there, and they got a hell of an all-you-can-eat Chinese dim sum buffet for four-ninety-five. Give me your cell number. I'll call you tomorrow when I get in."

"Make that two of us," Sharp Eddie said.

"Count on six of us," Marty said. "I'll call the others, too. We'll all come."

The next morning dawned sharp and clear, the hot, dry air carrying the tang of mesquite. As she ate breakfast, Hope realized that she had a spring in her step. The uncles were coming. And she had a shot at getting the ranch back.

As he'd promised he would, Marty called when he and Sharp Eddie arrived. When she drove in to meet them at the casino, she learned that the other four uncles were already at the tables.

"Did you call Big Julie?" Marty asked now, as they headed into the casino. "What did he say?"

Hope had wondered if she'd recognize Marty and Eddie, if they'd recognize her, and what she'd feel when she saw them again. But when she met them in the lobby of the Golden Palace, it was almost like old times. Except for one thing.

"You've grown up, Little Hope," Sharp Eddie had said. "Not so little any more."

Hope had given them each a hug, she was so relieved that they'd come.

"I'm meeting him at two this afternoon," she announced now, feeling happy and confident. "Thank you for setting up the meeting. Do you think he'll let me play?"

"He'll let you play," Marty said. "He ain't really got any options there. Come on, let's get to the tables. We got some card playing to do."

Hope followed Marty and Eddie into the card room, calling the other uncles from their high-stakes tables to the smaller-bet tables where Hope would relearn her game. Everyone settled in and bought some chips. The dealer brought out a new deck of cards.

Hope looked around the table at her uncles, men she hadn't seen in a long time, professional card players who'd dropped everything to revive her game and help her get the ranch back. They were the best.

They'd come all this way for her. She couldn't turn back now.

William Tanner Wingate, professional card player, consultant to federal law enforcement, and Tanner to his friends, was so startled by the scene in the Golden Palace card room that he stopped short, causing a waitress to bump into him and spill her drinks.

"Sorry," he murmured, slipping her a red chip, but he couldn't take his eyes off the table in the center of the room.

What was Marty the Sneak doing in Vegas? Marty came to Vegas only for poker tournaments, and there wasn't a tournament going on—because if there was a tournament, Tanner would be playing in it.

And it wasn't just Marty the Sneak. There was Sharp Eddie Toombs, Weary Blastell, Pete Wisniewski, Isaiah Rush, and Jim Thickpenny. The Jersey posse. And, even weirder than to see the Jersey boys all together at one table in Vegas when there wasn't a tournament, was to see them sitting at the three-dollar table. If they went all-out, they could make a six-dollar bet.

Any one of those players could and frequently did play in high-stakes games where a hundred thousand dollars or more could be bet in a single night—or a single hand. But today the high-rolling Jersey boys were all sitting at a three-dollar table.

With a blonde.

And what a blonde.

Not a kid, definitely thirty, somebody who'd looped the track once or twice. But she was gorgeous, with the face of an angel and the body of a showgirl, even if she wasn't exactly flaunting it in that navy suit. And who wore a navy suit to a card room?

Something was up. And whatever it was, Tanner wanted to know about it. And he definitely wanted to know about the blonde. He wandered closer and heard Marty say, "How much money you got, Hope?"

Hope. So that was the blonde's name. Well, he could hope, too.

"About forty dollars," she said.

"Enough for today," Sharp Eddie said.

"Yes, because I have to leave by one-thirty or so," Hope said. "Don't let me lose track of the time."

The blonde was calling the shots? A hot dominatrix blonde and the Jersey posse at the three-dollar table, like they were all having a tea party. Definitely a story there.

"Hey, Marty," he said approaching the table.

Marty the Sneak looked up, nodded, and stretched his hand out to shake.

"Tanner," he said.

The other men nodded, too. They'd all met many times over the years in clubs and casinos all over the world, although Tanner mostly stuck to Vegas because he hadn't wanted to travel much while his daughter, Troy, was young.

Tanner caught Hope's eye and then his breath.

Close up, her skin was luminous and lightly tanned, so clear and soft that she seemed to radiate light. She had high cheekbones and delicate ears with a beautiful curve to her neck. Who ever realized that bone structure could do that to a face? He felt a rush through his head and a yearning that was way deeper than attraction. More painful, too.

She has blue eyes. Big, blue eyes. Which were, he realized,

now that she was looking at him, expressive. She had opinions. Hope might not play cards, but she might play other games. Games that entailed whips. Handcuffs. Tight leather cutaway outfits.

He wanted to sit at her table, too.

"Let me introduce myself," he asked, when he'd been standing there way too long and it looked like Marty never would. He held out his hand to her. "Tanner Wingate."

"Hope McNaughton," Hope said, as she shook his hand. "Have we met?"

"I don't think so," he said, holding her hand, feeling a roughness that no amount of moisturizing could smooth over. She works with her hands. "I'm sure I'd remember."

"Your name sounds familiar."

"Well—I win sometimes. Maybe that's it."

"You're a professional card player?" Hope asked, taking her hand back, her voice suddenly twenty degrees cooler.

Now what brought that on? Tanner smiled, he hoped, winsomely. "I know a card player named McNaughton," he said. "Derek McNaughton. You related to him?"

"No," Hope said.

Tanner watched in amazement as the pupils in her eyes constricted. She was lying to him. She was sitting there with that angel's face and those you-can-trust-me eyes and butter-wouldn't-melt-in-her-mouth look, and she flat out lied to him. Her eyes—those big, blue, wide-open eyes— gave her away.

She was hiding something. What could it be?

He glanced over at Marty, to see if he could pick up anything from him. Marty was watching the green felt on the table. Marty knew how to hide his tells.

"So how do you guys know each other?" Tanner asked.

The men all looked at Hope.

"They're my uncles," she said.

The pupils of her eyes had enlarged, back to the size they were before they'd started this conversation. So now she was telling the truth? She lied about knowing Derek McNaughton, but she was telling the truth about these guys being her uncles? Because *no way* were these guys her uncles.

The "Jersey boys" were all in their fifties or sixties. Marty was single, and as far as Tanner knew, without family. Sharp Eddie was married with a couple of grown kids. Weary Blastell and Isaiah Rush were African-American and had met when they'd played football for Ohio State. Isaiah had been a fullback with visions of the pros until he tore out his knee, but Weary had played with the Green Bay Packers for seven seasons until injuries and cold weather forced him into retirement. Pete Wisniewski, despite his father's Polish name, got his looks from his Chinese mother. And Jim Thickpenny, the disgraced former Congressman, had gambled with his career and lost, which gained him a shock of prematurely white hair. Now he gambled for a living.

They were her uncles? No way.

"They're your uncles," he repeated. "Really. Everybody?"

"Yes," Hope said, her pupils now filling the normal amount of space in her violet iris. "Everybody."

"Listen, Tanner," Marty said impatiently. "We got to get going here. Call me later. You got my cell."

"You want me to join you?" Tanner asked, looking at Hope, wanting to stay with her. "You could use another player at the table."

"Another time," Marty said.

"Okay. Nice to meet you, Hope." He heard the blonde sniff as he walked over to a table that was getting a little action. He'd call Marty. And he was definitely calling Hope.

Chapter 3

"Let's go," Marty told the dealer. He turned to Hope. "Tanner's all right, Hope. But he's a player."

"I can see that." Hope glanced over to the table where Tanner was taking a seat. He pulled out a chair and dropped into it, all easy animal grace. He had an untamed look about him, with shaggy dark hair worn a little long, and his big body compact with muscle. His hands had been marked with many small scars and nicks. He didn't stay indoors all the time, and he used his hands for something other than playing cards.

She watched him ante up at the four hundred dollar table before she turned away. In the Hold'em game Tanner had just joined, four hundred dollars was the minimum bet. In the second round of betting, bets doubled. Eight hundred dollars. Just thinking about it made her feel dizzy. She didn't see how that kind of game could be fun, with so much money riding on each hand.

"I don't mean he plays cards," Marty said. "I mean he plays women."

"Oh." Hope picked up the two cards the dealer had spun her way, looked at them, and smiled. She turned back to Marty. "Don't worry about me. I don't date card players."

Isaiah, sitting to the left of the dealer, had been watching them. Now he glanced at his cards and tossed them back, folding his hand.

Pete Wisniewski was next. "Fold," he said.

"He's never serious," Marty said.

"Pete?" Hope asked.

"Tanner," Marty said. "Who we're talking about. He's not serious about the women he dates. And you're a family type of gal. Always were."

Sharp Eddie tossed his cards in. "Bing, bing, bing," he said to Hope. "Marty's right there."

"Are you taking over Derek's job now? I'm thirty-two years old, and I don't date card players," Hope said. "Thanks for the warning, though."

Weary tossed his cards in.

"Just so you know," Marty said, flipping his cards in.

"You're all folding?" Hope said. "You must have some cards. That's what you guys do—you bet. You raise. What's going on here?" It was her turn and she tossed a chip into the pot, the highest allowable bet, three dollars.

"If circumstances were otherwise, I wouldn't be at all adverse to investigating my potential positive outcome," Jim Thickpenny said, tossing in his cards. "But in this case, discretion has overcome valor."

"Jeez, we didn't even get to the flop, and I had great cards, too," she said, looking at the tiny pot that the dealer pushed her way.

Marty grinned. "Pair of aces?"

Hope turned to him, her eyes widening. "How did you know?"

"Thought so," Isaiah said.

Hope jerked her head his way, feeling a sudden rush. These guys were among the best players in the world, and they'd all spotted her first mistake right away. Somehow she'd given away her hand. Even though she'd played badly, the tingle that she'd felt when she used to play cards with Derek so long ago was back. She was getting her game back.

She felt thrilled. Terrified.

"What did I do?" she asked.

"You smiled," Sharp Eddie said. "When you picked up your cards."

Hope closed her eyes. The most basic tell in the world. The giveaway that anyone—the rankest beginner —would make and understand.

"That's stopping right now," she said. "Thanks."

Lesson one remembered and relearned.

If she'd played her hand better, they would have stuck in a little longer—made a few bets and fattened the pot—so she'd have earned more when she won. The first rule of card players probably was that winning was good, but winning big was better. And you didn't even always need the best cards to win. You needed the most confidence. The most courage. To bluff when the chips were down. And you needed to pay attention, figure out what the other players had, and learn their style of play.

In Hold'em, Big Julie's game, strategy and skill were as important—maybe more important—than luck. And that's what the uncles were here to help her with.

The dealer swept the cards into a pile, shuffled, and dealt.

This hand, Hope remembered the proper etiquette and left her cards on the table, just lifting the corners to see their number and suit. As she looked at them she spoke to the men. "I appreciate your time for this," she said. "I know it's got to be boring for you."

"Embarrassing, is what it is," Pete Wisniewski said.

"Yeah, the three-dollar table," Weary said. "In public."

Isaiah shook his head. "Could it get any worse?"

"You could lose," Hope said, scowling at them. "You could lose to a girl."

They all laughed.

"No chance of that, Little Hope," Sharp Eddie said, grinning widely.

"The tutoring session is only for a short duration of

time," Jim Thickpenny said soothingly. "We can manage our obligations so that in effect we are engaging in a high-stakes poker vacation. We anticipate that we'll enjoy the unique Vegas experience. And when you engage in your customary obligations, we'll play some serious cards."

Hope smiled at him fondly. Jim had never really gotten over being a politician. She glanced at her cards again, seeing a five of spades and a two of clubs. The only thing she could do with small, unsuited cards was fold, taking herself out of play and losing the chance to win the pot.

She tossed in her cards when her turn came.

She watched the play develop, trying to assess what the other players had and why they'd played their cards the way they did. She knew that on any given day, bad luck and bad cards could bring down a good player. But over time, a good player would make money playing cards because skill eventually and regularly trumped luck.

The dealer shoved the pot over to Marty.

"You looked at your cards twice," he said. "And you had a bad hand. You didn't look twice when you had a good hand. It's too soon to know if that's another tell, but watch out for that, Hope."

"Maybe she should wear bracelets," Isaiah suggested. "So that when she moves her hands, they'll jingle and she'll remember to hold still."

"Good idea," Pete Wisniewski said. "Maybe a hat, too. Or sunglasses. Something to hide the eyes."

"Do my eyes give me away?" Hope asked.

"Not that we can see," Sharp Eddie said. "Not yet. Just saying. Common problem. Eyes give away a lot of people. Eyes and hands."

The dealer scooped up the cards and shuffled, and Hope sat back, waiting for her two cards. A skitter of nerves ran through her fingers. She had a lot to learn—and a lot to shop for—before she'd be ready to play Big Julie for the ranch.

But she'd get there if she had to work twenty-four hours a day and buy out Las Vegas's entire stock of sunglasses, hats, and bracelets. Because she wasn't letting a little thing like accessories keep her from getting the ranch back.

By late afternoon Tanner was slumped in a chair in the interview room of the FBI's Las Vegas bureau, watching his future fade before his eyes. After the last time he'd worked for the agency, he'd hoped he'd never have to do another job for these hapless twerps. FBI demands didn't come often, but when they came he could never say no. Today his luck had run out, so here he was. Deep in the belly of the beast, with no chance of getting out or getting off.

"Face it, Wingate," Special Agent Roy Frelly said to him now. "We got you." He sat across from Tanner and leaned back in satisfaction. He was a big guy, with a spongy pot belly, beefy shoulders, heavy jowls, and short hair gone gray. Judging from his appearance, he was looking at retirement in two weeks at the most.

He's showing extreme confidence, Tanner thought. *Can't be good.*

"Yeah, I'm unclear exactly what you think you've got," he said. Where the hell was his lawyer? He'd called Jack a half-hour ago. But maybe traffic had held him up. Traffic could be a killer any time of day.

"We got a gig for you," agent Lee Gauger said. He was shorter, stringier, and younger than Frelly, but his hair was just as short, his confidence just as annoying. "You'll love it, because you love cheating at poker."

"I haven't cheated in almost twenty years, which you know," Tanner said, wondering what the agents wanted and not liking any of the possibilities.

"Tanner, not another word." Jack Sievers, his best friend since kindergarten and his lawyer since he graduated law school, breezed into the interview room and plunked his briefcase on the table. "Now, what's this supposed to be about?"

"Your client." Frelly stabbed a pencil in Tanner's direction. "We got a job for him. He's uniquely qualified because he cheats at cards. That's why we been enjoying his free consulting services for the last almost twenty years. Probation. Gotta love it." He chuckled, a sound Tanner found really irritating.

Just then the woman he remembered from last night's card game walked into the room. Last night she'd worn a tight, white dress, short, shimmery, and backless. Practically frontless, too. She'd sat next to him and leaned over one too many times and Tanner's brains had scrambled a little, but nothing that affected his play. There was something about her he didn't trust, and he'd wondered then if she was law enforcement.

Today he had his answer. Today she was wearing a tailored suit with a white shirt buttoned high, and her dark hair was twisted up, not down. No danger his brains would scramble today.

"Hey, Darla," he said. "Or is your name really Darla?"

"It's Darla." She smiled at him. "Nice to see you again, Tanner."

"Just one question. I've been thinking about where you could have hidden the camera. Can you help me out?"

Darla's smile thinned. "Keep dreaming, wiseguy."

So she didn't really like him after all. Well, not much of a loss. She had that body, but she didn't have much conversation. *Keep dreaming, wiseguy*? Who talked like that?

Roy Frelly leaned forward again. "So here's what we're gonna do," he said.

Extreme confidence, Tanner thought again. It looked like the feds planned to have their way with him.

"We want to get Big Julie Saladino," Frelly said.

Hell, Tanner thought. *And they picked me to lead the*

suicide squadron.

Guilio "Big Julie" Saladino was the biggest crook in New Jersey—a Mafioso with a major influence on most of the traditional Sicilian businesses—and, now that he was on an extended vacation, the richest card player in Vegas. Big Julie played only high stakes, no limit Texas Hold'em in venues where players could be assured that they'd be free of all the pesky surveillance and rules you found in the big gaming houses. That meant that Big Julie played in his suite—the penthouse suite, the five-thousand-square-foot, Polynesian-style, high-roller suite, with the hot tub and view and nothing-is-too-good-for-Mr.-Saladino room service.

Playing Big Julie would be fun, in a weird, once-in-a-lifetime way, but it was an experience Tanner was willing to sacrifice to keep all his body parts. He also had Troy to think of. His daughter, now eighteen, was leaving for college next week. She had realized long ago that the kinds of people the FBI put in her father's path could be violent as well as bent, and she didn't like the FBI's working requirements one bit.

I'll go down big time on this gig, Tanner thought. *Just my luck.*

"Big Julie's wanted on sixteen counts of murder and extortion," Frelly said now. "But to get Big Julie, we need somebody who can play cards and cheat. That's you."

No. Not this time. He didn't want to set Big Julie up for a fall. He'd be in trouble with the Mob for the rest of his life—his guaranteed short life. Next week Troy would be at UCLA, in eight months his probation would finally be over, and he'd have a whole new life to start.

He'd wondered what that new life would look like. He hadn't made any plans, but dying—even losing a limb—was definitely not on his personal menu of choices.

"Why don't you just arrest Big Julie?" Jack Sievers asked. "He's staying at the Desert Dunes. You've got the sixteen counts. Why does my client have to play cards with him?"

Frelly rubbed the back of head.

Distress. Tanner looked up. Frelly didn't like that question. And suddenly Tanner knew the answer.

"There are no charges against him," Tanner told Jack. "I bet there aren't any arrest warrants out on Big Julie at all. Right, Agent Frelly? You're just trying to fool me into going along with you. You can't make an extortion and murder case against Big Julie, so you want to get him on gambling charges."

Frelly leaned his head into his hand.

Very distressed. I was right.

"And you can't even get him on gambling without outside help," Tanner added. "So you're putting the squeeze on me. Not that I'm unwilling to do my patriotic duty, but why not Darla, here? You want somebody to nail him? She seems more than competent." And that way the FBI could worry about Mafia dons. He smiled cheerfully at the female agent, trying to beam confident support.

Darla gave him a thin-lipped sneer. Funny how great legs and big breasts just didn't compensate for a bad attitude.

"We tried that," Lee Gauger said from his stance in the corner. "Darla. Last week. Big Julie made her. Last night you, on the other hand, were clueless."

"He just looked down my dress all night," Darla agreed.

"You made it so easy to do," Tanner said. "But you notice I passed on the merchandise."

"The *point*," Frelly said as Darla opened her mouth in outrage, "is that Darla can't work Big Julie. He knows she's FBI."

Tanner shook his head. "Say what you will, the Mafia is smart. Smarter, evidently, than Darla. Not to mention, the rest of you."

"*So what we're gonna do,*" Frelly broke in, "is this."

Everyone looked at him expectantly.

Frelly leaned forward and jabbed his finger at Tanner.

Committed to a plan of action, Tanner thought.

"*You* are gonna play cards with Big Julie," Frelly said. "*He* is gonna win big. *You* will tape him. *Then* we got him."

"Yeah, not so much," Tanner said. "Even if he cheats, it's not a federal crime to cheat in a card game. You play anywhere—private game, card room, casino—and somebody cheats, management just throws him out and bars him from coming back. No arrests. No prison time."

"We're not talking about him cheating," Gauger said. "We're talking about you cheating—if you have to, to get Big Julie to win. The goal is to get him to win big. However it has to happen."

"Because?" Tanner asked. "I'm not following."

Frelly grinned in triumph. "Because if Big Julie plays regularly, which we know he does, he's operating a gambling establishment without a license."

"Class B felony," Darla said.

"Which the casino hates, not that they're saying," Frelly said.

Gauger nodded again. "Then, if you're operating a gambling establishment with earnings over a couple grand—"

"Which Big Julie is," Frelly said. "He's playing in the range of one-two hundred G's. So at your licensed gambling establishment, if you win big, you gotta report the winnings to the IRS right up front and withhold the taxes on it. Which Big Julie ain't doing. So now he's looking at two felonies. Minimum."

Tanner looked pained. "That old dodge? You're going to get him on income tax evasion? Come on, Frelly. That is so Al Capone. I expected better from you."

"Yeah, well, it still works, smartass. We got him for those two felonies for sure, and he's probably laundering money with the chips, too, if he uses chips. He use chips?" Frelly asked Tanner.

Tanner shrugged. "How would *I* know? Don't *you* know

that?" Tanner would be surprised, though, if Big Julie didn't launder money by using chips. Many people who acquired large sums of money in legally questionable ways went to the casino and bought chips with the dirty money, and then later cashed in the chips, asking for a check or wire transfer. After the money was washed through the casino's accounts, it was perfectly clean and legal.

"So we probably got him on money laundering, too," Frelly said. He leaned forward again, stabbing the air as he spoke. "If I get this guy, Wingate, I can look forward to a big retirement bonus, maybe a reward, even a plaque. I want this guy. And you're gonna get him for me."

"On income tax evasion," Tanner said. "You think that will work?"

Frelly nodded. "You know how much federal income tax Big Julie paid last year? We got his ten-forty from the IRS. One hundred six measly bucks. One-oh-six, total. That's what he paid. He probably earned millions."

"Man, that's incredible," Jack said. "Who's his accountant?"

"Two smartasses," Frelly said, leaning back. "I should arrest you both for being a pain in the behind."

"Tell him the deal," Gauger said.

"Please," Jack Sievers said.

"The deal is that your client snitches for us. On Big Julie," Frelly said.

"For how long?" Jack asked, at the same time that Tanner said, "No deal."

"No deal," Tanner repeated. He turned to the lawyer. "Can't do it, Jack. If I turned on Big Julie, the Mob would kill me." He turned and smiled winningly at Frelly. "And if I'm dead, I can't fulfill the terms of my probation."

Frelly shrugged. "Wouldn't happen. You might be doing the Mob a favor if you did help put Big Julie behind bars. The way I hear it, Big Julie's out here to take a break from the turf wars in Jersey. The Russians are trying to take over his territory. He goes to jail, they'll be grateful, and you'll be safe."

"You think his organization won't be upset if Big Julie got killed or went to jail?"

Frelly sat back and fiddled with his pencil. "You can break your probation and go to prison," he said finally. "Or you can play cards. Like you always do. Only now, you wear a camera and report back to us. Take your pick."

Tanner didn't like it. He didn't like getting face-to-face with the Mob. All of his assignments for the last nineteen years had been surveillance jobs from security offices, showing the FBI agents how someone was cheating or how a dealer was dirty. Nobody he'd ever turned over to law enforcement had known who he was. No suspect had ever seen him.

This situation was different. Now he'd have to play cards with and snitch on someone who'd be more than happy to do him serious bodily harm.

What were his choices? If he said no, he'd go to prison for twenty years. He didn't want to go to prison. He'd just have to take his chances that he could outwit the Mafia. If Big Julie was anything like Roy Frelly, maybe that wouldn't be so hard.

"Any money I win, I keep," he said.

"If you win it legitimately," Frelly said. "And pay taxes on it. Sure."

Tanner sat another minute, trying to think of a different way, a better way to get out of the FBI's deal. But he couldn't see it. He looked at Sievers, raising an eyebrow. Jack looked back, pursing his lips.

Pacification.

"For how long?" Sievers asked.

"Until we get the evidence against Big Julie," Frelly said. "Or until we say."

"Until you get the evidence, or one month," Jack said.

"Until we get the evidence, or three months," Frelly said.

Jack looked at Tanner, turning palms up. *Acceptance.*

"Okay," Tanner said, feeling the noose tighten. "It's a deal."

Chapter 4

Big Julie Saladino, wearing a white terry-cloth robe with the hotel's name stitched in blue over the chest pocket, sat at the dining room table in his penthouse suite at the Desert Dunes Casino and Resort and shoveled in his eggs. The table was set for two, but he was alone in the five-thousand-square-foot apartment except for a bodyguard, who lounged on a sofa, checking the stock market quotes in the newspaper.

Big Julie was in a bad mood. So far nothing had gone right today, and it wasn't even noon yet. He'd been woken up by his number-two lieutenant back in Jersey, who reported that one of the soldiers had a new girlfriend. That was the good news. The bad news was, she was the daughter of the Russian mob boss who was after Big Julie's business. To get Big Julie's turf, the Russians wanted to outfit Big Julie in a custom pair of cement shoes and take him for a long walk at the bottom of a deep ocean. Which was why Big Julie was in Vegas. Plenty of cement, sure, but no oceans.

The soldier was dazzled by the Russian girl's big bouncing boobies, which turned one part of his anatomy to steel but turned his brain to oatmeal. The lieutenant told Big Julie how it happened: the soldier's there enjoying an afterglow with the Russian girl and he asks her about her accent, and she says she's from Georgia, so of course oatmeal brain thought she meant Atlanta, but she meant Tbilisi. The soldier couldn't tell the difference between an effing southern accent and an effing Russian accent. That was the kind of help you got these days, where the oatmeal and the steel exchanged places when they shouldn't, and that was the other reason Big Julie was staying in Vegas. Better help.

So that was the first thing.

Then when he hung up the phone with the number-two lieutenant, Big Julie realized that Baby wasn't in bed and she wasn't in the shower, either. So that meant that she could be, one, out shopping, two, getting her hair done, three, getting her nails done, four, out shopping. And sure enough, the phone rings and it's the front desk asking him to approve a charge limit. And Big Julie wanted to know: what's the point of bringing a hot piece like Baby to share a love nest in Vegas if she don't want to stay in bed in the mornings and tempt him with her silicone-enhanced tits, her Brazilian-waxed legs, her organic rosemary peeled face, and her lipo-suctioned tummy? If he'd wanted to be sitting here alone approving credit charges like an effing Wall Street tycoon, he could've stayed in Jersey with his wife.

So that was the second thing.

Then he got up and ordered breakfast, and when it came, his eggs had runny whites, even though he'd *specifically* said, *no runny whites*. And they gave him that sourdough toast again. Who could eat that crap? It was enough to make a guy puke. So he'd ordered up a new breakfast, but that took a little while, and in the meantime, his coffee got cold.

So that was the third thing.

When Baby finally showed up, shortly before noon, carrying a half-dozen shopping bags, and with a starstruck bellboy carrying another dozen, Big Julie wasn't feeling very romantic.

"You have to see what I got!" Baby squealed as she tipped the bellboy, her smile sparkling for Big Julie alone.

"I can see you got plenty," Big Julie groused.

The bodyguard, glancing up over the stock market quotes, thought of something he needed to do somewhere else and glided out of the room, if a man who was six-four and weighed two-thirty in the buff could be said to glide.

Baby dropped the bags on the sofa and rushed over to Big Julie, throwing her arms around him. "Don't be mad, honey. I got everything for you. You want me to do you credit, don't you? And you were sleeping so hard, and I know how much those late nights take out of you. I couldn't wake you. And I got you a present. I hope you like it!"

Big Julie eyed her with disfavor. "If I'd wanted to wear out my credit cards in Vegas, I could have brought Marilyn."

And so, of course, that was the fourth thing. Because no self-respecting Baby would let a reminder of the wife back home go unchallenged.

"Marilyn!" Baby shrieked, dropping her arms from around Big Julie's shoulders and stomping off toward the bedroom with her shopping bags. "That's what you want? You want *Marilyn?* Well, go ahead and call her! Get her here! You don't spend time with me, you don't take me nowhere, we don't even go down to the casino or out to eat or *nothing.* And I go out to do a little shopping to kill some time while you're sleeping so you'll be proud of me, and now you bring *Marilyn* into it?"

Big Julie had spoken in haste. He really hadn't meant that he would rather have brought Marilyn. Ever since his wife had discovered that Baby accepted very munificent gratuities as well as a clothing and automobile allowance to entertain her husband, which she did regularly and energetically in a condo that he'd bought for her overlooking the ninth green of the Rocky Shores Country Club golf course, there'd been trouble at home. In fact, ever since Marilyn realized that every afternoon when Big Julie went out to the country club to swing his driver he was getting a hole in one, Marilyn had added murder to her daily to-do list. Big Julie's murder.

Not that the physical side of Big Julie's marriage hadn't been stale for some time. It wasn't Marilyn's tchotchke collection, her plastic-covered furniture, and her extra-large, frozen-from-Costco pans of lasagna that she served every Sunday at family dinners. It was Marilyn herself. That lasagna had packed on the pounds over the years, and although Big Julie liked a woman with meat, Marilyn had tried to rein herself in with the aid of industrial-strength undergarments. Her corseted figure was so rigid with elastic polymers that once when Big Julie found the courage to give one of her tits a little squeeze, there hadn't been any give to it at all. It was like squeezing a traffic cone strapped to her chest.

In short, Big Julie quickly realized that he had nothing to gain by alienating Baby's affections with talk about Marilyn.

"Baby," he said, his voice placating. "I didn't mean nothing."

Baby stopped behind the couch and dropped her shopping bags on the cushions in front of her, planting her fisted hands on her curvaceous hips. Her chin-length, blond, curly hair was tousled, her red lips were parted, and her breasts, those glorious globes of heavenly bliss, strained against the flimsy fabric of her sundress. Suddenly Big Julie didn't feel quite so oppressed.

"Baby, honey," he said again. "You know that everything I have is yours. I was just missing you. Come on, now. Give me a kiss."

He advanced to the sofa, but she backed up, her eyes stormy.

"*Marilyn,*" she said with contempt. "You told me you

were getting a divorce. Let's go to Vegas, you said. I'll divorce Marilyn. Six weeks and it's done, that's what you said. We'll get married, Baby. With flowers and a diamond ring. By an *Elvis impersonator.* Anything I want." Baby looked enraged. "Was that all a lie?"

"Baby, you know it wasn't. These things just take a little time," Big Julie said, trying to sound pleading. He didn't have to try very hard. He was feeling very urgent. Her cheeks were so flushed —her skin was so pink—he knew from enthusiastic experience how rosy those breasts looked when her skin was flushed, how her nipples stood up like sentinels on parade when she got excited, how they bounced when she was on top. If he leaped across the sofa, he could just about reach her.

"Have you even *started* the divorce?" Baby demanded, her voice rising. "Have you even *looked* for a lawyer? Because I'm telling you, Big Julie, if you're just messing with me—"

Big Julie couldn't wait any longer. He lunged forward, leaping over the sofa like an Olympic hurdler, unfortunately missing the top bar. His foot caught on the back of the sofa, but momentum carried him onward. As he stumbled over the top, he grasped wildly at Baby, getting a hand on her skirt and falling heavily to the floor as she staggered for balance. The dress tore in his hand, leaving him holding a ragged piece of bright cloth and showing a gaping hole at the waist where the skirt joined the bodice.

"Now look what you've done!" Baby shrieked, grabbing the remains of her skirt around her. "You've *ruined* my dress! You're a brute! I'm going to *kill* you! And you are *never* sleeping with me again until I see a marriage license!" She grabbed her shopping bags and stomped into the bedroom, slamming the door.

Still stunned from his fall and clutching the torn piece of Baby's sundress, Big Julie lay on the floor and watched her go. One thing he knew for sure: no elastic polymers there.

Not anywhere. Nothing but bounce, front and rear, on that one.

He heard the bedroom door lock turn.

Silence settled over the suite.

Big Julie lay on the floor, waiting for his breathing to restore to normal. He was fairly comfortable, all things considered. After a second, he heard a phone ring. Then Drake, the bodyguard, stuck his head cautiously around the door.

"It's your wife," he said, glancing at the bedroom door. "I think you should take it."

Big Julie sighed and rolled to his side, struggled to his hands and knees, and finally grabbed the back of the sofa to stand up.

"Not so young anymore," he said as he staggered toward the suite's den.

Drake wisely ignored this. "Would you like some more coffee?" he asked.

Big Julie tried to get his bearings, shaking his head like a wounded bear. "Coffee?" he said. "Way past that stage. Bloody Mary. And keep 'em coming."

"Sure thing." Drake disappeared into the suite's kitchen and Big Julie went into the den, collapsing on a leather sofa. He glared at the phone with its blinking light. *Marilyn.* Why was she calling? He'd left her with the checkbook, the family credit cards, the car, everything she could possibly want.

He picked up the phone, punched in the blinking light. "Marilyn?" he said, trying to sound cheerful and not like he'd just got his lights dimmed by leaping over a sofa after his girlfriend. "What's going on?"

"We need to talk," Marilyn said, triggering a sudden feeling of dread in Big Julie. "I've been feeling terrible ever since you left Passaic, and I know it's all my fault. When I said I'd kill you, I didn't mean it, Julie. I want to make it up to you."

"Oh?" said Big Julie, wary. "That's nice. I should be home—"

"So I'm on my way," Marilyn said. "I'm at the airport in Chicago right now, and I'll be in Vegas around three-thirty. Can you pick me up?"

"Unhg," Big Julie gasped, feeling that he was taking that walk on the bottom of the ocean after all.

"I want us to be *happy* again," Marilyn said. "Like we used to be. I'll see you this afternoon, Julie."

She hung up.

Drake came into the den with the Bloody Mary.

"Bad news?" he asked, glancing at Big Julie's face as he set down the glass on a smooth leather coaster.

"Marilyn's coming." Big Julie grabbed the glass and took a slug of his drink. "This afternoon."

"Oh?"

"Damn right, *oh*. What the hell am I going to do, Drake?"

Drake glanced out the window. *Jump*, his expression seemed to suggest.

"It's a problem," he agreed.

"You're no help," Big Julie said, fearing what might make his wife happy. The thought of having to get into bed with the flannel- nightgown-wearing, hair-curler-sprouting, face-cream-slathering Marilyn, while the ripe, luscious, soft, yielding, athletic, and best of all, naked Baby lay alone and neglected somewhere else, well, it was enough to weaken a man's resolve, if you got the drift.

"No," Drake agreed again. "And you have another problem, sir."

"Whatever it is, the answer is no," Big Julie said. "No more problems today."

"Well, this is a problem you have to take care of," Drake said. "You know how trouble comes in threes? I think problem number three is sitting in the living room."

"Right now? In the living room right now?" Big Julie asked.

Drake nodded.

"Is it a dame?" Big Julie asked. "Because I am done with dames."

"It is, ah, a dame," Drake said.

"And you let her in because—"

"Because, remember? You got a call from Jersey last night. From Marty the Sneak. And he's calling in his favor from last winter when he helped you with that thing in Atlantic City."

Big Julie remembered. Remembered it all—last night, the call, Atlantic City, the thing, and Marty the Sneak. He groaned.

"So what does Marty want I should do?"

"He wants you to talk to this nice woman who is sitting in your living room right now, and listen to what she has to say, and if you can, accommodate her. Marty says he thinks you can accommodate her."

Big Julie sighed. "Is she a looker?"

"She is indeed."

"Dammit to hell," Big Julie said. "I have really had it with good-looking women." And then he went out to the living room to deal with his third problem.

Hope stood up when Big Julie entered the living room. He looked terrible. He was wearing a big, white, terry-cloth robe, he was unshaven, and his hair was a mess. He looked pasty, like he was hung over or tired and hadn't seen the sun in any of his fifty years. He was holding a Bloody Mary, too.

This'll be bad, she thought.

She, on the other hand, had given a lot of thought to her appearance. Hope knew that she didn't have her mother's looks, but at least she had half the lucky gene pool. She was tall and blonde, and she was wearing her hair down, so Big Julie probably would like that, and her figure was decent and her features were regular bordering on pleasant. So she had that going for her, but she hadn't been sure what to wear. She wanted to look businesslike without looking prim. She'd settled on a navy suit with a skirt and high heels and a tight, bright pink camisole that had shrunk in the wash and never been worn again until today.

She hoped that would do the trick.

"Hello, Mr. Saladino," she said. "I'm Hope McNaughton. Thank you for seeing me."

"Yeah," Big Julie said, dropping into a sofa. The bathrobe gapped open over his bulk, and Hope quickly averted her eyes.

We've barely been introduced, and already I have too much information.

"Siddown, siddown," Big Julie said irritably, readjusting his robe. "Whaddaya wanna drink?"

"Oh, thank you, nothing," Hope said as she sat down again. She smiled, focusing on his face. "I don't want to take up too much of your time, but Marty said I should explain."

"Explain what? Drake, get her an orange juice. Or a Snapple. We got some good Snapple—lemonade, peach tea, whatever you want."

"Um, well, plain iced tea would be good if you have it."

"Drake, see if we got that. Okay, now explain."

Drake glided away again.

"I understand that at your poker game a week ago, you played with Derek McNaughton, and you won a ranch from him."

A smile lit Big Julie's face.

"I sure did. That guy don't quit, I gotta give him that. But he didn't have the cards that night. You know this guy?"

"He's my father," Hope said.

"Oh," Big Julie said. "Bad luck for you."

"You don't know the half of it." Hope paused while Drake brought in her iced tea, and she took a sip while he settled in a chair in the background.

"My family lives on that ranch," Hope said.

"So what is it you would like me to do?" Big Julie said. "Assuming I can do it, or want to do it, or will do it, which is not certain yet. Because I am guessing that if you know I got the ranch, you know I got a buyer lined up. A company that specializes in destination entertainment."

Hope nodded, feeling her stomach clench, knowing that she had to play her hand with everything she had, and be lucky, as well. And sitting across from this tired, hung-over, semi-naked Mafioso, she didn't believe that the odds were on her side.

"The lawyer I talked to said the place is worth two million dollars," she said. "My family doesn't have anywhere near that kind of money, Mr. Saladino, but we love that ranch. We've always lived there. We'd be heartbroken to leave it."

Big Julie finished his Bloody Mary with a slurp through the straw and put the empty glass on the end table.

"Yeah, see, I'm not in the charity business," he said. "Tell Marty I'm sorry about your loss and all, but I won that ranch fair and square."

"I'm not asking for charity, Mr. Saladino," she said. "I want to play you for the ranch."

Big Julie's eyes opened a little wider. "What?" he asked.

Go for it now. Hope unbuttoned her jacket and leaned forward, putting her glass on the table in front of her. She watched him while his eyes drifted toward the pink camisole. *Excellent.*

"In next Saturday's card game," she said. "I want to play. You win, you take my stake, you keep the ranch. I win, I get the ranch."

Big Julie stared, but he didn't budge.

"I don't think so," he said. "There's already eight in the game. Anyways, I got a buyer."

Hope took off her jacket, turning to lay it on the back of

the sofa, letting Big Julie get an eyeful of pretty much everything she had.

"I understand," she said, crossing her legs and smiling. "Still, the buyer wants concessions, right? Turning the property into an entertainment destination will be complicated. The sale isn't a simple cashout. There'll be leveraged stakeholders, stock options, maybe bonds to float, perc and land tests, permits, contingencies, covenants, restrictions, valuations, who knows what. You can't get it done in a week. You can't get it done in a *month*. Maybe several months. Even years. It's a lot of work. Maybe more work than the property's worth to you."

Big Julie had torn his eyes away from the pink camisole while she'd been talking, but now that she'd wound down, he was staring at her chest again. *Back in the game.*

"I'm just asking you to let me play." Hope recrossed her legs. Not that she had any evidence that Big Julie was a leg man.

"So what's this cozy little meeting going on in here?" a strident female voice asked.

Hope looked up to see a gorgeous, pampered, unhappy-looking young woman storm into the room. The young woman stared at her tight pink camisole and exposed thigh with deep suspicion.

Wrong outfit for her, Hope thought. *I blew it.*

"Hello," Hope said, trying to sound unthreatening. "I'm—"

"Baby, honey," Big Julie said, placating. "This here is—what did you say your name was again, Sweetheart?"

Hope blinked. "Hope," she said. "Hope McNaughton."

"Hope, here, is just asking me if she can play in next Saturday's game."

"Oh, is *that* what she's here for," Baby said, crossing her arms, glaring at Hope. "I thought it was for something else."

"Baby, you know I would never—"

"I'm watching you, Big Julie. You are never getting out of my sight until—"

And then, as Hope watched Big Julie gaze at the angry china-doll blonde, Hope saw an Idea enter Big Julie's head. His eyes went from desperate to smug in a second. And then she knew she was in the game—on Big Julie's terms, whatever they were.

He looked at Hope with a diabolical smile. "Hope here wants to play in the big leagues. And I was just about to tell her that she's in if she brings a stake of two hundred to the table and you take her shopping. Today. At *three-thirty*. And not a minute later."

"What? No," Hope said, confusion overtaking her surge of anticipation. "Shopping? Why?"

"Three-thirty today," Big Julie said. "Three-thirty *today*, you and Baby here go shopping. And you bring two hundred to the game next Saturday, and you can play."

Hope's heart pounded with excitement. *She was in the game*. And all she had to do was spend one afternoon shopping and bring a two hundred dollar stake.

"Me?" Baby said, incredulous. "Take her shopping? No way."

"Spend what you like," Big Julie said, uttering the magic words.

"Why do I have to take her shopping?" Baby asked, still suspicious.

"Are you kidding?" Big Julie asked, smug with victory. "She can't play cards looking like that."

"*What?*" Hope said, "Of course I—" But Baby looked at Hope, appraising her outfit. Evidently what Big Julie said made sense to her.

"Well, okay, I'll do it," she said. "But don't expect miracles."

"*Hey*," Hope said.

"So if you could just leave Hope and me for a second to settle some details, I'll be in to settle some details with you, too," Big Julie said. "Only yours will take longer."

Baby sniffed, but she tossed her head and left the room.

The second she was gone, Big Julie leaned forward.

"My wife is coming at three-thirty today," he said. "If you want to play next Saturday, you will take Baby shopping today and *every day* until then."

"What?" Hope said, her head spinning. "I can't. I have to *work*."

"Take it or leave it," Big Julie said. "I don't care. And don't forget, you need the two hundred, too."

"Shopping, every day," Hope said. She hated shopping, and Baby didn't like her. That should be fun. But at least she could afford the stake—Marty would be surprised. "And two hundred dollars. That at least I can manage."

"Two hundred dollars—you're a kidder," Big Julie said. "I like that."

Chapter 5

The next morning after breakfast, Amber dragged a dining room chair over to the desk in the corner and booted up the family's computer.

"What vegetables are you shipping this week, Mom?" she asked Faith, as the machine grunted and whirred. Amber helped her mom by typing up recipes and menus for the produce Faith packed and delivered. The two of them would be making a delivery run into Vegas as soon as everything was ready.

Faith put down the box she'd been filling. "Let me see," she said. "Chard. Carrots. Beets. Tomatoes, lettuce, spinach, onions, and potatoes—red and Yukon gold."

"Okay," Amber said. She pulled down the family's favorite cookbook and turned to the vegetable section. Her mom said that Amber needed to be original when she made up the recipes. She couldn't just copy something out of a cookbook—she had to create. Amber wanted to be creative, but when she altered the recipes, the customers usually complained.

Amber wasn't surprised that the recipes didn't turn out. She was ten. And she was guessing.

She sighed, looking for something that she could type up for this week. Here was one for "Spinach, Tomato, and Cheese Loaf" that used two of the vegetables in the box. Amber started typing.

Two cups cooked, drained spinach. Okay.

Two and a quarter cups drained, canned tomatoes. Oops. No cans allowed. Make that, okay, *three cups fresh, chopped tomatoes*, because she really hated typing fractions.

One-quarter cup chili sauce. What was "chili sauce"? Amber typed, *one cup catsup*. No fractions, no chili sauce.

One-half pound grated hard cheese or crumbled feta. Wasn't a half-pound an awful lot? Amber typed, *one cup grated cheese*.

One cup cracker crumbs. Okay.

Juice of one-half onion. What? How did you juice an onion? Amber wasn't typing that. But her mom said she had onions for the box. Okay. That would work. *One chopped onion*.

One-quarter teaspoon salt. No. Grammy said she had to watch her blood pressure, and she wasn't eating salt. So no salt.

One-quarter teaspoon pepper. Okay. Pepper didn't seem to have anything to do with blood pressure. But maybe she would add a little more, to make up for no salt. Amber typed, *one teaspoon pepper*.

Then she typed up the baking directions.

There. One creative recipe done. Five more to go.

"The first recipe is Spinach, Tomato, and Cheese Loaf," Amber said, struggling a little with the formatting.

"That sounds good, Sweetie," Faith said, carefully wrapping the beets in bio-degradable plastic wrap and placing them in the bottom of the box she was packing. "We should try that one ourselves one night."

Only if we follow the recipe in the cookbook, Amber thought. She didn't know how the recipe would go wrong the way she did it, she only knew that it would. That's what happened when you got too creative. You got a big mess. And she didn't know any way to fix that.

Hope met her uncles at the Golden Palace all-you-can-eat, four-ninety-five Chinese dim-sum buffet for a late lunch. They claimed a table and headed for the serving area, where steam tables and iced platters of dumplings, noodle dishes, meat morsels, and steamed seafood beckoned. Marty picked up a plate and contemplated the choices.

"How did the meeting with Big Julie go?" he asked as he piled some barbecued ribs onto his plate. "He must have said you can play. What's the stake?"

"Two hundred dollars." Hope looked over the cold shrimp, her mouth watering.

Marty shook his head, putting some of the ribs on Hope's plate. "Hope, I think you been out of the game too long. Is that what Big Julie said? Bring two hundred?"

Hope nodded, adding some shrimp to her plate. She should have taken a bigger plate. "Yes. So at least I can manage that."

"Honey, what he meant was, not you should bring two *hundred* dollars, but you should bring two hundred *thousand* dollars."

"What?" Hope felt disappointment like a blow, stopping so suddenly that Sharp Eddie ran into her, poking her back with his plate. "Two hundred thousand dollars? I can't do it then. Marty, I can't raise that kind of money in a week." Her credit cards were maxed out, and she couldn't afford a third loan. She was at her limit everywhere.

"Of course you can," Marty said, picking up a set of tongs and easing a red bean paste bun onto Hope's plate.

"That's why we're here," Sharp Eddie agreed, taking a heaping spoonful of steamed crab for himself and putting another on Hope's plate.

"You have to earn your stake, like everybody else does in these games," Marty said, moving on to the steamed dumplings. "Do you like these things? I hate cilantro. Tastes like soap. Here, try one. Everybody says they're delicious."

"I can't win two hundred thousand dollars in a week,"

Hope said, horrified. "I played for two hours today and I lost eight dollars." She looked at her overflowing plate. "Leave the dumplings. I don't think I can eat a thing."

"You gotta eat," Marty said, putting first the dumpling and then a miniature omelet on Hope's plate. "Nothing to be scared of. If you can't win even your stake, then you have no business playing Big Julie for a two million dollar ranch."

"Practice," Sharp Eddie agreed. "That's all it is."

"You mean gamble for the stake and then gamble for the ranch? I don't know," Hope said, feeling sick. Who could take those chances? Not her.

Marty stopped putting food on Hope's plate and turned to face her.

"Hope," he said. "What happened to you? Cards ain't gambling. *Slots* is gambling. Slots is you donating your money to the house which has rigged the game for you to lose. Cards is skill. You know that. And you got the chops for it—or you used to. You want to win this thing, you gotta be aggressive. Think big. You can do it, or we wouldn't be here."

Hope exhaled, pushing her hair back. She looked at him.

"We're here because we owe you," Marty said, still holding the tongs with the shrimp dumpling. "You held our marker. Now you called it in. We can get your game back. But you gotta play it."

"I held your marker?" Hope asked, confused.

"Don't get us wrong, Hope," Marty said. "We'd a come anyways. But it's up to you. You gotta decide right now what it's gonna be. Because whether you think you're gonna win, or you think you're gonna lose—either way, you're right."

By three o'clock, having dismissed cheaper ideas, Big Julie had a whole new wardrobe and a new suite to put it in. What else could he do? He couldn't put Marilyn in some cheap room and tell her that he was spending nights with Baby in the suite. He would be dead with his balls cut off before sunrise. He couldn't move Baby into a similar room and tell her that Marilyn deserved the suite. He would be dead with his balls cut off before sunrise. The only way out that he could see was to rent a second suite, put Marilyn in it, buy some clothes and hang those in the closet, pretend that he'd been there all along, and never, ever tell either one that the other one was there.

Where were those cement shoes? Walking on water with them would be simpler.

Marilyn's suite was on the fifteenth floor. Baby's was on the sixteenth. Way too close. Whoever designed this Desert Dunes place should have thought better than to put all the suites in the same place, like one on each floor. Damn stupid.

That was the first thing.

Then there was the coming and going. This broad who wanted to play in Saturday's game—what was her name again?—she'd take Baby off his hands every afternoon. But what about the other times? Mornings? Nights? Alternate nights, he could sleep with one and tell the other one that he had a late night card game someplace else. That would work, for a while anyway. Not for long, though. Neither one of them was stupid.

So that was the second thing.

And the *expense*. Two suites at the Desert Dunes didn't come cheap, and that would be the least of it. Marilyn would no sooner step out of the cab than she'd start waving credit cards at everything she saw, like the queen of Sheba waving at her servants to bring her stuff. Baby was burning a hole in his pocket. And he had major expenses for meals, drinks, facials, massages—not to mention his own new wardrobe.

Ten grand here, ten grand there, it added up. Big Julie prayed the mess with the Russian mob would resolve itself so he could stop paying lawyers and cops and snitches and start putting some money where it belonged—in the crawl space in the ceiling.

And that was the third thing. Somehow it seemed like it had to be more things than just three, but Big Julie was too exhausted to think of what they might be. He and Drake had bought out the shops downstairs, and now the suite on the fifteenth floor was full of clothes he wouldn't be caught dead in if he had a choice, which he didn't. He had to buy what the shops had. Like red sequin thong undershorts, for chrissake. Who could wear those without getting a cramp? And those floral shirts and those electric blue pants. They looked like something that exercise guy, Richard Simmons, would wear, if he ever wore pants.

Big Julie poured himself a drink and felt nervous sweat dampen his armpits. In thirty minutes he'd have to go down one flight to Marilyn's suite and pretend that he'd been staying there all along. He'd have to make nice with her, even when he'd rather make nice—make real nice, lots of times—with Baby. He'd have to keep the key cards straight. He'd have to restock the bar. He'd have to *remember*.

Big Julie sat on the sofa, thinking about everything he had to do and the disasters that would befall him if he did not do those things. He realized for the first time that maybe everything that happened in Vegas just might not stay in Vegas.

Punctually at three-thirty Hope went to Big Julie's suite to pick Baby up for their shopping trip. Drake opened the door.

"Hi," she said, eying Drake's sharp attire. "I'm here for Baby. Are you the butler?"

"Bodyguard," Drake said. "I opened the door because you're no threat."

"Yes, I am," Hope said, ruffled. "I'm a big threat. I'm getting my ranch back. Is Baby ready?"

"How should I know? Do I look like a butler?" Drake asked, drifting away.

"Yes," Hope called after him. "Just not a very good one." But Drake was gone, leaving Hope standing in the hallway. Some bodyguard.

She entered the suite, looking around until she found Baby in a huge bedroom putting things in a trendy leather purse adorned with buckles it didn't need.

"I don't know why I have to take you shopping," she complained when she saw Hope.

"Because Big Julie asked you to, because I need some accessories, and because you know where to shop," Hope said, eying the purse. Shopping with Baby, even for two hours, looked like an eternity. Who else had to do this just to play cards? She should be downstairs right now, earning her stake. But here she was, about to go shopping.

"Accessories? Just accessories?" Baby glanced at Hope's suit again, dismissing it.

"Yes," Hope said firmly. "Bracelets, sunglasses, and a hat."

"Well, if we have to, we have to," Baby said, giving herself a last glance in the mirror. "I do know a darling shop for jewelry."

"It has to be costume jewelry," Hope said, suddenly alarmed, as they left the suite. She had a vision that Baby might think a "darling shop" was Tiffany's. "I need something that's big and clanks."

"That's how you buy jewelry? Because it clanks? No wonder you look like that."

"How do I look? No, don't tell me." Hope had to admit that Baby looked terrific. She was like a porcelain doll, carefully made up in vivid colors—bright blonde hair, red lipstick, big blue eyes—and all the outfits Hope had seen her in were tight, short, and brightly colored. But Baby pulled it off. She looked stylish and modern and fresh and, well, hot.

Not Hope's look at all.

"You look like you never have fun," Baby said.

Hope blinked. She thought she looked fairly nice most of the time. She wore suits in neutral colors to work, and she wore jeans and tee-shirts at home. Hope thought she looked well-dressed and practical, but looking at Baby, she had to admit: she wasn't big on the wow factor. Whereas Baby was all wow, all the time.

"I have fun," Hope said, trying not to sound defensive.

"You look like you're going to the office," Baby said, as they got into the elevator. "On a Saturday. Where's the fun in that?"

True, Hope thought, there were more fun things to do on a Saturday than going to the office, but shopping with Baby wasn't one of them. The elevator deposited them on the lobby floor, and Baby headed toward a retail atrium.

"Down here," she commanded, leading the way.

Hope trailed after her, feeling resentful. They stopped in front of a shop. The window was full of sparkling, colorful costume jewelry. Some big, clanking bracelets were among the pieces displayed. Hope perked up. Those bracelets were cute. Baby knew her merchandise.

"Here we are," Baby said.

Hope peered into the glass, looking closer, and then saw the price tag of one item peeking out from underneath a faux jewel. She almost fainted.

"Baby, those things are nice, but I can't spend this much," she said.

"Big Julie said to spend what I want," Baby said, stepping into the shop.

"Yes, you can spend what you want, but I'm on a different budget." Hope sighed in frustration as Baby, already inside looking at displays, ignored her. Hope gave up and followed her into the shop.

Twelve hundred dollars for a bracelet? Hope knew she was out of touch with what nice things cost, but yikes. That was rent for a month. And this bracelet was plastic. Cute plastic, set with glass shiny things. But still. Twelve hundred dollars.

Inside, Baby was holding up earrings against her face in front of a mirror. Any of the earrings would have looked fabulous on her, and well they should, Hope thought, as she checked the price tags. Four hundred dollars. Hope put the earrings down.

"Baby," she hissed. "I can't afford anything here. We have to go to Target."

All nearby eyes swiveled to Hope. Conversation stopped, and all movement ground to a halt. The whole store locked in a freeze-frame.

Baby swiveled slowly toward Hope, her face a horrified mask.

"What did you say?" she asked.

"I said, we have to go to Target. I can't afford these things."

Baby blinked, her mouth open.

"I mean it," Hope said.

Baby's brows knitted in a look of consternation. "Go outside and meet me by the fountain in fifteen minutes."

Hope shook her head as she left the shop, congratulating herself on ditching an unwelcome shopping companion. But Baby rejoined Hope just a few minutes later, swinging a bright shopping bag and looking like she'd never heard of a cheapskate named Hope.

"You didn't like that store, okay," Baby said, sitting down next to Hope. "I don't get it, I think they have adorable things. But don't scare me like that again. Target." She shuddered.

"No, I meant it, Baby," Hope said. "I can't afford that jewelry. You're right, it's nice. But the bracelets I need are for the card games. They have to clank so that when I move my hands on the card table, I'll notice. And I need big sunglasses to hide my eyes and a big hat to hide my face. I need stuff that's functional. And cheap."

Baby stared at her in shock. "You mean, you actually want to go to Target? For real?"

"Or someplace like that."

Baby looked at Hope as though she'd just said she ate worms for breakfast.

"I have a car. Let's drive," Hope said finally.

"What kind of car?" Baby said, clearly not expecting much.

"Toyota Prius," Hope said, and Baby sighed in resignation, having had her worst fears confirmed.

"Do I have to?" she asked.

"Big Julie said."

"Let's go, then," Baby said. "But don't ever tell anybody I went shopping at Target."

Like she'd ever tell anyone she went shopping with Baby.

"My lips are sealed," Hope promised.

Tanner stayed at the four hundred dollar table for a few hours and left after he'd cleared three thousand dollars. When he stood up to cash out his chips, he glanced over at the three dollar table, but the Jersey guys and the mysterious Hope McNaughton who claimed she didn't know Derek McNaughton were all gone.

Uncles, my eye.

He glanced at his watch. He'd told Troy he'd be home for dinner, but he was hungry now. Maybe he could stop by the kitchen, see Kenji, and cadge a snack before he went home.

He walked through the casino, greeting the floor managers, pit bosses, waitresses, and dealers he knew, and went to the Ginger Palace, one of the casino's fancier restaurants that was open only for dinner. Kenji Hasegawa, the chef, would be in the back, getting ready for the evening.

Tanner said hi to the maître d' who was checking

reservations and asked if Kenji was working. Tanner was a familiar face in the casino, and the maître d' waved him past the red velvet rope that barricaded the entryway without losing his look of concentration. Tanner headed toward the kitchen and pushed his way into the double swinging doors, just in time to see Kenji handing a plate of niblets to a young girl.

"Hey, Kenj," Tanner said, sidestepping some sous chefs and bus boys who were flying around the kitchen, doing setups for the dinner crowd. He wondered whose kid that was. Couldn't be Kenji's. The girl was maybe ten and had blonde, wavy hair. Definitely she swam in a gene pool other than Kenji's. Kenji was built like a sumo wrestler, even if he was the most delicate chef in Las Vegas, maybe the west coast. Plus, he'd known Kenji for years, and the guy didn't have any kids, blonde or otherwise. "How's it going?"

Kenji Hasegawa stood up and grinned at his friend. "It's going," he said. "Amber, meet Tanner."

"Hey, Amber," Tanner said.

"Hi," Amber said. She barely glanced at Tanner. She'd put the little piece of sushi into her mouth and was trying to decide if she liked it.

"Amber's trying out something new," Kenji said. "What do you think, Amber?"

"It's very *unusual*," Amber said cautiously.

"Let me try it," Tanner said.

"Is that why you came in here?" Kenji asked, sliding a few pieces of sushi onto a plate for his friend. "To get something to eat?"

"That's one reason," Tanner said, taking the plate. "Also I wanted to see if you wanted to go to the UNLV game next week, after Troy leaves."

"Are you kidding? I'm their biggest fan." Suddenly he frowned at Tanner. "But I never thought you were. You're going to college sports now?"

Tanner shrugged, looking at Amber. "Gotta do something," he said. "You got any unagi? I don't think Amber likes this roe much, but she'll like unagi."

Amber glanced at Tanner, startled. "I didn't say I don't like it," she said.

"You'll like unagi a lot better," Tanner said. "It's the best."

"What is it called again?"

"Unagi. It's barbecued...fish." He didn't want to tell her eel until she'd tried it. But unagi was made for kids. It had a delicate, slightly sweet flavor and didn't look yucky at all.

Kenji slid a piece of the unagi roll onto Amber's plate, and she bit into it carefully just as a sous chef, carrying a load of bok choy from the refrigerator, bumped into Amber's stool. She clutched the wall for balance, but managed to hang onto her plate.

"Let's go into the dining room," Kenji said. "It's quieter in there."

Tanner took Amber's plate while the girl slid off her stool. "Is your mom going to miss you?" he asked as they left the kitchen. "We don't want her to worry."

"She's bringing in a delivery," Kenji said, ahead of them and already laying out his knives on the counter. "She knows Amber's safe with us."

"Okay. How'd you like that unagi, Amber?"

The girl looked at Tanner, nodding. "It was *delicious*."

"What did I tell you? The ones with crab and shrimp are great, too. Kenji is the best chef this side of the Mississippi."

Amber nodded again. "That's what my mom said. She was really excited when he started ordering her vegetables."

"So your mom delivers vegetables." Tanner watched the child, who was focused on Kenji as he sharpened his blades.

"She grows vegetables. And then she delivers them."

"She's an organic farmer out toward Mesquite Springs," Kenji said, taking his sushi knife and slicing carefully into a whole fish. Tanner watched Amber's eyes grow round as she watched.

"And you come with her," Tanner said, eating his own sushi.

"Sometimes. It's more fun now that she comes here. I like to watch."

Tanner watched Kenji's knife slash through carrots now, slicing them into narrow strips, curly shapes, oblongs with ruffled edges—whatever his creations needed.

"Do you want to be a chef when you grow up?"

At that, Amber looked away from Kenji and focused on Tanner, her mood suddenly different.

"No!" she said fervently. "I have to make up recipes for the vegetable boxes, and I don't understand anything. Nothing I put down tastes good. And look at Kenji. He's *awesome*. I could never be like that."

Tanner blinked. Amber had given this a lot of thought. And come to some bleak conclusions.

"Kenji's been to cooking school," he said. "And he's had a ton of practice. If you did that, you'd be good, too."

"I don't think so," Amber said, shaking her head, still looking upset.

"Of course you would," Tanner said, "if you wanted to. Okay, maybe you don't want to spend your whole life cutting the heads off dead fish. That wouldn't be the worst decision you'd ever make."

Amber grinned, glancing quickly at Kenji to see if he'd heard.

"Hey!" Kenji said. "There's nothing wrong with cutting up fish."

"Not for you. But for Amber—maybe you'd rather be a pastry chef," he told the girl. "The first thing you could work on is the perfect brownie. I'll volunteer to be your taster. I have a lot to say about brownies."

Now Amber giggled.

Just then the swinging doors from the kitchen flew open

and a blonde woman hurried through.

"There you are!" she smiled at Amber, coming up and smoothing the girl's hair. "Sorry I took so long. We should get out of here and let these guys get back to work." She turned to Kenji. "I hope Amber didn't get in the way. She loves to watch."

"She's never a bother," Kenji said, "as I've told you before. Bring her anytime."

Amber beamed, grabbing her mother's hand.

"Mom, this is Tanner. He thinks I should be a pastry chef."

"You could be a pastry chef, or a nuclear physicist, or a circus clown. Anything you want." The woman turned to look at Tanner, and Tanner felt a shock. He'd bet any money that this woman was related to Hope McNaughton. This woman was younger, for sure. But otherwise, they could be sisters.

"Tanner Wingate," Tanner said, holding out his hand. "I was telling Amber that I'm still searching for the perfect brownie. My hopes are pinned on her." He smiled at the girl, who grinned back at him.

"Faith McNaughton," the woman said, shaking his hand, and Tanner felt himself grin. He'd been right.

"You wouldn't be related to Hope McNaughton, would you?" he asked. "I just met her this afternoon. She was playing cards with some guys from New Jersey."

"Our uncles," Faith said. "Hope's my sister."

There was that uncles line again. Unbelievable.

"Come on Amber, let's go," Faith said. "I told Aunt Hope that we'd all have dinner together before she goes out to play cards tonight, and I have to move the truck out of Kenji's delivery space or he won't be so nice next time." The two of them started back toward the swinging doors.

"Next time bring me more cabbage, and all will be forgiven," Kenji said, lifting his hand in farewell.

"Next time I'll bring you a mountain of cabbage, Kenji,"

Faith said.

"Mom, we don't have a mountain of cabbage," Amber whispered, looking worried.

Tanner grinned. He hoped Amber would become a pastry chef. She seemed much too practical to be a circus clown.

"See you, Amber," he said. The girl turned around to give him a wave.

"You were right!" she called. "The unagi was the best!"

Tanner watched the two of them push through the swinging doors, and just as they disappeared into the kitchen, he heard Faith say, "So, Amber, have you decided what you want to do for your birthday next Tuesday?"

Nice kid. And now she was having a birthday. They grew up so fast.

Tanner collected his pickup and drove home to the well-maintained ranch-style house he shared with his daughter. Troy was in her bedroom trying to squeeze three cubic feet of personal items into a two-cubic-foot suitcase.

"I'll never get everything packed," she wailed in frustration, flopping down on her bed. The pink chenille spread, normally smoothed over the frame, was disheveled and wrinkled, much like his daughter. The open, uncooperative suitcase bounced on the mattress.

"I guess you can't go then," Tanner said with a grin.

"Oh, Daddy." She scowled at the suitcase, a young woman with major packing problems, and then looked at her father, leaning against the doorframe. Suddenly her face changed, and she looked not much older than Amber, more like the little girl he had helped get ready for camp too few years ago.

"It's so soon," she said, her face twisting a little.

Tanner came into the room and sat down on the bed, edging his eighteen-year-old daughter over to make space. He stroked her hair.

"College is a lot different," he said. "But you're ready

for this. You're going to do great. You'll make a lot of new friends. I'll still be here. You can always call. You'll come back at Thanksgiving. And you won't go on any dates until you're twenty-five."

"Oh, *Daddy*."

He laughed, standing up. "Are you hungry?" he asked. "I think there's enough stuff for salad and spaghetti."

"No, there isn't," Troy said, bouncing off the bed. "I ate that for lunch. And I've been here all day, packing and stuff. And I went for a swim and I'm starving. Can we go out for Chinese?"

"Out it is. Give me a minute to change."

When he came out of the shower a few minutes later, Troy was still getting dressed, so he wandered into the kitchen and looked up "McNaughton." There were no local listings for Hope. Faith lived in Mesquite Springs, Kenji had said, but the Las Vegas directory didn't cover small towns forty miles away. Maybe the sisters lived together.

"What are you looking for?" Troy came into the kitchen, looking so fresh and young that his heart ached.

"Oh, nothing, really."

Troy just stood there, her head tilted to one side, watching him.

"Okay, then, smartypants," Tanner said, sighing in mock resignation. "I met a card player today, and she's got the same last name as another card player from Vegas, and she denies knowing him. And that seems weird. I mean, what are the odds? So I wondered if I could find her online."

"Do you want to ask her out on a date?"

"What did I tell you?" Tanner asked, picking up his keys. "No dating for anybody until they're twenty-five. Now, if you're ready, let's go."

Chapter 6

After Tanner and Troy finished dinner, he dropped her at her best friend Lizbeth's house. The two girls planned to go to a movie, and if Tanner knew anything about teenagers, flirt with boys. At least he hoped that's all they'd do.

"Remember that I'll know everything you do," he said. "So be careful."

"I will. Jeez, Dad. Lighten up! I'm going to college next week."

"It's not too late to rethink that plan."

Troy grinned as she got out of the car. "Lizbeth will drive me home. We won't drink, do drugs, or have sex. I'll be careful."

"Okay. Have fun."

"If that's even possible if you know everything I do." She laughed, tossing him a saucy glance, her ponytail bouncing, as she turned and ran up the lawn of her friend's house.

He watched her go, remembering how his own parents had given him the same warnings. And just like Troy, he hadn't really listened, never thinking that anything could happen to him. And as a consequence, he'd become a father at nineteen, his whole world turned upside down.

Not that he would alter anything if he could. He'd wanted his daughter with a fierce protectiveness ever since the day she was born, when she'd wailed and clutched his finger as the only safe haven in a cold, cruel world. He'd been surprised at the depth of his emotions then, but never doubted them—not when his girlfriend's parents came to put the baby up for adoption, not when, in desperation, he'd asked Jack's father, a corporate attorney, to represent him when he asked for permanent custody. The court case had seemed to drag on forever, but in the end, Troy was his.

And that's when the work had really started. He'd moved back home, finished college at night when his folks could watch his baby daughter, and he watched her in the daytime when they worked. His parents had really come through for him.

Those first few years were tough for all of them, but it had been more than worth it. Raising Troy had been incredible, the hardest, most fun, best thing he'd ever done. Troy had made him the man he was. A better man than he'd started out to be.

He drove home, believing, hoping, that Troy was smarter at eighteen than he'd been, and let himself into the house. He checked his messages. One. From agent Frelly.

"Call me when you get in," Frelly growled.

Tanner sighed. What were the odds? Frelly would want him to go back to the casino. Maybe he'd found a way for Tanner to get in Big Julie's game tonight.

He called the number the agent had left and Frelly picked up on the first ring.

"You gotta get over to the casino," Frelly said. "We can fit you into Big Julie's game tonight."

"So soon?" Tanner asked. He tried to keep the doubt out of his voice. He'd only talked to the agents this morning. Surely replacing one of Big Julie's regular card players with a total stranger couldn't be that easy. Big Julie would be suspicious of substitutions.

"Yeah," Frelly said. "One of his regulars ate a peanut. Guy's allergic to peanuts. They hadda call an ambulance. Darla's at the Desert Dunes waiting for you. We hid a camera in Big Julie's bathroom. You go in pretending to take a leak. You take out the camera and hide it someplace in the room where they're playing. It's tiny. You won't have no problem. Darla will show you how it works."

"How am I getting into the game?" he asked. "I can't just show up at the door and ask if Big Julie wants to play."

"No," Frelly agreed. "The floor manager will call Big Julie and ask him, since his seventh player is in the ICU, if he wants to play with you, because you are in the house and you're not bad but not that good, either—"

"Hey!" Tanner said. "I'm very good."

"Yeah, well, the point to remember here is that you won't be playing that good with Big Julie, because we need him to win."

Tanner thought. It sounded thin, but the point was to get him in Big Julie's game. If this half-baked subterfuge got him there, fine.

"Okay," he said. "I'll go down there. You're staking me, of course."

"Much as I hate to do it," Frelly said.

Tanner rolled his eyes. "Then it's showtime."

But when Tanner got to the casino and went to the manager's office, Darla told him the gig was off.

"Big Julie is too despondent to play because his regular has gone into anaphylactic shock with the peanut," Darla reported. "Tonight's game is cancelled. Sorry about that."

Tanner thought about the chores he might have done that evening instead and felt philosophical.

"Will Big Julie still be feeling despondent next week, too?" he asked.

"I think he'll be feeling better," Darla said.

"I'd like to know how you guys do it," Tanner said, as he opened the door that lead out to the floor. "That peanut was no accident."

"Hey," Darla said, grabbing her purse, preparing to

follow. "Peanuts are everywhere. A person's got to be careful."

Tanner cut through the casino, thinking that if the action looked good he might as well play a few hands, when he saw Hope McNaughton sitting alone at the bar, still wearing that ridiculous navy suit, clutching a glass, and looking like she was going to throw up.

It was a man's duty, not to mention his pleasure, to rescue a damsel in distress, so Tanner changed course and headed her way. Not that Hope, who must be five eight at least, was his idea of a damsel, exactly. In that suit, with that bright pink top underneath, she looked more like a really hot accountant, who, when she wanted to balance her ledgers with you, just took off her glasses and let down her hair before she really, really cooked your books.

Tanner shook his head, trying to get a grip, and then he slid onto the stool next to her, signaling the bartender for a beer before he nudged her elbow gently with his own.

"Tanner Wingate, remember me? We met today? Friend of Marty's?"

Hope turned and looked at him blankly.

"I guess I didn't make that good an impression."

Hope blinked and seemed to come back into focus. "I'm sorry. What?"

"Tanner Wingate," Tanner said again. "We met earlier."

"Oh, right." She sat up a little straighter. "The card player."

"That's me. So, what's up?"

"Not much." Hope took a pull out of her drink and set the glass back on the bar, smacking it against the edge as she did so. Some of the drink slopped onto the polished surface, and the bartended wiped it up as he set down Tanner's beer.

She was just unbelievably beautiful. She looked like a tipsy Botticelli angel as she sat there, all lush hips and thighs and breasts and wavy blonde hair. But Botticelli angels rose naked from the sea and plucked spring fruit under the threat of cupid's bow. They didn't wear navy suits and camp out on bar stools, and now that he thought about it, Botticelli angels didn't seem so cranky, either. The Botticelli vision faded, but duty still called. And if he rescued Hope, maybe she'd be really, really grateful. Another vision—one of black leather thongs and whips— entered his mind.

"I know something's wrong," he said, trying to exude empathy. "Want to tell me what it is?"

Hope closed her eyes and leaned into the bar, holding her head in her hands. "I'm fine," she said. "Really. Thank you for your concern. I don't need any help. You can go now."

Oh-kay. No Botticelli angels. No leather thongs. Not for him, not tonight. One of the cable TV stations had scheduled a weeklong marathon of Perry Mason reruns; maybe if he went home now he could catch the start. Old television programs and a bowl of popcorn were starting to look good compared to his evening so far.

"You want me to call Marty for you? Since you're, well, upset."

Hope took another pull from her drink. "I'm not upset," she said. "Don't call Marty on my account. I have to do this myself."

Tanner looked at her. Hope was an adult, and she was a friend of Marty the Sneak and all those Jersey people, so she had to have a head on her shoulders because Marty was a pro and he didn't fool around with losers. But people who sat on barstools clutching drinks and telling others that they can handle their problems themselves, usually couldn't.

Tanner took a sip of his beer, wondering what he could do, what he should do. He probably should just call Marty and have him come and take care of Hope. Whatever the problem was, Marty clearly was already involved in it.

"It's a long story," Hope said.

Finally. "I love long stories," Tanner said, smiling to encourage her. "Tell me."

The bartender hovered and Tanner waved him away.

"I need to raise a lot of money," Hope began.

Tanner's heart sank. Too many lives had been ruined by people who thought they could get rich by gambling or playing cards. It just didn't happen. In the casino games like roulette, the game was slanted so the house usually won. In cards, winning depended on the players' skill and the luck of the draw. Tanner himself had played professionally for almost twenty years and had done very well overall. Still, he'd had many, many losing nights. All professional card players had ups and downs.

And now here was Hope McNaughton, with her sister Faith, the organic farmer, and niece, Amber, who wanted to be a chef—her nice family no doubt at home, and here was Hope, sitting inebriated on a bar stool, thinking she'd get rich quick.

Gambling could be a sickness, and when he saw people throwing their lives away, it made Tanner angry.

"Go home, Hope," he said, trying to be gentle. "You don't need a lot of money. You need to spend time with your family."

Now Hope sat up very straight, and her eyes blazed. " 'I love long stories,'" she mocked his words in a high-toned voice. " 'Tell me.'" She brought her voice back to normal, if strident with contempt could be called normal. "First you ask me to tell you, and now you won't listen. You don't know what I need."

"I know that playing cards to get rich quick isn't the answer."

"There's nothing you can tell me about card players," she snorted. "Vegas would be so much nicer without them."

"So you want to join the ranks?" Tanner asked, annoyed in spite of himself. "Think about what you're doing. But think about it at home."

Hope dug a bill out of her purse and dropped it on the bar, sliding carefully off the stool.

"I'll go home," she said, as she walked away, "if you'll go to hell."

Tanner watched Hope walk a little too carefully toward the ladies room. That went well. From the moment he'd thought about hot accountants who could cook a guy's books to the second she told him to go to hell not five minutes later, Tanner had reached a new record in alienating women. Not even Troy could get that mad at him that fast.

The door to the restroom drifted shut after her. She'd probably be all right, but he pulled out his cell phone and called Marty. And then while he waited to make sure that someone came and took care of her, he pulled out a deck of cards and started practicing his old tricks. He needed to be ready next week, when Big Julie would not be too despondent to play cards.

Hope splashed water on her face in the ladies room, feeling the coolness take some of the heat from her cheeks. She was furious with Tanner Wingate, but she knew she was angry because his cautionary words reflected her own fears. She'd been sitting at that bar nursing a drink, terrified and upset at what she'd done.

She'd lost two thousand dollars.

She'd needed to earn the two hundred thousand for her stake, so she'd played at the thirty-dollar table. Then, faster than she could have imagined, she lost a couple of big pots, and when she looked down and saw her chip pile, how small it had shrunk, she felt sick. She'd jumped up and left the game.

From her own experience she knew that every card player, even the very best, lost a lot—a lot of hands, and a lot of money. But if you brought your skill to the table, if you were good enough, you'd win.

She knew that. But when she realized that she'd lost two thousand dollars in a half-hour, she'd panicked. Run.

Two thousand dollars! All that money, just gone. At that rate, not only would she not raise her stake to play Big Julie for the ranch, but she'd drive her family into the poorhouse before the night was over. They'd wind up worse off than before, if that were possible.

She went into a stall and sat on the toilet seat, looking at the blank metal door. Tanner Wingate had a patronizing, know-it-all attitude, but maybe he was right. Maybe she shouldn't play cards. Maybe she should just let the ranch go. Two thousand dollars could have bought a lot, if she hadn't just thrown it away.

On the other side of the stall door, she heard the restroom door open, water run, footsteps recede. To her relief, no line had formed for her stall.

Should she keep playing? Maybe she'd lost her skill, as well as her money. If she couldn't win, she shouldn't play.

She heard the door open, an exclamation, the door closed. The restroom was very quiet.

Well, she was done for now. She'd played, she'd lost, and now she was tired and discouraged. This wasn't the time to push her luck. Tanner Wingate was probably right about one thing: she should go home, at least for tonight.

Opening the stall door, she nearly bumped into Weary Blastell, who was leaning against the restroom wall, his arms crossed over his barrel chest. His shaved black head gleamed in the fluorescent lights of the restroom, his six-foot-five frame seemed to fill the small space.

"So, Little Hope," he said, uncoiling himself from the wall, "how you doin'?"

Sympathy made her crumble the way anger never would. Tears sprang to her eyes and she felt her chin tremble.

"Oh, Weary," she said, wiping her eyes, hearing her voice break. "I lost two thousand dollars. And Tanner said— Tanner said—"

Weary Blastell was the happy father of four and grandfather of ten, and a woman's tears didn't upset him. He grabbed a handful of tissues and handed them to her.

"Don't you fret none about what flea that no-good, loudmouth De-troit carpetbagger's got in his ear," he said. "You listen to us. That's why you payin' us the big bucks."

Hope laughed, a thin, watery chuckle. She swiped at her eyes with the tissues.

"Okay. But—"

"No buts. You want to do this thing, Hope, you got to go for it. No negative thinking. You get some ups. You get some downs. That's the business."

Hope nodded, tossing the tissues in the trash. The uncles had good sense. And guts. Weary seemed to have no discomfort at all waiting for her inside the women's restroom. That kind of adaptation to circumstances was probably what made them such good card players.

"I keep thinking of it as grocery money," she said. "Not venture capital."

"Makes sense," Weary said, "since you're underfunded. But you gotta get past that. You need a big stake, so you gotta play big. Playing cards has risks. Like life. You gotta be prepared to lose some. It's part of winning."

Hope stared into the mirror for a minute before she answered. "I've managed the family finances for so long—I don't know if I can lose our money this way."

"Sure you can," Weary said. "What you talkin' about? I seen you do it a million times. You just momentarily forgot how is all. That's what we're here for. Make you remember the groove. Well, that and the big bucks."

Hope did remember what it felt like to play cards. She remembered the glow, the rush, the moments of triumph, the times when it seemed like she could do nothing wrong even when she lost a few pots, because she knew before the night was over, she'd be back up again.

She remembered the groove, all right. That was the

second thing she was scared of.

Her biggest fear was that she'd lose, and then they'd lose their home. That would change all their lives in ways none of them wanted. And it would be all her fault.

But she was afraid to win, too. Afraid that if she played too long, she'd like it too much. That if she remembered the groove too clearly, she'd never want to leave it. Afraid she'd turn out like her father, with no family, no friends, no roots.

Afraid she'd become addicted, just like her father.

Hope dried her hands on a towel and tossed it into the bin just as a woman entered the restroom. The woman stood there, looking at Weary, the space he took up. Looking uncertain.

"We're havin' a conversation here," Weary said. "You gotta come back later."

The woman fled the restroom.

"Tell me the truth, Weary," Hope said. "Can I do this?"

Weary rolled his eyes. "What have I just been sayin'? Yes, you can. We know you can. But not if you don't stop fussin' and start playin' cards. How bad do you want the ranch? You want it bad enough, you got to set your thinking straight."

"I don't know how to do that, Weary."

Weary paused, considering. "Okay. First thing. You can't hold on to your losses. Forget the last hand. You got to approach each hand as fresh."

"But that's how Derek played! And he sucked. He played himself into a hole and then he pretended he wasn't there, so he never came out. He just dug deeper and deeper. Until he'd lost everything."

"Did I say play like Derek? No. I'm telling you, play each hand with a clear mind. You lost the last pot, you figure out why if you can, but you play your strategy. You try to make up for the last lost pot—yeah, you're always gonna lose."

Hope thought about it. Weary was right. She'd fallen into Derek's bad habits—chasing bad hands when she was down. She'd never played that way before, and she wouldn't start now.

"Thanks, Weary. I'll remember that, to play my strategy. Because I'm not going to lose here. I'm going to win." She had to win. Losing just wasn't an option.

"That's the girl." Weary put his arm around her shoulders and walked her out of the restroom. As they headed for the exit, they passed Tanner at the bar. He was fooling around with a deck of cards, and Hope saw with shock that he was practicing card tricks—dealing off the bottom and palming cards—that were illegal to use in play. She never would have recognized the slight movements for what they were, except that Derek had used—and taught her—those same moves many years ago.

Not that she should jump to conclusions. Lots of people practiced card tricks that they never planned to use in real card games. Lots of people practiced card tricks to wow their friends at parties. Not everyone who could cheat at cards, did cheat.

But for other people, playing was an addition, and cheating was an option when winning didn't come naturally. When Tanner had lectured her, he'd obviously known what he was talking about. Not that he was in a position to preach.

She was glad she'd never have to play him. She'd never be able to compete against a card cheat.

Chapter 7

Refreshed and relaxed after a vigorous hour with a personal
trainer followed by a ninety-minute hot stone and aromatherapy
massage and a soothing eucalyptus sea salt body wrap and
exfoliation, Marilyn Saladino stepped into the elevator at
ten-thirty on Sunday morning feeling in need of breakfast.
Although the trainer had advised a wheatgrass smoothie
enhanced with probiotics for her first meal, Marilyn was
thinking more along the lines of bacon and eggs. There was
nothing like protein for long-lasting energy.

The Desert Dunes casino was almost quiet, and the
elevators that served the upper suites for special guests
were empty, except for one young woman who got off as
Marilyn got on. The blonde was wearing a pair of white
Capri pants so tight they looked like they'd been sprayed
on, with a bright turquoise and yellow print blouse tied at
her navel. Her fingernails and toenails were painted tangerine,
she wore big, colorful earrings, she had a hat, she had a bag,
she wore little mules with clear plastic high heels.

Marilyn sighed as the young woman stepped off. What
she wouldn't do to have that kind of figure again. That hair.
That complexion. The young woman was a tramp, of
course. Only someone who was looking for a sugar daddy
would dye her hair *that* color and wear her clothes *that* tight.
But Marilyn knew from bitter experience that men loved
such brazen flaunting. Just weeks ago she'd learned that her

own husband had had a fling with just such a hussy. Of course Marilyn had put a stop to *that*. But Big Julie had been so—

Marilyn slammed her hand between the elevator doors just as they were about to close and forced them apart. Just how many high-roller suites did the casino have? And what were the odds that a blonde tramp was there with someone else? Marilyn felt the seeds of suspicion grow. Had she really succeeded in halting Big Julie's little fling? If he'd brought his tart to Vegas instead of her, his lawful, loving wife, she was going to kill him.

She hesitated for just a second. And then she took off after the blonde. She'd never seen the floozy Big Julie had been keeping out at the golf course, but the private detective she'd hired had taken some pictures. The image of the tart was grainy, but Marilyn had recognized her loving spouse when he was in flagrante delicto. Or even when his delicto was not so flagrante, as had been the situation last night. Last night, his delicto had practically gone into hiding, and after Marilyn had put all that effort into coaxing it out, too.

But Big Julie's delicto had been flagrant enough for the blonde in the photos, and here was a blonde again. Even as Marilyn trailed after the woman in the white Capri pants, she realized that she might have overreacted. America was full of bottle blondes, and they probably weren't all sleeping with Big Julie. Some of them probably just happened to be staying at the Desert Dunes when Big Julie was and happened to come down the same elevator he used and it didn't mean a thing, even if she looked more or less exactly like the grainy photo of the blonde at the golf course.

The blonde turned into a dress shop and, with no hesitation whatsoever, Marilyn followed her in. The blonde tart at the golf course had never seen Marilyn, would have no idea what she looked like. Marilyn wasn't worried.

Marilyn browsed jewelry while the blonde browsed

clothes in sizes Marilyn hadn't seen in twenty years, finally taking a few outfits into a fitting room and trying them on. Just as Marilyn thought she couldn't pretend for one more second to be deciding between pairs of rhinestone bangles, the blonde decided on an outfit and took it to the register.

"Charge it to room sixteen-oh-one," she said.

Sixteen-oh-one, Marilyn realized, was the penthouse directly above hers. Hers and Big Julie's.

The blonde signed, the clerk smiled, stapled the receipt, closed the bag, and handed it to the woman, who sashayed past Marilyn and went back the way she'd come. Smiling at the clerk, Marilyn followed her out of the store and watched her head back to the elevator banks.

But instead of following her, Marilyn turned to the right and went to the line of house phones across from the concierge desk. She picked up a phone and an operator came on.

"Can you tell me which room Julie Saladino is in?" she asked the operator.

"I yam sorree," said the operator. "I yam not allowed to give out that infor*may*shun."

"Please connect me to sixteen-oh-one," Marilyn said, expecting the worst.

The phone rang.

"Yeah," Drake answered.

Marilyn thought that at ten-thirty in the morning, Big Julie would still be lying snoring on the big king bed in fifteen-oh-one where she'd left him. But she could still find out if he was registered with the blonde in sixteen-oh-one *and* with herself one floor below.

Marilyn clenched her teeth and spoke through them, hoping to disguise her voice. "Can I pleazhe zhpeak to Big Chulie?"

"He's not here," Drake said. "Who's this?"

"I'll call back." Marilyn hung up.

So. Her lousy, two-timing creep of a husband had not

only lied to her about dumping that tramp, she was here in Vegas! Staying with *her husband!* In the suite directly above hers!

All thoughts of bacon and eggs, not to mention wheatgrass and probiotics, fled her mind as Marilyn stormed back to the elevators and viciously stabbed the call button. When the elevator doors opened, Marilyn leaped in, jabbing the button for the fifteenth floor. As Marilyn gnashed her teeth, the doors closed majestically, in their own time, and the car rose. By the time the doors finally opened on the fifteenth floor, Marilyn was in a frenzy. She slashed her access card through the key slot and flung herself into the suite, barreling through the rooms until she got to the bedroom, where Big Julie lay in semi-naked somnambulance.

"You big—big—*jerk!*" Marilyn yelled, not finding a word bad enough to call her life's mate.

"Wha—?" big Julie said, struggling to sit up. "What's the matter, Baby?" And then realizing who he was talking to, added, too late, "Marilyn. Sweetheart."

Marilyn picked up the lamp from the side table. "You lying," she heaved the lamp at him "cheating," she picked up the clock radio "two-timing," threw it at him "scum!" She picked up a small vase holding an artificial flower arrangement and held it before her, vibrating in fury.

"You brought that tramp out here! You've been staying with her upstairs! Don't deny it! I *saw* her!" She pitched the flower vase at him, looking for something else to throw.

Big Julie had dodged the lamp purely by instinct and had fully awakened by the time the clock radio whizzed by his head. Training and experience kicked in, and he watched his spouse warily, ducking flying objects as they smashed on the wall behind him. Marilyn had lousy aim, but if she hit him she could do some damage. He didn't want to get hurt—especially not if injuries to sensitive parts of his anatomy cut into his time with Baby.

But what a throw! Marilyn was putting a lot of force behind her delivery, and if she wasn't getting results, it wasn't for lack of trying. Her skin was flushed from the effort. A deep V of sweat stained the front of her leotard. Her pink athletic socks sagged around her ankles, her carefully tinted red hair escaped its pony tail and flew around her head. She was pulsating with fury.

"Now, Marilyn," Big Julie wheedled, evading the flying flower arrangement. "Sweetheart."

"Don't 'Sweetheart' me," Marilyn yelled.

Big Julie was getting turned on by all of Marilyn's passion and sweat. Not to mention the way the edge of the exercise leotard bit into the curve of her ass. If it was one thing he liked, it was a passionate woman, and Marilyn, okay, she was meaty, but her curves still had plenty of velocity, and she was wearing a skin-tight leotard, her nipples showing through it like hard little points on a pencil. Her rump was quivering, her thighs were trembling, and best of all, there were damn few elastic polymers in sight. A woman in full bounce was a glorious thing.

Marilyn picked up the bedside phone and pulled her arm back, ready to throw.

Big Julie hadn't been married for twenty-five years and been a made guy for the same without learning something about self-preservation. He rolled off the mattress away from Marilyn's aim and thundered around the end of the bed. Marilyn dropped the phone and turned to run, but Big Julie tackled her, flinging her onto the bed and jumping on top of her. Marilyn tried to knee him in the balls, but Big Julie was ready for that, clamping her legs with his and grabbing the one hand of Marilyn's he could reach. She swacked him on the head with the other, but she didn't do much damage because his head was plenty hard and now he was getting hard elsewhere, too, which also was a glorious thing.

Marilyn pulled back in shock and then struggled harder,

but Big Julie grasped Marilyn's sweat-soaked boob with his hand and pinched her nipple. It gave him a nice rush, not as nice as Baby, but still really, really good, and when he realized that he couldn't get his hand inside the leotard, he grabbed it by the neck and yanked, tearing it open and leaving exposed a naked breast the size of a small cantaloupe.

He gazed at it, feeling his breath quicken. Marilyn's boobs weren't anything like Baby's. Baby's firm titties stood up straight when she was on her back, thanks to surgical intervention, but Marilyn's exposed breast slid sideways on her chest. It was bigger and pinker than Baby's and a lot softer. He put his hand on it and molded it, seeing how her generous flesh swelled out from between his fingers as he squeezed.

Marilyn had stopped struggling and was staring at him in surprise but not horror, her breath coming in shallow gasps, the skin on her chest rosy with exertion and extra blood flow. Big Julie took note of the change in posture, activity level, breathing, and speech, and took advantage, settling himself more comfortably and letting her know with other movements just how vigorous and refreshed he was feeling this morning after a good night's sleep. In a very short time, he had the satisfaction of seeing Marilyn's eyes close. She sighed—a melting sigh—and when her back arched, Big Julie smiled in triumph, knowing that he was about to enjoy a very nice marital workout.

Sometime later, Marilyn got up to take a shower, careful not to wake her spouse, who was gently snoring. Her hair was a mess. She had beard burn on her chest. But she felt great. Her skin tingled. Her thighs throbbed with a gentle ache she hadn't felt in months, if not years. Her vagina hummed. Every nerve ending sat up and saluted.

She stepped under the warm water, bathing quickly and washing her hair. When she got out, she combed her hair and put on one of the bathrobes that the hotel thoughtfully provided its guests before she went back into the bedroom to dress. When she stepped into the luxurious space, now strewn with discarded athletic clothing, Big Julie was awake and watching her. She felt the hum escalate to a full choir belting out the Hallelujah Chorus.

Big Julie watched Marilyn come back from the bathroom, her wet hair hanging in dark hanks around her shoulders. The bulky white bathrobe was crossed tightly over her chest and knotted around her middle. Marilyn right out of the shower looked nothing like the hot, ferocious, no-holds-barred, wild woman whose clothes Big Julie had torn off just a short time ago. She looked, in fact, like the Pillsbury dough boy if the Pillsbury dough boy had fallen into the dishwasher and survived the pot-scrubbing cycle.

"Julie," Marilyn said. Her eyelids drooped as she looked him over, but her mouth looked good, soft and slightly swollen. "We should do that more often. *Way* more often."

Big Julie felt his heart sink. Under the best of circumstances, like say if Baby was wearing her black leather chaps and spurs and riding him harder than a cowgirl in a rodeo barrel racing competition, he could go two full rounds before he was knocked out. But with Marilyn looking like Mortitia dragged from a lake, he was done.

"That was great, honey!" he said, trying for enthusiasm. He jumped out of bed and pulled on his shorts. "I could eat a bear after that. What do you want for breakfast? They got everything here."

Marilyn turned to the dresser, disappointed, and pulled open the bottom drawer.

"Whatever you're having is fine," she said, pawing through her clothes. "Eggs, maybe. Coffee."

Big Julie grabbed the phone that Marilyn hadn't thrown at him to call in the order, but when he looked up to ask Marilyn when should they bring it, he stopped. Marilyn was still bent over the drawer. The bathrobe was clinging to her butt and stuck between her thighs. He remembered once with Baby in and out of the hot tub, when her robe had been sticking just like that. And that hadn't been once with Baby so much as three times, he'd been so damn hot for her, what with the water and everything.

Just thinking about Baby and the hot tub, he felt himself stir underneath the shorts.

Marilyn's bathrobe gapped at the chest, and Big Julie could see a curve of breast. It looked nothing like one of Baby's tits, which were round like halves of a baseball, big and symmetrical. When Big Julie rubbed his face on them, it was like his nose was gliding over a ski jump covered with soft, new snow, they were so firm but her skin was so delicate. When Marilyn was bending over, though, her tits looked more like Japanese eggplants, full, but more oblong. Except Marilyn's tits weren't purple like Japanese eggplants.

He imagined his face buried in the valley of Baby's perfect tits. He could just about smell the new snow now, his tongue reaching out to catch a fresh snowflake.

"Open your bathrobe a little," Big Julie said, his voice husky. "Let me see you more."

Marilyn blushed. "You are *bad,* Big Julie," she said, but she loosened the tie on her bathrobe and pulled on the crossover fabric. She glanced at him, at the ski pole in his shorts.

"Bend over like that again," Big Julie asked. "Like you were. I like to look at you like that."

"I think you're ready to do a little more than just look, Julie," Marilyn said, crossing over to the bed.

Big Julie thought about ski slopes and watched Marilyn approach, his eyes half-closed.

"Oh, Baby," he said. "I am ready to jump."

Chapter 8

By the time Hope shuffled yawning into the kitchen, looking for her first cup of coffee, Faith and Amber were in the kitchen making waffles for breakfast.

"We just need about another five minutes and we'll be ready to eat," Faith said.

"I wish we could put recipes for waffles in the vegetable boxes," Amber said. "At least that's not hard to mess up."

"What you do is fine," Suzanne said, coming into the kitchen and giving her granddaughter a smacking kiss before glancing at Hope, who had pulled a chair over to the computer and turned it on. "What are you doing, Sweetie?"

"Just looking something up quick," Hope said.

"Before breakfast? What's so important?" Faith asked, pulling up the cover of the waffle iron and turning out a perfect golden orb, fragrant with butter and sugar.

"I met a card player yesterday," Hope said. "I think I must have met him before. He said no, but his name is so familiar."

"Tanner Wingate?" Faith asked.

"He said he met you," Amber said, perking up.

Hope looked at them, astonished. "How did *you* guys meet Tanner Wingate?"

"He was in the Desert Dunes when we were delivering the veg," Faith said.

"He got a snack from Kenji. He's the chef," Amber said.

"Unagi. I had some. It was fantastic. He's cool. Tanner, I mean. And Kenji is, too."

"Tanner's cool?" Hope typed Tanner's name into the search engine and saw more than a dozen hits scroll down the screen. She clicked on the first one. "He's a card player."

"He's *very* cool," Amber said. "He knows stuff."

He knows how to cheat at cards, Hope thought. She started to read the first article, a news story from a Detroit newspaper. "College Student Arrested in Card Scam" the headline read. She skimmed it, then went to the next one, as the story came back to her.

She'd been just a kid at the time, thirteen or fourteen years old, but in Vegas, the story had been all over the papers. Back then, she'd admired the daredevil teenaged card shark who'd taken his tricks on the road to Atlantic City and Las Vegas, cheating the casinos and card rooms out of almost a million dollars. His sleight of hand had been so subtle that it had taken the security systems months to catch him. But finally, they did.

The kid's high-priced lawyer had used his client's youth to play on the judge's sympathy, and ultimately William Tanner Wingate had received only probation for his crimes, plus restitution to the casinos. The restitution had been the easy part. He hadn't spent any of the money.

The probation would have been harder. *Twenty years.* Hope looked at the date on the news story. It had all happened nineteen years ago, and Tanner Wingate was *still* on probation—would be on probation for another year, it looked like.

He was probably still cheating, too. She'd seen him practicing those card tricks at the bar, and in her experience, once a cheat, always a cheat. A leopard couldn't change his spots.

At least that explained why she'd recognized his name. As a nineteen-year-old, he'd probably been the most famous card player in the country.

"Breakfast is ready," Faith said, putting a platter on the table.

Amber put the pitcher of maple syrup on the table. "What did you find out about Tanner?"

Hope switched screens before Amber could see any of the headlines.

"Not much. Come on, let's eat."

There wasn't any reason to sully Amber's heroes. After all, she'd probably never see him again.

Hope was back at the casino, ready to play, by eleven a.m. That would give her a solid four hours before she had to take Baby shopping *again* at three-thirty. Her remaining chips dug in her jeans pocket. She would not fixate on the two thousand dollars she'd lost yesterday. That was old news. Today she'd start fresh.

She met Marty at the gaudy floral arrangement in the hotel lobby as they'd arranged. When she arrived, he was already there, sitting on one of the hotel's small, gilt chairs, drinking coffee out of a paper cup and looking as out of place as a bookie at a dance recital.

"Little Hope," he said, when he saw her. He patted her shoulder and smiled affectionately. "Hey. Let's go."

"Weary told me about last night," he said as they entered the casino and headed for the card room. "Sorry I couldn't make it. I was in the middle of something."

A straight flush, Hope thought, smiling. It was probably just as well Marty hadn't seen her meltdown, too. Fortunately the women's restroom off the card room was way too small to have accommodated all the uncles at the same time. If they'd all squeezed in there, they'd have looked like a Marx Brothers routine.

"But I was thinking. About the two large," Marty said. "Especially now, when you gotta pump up your stake."

That's what Weary had said last night, Hope realized.

Figure out what you did wrong. Evidently Marty had a plan.

"I gotta plan," Marty said.

Hope stopped in the middle of the casino floor and beamed at him. "You're the best," she said. She put her arms around him and gave him a hug.

"Hey, what?" Marty said, startled and embarrassed. "What did I do? Come on. Stop."

"Okay," Hope said, letting go. "What's the plan?"

"We gotta be careful about it," Marty said, and Hope felt her dreams fade.

"Nothing illegal," she said.

"Oh." Marty looked thoughtful. "Well, it's not *illegal.*"

"If it's not illegal, what is it, then?" It would have to be *something.*

Marty glanced at her, cleared his throat. "Well. Ah. It's, ah, disliked. Probably. Yeah. Disliked."

"Disliked?"

"Here's the plan." Marty took Hope aside. "You know about them kids from MIT."

Hope nodded. Who didn't? In the eighties and nineties, a bunch of really smart kids at MIT had figured out how to win at cards by beating the odds. They watched tables and counted which cards had been played. When tables had a disproportionately large number of high-value cards left to play, they placed big bets, knowing that although they would lose sometimes, they had a higher proportionate chance of winning big, too. The students won possibly millions of dollars before they were discovered. But when the casinos finally figured out the scam, the students were banished for life from all the gaming establishments in the country.

"*Jeez,* Marty. We can't do that." Once she won the ranch back, Hope didn't much care if she herself was banned from the casinos and never saw another card room again. But she couldn't let the uncles jeopardize their careers for her.

"It's nothing like that. Don't worry."

"What *is* it like, then? You're scaring me. What exactly is the plan?"

"First off, you're gonna move back to the twenty dollar tables until you build up your stake."

Hope nodded. "That was my plan, too."

"Okay, then we're on the same page. We'll split up. All of us. We'll watch the tables. Here at the Desert Dunes, across the street at the Golden Palace. At the Casbah. Six casinos, one guy each. We'll be looking for a full table with a couple of lousy players. When we see a setup like that, we'll give you a call, and that's the table you play. You got your cell?"

Hope nodded.

"Okay. You play the table until you get too much competition or you beat their socks off and they walk away, whatever. When the table's done, you walk away. Then you call me, and we'll pick you a new table. You gotta be ready to move around."

"You think that'll work?"

"Worked for the MIT kids," Marty said. "Two worse-than-average players in a standard Hold'em table of nine means that the guy who wins takes home twenty times the income than he would if everybody was evenly matched."

"Really?" Hope said.

"Yeah," Marty the Sneak said. "You wanna win these days, you gotta study. Statistics. Probability theory. Regression analysis."

"Regression analysis?" Hope said, amazed at Marty the Sneak's apparent intellectual bent. "Really?"

"No," Marty agreed. "I'm just kidding about that. But that other stuff—that's part of the game now. You gotta know what your odds are to win a pot, what you have to win to make the bet worthwhile, like that."

"Won't the casinos notice you guys staking out their tables?"

"We have Little Hope they'll discover us," Marty said with ponderous humor.

Hope grinned at him. The jokes on her name were silly, but she liked them anyway. If her father had to have been a card player, why couldn't he have been Marty the Sneak? Marty probably was too involved with organized crime and he probably broke some laws, too, and he might have made a bad father, but here he was, helping her.

"You be careful," she said. "All of you. I don't want to spend my stake bailing you out of jail."

"When did I get in trouble for something like this?" Marty asked, justifiably miffed. "You just pay attention to your cards. Concentrate. Remember what Weary told you last night."

"So where do I start?" Hope said.

"Eddie said a couple minutes ago he had a good table for you in here. Lemme check with him it's still going." Marty punched a number on his cell phone.

"Eddie? What's happening?" He listened. Then he nodded.

"She's on her way," he said into the phone. "These things are great," he said, closing the phone and putting it into his pocket. "How did we get by before we had cells? Them and ATMs. They're a bonanza for card players. Okay. Over by the north door, about two tables in. You're looking for the table with the guy in the red check shirt, a second guy with a Dodgers baseball cap. They both play too loose, Eddie says."

They bet on bad hands, Hope thought. "That should help rebuild my stake," she said.

"That's the plan," Marty said.

By three o'clock Hope had won seven thousand dollars at the twenty dollar tables. She beamed at the uncles while she banked her winnings.

"I love this plan! Are you sure no one spotted you?"

"We're good, Hope," Pete Wysniewski said.

"Well, they *spotted* me," Weary Blastell said. "But no one *suspected* me."

At six-foot-five, with his former-football-player's build, a person would have to be blind not to spot Weary, Hope realized

"You be careful, Weary," she said. "You don't exactly blend."

"I blend better than Cuisinart," Weary said. "Don't worry about me."

"Plus, now we know every card player in Vegas who's sitting at the twenty- and thirty-dollar tables," Isaiah Rush said. "And we know how to beat them."

"Speaking for my colleagues here, I feel confident in saying that we plan to increase our own earnings by substantial margins," Jim Thickpenny said. "We anticipate major breakthroughs in profitability."

"Bing-bing-bing!" Sharp Eddie concurred.

"You're doing good," Marty said to Hope. "Tonight you go back to the thirty-dollar tables. What time you coming in?"

"Seven o'clock?" she asked. "Does that work? At the flower arrangement again?"

"Someplace different," Marty said. "The little coffee shop. We gotta talk strategy anyway, before you go out there."

Hope nodded. "Maybe I can teach you about regression analysis," she said.

Marty looked thoughtful. "If that works for seven card stud, eight or better, high-low split, count me in."

Chapter 9

Tanner was home putting a new washer in the kitchen sink faucet when his cell phone rang.

"Yeah," he said. He could hear noise in the background; it sounded like the casino.

"Tanner, it's Marty."

Tanner put down the wrench and pulled out a chair. Apart from poker tournaments, he hadn't had as much face time with the Jersey crew in his entire life as he'd had in the last two days.

"Marty. What's up?"

"Listen. About last night. What you said to Hope."

"What I said to her? I just told her to go home."

"Yeah, I know what you said. Weary told me. Don't say crap like that no more to her."

"What do you mean, Marty? She was at the bar, she was on her way to having too much to drink, she'd lost too much money. People got problems with losing, they shouldn't play." Tanner shook his head. It was probably a good thing he didn't see more of the Jersey gang. He was starting to talk just like Marty.

"Not Hope. She got scared a little, is all. She's out of practice, but she's a fine card player. And now she needs the money."

"What's so important that she'd jeopardize everything?"

"She isn't jeopardizing everything, you numbskull. That's

what I'm telling you. She played cards and she lost a few hands. That's it. Now listen to me. You made her cry, and that ain't right."

"I made her cry?" Tanner was shocked. He was used to Troy's tantrums and tears, and sometimes to his dismay he'd evoked tears from women he'd dated when he failed to meet their expectations. But when he'd seen her, Hope hadn't cried. She'd told him to go to hell. He hadn't thought he'd gotten through to her. Maybe he had. But he sure as hell didn't want to bully women in bars until they cried. Even if it was for their own good. Which, apparently, Marty the Sneak didn't think it was.

He wouldn't have wanted to make Hope cry in a million years.

"She cried because of what you said," Marty went on. "You made her feel bad. Question herself. And you set her back a half-day. She's playing on a clock here, and we all gotta pitch in. If you're gonna help, okay. If not, find somebody else in the card room to preach to."

"Marty, really, I wasn't preaching, I just—"

"Yeah, yeah, I know, you saw Hope, a real pretty girl, and you got an itch you wanted to scratch. I understand that. But she ain't your type. I known her a lot longer than you, so you can trust me on that."

"Marty, hold on here," Tanner said. "You're way ahead of the game. I—"

"No, I ain't," Marty said. "I seen the way you look at her, and I know how long you date somebody, about twice each one, am I right?"

"That's a little exaggerated. I—"

"I got nothing against you, Tanner. I like you, even, as much as I know you. You straightened up. You're a good card player. But right now, Hope don't need no distractions. She's in the casino to work. So either help her or butt out."

"Well, I could help," Tanner said, feeling flattened.

"Just so you understand," Marty said, and hung up.

Tanner blinked, staring at his phone, before he finally hung up, too. *What did I do? I just wanted to save a damsel in distress.* And before he knew it, Marty had torn a strip off him.

At least now he understood why the McNaughton sisters called the Jersey crew their uncles. Nobody could have protected Hope better.

That's what he'd tried to do last night, too, but evidently he'd been on the wrong track. *Help her*, Marty had said. Tanner picked up his wrench. Well, okay then. He'd help.

Promptly at three-thirty, Hope rang the bell on Baby's suite, and Drake opened the door.

"Oh, you," he said. "The comedian." He walked away, leaving the door open for her.

"Anybody could get in here," Hope called after him. "I could be somebody *dangerous*."

"I wish," he called back, and Hope heard the television in the background. *Sports*, she thought, but when she walked through, looking for Baby, she saw it was an investment program on cable.

"Grain futures tanked," Drake said. "Too late now, if you were in deep."

"Not me," Hope said. "The only thing I'm deep in is unpaid bills."

"Better than grain futures," Drake said, as Hope moved on to the bedroom, still looking for Baby.

Baby was standing in front of the mirror, staring at herself but not making any adjustments.

"Baby?" Hope entered the room. "Is something wrong?"

"I think so," Baby said. "Big Julie, he always wants to do me in the morning. I dint even *see* him this morning. He said he was out all night playing cards, and he fell asleep drunk at the game. Do you believe that?" She turned to look at Hope.

Hope blinked, not sure if Baby was being rhetorical or

really wanted an answer. "Um," she said.

"But then he finally shows up like at noon, and he doesn't want to do me? That's the best time for him." She lowered his voice. "He's not young anymore, you know? He used to take Viagra, but then he didn't need it with me. That's what he said. But he sure needed it this morning."

"Maybe you shouldn't be telling me this," Hope said. "Big Julie probably wouldn't like it." *As much as I don't.*

"I shouldn't say he didn't *want* to do me," Baby said. "We got naked, all right. He was all, Baby, take your clothes off, and I was all, anything you want, Big Julie. So he goes, do me a little dance, and—"

"Baby," Hope said. "Maybe we should go shopping?" But even the magic word failed to penetrate Baby's misery.

"So I'm doing my little dance but it's going nowhere, if you get the picture, and after a half-hour at least, he just rolls over and falls asleep! What does that mean?"

"I think there's a sale at the premium outlets, if you want to go there." Hope tried to keep the desperation out of her voice. She'd gotten much more of a picture than she wanted.

"I'll tell you what I think it means," Baby said. "It means he don't want me no more."

"Sixty percent off!" Hope said.

"Or it could mean that he did somebody else this morning." Baby paused, thinking. "If he did, I'll kill him."

"Or we could go to your favorite places, wherever you want," Hope said. "You could show me."

"I don't see how it could have been some young chick." Baby looked at her flawless, twenty-five-year-old face in the mirror with no apparent irony. "Where did he meet her? He's been with me all the time. I been keeping him totally satisfied."

"It's a mystery," Hope said. "You want to go now?"

"Marilyn knew he was here," Baby said. "But how could he be doing her? She's back in Jersey and she must be fifty at *least*. You think maybe she came out here and put a hex on him or something?"

"If she did, you'll need a new outfit," Hope said. "Probably more than one."

"You know, you're right," Baby said, determination glinting in her eyes. "What are we waiting for? Let's get out of here."

Hope soon realized that Baby's fears about the extent of Big Julie's affections had put her in a fiercely competitive shopping mood.

"That plastic is gonna *melt*," Baby declared as Hope parked in the premium outlet mall parking lot. "We are gonna do some *damage*."

Hope could already feel the pain her feet would be in by the time Baby got done melting Big Julie's credit cards. "I don't really need anything," she said, grabbing her purse from the back seat. "But I'll tag along."

"Big Julie said you need new clothes," Baby said, pulling down the visor and frowning into the mirror on the back to check her lipstick. She turned and glanced at Hope. "And no offense, but he's right. You could do better."

Hope glanced down at her clothes. She was wearing a white tank top and loose khaki cargo shorts that came to her knees with sport sandals. In the desert heat of Las Vegas, which was at least fifteen degrees hotter than the ranch, nothing else made sense. She didn't look as fantastic as Baby, but she didn't require as much upkeep, either, and she was as cool as she could be. That had to count for *something*.

"Baby, it's too hot to wear anything else."

"I've seen what you wear," Baby said. "You always wear stuff like that."

"It's *practical*," Hope said, knowing that to Baby, practicality had about as much appeal as dumpster diving.

"Practical," Baby sniffed. "We're getting you an outfit.

It'll be fun." Her voice had the iron will of a marine drill sergeant.

Hope sighed and followed Baby into the outlet mall.

"Baby, you can't pick out clothes for me," Hope said, feeling harassed. *I'll wind up looking like you. Like a, a— cupcake.*

"We're just looking," Baby said, pausing at the mall directory, "but you're sticking with me because you got the fashion sense of a dishrag."

"That's harsh," Hope said, a little stung. "Come on, Baby. Clothes aren't everything. I'm *comfortable*."

"Yeah, you and Santa Claus. So you wanna wear a red pantsuit with white fur trim? I didn't think so. They got some good stuff here. Let's check it out."

At the first store, Baby stopped in front of the window and shook her head. "Look at that," she said. "Bows and sailor collars! Like we're five years old."

"The bows look stupid," Hope agreed. Baby looked at her suspiciously.

"They *do*," Hope said.

"Well, that's something," Baby said.

They moved on to the next window.

"Never wear anything with writing," Baby said, dismissing a famous designer in five words.

At the next store, Baby stopped. "In here," she said.

They went in. Hope had heard of the designer, but she always shopped online from catalog retailers. She idly browsed the racks, fingering the softness of the fabrics. *It wouldn't be hard to get used to this,* she thought, putting the garments back.

Baby flipped through the clothes, checking sizes and pulling out colors. Then she took an armload of selections back to the fitting room. "Pick something out," she ordered Hope. "You're getting an outfit. At least one."

Hope laughed as she watched Baby disappear into the back of the store. *Well, why not?* She'd made seven thousand dollars this morning. She would win another seven thousand tonight. If she bought an outfit, she'd still be way ahead. And here was Baby, her personal shopper, more than willing to help.

She looked more seriously at the clothes. They had a lot more flair than the things she usually bought. She went through the racks, considering, and finally picked out a cute linen blouse in chocolate brown and a pair of tan slacks with notches at the ankles, both of which were on sale, and went back to try them on. There she found Baby in the hallway, inspecting herself critically in front of the mirror.

"What've you got there?" Baby asked, looking at Hope's choices, and then recoiled almost in horror. "No, no, no! Beige? Is this what they teach you at whatever college you went to? You should not be allowed to shop alone."

Personal shopper with attitude, Hope thought, annoyed.

"What's wrong with this? It's neutral. I like it."

Baby rolled her eyes and spun Hope around until she faced the mirror. "Look at you," she said. "You got a nice body. Okay, not as good as mine, goes without saying. But you got nice boobs, hardly sagging at all yet."

"Hey," Hope said. Her annoyance flared higher.

Baby leaned back to look at Hope's rear. "Pretty good butt—"

If she says, 'hardly sagging at all yet,' Hope thought, *I'm going back to the car.*

"—and pretty good legs. You're maybe, what? A little short-waisted. So, really, you can wear almost any style. And look at your coloring. Blue eyes. And your skin's good. I bet you don't even do anything to get that, do you?" Baby's voice had taken on an accusing note.

Hope blinked. "Moisturizer. I moisturize. A *lot.*"

Baby snorted in disdain. "Moisturizer. Your skin's almost as good as mine. And you're a lot older than me! And look at your hair. I bet you're a natural blonde."

"Well, yeah, all my family—"

"So you're a blue-eyed blonde with a peaches-and-cream complexion, and you got a showgirl's body and you want to wear beige. Hello? Is *anybody* home at your personal fashion mall?"

"*Hey*," Hope said.

"Seriously," Baby said.

"I don't want to be a slave to fashion," Hope said, feeling dumb even as she said it. Not only had she never been a slave to fashion, she'd never even gone to work for it, not even as a temp. She barely had a nodding acquaintance with fashion. If fashion showed up looking like a movie star and wearing a name tag, Hope probably wouldn't recognize it.

Baby, on the other hand, *was* a slave to fashion, and what did it get her? Boyfriends. Money. Glamour. Trips to Vegas.

"Don't be dumb," Baby said now, taking the clothes away and handing them to a passing clerk to restock. "Nice clothes feel better. They look better on you, and looking good gives you confidence. They last longer, too." Then she relented.

"Come on. Let's see what else they have."

The next two hours were eye-opening for Hope, who had never shopped for clothing that was anything but basic. First came the sleeveless, cowl neck knit top in deep cobalt blue. The cowl dropped in the front, exposing a deep V of cleavage.

"That outline is perfect on you," a clerk said, nodding to her as she bustled by.

Hope stared after her. Was she *nuts?* She felt utterly, completely exposed in the clingy, silky top.

"I can't wear this," she said.

"Yes, you can," Baby said. "It's perfect." She stood next to Hope and twitched the hem. "See how it shows off your boobs?"

"Yes," Hope said. "That's what I mean." She looked at her breasts, which seemed eager to burst through the top. Like her body had a point team, two of them, moving in front of her at all times to clear the way before she got there. All Hope could see when she looked at herself was breast.

A second sales clerk breezed by, holding an armload of hangers. "That top looks great on you!" she said.

"See?" Baby said.

"She's paid to say that," Hope said.

"You are making me mad," Baby said. "Go out to the front and walk in front of anybody. See what happens."

I'm making her *mad?* Hope scowled, but she went out to the front of the store and jammed some of Baby's rejects back onto a rack.

"What a lovely top," another shopper said. "Is it on sale?"

Hope glanced at Baby who smiled in smug satisfaction.

"It is," Hope said, feeling trapped. "Right over there. More colors, too."

"It's terrific," the shopper said, going over to the rack Hope pointed out.

Hope headed back to the fitting rooms.

"That settles it," she said to Baby. "I can't buy it. People will stare at me."

"You will buy it, and you will wear it," said Baby, the marine drill sergeant. "It looks fantastic on you. And it's washable. You'll like that. It's—what's that word again? *Practical.*"

Two hours later, Hope was burdened with shopping bags. *How did this happen? And how much did I spend?* Thanks to Baby's forcefulness, Hope had bought several new outfits—halter tops and wraparound tops and camis with spaghetti straps. She owned a new pair of Bermudas, a pair of cropped pants, a pair of loose linen slacks, and a perfectly tailored pencil skirt. She had accessories. She had shoes. And she had an utterly fantastic sundress with a sweetheart neckline and a pattern of orange butterflies down the front. She didn't know where she'd wear it, but the second she saw it she couldn't resist it. She loved it. She couldn't believe it, that she could love a dress like that.

"Everything was on sale," Baby said soothingly as they headed back to the car. Hope's shopping bags banged against her legs as she trundled her purchases out to the parking lot. She felt acutely anxious. The clothes were pretty, and she had to admit that they'd looked great on her. But she'd never worn clothes like this. Revealing, body-conscious clothes. They seemed too—risky. Not like her. She felt like a sailor charting unexplored seas.

"I've never done this before," Hope said as they got into the car. "Gone shopping like this, I mean. For fun. With a, a friend. And bought clothes like this. I've never worn clothes like this."

"I never would have guessed," Baby said, rolling her eyes. "Aren't you glad? You gotta know how nice those things are."

"I guess." Hope glanced doubtfully at the load of shopping bags in the back seat of the car. *But will I have the nerve to wear them?*

Chapter 10

Tanner had had an idea how he could see Hope again, almost like a date. But he'd need help to set it up. First from Kenji. Then Faith.

Faith he was sure of. Kenji would be more of a problem.

"I don't know about this, Wingate," Kenji said now.

"You're always saying I should go out more. Now here's someone I want to go out with. I'd think you'd want to help."

"It seems a roundabout way to get there," Kenji said. "You can't just call—what's her name? Hope? You can't just call her and ask her out to dinner? Like normal people?" He stood by the phone in the Ginger Palace kitchen, not making a move to pick it up.

"If I ask her out, she'll say no," Tanner said. "So I want to get her family involved. She likes her family. You like Faith, right? And her little girl. You'll have fun. And I'll get some quality time with Hope."

"I don't want to screw up my vegetable deliveries just so you can go out on a date. You're getting me UNLV basketball tickets, right?"

Tanner sighed. "Yes. I told you. *After* we make the call."

It was Kenji's turn to sigh. "Okay. If Faith says no, do I still get the tickets?"

"Don't let her say no. *Persuade* her. But you're making her a great offer, Kenj. She'll want to do it for her kid. Trust me."

Kenji shook his head, but he picked up the phone and dialed. He was relieved when Faith answered.

"Hi, Faith? It's Kenji Hasegawa, down at the Ginger Palace, how are you doing?"

"Kenji, yes, hello," Faith said. "Is something wrong with the vegetable delivery?"

"No, no, nothing like that," Kenji said. "Everything is great. Listen. I was talking to Tanner Wingate—do you remember him? He was in here yesterday when you came in with the delivery. We had an idea for Amber's birthday. It's her birthday on Tuesday, right?"

"Yes," Faith said. "You had an idea? Really? What? And maybe, why?"

"Amber mentioned that she wants to learn how to cook. Did you hear her talking to Tanner about becoming a chef? She said she's been working on the vegetable boxes, but she seems frustrated by that."

"Boy, that's the truth," Faith asked.

Tanner prodded Kenji. The chef rolled his eyes, grabbing the phone away.

"We—Tanner and I—thought Amber would enjoy it if I gave her a cooking lesson on Tuesday when the restaurant's closed. She and I could make something together, and then you and Hope and your mom could come for a lunch party. Tanner says you have a bunch of uncles in town right now? They could come, too."

"Are you *kidding?*" Faith asked. She lowered her voice. "A cooking lesson? You'd *do* that?"

Kenji smiled into the phone. "Actually, I sometimes teach cooking classes at the Ginger Palace. If you can believe it, the resort thinks that's a selling point. That's how I met Tanner, in fact. He came to one of my classes. He had his little girl, and he wanted to learn to cook a few things."

"You don't think a cooking lesson from you would be too hard for Amber?" Faith was still whispering.

"Nah, I've got this teaching gig down cold. I've given lessons to kids, too."

Tanner poked Kenji again.

"I think she'd enjoy it," Kenji said again. "She shows a real interest. It would be fun. What do you say?"

"Kenji, it seems so—generous."

"Not when you see how much hero worship I get from it. It's not generous at all."

Tanner nodded encouragingly.

Faith laughed, keeping her voice low. "Well—Amber would *love* it. You're awfully nice to do it. I think you're my hero now, too."

Kenji reddened. "Really, it's nothing. She's a nice kid. We'll both have fun. If you can get her here at nine, we can go to the market first. And then you can all come for lunch at twelve."

"I'll let everyone know, or Hope will," Faith said. "She's at the Desert Dunes with Marty. She's meeting him at the coffee shop for supper. I can call her and she can spread the word."

"I'll see you on Tuesday, then," Kenji said.

"Thank you for the cooking lesson. This will be her best present ever."

They said goodbye and Kenji hung up the phone. He turned to Tanner, waiting impatiently.

"My friend, you're in luck," he said as he put the phone back on the shelf. "The party's on, *and* you can run into Hope at the casino tonight, if you want to."

"If I *want* to," Tanner said. "Just tell me when and where."

After their daily midafternoon shopping expedition, Baby invited Hope up to the suite.

"You gotta put on one of your new outfits," Baby said. "Bring this—" she grabbed a bag, "—and this. And maybe this, just in case. And these shoes."

She'd taken a half-dozen bags and handed them to Hope.

"What if everybody stares?" Hope asked. "What if nothing looks good now?"

"I don't get what your problem is," Baby said, exasperated. "Come on."

My problem is that I'm not used to trying to look good, Hope thought. And to be honest, she didn't feel secure showing herself off, either. She followed Baby into the elevator and up to the sixteenth floor, feeling like a doomed woman. Drake met them at the door.

"The meeting of Shoppers Anonymous is downstairs tonight," he said, swinging the door open.

"The only thing we bought is grain futures," Hope said, brushing past him with her bags. "Buy low, sell high."

"They sell grain futures in the Kate Spade outlet?" Drake said, walking back to wherever he spent his time.

Baby walked down the hallway and flung open a door. "Here, use the bedroom to change. I'll get scissors for the tags. Drake, where's the scissors?"

"I can't do everything around here," Drake said from the next room. "I get a day off, you know."

Baby's face turned mutinous. Hope said, "Maybe there's a pair in the end table."

She pulled open the top drawer of the small table by the bed. The only thing in there was a large, pink dildo.

Hope had never seen a dildo up close and personal, much less such a large and pink one, but that's what it had to be. The shape was unmistakable. It was *huge.* Way too big for—whatever you wanted to do with it. It looked like it was made out of leather. She reached out and touched it experimentally with one finger. It *was* leather. Soft, but firm, too. Just like— It looked like it could do a lot of— well, a lot. She slammed the drawer shut, breathing quickly.

"Anything there?" Baby called from the den, where she'd gone to deposit her bags.

Just a giant dildo. "Not so far," Hope croaked. She

opened the next drawer, which, to her relief, was full of junk, including scissors.

"Here we go," she said, trying to sound normal.

"Oh, good. Can you help me with this?"

For the next half-hour, she and Baby cut off tags and examined their purchases, and when Hope was finally dressed in her new clothes with her old cargo shorts and tank top tucked into the shopping bag, she looked at herself in the mirror.

"I look totally different," she said, pivoting slowly in front of the mirror.

"That's the *point*," Baby said, rolling her eyes.

Hope stared at herself. The clothes really showed off her body. She still looked more conservative than Baby—a lot more. But that was like saying she looked more conservative than an avant-garde rock star. She looked—well, not *wow*. But she had definitely upgraded to *huh*.

The change was scary. But Baby had insisted, and Baby knew what she was talking about when it came to fashion. And Hope had to admit, she sort of liked the new look. She wondered if anybody would notice. After she said goodbye to Baby, she went down to the casino coffee shop to meet Marty, gazing in wonderment at herself in the elevator mirror as she rode down to the lobby.

Before Tanner left for the casino, he called Troy, who was babysitting that night for the neighbors. When she picked up the phone, he could hear the squalling of an angry two-year-old in the background.

"So how's it going?" he asked. He was glad that she'd had this regular gig for the last two years. Maybe it would make her think twice about the consequences of unprotected sex.

"Anthony doesn't like strained pears," Troy said, sounding as if she were at the end of her rope. "Or cereal. Or banana. Or sweet potato. Or *anything*."

Tanner laughed. Maybe she'd put off kids until she was at least thirty. She could finish her education, work, maybe travel, before she even thought about starting a family.

"It's not funny." Her voice changed, moving into a wheedle. "Can you come over, Dad? You'd know what to do."

"It sounds like you're doing great," Tanner said, trying to keep the smile out of his voice. "Here's my advice: don't give him anything. He won't starve. Why force it? Anyway, I can't come over. I have an appointment at the casino."

"On a Sunday? You never go to the casino on Sundays. And I need your help. Anthony, here, want your duck? Take your duck, Anthony."

"I'm not sure when I'll get home, but it won't be too late." *Unless I find Hope McNaughton, and she wants to play naughty games with me.*

"Is this about that woman you're interested in?" Troy asked, making Tanner blink, certain that Troy had read his mind. "The one you were looking up in the phone book? Have you asked her out yet?"

"It's not about a date," Tanner said, glad she couldn't see his face. "I just have something to do."

Troy exhaled. "Dad. I wouldn't mind. At least, I don't think so. If that's what you're worried about. Not if you went out with someone nice. If I could, you know. Like her."

Tanner wasn't sure he could call Hope "nice." Interesting, yes. Tense, for sure. Maybe even edgy. She might be nice, too, once she got past whatever it was that made her want to play cards like a dervish. But he was touched by his daughter's openness, all the same.

"It's just you and me, kid," he said.

"But if you want to—I don't know—get married. It'll be okay. I don't want you to grow old alone."

Old? Now he was *old?* He was *thirty-eight.* Marty talked to him like he was a randy teenager, and his daughter talked to him like he had one foot in the grave. Between the Mafia and a teenager, a guy couldn't win.

"Don't worry about me," he said. "I'll shuffle along somehow. But what about you? Anthony seems awfully quiet all of a sudden."

"Oh, no!" Troy said. "*Anthony! Stop* that! Dad, I gotta go."

Tanner glanced at his watch as he looked around. Hope wasn't in the casino coffee shop. Neither was Marty the Sneak. So where were they? Faith hadn't said when Hope would be there, but surely it wouldn't be late. If she was trying to earn a big stake, she'd need to play early and often.

Then he turned, and there she was. Hurrying toward him.

Tanner's heart started to pound. Hope was striding down the hallway, as other people made way for her, following her with their eyes. *And she was coming to him.*

His mouth went dry as he watched her approach. She looked fantastic. She glowed brightly in the casino, like she had an aura. Her blonde hair, hanging loose around her shoulders, bounced as she walked. She was wearing some kind of blue sleeveless top and long, white shorts—and what he wouldn't do to slide his finger under that hemline to find that sweet spot behind her knee.

She looked a lot different than she had yesterday when she'd sat at the bar, shellshocked, in that silly navy suit. Tonight she looked hot, and cool. Confident, but approachable. Infinitely desirable. Utterly beautiful. Radiant.

He let her come right up to him, waiting for her at the door of the coffee shop.

"Hope," he said.

She glanced sideways, both ways, startled, before her eyes settled on him. Then her eyes turned wary.

She hadn't been coming to him. She hadn't even noticed him.

His disappointment was so acute it felt like kick to the gut.

"Hi," he said, trying to get breath back in his lungs. "You look—great."

She stopped. "What are you doing here?" she asked.

She *so* hadn't been coming to him.

"Marty called me," he said. "He said I was out of line yesterday. About what I said to you."

"*I* told you that you were out of line," she said, looking like she was already getting mad. He *really* didn't want that to happen again.

"Yes, but I needed confirmation from an impartial outside observer," he said. "Not that Marty is exactly impartial."

"What did he say?" Hope asked, suspicious.

Tanner felt inspired. "He said I should help you," he said. "So here I am. Ready to help."

"I don't need your help," Hope said.

"You said that last night at the bar," Tanner said, nodding to the hostess who had approached them, holding menus. "I hate to say it, but you do need help if you're losing at the thirty-dollar tables."

"I won today," Hope said.

"That's great, but one afternoon's success at the thirty-dollar table—"

"Twenty-dollar table," Hope admitted.

Tanner raised his eyebrows. "Right. One afternoon's success at the twenty-dollar table does not put you in the ranks of the pros."

"I *know* that," Hope said. "That's why the uncles—"

"Said you should take all the help you can get," Tanner said. "That's what Marty said. Here he comes now. Ask him."

Hope looked up to see Marty approaching. "We're having something to eat before we play," she said, obviously trying to give Tanner the brush-off.

"That's great, because I'm hungry," said Tanner. "Hey, Marty. I'm here to help, like you said."

Marty looked at him and sighed before turning to Hope. "He *does* know how to play cards."

Hope didn't look thrilled at the prospect of having Tanner in her corner, but she didn't say no. "Okay," she said grudgingly, nodding to Tanner.

So okay, he was the only happy camper out of the three of them. Not terrible odds.

Tanner turned to the hostess. "Table for three," he said. "Nonsmoking."

He followed Hope into the coffee shop, watching her hips under the white shorts, feeling like a liar.

Smoking was the only way to describe the air *he* breathed.

"Okay," Hope said, when they'd finished eating and the waitress had cleared their plates. She'd rather not be sitting here with Tanner. She didn't know him, he was a card player, he knew how to cheat, all the signs pointed to *get him out of here.* But Marty vouched for him, so she'd accept his help. She might not want Tanner around, but more than that, she wanted to play better. She *had* to play better. She had less than a week to win her stake so she could win the ranch back from Big Julie.

Too bad Tanner was a card player. She'd be tempted otherwise. Those shoulders. He didn't get those by sitting indoors all the time. Those hands, too. They were big. Calloused. Nicked. They were hardworking hands, although his nails were clean and trimmed. His arms, what she could see of them, were tanned. Strong-looking.

But she knew what card players were like. They played fast and loose, in more ways than one. And she'd had enough of that to last a lifetime.

"Do you think they'd mind if we spent twenty minutes just playing?" she asked, glancing around to see how crowded the coffee shop was. "It's time to step up my game. I want to move to the thirty-dollar tables."

"You want to play just to ask questions, right?" Tanner

asked. "For practice. Not for money."

"We can play for money." Hope swallowed. They'd take her, that was for sure. They were both pros, much better than she was. She didn't mind losing to Marty, but losing money to Tanner would bite.

"*Not* for money," Marty said, scowling at Tanner. "We're here to *help*."

Hope dug a pack of cards out of her new straw bag. It had a wooden toggle clasp and embroidered blue flowers. Hope hadn't been sure about the bag, but Baby had insisted. And now Hope saw she was right. It *made* the outfit. That and the blue wooden bangle bracelet she wore.

She shook her head to clear it and dealt the cards just as the waitress came by with the water pitcher and an inquiring look. Tanner slid her a twenty.

"Just twenty minutes," he said with a slow smile, and the waitress smiled back, pocketing the money and walking away.

Fast and loose. A good reminder to stay away, no matter how broad the shoulders were.

"You can pay me back later," Tanner said, glancing at Hope before he picked up his cards.

"Ha," Hope said. "You tip waitresses for table time, you're on your own. I only tip dealers."

Tanner slid a second twenty to Hope. "Twenty for the dealer, too," he said, "if I get twenty minutes alone with her."

"Does that kind of line usually work for you?" Hope asked, irritated, pushing the twenty back and finishing the deal. She pointed to the cards in front of him. "We're here to *play*. So—play."

They played ten quick hands. Hope lost them all.

"Okay," Hope said, sitting back, ready to learn from the experts. "My cards aren't bad. I don't see what I'm doing wrong. What did you see?"

"You have to be more aggressive," Tanner said. "Bet instead of call. Call instead of fold."

Marty nodded. "He's right, Little Hope. You gotta go for it."

Yes. She might not like the messenger, but she wanted to hear the message. "When?" she asked.

Tanner shook his head. "In the third hand—you couldn't decide if you should call or fold when all the cards were out. Marty had bet into a big pot. What did you do?"

Folded. "I thought Marty had a full house. Jacks full of sevens."

"But he didn't. He had two pair. *You* had the winning hand."

She nodded. "Two pair. Kings and nines."

"Okay. So how much did that pot cost you?"

She remembered. "One hundred fifty dollars. If we'd been playing for money."

"Right. When you're not sure—call. You might lose the bet. In fact, you'll probably lose the bet. But when you fold the winning hand, you lose the *entire pot.*"

She glanced at Marty for confirmation.

Marty shrugged. "Yeah," he said. "If your bet is ten bucks and you *call* and you lose, you're out the ten. But if there's a hundred in the pot and you *fold* the winning hand, you're out the hundred. So you can call nine times and be wrong and make it good with the tenth call. So call."

Tanner nodded. "In general, you have to be a *lot* more aggressive," he said. "You want the other players to fear you. Respect you. When they do, you can control the game better. You won't win otherwise."

Hope nodded. He would be a formidable player, she realized. She wouldn't want to face him in a showdown.

"He's right," Marty said. "And you gotta work the pots better. Control them better."

Hope frowned, turning to him. "What do you mean?"

Marty thought a minute. "Say, you hold king-queen. The flop shows king, jack, nine. The next guy bets. What do you do?"

Hope looked at him, not sure.

"You *raise*," Tanner said.

"Right," Marty said. "You used to know this, Hope."

Hope shook her head, feeling exasperated with herself. "I never really *knew* it, Marty. I used to *feel* it. When I was a kid, I just played my guts out."

"You should still play like that," Tanner said. "What happened?"

"Life, I guess," Hope said, looking at Marty, not wanting to say, *my card-playing, card-cheating father abandoned me and we got poor and I shut down.*

"You should have seen her," Marty said, a dreamy smile on his face. "Just a kid, and she could play your socks off. Well, don't you worry, Little Hope. You don't ever really forget how to play. We'll get it back for you."

"I hope so," Hope said. "Anyway, I'm pretty sure that in that situation I'd know to raise. That's a good hand."

"Right," Marty said. "It's a good play, so you raise. And it's good strategy, because you flopped the top pair. When you raise the other bettor, you cut down his pot odds by making him put in more money to win less."

"Pot odds," Hope said.

"The amount you bet relative to the amount you'd win," Tanner said.

Hope was amazed. "You *think* about that?"

Marty nodded. "You got to," he said. "If you're gonna make your play count."

"Explain, please," Hope said, feeling like she was on the cusp of something big—graduating from high school. Buying a clingy top. Whatever.

"Okay," Marty said. "Suppose there's forty bucks in the pot when your guy bets ten bucks. If you *call* with your ten dollar bet, there's sixty bucks in the pot for his ten-dollar bet. Six to one. You with me?"

"So far," Hope said, waiting for the payoff.

"Okay. If you *raise*, there's eighty dollars in the pot for his twenty-dollar bet. Four to one."

Tanner tapped the table. "And if you raise, you might drive out other players, which is good. You don't want anyone else to benefit from lucky draws on the turn or the river."

Hope put the cards back in her bag, grateful to them both. "You don't need regression analysis, Marty. There's nothing wrong with your math. Thanks for your help. Tanner, you too. I'm thinking they don't teach the right stuff in business school."

Marty looked embarrassed. "It's just what we do, Little Hope."

Tanner shrugged. "I'm here to help. At least after losing this game you're not sitting in the bar crying over your beer."

"I wasn't crying before," Hope said, annoyed with him all over again, sliding out from the booth.

"Of course not," Tanner said, rising and picking up the check. "And I don't drink beer."

Chapter 11

On Monday morning Hope called her boss. She'd only phoned the uncles on Friday, just three days ago, but already the software company seemed like a million light years away. The thought terrified her. She'd worked so hard to get her job—and in three days she'd forgotten all about it.

"Brian," she said when her boss answered. "Listen, I know it's sudden, but I have to take my two weeks' vacation now, starting today. Something's come up."

"Is everything all right?"

"Yes, it's just—well, some family came into town unexpectedly" —*the uncles, so it wasn't really a lie*—"and I have some related business to take care of." *Like win two hundred thousand dollars and then the ranch in a poker game.*

How could the chief financial officer of a software startup tell the CEO *that?*

"Anything we should know about before you go?"

Don't bet long shots. When in doubt—call, don't fold.

"Just—I've got the annual report done, and the one- and five-year projections are complete except for the graphics."

"Yeah, I saw them on the server," Brian said. "No problem, Hope. We're all set. Take the time. See you in two."

She thanked him and sighed as she hung up. *That was that.* Now at least she'd have the time to play and earn her stake. Whether she *would* earn it was another matter. She'd played the thirty-dollar tables last night and she'd come out about even. The play was much tougher at that level. Professionals played the thirty-dollar tables, and they weren't fooling around.

Of course, neither was she.

The uncles had watched the action for most of the evening, just as they'd watched in the afternoon, looking for tables with a few weak players. Even so, Hope was only three hundred dollars ahead, and that was mostly a fluke. She'd have to do a lot better than that—and soon. She had to succeed at the thirty-dollar tables, because if she played day and night for the rest of the week at the twenty-dollar tables and won every hand, she still couldn't earn two hundred thousand dollars in time to win the ranch back.

But she'd held her own at the thirty-dollar tables. She'd played hard and she'd done okay. Today she'd have to do better.

She had seven thousand dollars, and she needed only one hundred ninety-three thousand more.

Hope had dressed for the casino and was rinsing out her coffee cup at the kitchen sink when she looked up and spotted a strange car in the driveway and two men she didn't know push open the barn's heavy sliding door and step into its dim interior.

Why were strangers entering the barn? They couldn't be up to any good. She thought of the Mafia and the horses and what a lot of dry hay in hot weather could do, and she dropped the cup, leaped for the screen door and sprinted over to the barn, fear and anger making her run faster than she ever had.

When she got to the barn, she slid in as quietly as she could and grabbed a pitchfork that hung by the door. She couldn't see the men, but she could hear their voices. They were in the tack room.

Holding the pitchfork in front of her, she approached the

small space where she stored riding gear, rags, saddle soaps, and leather. A young man had pushed aside some equipment and was thumping the panel on a cupboard; a middle-aged man was holding a tape measure against a wall.

"Who are you and what are you doing?" Hope demanded from the doorway.

The men jumped. The older man dropped his tape measure.

"Jesus, you scared me," he said, reaching down to pick it up. "We're appraisers. Didn't somebody from Cantwell, Lederer, and Sharp call you? The law firm? That guy Sharp said he'd talked to you, and he'd get in touch."

"Nobody called," Hope said, her voice tight. "What's this about?"

"We're supposed to assess the buildings," the man said. "For the sale."

Hope's anger surged. *They sure didn't waste any time.*

"The place isn't sold yet," she said. "And until it is, you'll have to leave."

"There's just been a misunderstanding," the man said, taking out his phone. "You can put down the pitchfork. I'll call—"

"No, you won't," Hope said, taking a firmer grip on the pitchfork. "The place isn't sold, the deed isn't transferred, and until it is, you have no business being on our property. I haven't given permission, and I won't. Now, you'll have to leave."

"But—" the man started.

"I have my own lawyers to call," Hope said, bluffing. "You really want to get tied up like that?"

The man sighed.

"Come on, Jimmy, let's go," he said to the younger man. "Looks like we'll have to come back later."

Yeah, a lot later. If she had anything to say about it, they'd *never* be back.

Hope brandished the pitchfork at them as they preceded

her out of the barn, feeling better as she did. Could she be arrested for assault if she poked them in the backside? Probably, more's the pity.

She marched them over to their car and watched them get in and drive away. There, that was that. Although next week would be a long one if she had to play cards *and* drive away the greedy vultures trying to make a buck off her family's misfortunes.

Tanner waited for Hope at the concierge desk, reading a brochure about Las Vegas points of interest while he passed the time. He was filling in for Marty, who had been unable to tear himself away from a lucrative no-limit game that had run unexpectedly long. Tanner was only too happy to oblige. If he'd known that his acquaintance with the Jersey players would have yielded the incredible payoff of getting closer to Hope, he'd have pushed sooner to get to know his east coast competition better.

Tanner glanced up and saw Hope approach—and had the breath knocked out of him again. She had that glow. That drop-dead radiance that made his heart stop. It wasn't anything she wore. Clothes had nothing to do with how beautiful she was. It was like a golden aura that surrounded her.

"If you're tired of playing poker, we could do the Big Shot," he said as she neared, trying to sound normal. "Might be good for a cheap thrill." He squinted at the brochure. "Or maybe not so cheap. Thirty bucks to toss your breakfast. There's a concept."

"Isn't that the bungee jump? From forty stories up, or something?" Hope said, coming up and looking over his shoulder at the brochure. "Just what I need—more free fall. Where's Marty?"

Tanner shrugged, enjoying how close Hope was. "He got into a game that didn't end on time. He should be done in a while. The other guys are in place."

"Why didn't he call me?"

"Because he called me."

She looked at him, uncertain.

"I guess because I've got the cell plan with the fewest dropped calls. Look, you're covered, Hope. You want to do this or not?"

She exhaled, looking a little embarrassed. "Yeah. I do. Sorry. I just have to get a quick cup of coffee first."

"Fast coffee, our specialty." He put the brochure back in the rack and led her into the casino. "If you're not too fussy about locale, they have decent brew at the bar."

They pulled up two stools at the nearly empty bar. Tanner nodded to the bartender and ordered plain coffee. They made it the way he liked it: strong and hot, and it tasted good going down. Hope sagged onto a bar stool and sighed in relief while she drank. Tanner eyed her over his own cup.

"So how are you doing so far?"

Hope frowned, taking another swallow. "I did okay last night. I didn't win, but I didn't melt down."

"Any thoughts on why you didn't win?"

"The thirty-dollar tables are a whole different level of play. Everything is stepped up."

"Got that right. You playing into any inside straights?"

Hope snorted. "I know better than *that*."

Tanner grinned. "Just checking. Okay. Take a look at that table over there. The one with the Harley Davidson tee-shirt. The dealer is just starting out. Tell me how the players will bid."

Hope stared at him. "How can I tell? I'm not in the game."

"Not the amounts. Just how they'll play."

Hope stared at him and then turned her back to him to watch the game twenty feet away.

With her back to him, he could see the curve of her neck, the strong set of her shoulders. Shoulders? He'd never bothered to notice a woman's shoulders before. *Crap.* He

127

had it bad.

"I know I'm supposed to be looking for tells," she said, turning back to him. "But I don't see how I can see anything. Don't you have to study the players for a while to know how they'll play? Like several hands? Or several years?"

"Not necessarily." Tanner took a deep breath and regrouped, putting all thoughts of Hope's shoulders temporarily aside. "Okay, the Harley tee-shirt. What's he all about?"

Hope looked at the player at the end. "He likes motorcycles?"

Tanner laughed. "Are you *sure* you're not playing into any inside straights?" he asked. "Look at his hands. His fingers. He's got them laced together."

Hope looked again for a few seconds. Then she turned to Tanner, her eyes bright with anticipation.

"What does that mean?" she asked.

Tanner smiled, warmed by her infectious enthusiasm. "Generally speaking, it means the player has low confidence. It's not much to go on. Low confidence could mean he thinks he has a bad hand, or he thinks he has a good hand but he doesn't know how to play it. And there's all kinds of exceptions. He could be bluffing. He could have some other tell that he's trying to conceal by locking his fingers together like that. But when you sit down at a table and you're first gathering information, go with the customary read. Interlaced fingers means low confidence."

"So I could bluff him."

"You could."

She beamed at him, and Tanner felt himself fall into her smile. "What else?" she demanded.

"What else," he said, glancing at the table, wanting to find something that would make her smile at him like that again. "Guy in the blue shirt."

Hope looked at the man in the blue shirt for several seconds. Tanner watched her narrow her eyes and glare at the unoffending player before she turned back to him.

"What?" she said.

"Thumbs in waistband. Tell you anything?"

"He ate too much breakfast. *What?*"

Tanner grinned. "He ate too much breakfast."

"Hey!" Hope said, but she laughed. "You're supposed to be teaching me here!"

Tanner shook his head. "He ate too much breakfast, *and* it's another low-confidence tell. Thumbs in waistbands or pockets generally are low-confidence tells."

"Thank you. Was that so hard?"

"Good thing I'm so trustworthy. I could be telling you this stuff all wrong."

Hope leaned back, an arrested look on her face. "I probably shouldn't listen to you at all. I have to go." She jumped off the stool.

"Wait a minute." Tanner put out his hand to stop her, feeling her flesh, firm and smooth under his fingers. "I was just teasing you. But that reminds me—one thing you do need to learn, and the sooner the better—patience. What's your starting hand?"

Hope jerked her arm away. "It depends."

"If you say it depends on your position at the table, that's the right answer. Even so, you need to decide what your opening hand is for where you sit in the betting round, and then stick to it. It'll save you a lot of poor decisions down the road."

Hope was looking at him like he was pond scum. What had he said that had made her mad?

"You have to be aggressive, like we talked about, but selective. Wait for the right hand, and then play the hell out of it. You'll be better off."

She was still frowning at him. He couldn't believe it. Here he was, *helping.*

"You can trust me, Hope. Marty does."

She looked at him for a long moment and then took a deep breath. "Yeah, I trust Marty. For some things. He's my *uncle*, after all. But he's not exactly a pillar of the community, either. Where am I playing first?"

Tanner felt disappointed, but he pulled his phone out of his pocket and checked his messages.

"Isaiah says he's got a ringer over at the Casbah. Let me check if that game is still in progress."

He called briefly, listened to what Isaiah had to say, then hung up.

"You're due at the Casbah," he said, "the game at the east corner, guy with the Hooters cap." Hope rolled her eyes, picked up her bag, and headed out of the casino.

"Also a sign of low confidence," Tanner called after her.

Tanner sat on the bar stool, drinking a second cup of coffee while he watched the tables. This job was incredibly boring. He was sitting alone indoors on a beautiful morning, watching tables for bad players so that he could coordinate with six other guys who were also watching tables, so that a relative novice could move in and score.

The only reason he was wasting his time this way was because he wanted to get some nonworking time with Hope as a reward. She must have been holding a huge marker on these guys, to get six professional players to fly out from Jersey for a week and help her out this way, without payment or even the expectation they could earn back their expenses.

Interesting, though, how she didn't seem to trust any of them fully—certainly not him, but not even Marty.

He'd give a lot to know what *that* was all about.

With one eye on the tables, he fielded calls from Sharp Eddie Toombs, Pete Wisniewski, and Jim Thickpenny, which is why he didn't notice when Agent Roy Frelly of the FBI came up from behind him and slid onto the stool Hope had recently vacated.

"Wingate," Frelly said. "Tell me what the hell you're doing here, and make it good."

"It *is* good," Tanner said, taking a sip from his cup. "The coffee, I mean. I recommend it."

"I know what you're doing, and you're not just drinking coffee," Frelly said. "You're scoping out the tables."

Tanner felt his heart sink. Watching tables wasn't illegal. You could watch all you liked, and you could play based on your observations, and you'd never break a law. Laws were broken only when you'd done something to artificially alter the outcome of the game—like when he'd used card tricks when he was nineteen. But he hadn't played crooked since then—almost twenty years.

That didn't mean the casinos liked it when you won based on watching tables. Just ask those MIT kids who were banned from all casinos for playing in teams and betting high when the cards would stack—entirely legitimately—in their favor.

If there was one thing Tanner didn't want, it was to be kicked out of the casinos. He earned his living in the card rooms here. And he didn't want the Jersey players and Hope kicked out, either. Frelly might not be able to accomplish that, but he could certainly make trouble for them. And Tanner didn't want to give Frelly any more power over his life than he already had.

"Like I said, just enjoying the coffee," Tanner said. "What are you doing here?"

"I'm looking for trouble," Frelly said. "Like I always do. And I think I found me some."

"Not me," Tanner said virtuously, hoping his phone wouldn't ring, announcing the losing attributes of a poker table at another casino. "I am as clean as the driven snow."

"Yeah, tell me another one," Frelly said, snorting. "You're so clean, that's why we got you by the short hairs for twenty long ones."

"Frelly, did you come by just to annoy me, or do you have something to say? Because if not, I'll be going."

Frelly raised his finger and the bartender brought him a cup of coffee. The agent took a careful sip.

"You're right. This stuff ain't half bad," he said. "Okay,

we got a tip that we should be expecting trouble. Mafia-type trouble."

Tanner rolled his eyes.

"But Agent Frelly, we're in *Vegas*. Is there *gambling* here? There *is?* I'm shocked, *shocked*, that organized crime wants a piece of it."

Frelly shook his head. "Once a smartass, always a smartass. No. What I'm asking you now is whether you seen anybody unusual or people shouldn't be here who could be a part of organized crime."

The Jersey crew. They weren't exactly *organized,* but some of them probably were criminals. More or less.

"So I'm a snitch now?" Tanner asked. When he thought about it, Frelly had just insulted him. "I get paid extra for that."

Frelly snorted again. "You get paid nothing, like always," he said. "I'm asking you, as a respon—as an *observant* member of the general public, have you seen anything that can cause trouble."

The bartender came by with the coffee pot and refilled their cups. Tanner turned to him.

"Skip, you seen anything that can cause trouble around here?"

The bartender shrugged. "Just that blonde you were with earlier. She looks like big trouble to me."

Tanner winced. So much for keeping Hope out of it.

"What blonde?" Frelly asked.

"Somebody Tanner here has the hots for," Skip said obligingly. "But she's got marriage and kids written all over her. Not our Tanner's type at all."

Frelly shrugged, losing interest. "I got a photo." He reached into his jacket pocket, briefly exposing his sidearm, and pulled out a sheet of paper. He unfolded it and showed it to Tanner and Skip. "You seen this guy? Russian. Goes by the name of Johnny Red."

Not one of the Jersey crew. Tanner felt his tension fade.

But Skip staggered back in feigned astonishment. "Johnnie *Walker* Red? We got him right here on our shelf."

Frelly glared at him and then Tanner. "A bunch of smartasses. This guy's trying to take over the Jersey action. The office in Newark sent us a tip that he came out here. For business or pleasure is what we're trying to find out."

He came out here for Big Julie Saladino, Tanner thought.

"I think he's coming to take out Big Julie Saladino," Frelly said. "What are the odds?"

If Johnny Red does take out Big Julie, I won't have to play cards with the Mob, Tanner thought. *Works for me.*

"Haven't seen him," he said.

"Just my luck," Frelly said. "I'm two damn weeks from retirement and I got some Jersey goons gonna duke it out on my patch. They couldn't go to Atlantic City? This is gonna mess up my pension, I can feel it."

"Well, everybody's got problems," Tanner said, edging off the stool. "Gotta run." Over Frelly's shoulder Tanner had seen Marty enter the casino and head toward the bar. On his home turf Marty counted most of the police force from Passaic to Piscataway among his friends and beneficiaries. He wouldn't normally worry about running into one depressed FBI agent. But Marty might not be so relaxed about meeting an FBI agent when they were casing tables for Hope.

"You lemme me know if you spot something," Frelly called after Tanner as he headed toward Marty.

"Sure thing," Tanner called back. Marty had stopped, seemingly engrossed in a blackjack table.

"Concierge desk," Tanner said as he brushed by Marty without stopping. Five minutes later both men stood at the concierge rack, perusing brochures for helicopter flights over Hoover Dam.

"That was Frelly, my FBI shadow," Tanner said. "I wasn't sure you'd want to meet him."

Marty glanced up. "We're not doing nothing wrong."

"No. But you're not on probation." Tanner looked at him when Marty didn't respond. "Are you?"

"No. Dammit. Is this going to be a problem? You scoping the tables for Hope? I don't want her getting into trouble because of you. What did he want?"

"He wanted to know if I'd seen anybody from out of town who could be connected to organized crime."

Marty the Sneak flinched.

"Yeah, that's what I thought too, but he meant somebody named Johnny Red."

Marty relaxed. "He's the Russian wants to take over Big Julie's territory. He's out here now? He planning to go after Big Julie?"

"Frelly had a tip that Johnny the Red is here, that's all he said. Nothing about killing. But I'd bet good money he's not out here to see Hoover Dam."

Marty put the brochure for the helicopter ride back into the rack. "Well. That makes the game more complicated. Because I've had some, ah, business dealings with Big Julie, and it would be in my best interest to keep him alive, if possible."

"Mine too."

The two men eyed each other.

"Okay," Marty said finally. "Enough said. Let's go watch us some tables."

Chapter 12

At three-fifteen, Hope was still sitting at the table in the Casbah, now twenty-five thousand dollars to the good. She watched Bob Olsson, a very successful professional player and the chip leader in this game, lick his lips. She didn't need Tanner to tell her that the chip leader was nervous.

She led the betting. Not the best position to be in. She had only a jack high. Not the best hole cards. It was her last hand before she had to go meet Baby. She had a healthy chip count. She could get out now and be proud of what she'd earned today. Twenty-five thousand dollars was *great*. Anybody—the uncles, Tanner, even Phil Hellmuth—*anybody* would be proud of earning that much money in one day.

Bob had about thirty-five thousand dollars in chips. So he had the depth to challenge anyone. He bet last—the best position. Still, he'd licked his lips.

He definitely was nervous.

What did that mean? If he had a bad hand, why would that make him nervous? He could just fold. No real money lost. If he had a great hand, he could just go for it. If he had a mediocre hand—would that make him nervous?

Two mediocre hands, fighting it out. Hardly the stuff of romantic poker legend. She bet, a nice conservative bet.

The play went around. Bob called.

Hope watched the flop. A king, a nine, a two. That

combined with what she had in her hand, could go somewhere.

She considered Bob. He was still nervous. The flop hadn't relieved his anxiety. What could he be holding? She felt herself breathe, felt a humming in her brain. She could win this. If she played her cards right. If she had some luck. If Bob bought her bluff.

She checked.

The chip leader toyed with his chips, letting them flow through his fingers. Hope kept her eyes locked on the dealer, but she could tell through her peripheral vision that Bob glanced at her, trying to read her.

Hope wished she'd gotten the glasses and hat. What had she been thinking? She needed to disguise her face more. Today when she went shopping with Baby, that's what she'd buy. A giant hat. A *sombrero*. And sunglasses only Mr. Magoo could love.

The chip leader pushed ten thousand dollars' worth of chips into the center of the table.

He thinks he has a better hand than I do. He might. What's the best he could have? Hope glanced at Bob. His lips were slightly pursed. Hope thought about it. She called.

The card on the turn improved Hope's hand again.

Hope checked. The chip leader checked.

The last card, the card on the river, did nothing for her. Hope checked again.

Bob openly stared at her this time. Hope resolutely looked away. By checking on the turn and the river, she'd given up her chance to bet again. She wanted the leader to take advantage of that.

Go for it, Bob.

The chip leader shoved the rest of his chips into the center of the table—another twenty-five thousand dollars' worth.

"All in," he said.

She had him. Maybe. Bob was counting on having a

better hand than she did. He'd been lead to believe that he did because, although Hope had stayed in the game, she hadn't bet or raised. She couldn't have been that confident of her cards.

And, because she had the second most number of chips, by going all in, if he won—*when* he won—he could wipe her out with this one hand. He wouldn't have to play her for hours, whittling her down.

Anyway, that's what she hoped he thought.

Of course, he truly might have a better hand than she did. Hope inhaled deeply and felt her heartbeat slow. If he had the better hand, she just lost everything she'd won tonight. Twenty-five thousand dollars, gone.

If she lost, she'd be back to square one.

Hope turned over her cards. The chip leader groaned.

Hope's king, queen, and nine from the board combined with her own jack and ten to give her a straight, beating the chip leader's three queens.

Hope was up by fifty thousand dollars.

A thrill of joy bloomed in her chest and spread through her bloodstream, going straight to her head. *She'd done it!* She'd won *fifty thousand* dollars in four hours. She'd *won!* And the ranch—well, her stake in Big Julie's game, anyway—was that much closer. Maybe she could do this after all.

She managed to keep her expression neutral. "Thank you for the game," she said to the table, standing up and shaking hands all around, tipping the dealer. "I'm sorry I have to leave for another appointment."

As she rose, gathering her chips and bag, she turned and saw the uncles and Tanner Wingate, standing just outside the card room, all watching her and grinning.

"Way to go, Hope!" Marty said.

"Bing-bing-bing!" said Sharp Eddie Toombs.

"Yowza," said Isaiah Rush. "Bobby Olsson. Good going!"

"Hell of a game," Pete Wisniewski said.

"We knew you could do it," Weary Blastell said.

"That was an astonishing display of card mastery and concealment, comparable only to play seen at the highest echelons," Jim Thickpenny said. "You are to be congratulated on your outstanding performance."

Hope walked over to them, beaming. She could feel the bounce in her step.

"I couldn't have done it without you," she said, hugging first Marty and then going down the line, hugging each uncle in turn. When she got to Tanner, she hesitated.

"You're not going to hug me?" he asked. "I helped." He was smiling, and she knew he was teasing, but for an instant, she thought she saw something else reflected in his brown eyes.

Hope put her arms around him and hugged him. *My first mistake today,* she realized.

Tanner was tall, a lot taller than she was, which was way too appealing. And he had broad shoulders and well-defined muscles. And his back, as she put her arms around him, was warm, the fabric of his blue chambray shirt smooth under her fingers. Even after a long day in the casino, he still smelled fresh, like soap and mint. With her head pressed against his chest, she could hear the steady thump of his heart. His hands were big and strong around her, holding her close. His thumbs circled slowly on her back, gently feeling out the bumps in her spine. She liked it. It felt hypnotic. She could feel his cheek resting against her hair. She liked that, too. It had been a long time since she'd broken up with her last boyfriend. He'd been smart with a dry sense of humor, but he'd had no sense of the physical.

Tanner had a *great* sense of the physical.

The thought flooded her mind with panic.

No, no, no! No physical! No distractions! No card players! No broken hearts!

With an effort, Hope lurched away, feeling her own heart pound in her chest, knowing she looked flushed.

"Little Hope?" Sharp Eddie asked, looking confused. "Are you all right?"

"What's wrong?" Tanner asked, dropping his hands, a question in his eyes. Those melting brown eyes, darker than the very best chocolate. Why hadn't she ever noticed what color his eyes were?

"That was an incredible bluff," Weary said. "That your hand was *worse* than it was. All that checking so he'd stay in the game."

"Learned from the best," Hope said with an effort, smoothing down her hair.

Marty took her arm and led her toward the cashier's window. "Whaddid I say, Little Hope? You played a fantastic game. Fantastic. Never saw anything like it, except that one time out here years ago. Well, and then that time in Atlantic City, during the hurricane. And then at that private party out in Teaneck—but never mind that. I knew you could do it. Now, bank your winnings. You don't want to walk around with all that money. You have just enough time before you go upstairs for your shopping trip."

Hope had regained her equilibrium. "I'm all right, Marty," she whispered as she handed in her chips.

"Of course you're all right, and you just won a lot of money, too, so we'll be celebrating with you or without you," Marty said cheerfully as they stepped away from the cashier's window. "Now you go shopping and when you come back we'll go to the Chinese buffet for supper and celebrate before you play tonight."

"Okay," Hope said. She gave him a little grateful squeeze. "Thanks, Marty."

She and Marty had paused in the hallway leading to the elevators, and Hope smiled at the uncles as they wandered up.

"Thank you again. Everybody," she said, glancing at them all. Even Tanner. "I couldn't have done it without you."

"We know, Little Hope," Pete said, grinning.

"You're a credit to our teaching," Weary said, nodding.

"Bing, bing, bing!" Sharp Eddie said.

"You can play on my team any time," Isaiah said.

"Your previous experience combined with your renewed enthusiasm and our strategic investments of time and resources have brought us to the happy circumstances we enjoy today," Jim Thickpenny said.

Hope beamed at them again. *Fifty thousand dollars*. And they'd all come out here just to help her make it happen.

The elevator doors opened and Hope stepped in. Punched the keypad. The doors closed.

As soon as Hope's face disappeared behind the doors, Marty slugged Tanner in the arm.

"*Ow,*" Tanner said. "Cut it out! What's that for?"

"Just remember what I said," Marty said, narrowing his eyes.

"I remember. You said, help. I *helped*."

Marty scowled at him. "No distractions. She's here to work."

"What did I do? She's working. She's doing great."

"Just so you remember. Want to get a drink?"

"Are you done with the hitting?" Tanner asked, rubbing his arm.

Marty shrugged. "Sure. For now anyway."

Tanner flexed his shoulder, massaging his arm again. "For *now?* What's that supposed to mean? I'm going to have a bruise, you know that? *Jeez.*"

"Come on, don't be a whiner. We got a hell of a play to celebrate. I'll buy you a beer, how about that?"

"Scotch," Tanner said, walking back to the bar with the uncles. "You are buying me a twenty-five-year-old, very expensive Scotch."

At the bar, Marty turned to Tanner and they clinked whiskey glasses. They each took a sip in silence, giving the smooth blend the reverence it deserved.

"I realize that situation back there, where she panicked a

little, that wasn't your fault," Marty said. "Not all of it, anyway. But I gotta watch out for her. You understand."

Tanner nodded. Marty could watch out for Hope all he wanted. Tanner intended to watch out for Hope, too. And Tanner didn't intend to interfere with Hope's game in any way, whatever she was playing for.

But Tanner had seen Hope's eyes. Those blue eyes, warm and dark, almost navy, as she'd looked at him.

She might have panicked, but being close to Tanner, holding him—his holding her—she'd liked that. She'd *liked* Tanner close to her. She'd denied it to herself. She'd jumped away. She'd been scared. But she'd liked it nonetheless.

And there was nothing Marty could do to stop that.

"So, Baby, can I ask you something personal?" Hope asked. She and Baby had gone to Target for more accessories, where they'd struck gold—or at least gold plate. All the merchandise, normally very reasonably priced, was now on sale. Baby was having a field day at the sunglasses display.

Hope tried on a pair of sunglasses with huge frames and looked at herself in the tiny mirror that hung over the rack. No. Too big, too square, definitely too much flash and not nearly enough class.

"Something personal? Sure," Baby said, looking deeply into her own teeny mirror at the sunglasses she had on. The narrow, cats-eye frames were turquoise, edged in rhinestones. "These glasses are so cute! I can't believe I never shopped here before. This store is fantastic for accessories. Okay, it's got no atmosphere at all, but the selection! And the *prices!* I'm definitely getting these."

Hope glanced at her, assessing. "You definitely should. If you don't, I will."

Baby snorted as she took off the glasses and put them into their basket. "As if. So whaddaya wanna know?"

Hope hesitated, putting the big frames back on the rack.

"I don't want to offend you. But Big Julie's not an obvious choice for a, a boyfriend for you, I guess. And I wondered, why did you pick him?"

Baby handed a pair of glasses to Hope to try on. "You're thinking, hot young chick and old fat man. He's rich and I'm out for what I can get. Right?"

Hope swallowed, putting on the sunglasses to hide her eyes. *In a nutshell.* "Well, something like that."

Baby nodded. "It's not real obvious, but Big Julie's sexy. I think it's because people do what he says. I'm not saying I won't take what Big Julie wants to give me. But you know, giving me stuff makes him feel good. It's more like, it's not about me. It's about him, you know?"

Hope thought about that. "So you'd be his girlfriend even if he didn't give you a lot of presents?" She took another look at her face with the squarish tortoiseshell glasses. They were a bit glam. But not too glam.

"Well, probably not," Baby conceded. "But with Big Julie, it's not either or. He's got the money to buy a nice apartment on the golf course, and he's got the pull to buy it, too, even though he's not a member. See? He can get your street light fixed first. Like that."

"You care about *street lights?*" Baby was showing unexpected depths.

"*Of course* I care about street lights." Baby was indignant. "The other night we came home from dinner and a nice night out, the street lights were dark, what is *with* that? And I stepped into a crack in the sidewalk and broke the heel off my Jimmy Choos. They're *ruined.*"

"Ah."

"So why are you asking all these questions, anyway? Not that I mind. And by the way, those shades look very classy on you."

Hope took off the sunglasses and dropped them into the basket. "Well. Is there something about Big Julie's—associations—that attracts you? When you met him, was it—appealing somehow?"

"Oh, *now* I get it," Baby said, a knowing smile lighting her face. "You met a bad boy, right? They're the best kind."

Hope frowned and started to push the cart toward the checkout. "I wouldn't know. And I've never wanted to find out."

Baby rolled her eyes. "Oh really? Beige Girl never went out with a bad boy? Why does that so not surprise me?"

"Hey," Hope said, jerking the cart to a sudden halt at the end of line ten. "I've gone out with plenty of troublemakers. *Plenty.*"

"All of whom dressed like they went to the office on Saturday."

"It doesn't matter what they *dress* like," Hope said, exasperated. "What matters is what's in their *head.*"

"What's in their head is what they dress like! And that's why we're shopping for *you*. If you dress like you have fun on Saturday, you might actually *have* fun."

The woman pushing the cart ahead of them in line turned around and gave Hope the once over. "She's right, honey," she said before she turned back to her celebrity tabloid.

"I *am* having fun," Hope said, jamming the cart between the checkout counters. "See? *Lots* of fun."

"You could be," Baby said with that irritating, knowing smile. "You're all hot and bothered about that bad boy you don't want to think about."

"I'm not thinking about anybody," Hope said, putting her sunglasses on the checkout counter and watching them roll toward the cashier.

Not much I'm not.

Chapter 13

When Baby and Hope got back to the casino, they met Tanner by the elevator that went up to the suites.

"What are you doing here?" Hope asked.

"Marty sent me to take you to buy a hat," Tanner said. "Assuming you didn't get one yet. You could act happier to see me."

"I'd be happier," Hope said, glaring, "if I weren't so busy having so much incredible *fun*."

"What?" Tanner asked, looking confused, but Baby had stepped a little closer and was looking him over, blatantly assessing him.

"Are you bad?" she purred, leaning forward slightly, giving Tanner a spectacular view of everything she had, which was quite a lot. "You look like a bad boy."

Tanner assessed her too, a faint smile on his face. "I can be bad," he said. "How bad do you need me to be?"

"I can see that introductions are probably superfluous here," Hope said, feeling waspish, "but let me make the attempt. Baby, this is Tanner Wingate."

"The bad boy." Baby licked her lips.

"Very," Tanner said, smiling into Baby's eyes and then glancing at Hope. "I especially like to be bad with two beautiful women."

"You'll have to save all your badness for one, because I have plans for my own bad boy," Baby said. "I was just curious. See you." She stepped into the elevator car and waved at Hope as the doors closed.

Hope watched Tanner watch Baby disappear from view. Baby had her ways with men. They certainly had worked on Tanner.

Feeling unaccountably depressed, Hope turned around and walked away. All this shopping was pointless. She was the heads-down, focused-on-the-future one. The one without the silicone breasts, the tummy tucks, the extra peroxide lift. The one who dressed like she went to work on Saturdays. The one who—if she faced facts—would acknowledge that she didn't have any fun.

"Hey, Hope, wait up!"

Hope glanced at her watch as she strode down the hall. Five-thirty. She was meeting Marty at six for the all-you-can-eat Chinese buffet to celebrate her big win that afternoon, which now seemed a long time ago. She'd check in at home first. She didn't want to spend any more time with Tanner Wingate, who was probably drooling on the elevator doors right now, wishing Baby's breasts would come back.

A hand snagged her elbow.

"Hey. Didn't you hear me yell to wait up?"

Hope scowled at Tanner's hand on her arm until he dropped it. "Oh, you thought I was a dog in training? I come when you call?"

Tanner stared at her. "We're going hat shopping. For your game. What's the matter with you?"

"Nothing. But I'm not in the mood to go hat shopping." She started to walk again, and Tanner went after her.

"We have to. Marty will rip me a new one if we don't come back with a hat for you."

"I've done all the shopping I can do today. Maybe you can take Baby. She likes to shop."

Tanner stopped her again. "What? Don't tell me. Is that what you're pissed off about? Because Baby showed me her goods?"

"I'm not pissed off. Whatever Baby showed you, I'm sure it was very nice. I wasn't paying attention."

Tanner laughed shortly, looking exasperated.

"You *are* mad. Jesus. She was yanking my chain. You have to know that, right? And now *you're* yanking it. Well, at least the two of you are having fun."

Hope looked away. Baby *had* been kidding. Or—Baby had been teasing both of them, trying to find out if Tanner was the "bad boy" Hope had been thinking about. Tanner, though—Hope didn't think Tanner had been kidding when he'd stared at Baby's breasts.

But Tanner didn't matter. He was just another card player, out for the quick score. She didn't care about him. Once this game was over, she'd never see him again.

"Okay, whatever," she said, focusing on the future again. "Here's the deal. I'm meeting the uncles at six for dinner. I'm not going hat shopping. There's no time and I don't want to. Goodbye."

"Whoa," Tanner said, putting out a restraining hand again. "Change of plans. Why do you think I was waiting around down here for you in the first place? Marty called. He said, meet him at seven. And until then, we're going hat shopping."

Hope frowned. "Why didn't Marty call me?"

Tanner rolled his eyes. "Maybe your phone needs a charge? Maybe it's turned off? How should I know?"

Hope dug through her purse and pulled out her phone. It was turned off.

"I can't believe I did that," she said.

"Can we go hat shopping now?"

Hope sighed. "I suppose."

"Gracefully said. The car is this way."

Hope trailed through the casino after Tanner, feeling rebellious and immature. She dug the phone out and turned it on. She called home.

"Hey, Mom, it's me," she said when Suzanne answered the phone. "What are you doing?"

"We're just making dinner," Suzanne said. "We're having spinach lasagna and salad, and then we're going to have hot fudge sundaes while we watch that new reality singing show. How are you, sweetie? How did it go today?"

Hope felt a pang of longing. She'd had a great time—a really great time—winning that fifty grand today. But now she wished she could go home and eat dinner and watch television with her family.

"I did good," she said, hearing the happiness bubble back into her voice. "I won fifty grand."

"Fifty thousand dollars? Hope, that's fantastic! Faith, honey, Hope won fifty thousand dollars!"

Even through the noise of the casino, Hope heard a whoop in the background.

"Faith says, way to go. What's that, Amber?"

Hope waited.

"Amber says, say hi to Tanner."

"Tanner gets quite enough female attention," Hope said, feeling snarly again.

"What's that, Hope?"

"Nothing, Mom. Listen, I've got to go. You have fun. Save me some leftovers, okay? And don't wait up. I'll probably be late again."

"Break a leg, dear, or whatever they say to poker players."

Hope closed her phone and looked up to see Tanner watching her.

"Amber says hi," she said, shoving the phone in her purse.

"She's a nice kid," he said. "Come on, let's get that hat."

They drove north of the airport until Tanner pulled into the huge parking lot of a giant, brightly lit store.

"You ever shop here?" he asked.

"No," Hope said, looking at the Western insignia on the outside. "And I don't want to start. I don't want a cowboy hat."

"They sell all kinds," he said.

Hope sighed and got out of the truck.

"That's the spirit," Tanner said.

They went into the store and Hope blinked at the bright lights and rows and rows of shelves, all crammed with Western wear. Jeans, shirts, jackets, boots and shoes, and most of all, hats.

Hats of all types. Fedoras, toques, caps, bowlers, berets, sun hats—even stovepipes, top hats, and deerstalkers. But most of all, cowboy hats. Hats in all colors. Hats in straw, wool, and felt. Cowboy hats with bands of contrasting fabric, beads, conchos, feathers, rhinestones, metalworking and leather braiding. The sheer numbers, the fabrics, the styles of the hats made Hope dizzy.

"Wow," she said.

"Yeah," Tanner said. "They've got everything here."

They went over to the women's hats, and Tanner looked at Hope. "What do you like?"

Hope looked at all the dozens—probably hundreds—of hats.

"I don't know," she said. "Baby's been modifying my taste. Something with a wide brim." Suddenly she frowned.

"Maybe we should have brought Baby," she said. "You'd have liked that."

"Stop busting my chops," Tanner said, picking up a tan wool Western hat with a braided band in dark brown leather. "I can't imagine anything less fun than the two of you hassling me all night. Here, try this one for starters."

He handed the Western hat to Hope who slapped it on her head. "What do you mean?" she said. "You *liked* Baby."

Tanner sighed. "She's all right. But I'm done talking about Baby. Do you like that one at all?"

Hope looked in the mirror. "Does it look like I can have fun in this hat?" she asked.

Tanner looked at her. "You can have fun wearing anything. It isn't the accessory, it's the attitude."

Hope twisted in front of the mirror to get a different view. "Baby doesn't think so. She thinks if you have a fun attitude, it will come out in what you wear. And I'm thinking, maybe something with a little more color."

"That's what I said. Mostly. This one's nice." He handed her a dark hat with a band of rust-colored feathers. Hope dropped it on her head.

"I don't know," she said, turning her head in the mirror.

"Nothing's going to look good that way. Here." He stepped closer and lifted the hat slightly, adjusting it to slant forward over her forehead, curling down one side of the brim, nudging the crown into a sharper crease. He brushed a strand of hair off her cheek, looked into her eyes, and smiled.

"There," he said.

Hope stepped back, feeling a little breathless, and looked into the mirror. The hat *did* look better.

"Um, maybe," she said. She glanced at Tanner, who scrutinized her.

"Look down," he said.

She looked down.

"I think I need a—" she started.

"Bigger brim," he finished.

She looked up and smiled at him. "Yes," she said.

Damn, she was pretty. When he'd adjusted that hat, it was all he could do not to kiss her. Except of course if he'd tried, she probably would have ripped his head off. Or accuse him of thinking about Baby.

But how interesting was it that she was all whacked out of shape about Baby, for some reason? Baby was hot looking, for sure. He'd met hot women hundreds, maybe thousands, of times in his career. Shit, even FBI Special Agent Darla was hot. And twenty years ago—even ten years ago—hot would have been enough. But he was a lot older now and, he hoped, somewhat wiser. Hot didn't get him there anymore. Hot was nice, but he needed more than just sizzle now. He needed substance. He needed someone smart, complicated, interesting, testy, insecure, and confident. Someone with goals she was willing to work toward and people she intended to celebrate her achievements with.

He needed someone who needed a hat.

He picked up a pale straw hat with a band of bright turquoise stones.

"Try this one," he said.

Hope took the hat and put it on her head. She tilted it forward over her forehead the way Tanner had done. She bent the brim down. *Tried* to bend it down. The brim was too crisp. It didn't curl right.

"Let me," Tanner said.

He stepped closer, putting his hands on the hat brim just above her ear. She could feel his fingers brush her ear lobe as he gently curled the hat brim down. He stroked his hands along the brim toward the front and back of the hat, smoothing it carefully, bending it the way he wanted. His fingers brushed her hair, her cheek, her neck as he shaped the straw.

She stood very still and watched him in the mirror as he concentrated on the hat. He frowned slightly as he worked. His hair was overgrown and shaggy, his eyes glued on what he was doing. She felt his attention like a beam of light. Every inch of him was focused right this minute on her, on making this hat the best it could be for her.

His touch was as light as thistledown. She felt a little shiver even as her skin grew warm. Her breath became light, shallow.

He took a long time getting the curve just right. He urged the straw to curl down, the crown to stay sharp. He nudged the hat just a little lower over her eyes. The whole time, she couldn't move. Her feet were rooted to the spot as Tanner nudged and brushed and floated his fingers over her face, her ears, her hair, her neck, always adjusting the hat.

Finally he turned her to face the mirror. His hands were warm on her shoulders, and then they were gone. But he stood so close behind her she could feel his heat against her back as they both looked at her reflection.

"There," he said.

The hat was fantastic.

The color, a pale golden straw, lit up her hair and skin. The wide brim framed her face, the turquoise stones on the hatband set off her eyes, now almost navy as she looked back at him in the mirror. The crown added a good three inches to her height, so now she appeared only a few inches shorter than Tanner, who must be six two if he was an inch. She looked tall and strong and ready for anything. She looked adventurous and daring. She looked *hot*. She was grateful to Tanner for taking her here and picking out this hat.

"Pumpkin, that's the hat."

The warm and grateful moment faded.

"The hat is great," she said. "Don't call me pumpkin."

"Why not? You are a *total* pumpkin."

She turned to frown at him. "No endearments. Plus— orange, fat, round. That's why not."

"That's how you see pumpkins? Orange, fat, and round? And your sister an organic farmer. It's sad, that's what it is."

"What on *earth* are you talking about?"

"Pumpkins. The most beloved item at the farm. When everybody goes out to the country in the fall to pick vegetables, what do they look at first? Do they run to the corn field? No. To the tomatoes? No. Do they go and shriek with happiness at the green peppers? No. They rush to look at the pumpkins. Why is that?"

"I'm not following you."

"The pumpkins. People want their special pumpkin. Each is separate and distinct, unique. Their color is glorious, the color of kings, of riches, of sunsets."

Hope rolled her eyes. "Jeez, Tanner. You are so full of it."

"And the pumpkin is the hardest working vegetable in the garden. It can be soup, or soufflé, or pudding. You can mash them, boil them, or bake them. Even fry them. For something sweet, there's nothing like pumpkin pie. Or cake. Or bread. Muffins. Pancakes. You want a vegetable that will feed you forever, in more ways than you can count, in ways you never will tire of, you go with pumpkin."

Hope blinked. Tanner's voice was soft and hypnotic. They were alone in the aisle, facing the mirror, and he was looking into the mirror at her, and she was looking back at him. He was standing so close behind her that she could feel the roughness of his shirt against her bare back. She was too warm. She couldn't breathe. And she couldn't make herself look away.

"And when you go to the field to pick out your pumpkin—well, you've seen how it happens. You've probably done it yourself. You don't pick the first one. You look at them all. You hold them. You feel them. You stroke them. Are they the right fit? The right size and shape? A good color? You have to be sure."

"Oh," Hope said. She felt herself swallow. Tanner's voice was very soft.

"And then, you see it. The pumpkin that's yours. The one you've been looking for. The one with the glowing skin and a few bumps to make it interesting. The one with luscious, perfect curves. Shaped by creases and folds and indentations, so a man's hands can stroke it and always find something new."

Hope felt her breath catch.

"Maybe it's not a perfect pumpkin. Maybe it's got a few little flaws. But you know when you see it, when you touch it, that's the one you want to take home. That one and no other."

For a second more, they faced the mirror. Hope's feet were frozen in place, her whole body electric, her breathing shallow. She saw her own blue eyes wide and dark in surprise, Tanner's brown ones alight with heat. When he leaned into her and kissed her softly on the neck, Hope thought she'd melt completely away and leave nothing but a big messy puddle right there in aisle five.

Chapter 14

Johnny Red, so named because he'd had the luck, good or otherwise, to be born in Moscow before the collapse of Communism, strode out of the terminal at McCarran airport in Las Vegas with the other business travelers. Like them, he wore a dark suit and carried a cell phone. He had a large rolling suitcase that he'd checked, a briefcase that he'd carried on the plane, and a business plan that he intended to execute on this business trip. But Johnny Red wasn't planning to use time management to execute this plan. No, when Johnny Red was ready to execute his agenda, he'd use his Glock, now packed away in his checked baggage.

Johnny Red arrived with an entourage of four men who would help him execute the plan. One of them was young and strikingly handsome, medium height with dark, wavy hair, blue eyes, and the physique of a Greek god. The other three men were older and bigger, resembling ex-professional athletes who'd stayed in shape and turned to security work, which is what they were. All three wore identical bad suits and could have passed as triplets.

Johnny Red exited the airport terminal with his arm raised for a cab and stopped in the middle of the sidewalk so suddenly that the four men following him piled into each other, like ducklings following a cautious mother to the water.

"By the purity of all the saints and the holy Russian motherland they walked on, it's hot out here," he said.

This observation was dutifully confirmed by the triplets.

"Not like Moscow," said Yakov. "Nice and cool in Moscow."

"Forty degrees Celsius here," said Markov.

"At least," said Igor.

"Around here, they would call that a hundred degrees Fahrenheit," observed the young and handsome one. "More like a hundred and four."

Johnny Red grinned suddenly and reached out, ruffling the young man's hair. "That's Alexei for you," he said, grinning at the triplets. "Always the scholar."

Alexei grinned back. "Success is in the details," he said. "That's why you're sending me to law school."

"*Da*," Yakov said. "And to keep us oudda trouble."

There was a murmur of agreement around the circle.

"Okay, enough with the standing around like the peasant representatives to the First International," Johnny Red said. "We must get to the hotel. We need to plan. Comrade!" He beckoned imperiously to the next cab in line.

The cab inched forward, and the driver, a dark-skinned man wearing a turban, got out to help them with their bags.

"Comrade," Johnny Red said as they got in, "are you from one of the great Soviet Socialist Republics? Perhaps one of the Asiatic republics?"

The cabbie glanced in the rear view mirror. "New Delhi," he said.

"Ah, well," Johnny Red said. "Can't be helped. You know the Desert Dunes Resort and Casino?"

"Very nice place," the cabbie said obligingly.

"It's a pleasure palace for the decadent bourgeoisie," Johnny Red said, "but we must go where duty lies. Onward, my friend!"

The cabbie nodded, thinking that in Vegas, decadence usually trumped duty. Still, as this fare demonstrated, it took all kinds. He glanced over his shoulder and edged into the lane of traffic.

The Desert Dunes Casino and Resort was everything the Russians wanted in a Las Vegas accommodation.

"Look at this place," said Alexei, swiveling to catch the murals on the ceiling, the Carrera marble on the floor, and the Tiffany glass behind the concierge desk.

"Look at the action," said Johnny Red, checking out the entrance to the private baccarat room, the poker tables, slots, and roulette wheels. "We could make a killing here."

"We *will* make a killing here," said Markov, surprised.

"Shut *up!* Jesus! Tell the world," said Johnny Red. "Call the cops, why don't you."

"Look at the broads," said Igor, the most awed of all. "Even the ugly ones is gorgeous."

They all paused for a moment in reverent silence to the gorgeous broads.

"Boys, we have found Paradise," Johnny said, as they stepped up to the check-in clerk.

"Can I help you?" the young woman in the tangerine suit behind the desk asked.

"Yes, you can," Igor said reverentially. "You can come up to my room, whatever it is, when you're off."

The woman smiled professionally.

"You're here to check in, Mr. –?"

"Rudnitsky," Johnny Red said. "Call me Johnny Red. I reserved the suite."

"*You're* sweet," Igor said to the clerk.

"For a week," said the clerk, not smiling. "You'd like to keep it on your card? How many keys?"

"Three," Johnny said. "One for me, one for Alexei, and one for the morons here."

They finished their transaction. The clerk slid a small envelope with three keys over to Johnny Red.

"You're in suite seventeen-oh-one," she said. "Take the elevators to the left."

"When are you off?" pleaded Igor.

"Have a pleasant stay," said the clerk.

"Come on," said Johnny. "Let's go up to the suite, get cleaned up, and see what's happening."

"Did you see her?" asked Igor, as he walked backwards toward the elevator, keeping his eye on the clerk. "She was gorgeous." He smacked into a pillar.

The others laughed.

"Seventeen-oh-one," Johnny Red said, hitting the button on the elevator.

The car arrived, and they all stepped in, shoving their luggage into the small space. Alexei, standing closest to the buttons, hit the button for seventeen.

"This is quite a place," he said as the car rose.

"I could fall in love here," said Igor.

"You got to develop some finesse first," Yakov said.

"I got finesse," Igor said.

"You got the finesse of a supervisor at a Siberian labor camp," Yakov said.

"Remember why we're here," Johnny Red said when the car stopped at the seventeenth floor and he stepped out. "Falling in love is for the bourgeoisie. The job's gotta come first. I expect everybody to pull his weight on this trip. You hear me?"

He stopped suddenly, his key card poised above the lock on his door, his nose pointed into the air like a bird dog.

"What's that?" he asked.

"What?" shouted Yakov, whipping out his Glock and crouching low, as he whirled to face the elevator.

"*That*," Johnny said, sniffing.

"Where?" shouted Markov, whipping out his Glock and crouching low, like a synchronized swimmer next to Yakov, as he faced the opposite direction down the hall.

Johnny shook his head. "As I honor Lenin, the father of our glorious revolution who struggled to free the masses from their chains of bondage and despair, I can't believe I brought you amateurs along," he said in disgust.

"You smell something?" Alexei had seen his uncle sniff the air, and he had not been sent to law school for nothing.

"*Varenikis*," Johnny said.

There was a moment of silence almost as profound as the one for the broads.

"Where?" said Alexei.

Johnny sniffed. "Downstairs," he decided.

The five dropped their luggage outside the door of their suite and headed for the stairs, Yakov and Markov shouldering their weapons.

"What kind, boss?" ventured Markov.

"Apple cinnamon," said Johnny. "Can't you tell? The crust, as light as a feather, as rich as a Belarus banker. Dusted with cinnamon sugar, grainy and sweet. The filling—apples, tart, softened with butter, sweetened with raisins and honey, brightened with lemon juice, cooked to perfection. The whole thing fried to a golden brown and dunked in sour cream. *That*," said Johnny Red, east coast mobster and devotee of Russian cooking, "is gorgeous."

By now the five had reached the sixteenth floor, which contained only two suites. Johnny sniffed.

"Here," he said, stopping at sixteen-oh-one.

He rang the bell. Waited.

"Come on, come on," he said impatiently, slapping his hand against his leg.

Just then the door was flung open, releasing a gust of air so warm and moist, so redolent of butter, of sugar, of apple-cinnamon varenikis, that Johnny Red almost swooned. And when he had put out his hand to steady himself and opened his eyes to view this heaven, he saw the Angel of Russia framed in the doorway.

Her hair was a blonde halo, an aura of pale curls fluffed from heat. Her cheeks were pink, flushed with the vigorous beating she'd given her dumplings. Her eyes were the color of the Volga on a stormy day. Her tight white tee-shirt was pulled low, exposing the edge of her lacy red bra on the curve of her breast and the strap over her shoulder. She wore an apron that did nothing to conceal her perfect tan legs.

And, best of all, her face was dusted with flour and she held a wooden spoon in her hand.

"Well, hello, boys," Baby said, smiling at the five stupefied Russians. "What can I do for you?"

An hour later they were eating out of her hand.

"Here, have another," Baby said, leaning over Alexei's shoulder as she reached around him and placed two tender varenikis on his plate. He'd already had six, but he would have eaten a hundred if this beautiful baker of heavenly varenikis would continue to press her voluptuous breasts against his shoulder the way she was doing now. He sighed, letting his head drift toward Paradise.

"Oh, I can't," he said weakly, feeling the buckle of his belt press too tightly against the firm, muscled contours of his stomach. "I'm stuffed."

"You'll hurt my feelings if you don't try the apricot," Baby said, her luscious red lips pouting. She reached forward toward the bowl of sour cream, which did amazing things to her chest and caused Alexei almost to pass out from bliss. And then she held the apricot vareniki just an inch from his lips and brought her face down to his.

"Taste," she said. "This you will love."

Alexei did, indeed, love.

Johnny Red looked at the sugary remains on his plate with gluttonous satisfaction as Alexei struggled to please the goddess at the table by eating the apricot vareniki that she wanted him to eat.

"You cook like an angel," Johnny Red said, watching Baby's breasts with a fascination almost equal to Alexei's. "Where did you learn to make varenikis?"

"From my grandmother," Baby said. "Born in Minsk. Raised in Moscow. She cooked for generals. For bishops.

For presidents even."

"Lenin?" Johnny Red breathed.

"Not Lenin," Baby said. "She was too young for Lenin."

Johnny Red kept silent. He would ask no more. This angel was here now, cooking the varenikis. For him, Johnny Red. That was what counted.

He licked some crumbs off his plate and glanced up. Baby's breasts all but spilled out of the lacy red bra over her tight tank top.

"Magnificent varenikis," Johnny Red said.

"Don't I know it," Baby said.

That night in bed Baby warned Big Julie about the Russians.

"There are five of them," she said. "But only four of them carried guns. The youngest one was sort of sweet."

Big Julie struggled to come out of the deep post-coital stupor he'd fallen into. What Baby couldn't do with just her fingers and a rubber band.

"Hey," he said, opening his eyes on a wave of possessiveness. "Who?" And then after a second to gather his thoughts, "How do you know they got guns? How did you know they was even coming here?"

"The Russians who are after you," Baby said patiently. "I knew they were coming because one of your guys called when you were out, I don't even want to know where, you never tell me *nothing*. I told you before but you didn't listen. I saw the guns when they were eating the varenikis."

"The Russians were *here?*" Big Julie said, struggling to sit up. "Did they threaten you? Why didn't you tell me?"

"I *am* telling you," Baby said. "*Again.* I made varenikis for them. They liked them."

"You cooked varenikis for them? You invited them *in?*" Big Julie asked, all memories of exploring fingers and rubber bands vanished. "Are you *crazy?*"

Baby pouted. "You always said, keep your friends close

and your enemies closer."

"But, Jesus. I didn't mean the Russians."

"Well, you should have been more clear, then." Baby turned away, hurt. Her flounce and the way she crossed her arms over her chest thrust her breasts out in such a way that Big Julie was momentarily distracted.

"Aw, Baby, you know I didn't mean nothing. What you found out—that was a big help." Big Julie lost focus. Baby's breasts—full, round, firm, pink, luscious—called out to him like dessert at the buffet table. He reached out, helping himself to their sweetness.

"What did you tell them?" he asked, his voice a little strained.

"*Nothing*," Baby said outraged, turning a little so Big Julie could reach better. "But they know you're here. A couple of them spoke Russian. They thought I didn't understand."

"Uh," Big Julie said, feeling Baby's warm, taut flesh under his fingers.

Baby arched her back a little. "They said they were staying for a week. So whatever they've got planned—" She stopped momentarily, drawing in a breath as Big Julie's hands found what they'd been seeking. "Whatever they got planned, Big Julie, you should be careful," she finished on a gasp.

"I'm being careful," Big Julie said, breathing in her warm freshness, the firm, soft breasts. "See how careful I'm being?"

He slid his hands under the sheet, reaching lower, finding her heat. He raised his head, as a new thought occurred to him.

"You made *varenikis*? You can *cook?*"

Chapter 15

Kenji Hasegawa, a world-famous chef whose last restaurant had earned three Michelin stars and whose current restaurant was fully booked through Christmas, looked down at the blonde girl who was perched precariously on a stool at his stainless steel counter. Why on earth had he let Tanner Wingate talk him into this? But he'd said he'd give this child a cooking lesson, and he would do his best. She was a nice kid, well-mannered and interested. And he'd gotten season tickets to the UNLV basketball games out of the deal, so that was something.

"Have you thought about what we should make for your birthday lunch, Amber?"

She beamed at him. "This was a total surprise! Thank you *so much* for the lesson. You are totally the *best*. Anything we make will be *awesome*."

Kenji found himself smiling back. At least she'd be easy to please.

"Well, what do you like to eat?" he asked.

"I like *everything*. Except for totally weird stuff."

Kenji grinned. "You want to stay away from totally weird stuff," he agreed.

Amber grinned back. "You're a sushi chef, right?" she asked. "That's all fish? Let's do fish."

"That will be easy, then. We'll go to the market to pick out something fresh. What would you like to have with it?"

Amber's forehead furrowed while she thought. "Potato salad?" she asked. "Like a picnic."

"Good choice," Kenji said. "There's lots of variations with potato salad. What else? Remember, we've got the protein and the starch, so now we need a vegetable that adds color to the plate."

Amber tilted her head at him. "This seems so easy," she said. "When I'm making up recipes for the vegetable boxes, doing a menu seems really hard. How about cole slaw? That's green."

"Cole slaw it is. Do you want birthday cake for dessert? I'm not a baker, Amber, so it wouldn't be real fancy."

"Brownies," Amber said firmly. "With nuts."

"That's the menu, then," Kenji said. "We have a lot of the stuff we'll need here at the restaurant, but I thought it would be fun to shop. Are you ready to go?"

They went to the natural foods store and bought the chocolate, nuts, and flour. They went to the Indian food store and bought spices. Last they went to a seafood market. Before they drove back to the restaurant, Kenji dug through one of the grocery bags, pulling out a small cellophane package and tearing it open.

"What's that?" Amber asked, looking at it.

"I got it in the Indian grocery shop," Kenji said. "It's green mango candy."

"Mango," Amber said. "That's a tropical fruit, right? Cool."

Kenji handed a piece to Amber, who unwrapped the morsel and popped it into her mouth. Her eyes widened.

"Juicy," she said, focusing on the horizon while she tasted. "It's good. Sweet, but sour, too."

They got in the car, and Kenji started to drive. "They've got a lot of good things there," he said. "The trick is to learn how to use them. The candy, though, isn't so hard to figure out."

Amber giggled.

Back at the restaurant, Kenji handed Amber a big white apron, looping the strings around the girl three times to tie it snugly. But when he gave her even the smallest chef's hat, it fell down over her eyes. He dug through a drawer and found a clean but worn pink bandana and tied it around Amber's forehead over the hat, pleating the brim in back to make it fit.

"Now it looks like you work here," he said, as he tied the bandana securely behind her head.

Amber beamed, feeling the tall white hat towering over her head. "I'm ready to cook," she said, and Kenji laughed.

"First we'll make the side dishes," he said. "Let's start with the potato salad."

Hope, dressing for Amber's birthday lunch, put on her new butterfly sundress. She brushed her hair and slipped into the new high-heeled sandals that she'd bought with Baby. She pulled on two orange-and-white bangle bracelets and stepped back to look at herself in the mirror.

She looked good. Not that anyone would notice. Not that she cared whether they did or not. She wasn't dressing to please people. People who liked flirting with everybody were not serious about anybody. She was wearing her sundress because it was Amber's birthday, and she wanted to do justice to the occasion. And that was all.

Hope almost rolled her eyes at herself as she grabbed the present she'd picked out for her niece and left the house. Who was she trying to kid? People who flirted with everybody might not be serious about her, but she was trying to impress them anyway. *More fool her.*

When she got to the casino restaurant, Weary was waiting at the entrance. His eyes widened when he saw her.

"You look mighty fine, Little Hope," he said. "As pretty as a picture. Like a canary set down in a field of mud hens."

"Thank you, Weary," she said. "I've been shopping."

"It paid off." Weary held out his arm to her. "Okay,

well, now that you're here, we can get this shindig off the ground."

"Am I late?" Hope took his arm. "I didn't mean to keep everybody waiting."

"Nah, you're not late, just the last to arrive. And with you lookin' so pretty, it was more than worth it. I just been standing here to keep out the undesirables," he said, ushering her into the closed restaurant.

"Has anybody tried to get past you?" Hope asked.

"Hell, yes. Somebody slipped me a Jackson to get a reservation for dinner tonight."

"Did you take it?"

"Sure, I took it," Weary said. "If people be so foolish as to think I'm the maître d', I'll take their money. Do I look like a maître d' to you?"

"Only if maître d's wear Hawaiian shirts and look like ex-professional linebackers."

"Exactly."

They went into the dim restaurant and crossed the dining room to a table in the back beautifully set for twelve. Tanner, who'd been uncorking a bottle of wine, turned and, when he saw Hope, his eyes widened just as Weary's had. He put the wine down and went to join them.

"You look fantastic," he said. "Like a—I don't know. Butterfly garden." He leaned forward and kissed her gently on the cheek.

Hope felt herself blush. *A butterfly kiss*, she thought.

"Weary, I'll take it from here," Tanner said. While Weary grinned in amusement, Tanner gently untucked Hope's hand from Weary's arm and tucked it into his own.

"There. That's better," he said.

Hope's pulse speeded up. She must be flushed, because she was way too warm.

Tanner leaned into her. "There's no name cards on the table," he said, his breath soft against her ear. "I already checked. So I can sit next to you."

"Maybe Amber has other ideas," Hope said. When she turned her head to speak, her cheek brushed his. Her heart fluttered and lurched inside her chest, like a moth bumping around a light bulb.

"She'll let me sit next to you," Tanner said, so softly it was almost a whisper. "She and I are buds."

"Hey, Hope, get over here," Marty called from where he stood at a sideboard. "You have to try these appetizers."

Hope jerked her head up. "Coming," she said.

"What does Marty think I can do to you in here?" Tanner asked, but he followed Hope as she joined the group getting drinks.

"Now everybody's here," Marty said, handing a glass of wine to Hope.

"Just like the old days," Pete Wyzniewski said.

"Bing-bing-bing!" Sharp Eddie said.

"Where does the time go?" Isaiah Rush asked. "Hope and Faith, all grown up. Now Amber, just starting out."

"It's great to see you all again," Weary said. "It's been too long."

"The unexpected pleasure of reanimating treasured acquaintances cannot be surpassed by any other companionable entertainments," Jim Thickpenny said.

"Hear, hear!" Tanner said.

Amber burst out of the kitchen, waving a wooden spoon, her white chef's hat askew, barely held in place by the pink bandana. She looked flushed.

"We're ready!" she announced, and then she saw her mother. "Mom! I'm having *so much* fun! Everybody sit down! Time to eat!"

And then she dashed back into the kitchen.

"Maybe the presentation could do with a little polish," Faith said, laughing as they sat down at the table.

"She's excited," Suzanne said.

Amber came back into the dining room, carefully carrying a big bowl. "We're having grilled sardines with potato salad and fancy cole slaw," she said, putting the bowl on the table. "And brownies!"

"My favorite!" Tanner said. He grinned at her, and Amber grinned back, giving him a thumbs up before she disappeared back into the kitchen.

Kenji and Amber brought out the rest of the food. The meal was simple, but all the dishes looked good. Hope realized how hungry she was. Tanner did indeed sit next to her, and as he handed her the warm plate of grilled sardines, she took three of the small fish, glistening on the platter and cooked to a dark golden color.

"They smell delicious!" she said to Amber.

"But no more delicious than you," Tanner whispered to Hope before he took the potato salad from Weary on his other side.

"Stop it," Hope said softly, even as she felt herself flush. She watched as Tanner helped himself to the potato salad. His hands were big, the knuckles stood out on his long fingers. His nails were clean but short. He'd worn a long-sleeved shirt, and he'd rolled up his cuffs, exposing ropey tendons and sinews in his tanned forearms.

Tanner glanced up and caught her looking. He grinned at her, mischief in his eyes.

"The potato salad looks good," she said, feeling trapped, feeling her cheeks turn even hotter. Now that she looked at it, the potato salad did look good. The potatoes were dotted with green specks—parsley, Hope thought—and lightly coated with something brown.

"You like potato salad?" Tanner asked softly. "I've been known to make excellent potato salad. Tender, moist, sweet. Just ask me. I can give you all the potato salad you could ever want."

He *so* wasn't talking about potato salad. Hope reached for her water. If only she could splash it against her face. Or dump it in his lap.

"In fact, I'd like to give you some potato salad right

now," Tanner said.

Hope choked on her water, and Tanner grinned, handing her his napkin. "Careful there," he said.

"*Tanner!*" she said, glaring at him. "Cut it out *right now!*"

Several heads turned their way.

Tanner dipped the serving spoon into the potato salad and piled some onto her plate. "Here, have some potato salad," he said, his eyes dancing. "It's delicious. Just try it. Take your time. Let it work its magic."

Hope yanked the bowl away from him, still glaring.

Tanner laughed.

Kenji clinked his spoon against his glass. "To the chef!" he said. "To Amber, on her birthday!"

Relieved, Hope picked up her glass with everyone else. "Happy birthday, Amber!" they all said.

Amber looked flustered. "Thank you!" she said. "Please eat!"

Marty and Eddie didn't need any urging. They dug into the sardines with gusto.

Hope saw that Amber was watching her expectantly, waiting for her verdict. The fish certainly *looked* wonderful. Hope picked up her fork and knife and carefully slit down the back of a sardine, laying open one side. Then she pulled out the bones in one easy tug. The flesh of the small fish was delicate and had a faintly smoky aroma. Hope cut a piece and took a bite. And then she felt her eyes open wider in surprise. The sardine was heaven on a fork. The little fish was so light and flavorful, the seasonings—what? Garlic? Salt? Something else she couldn't identify—just perfect. The skin had just a hint of a crunch.

"Amber," Hope said, putting down her fork. "The sardines are absolutely fantastic. The best I've ever eaten."

Amber beamed at her. "Do you really think so? We put a little coating on before grilling. Kenji says it's our secret."

"Sweetie, you did a wonderful job on everything," Faith said. "Hope, have you tried the potato salad? Unbelievably good."

Hope felt Tanner's leg nudge her thigh under the table. She felt color flood back to her face.

"That's just what I was telling her," Tanner said. "How good the potato salad is."

"Everything far supersedes expectations," Jim Thickpenny said, digging into the cole slaw. "I might say that the ingredients defy categorization. Can I ask what you've added to create this phantasmagoric experience?"

Amber, confused, looked at Kenji.

"What we put in it," he explained to her. "Miso," he said. "And other things."

"Amber, did you really make all this?" Hope asked, finally trying the potato salad. "Everything is *delicious*."

"Big, big, big!" Sharp Eddie said, his voice thick around a mouthful of potato salad.

"I did!" Amber was all smiles. "Kenji showed me stuff. And he did a *lot*. But I did a lot, too. Didn't I, Kenji?"

Kenji nodded. "Amber, I was thinking—" he said.

"Did I put too much cumin in the potato salad?" Amber asked, suddenly worried. "I wondered."

Kenji laughed and reached out, straightening her hat. "Listen to you. Too much cumin. You're funny. No, this potato salad is perfect."

"Absolutely," Isaiah Rush said. "Would you pass it again, please?"

Tanner leaned into Hope while he picked up the bowl of potato salad. "See?" he whispered. "Everybody likes the potato salad."

Hope kicked him under the table.

Tanner grinned and started the bowl of potato salad around the table for the third time.

"This is what I was thinking," Kenji said. "My publisher has been asking me when I'll turn in a proposal for my next cookbook, and so far I haven't had a good idea. But today it occurred to me that a kids' cookbook is a good idea. Simple recipes with a twist to get children interested in food. But I have a big problem." He turned to face Amber, looking somber.

Amber looked at Kenji, her small face worried. "What?"

"I need a kid for a co-author. If I could find one—someone with talent, who knows something about food already because her mom has an organic farm—who could help me write it, I'd be all set." He grinned at Amber. "If her mom said it was okay."

Amber's eyes got huge. "You mean *me? I* could help you write it?" When Kenji nodded, smiling, she turned to her mother. "Mom, could I? *Please?*"

Faith looked from Amber to Kenji, her forehead furrowed. "That's a huge honor, Amber, Kenji asking you to help, but I don't know. It's a big commitment. School's starting soon. You'll have homework."

"I can do it! I know I can! Please, Mom!"

Kenji turned to Faith. "Amber would be a perfect partner. She already has a lot of background from the farm. She's an adventurous eater. And she's got good instincts. She'd be cute on the cover. We could do the testing at your house, if that's easier."

"I could be on the *cover?*" And when Kenji nodded again, Amber turned pleading eyes to her mother. "Mom, did you hear that? I have *instincts.* I could be on the *cover.* With *Kenji. Please* say yes. Please, please, *please.*"

"It will be a lot of work, I won't mislead you about that," Kenji said. "But I think we'd have fun. And of course she'll get half the advance and royalties."

"I don't care about that," Amber said, and the others grinned. "*Please,* Mom."

"Well, okay, sweetie, if Kenji's sure," Faith said, "but it can't interfere with homework."

"It won't. I *promise.*" Amber threw her arms around Kenji, giving him a hug. Her smile was so bright and so wide, so rapturous with pleasure, Hope thought it would split her face.

Was I ever that happy about anything? Hope thought about it. Not in a long time, if ever. Not that she could remember.

"Here's to collaborations," Marty said and raised his glass.

Tanner leaned into Hope as she raised hers with the others.

"Collaborating on potato salad, that's the ticket," he said softly.

Hope rolled her eyes at him.

"To collaborations," she said firmly with the others, avoiding Tanner's eyes, and drank.

When the lunch was done and the table cleared, Amber opened her presents. Her first present was a set of knives from Kenji.

"They're too small for me," he said. "I hope they're not too heavy for you. If you use them, Amber, you have to be very careful. They're sharp."

"Oh, I will!" Amber said reverently, holding one of the knives. "I can't wait to try them! For the cookbook! Thank you."

Tanner gave her a hand-carved chess set. All the pieces were from Alice in Wonderland.

"It's fantastic," Amber breathed, stroking the White Rabbit.

"Do you play?" Tanner asked.

"No," Amber said. "Not yet. Will you teach me?"

"Sure," Tanner said. "Whenever you're ready."

The uncles had chipped in to give her a helicopter ride over Hoover Dam.

"Wow." Amber blinked at the uncles. "I've never been in a helicopter." Suddenly she turned shy. "Maybe you could come with me?"

"We would love to, Bright Amber," said Sharp Eddie, and all the uncles nodded. "If we can all fit," he added.

"If not, we'll play a quick round of seven-card stud 8 or better, high-low split to see who goes," Marty said.

"Okay," Amber said, looking confused. But when she opened Hope's gift, she became speculative.

"It looks like a food dish," she said. "And a collar. And leash. For a dog."

"Yes," Hope said.

"I guess it's time for you to get my present," said Faith. "But you have to come with me."

"Mom?" Amber asked with mounting excitement as she scrambled out of her chair to follow her mother. "Is it a dog? You got me a *dog?*"

Everyone stood up as Faith and Kenji led Amber out of the dining room, through the kitchen, and out the back door to the restaurant's loading dock. There, tied up in the shade of an overhang, lying on a thick mat with a bowl of water and another of kibble, sat a largish brown and white dog that wriggled and whined, almost dancing in eagerness and anxiety, as they came out the door.

Amber dropped to her knees on the hard concrete loading dock next to the mutt, and the dog flung itself into her arms, licking her face and almost knocking her over. She hugged the animal, laughing while it wriggled against her. Kenji leaned over, trying to get a grip on the squirming dog to put the new collar on it.

Amber looked up at her mother as everyone smiled. "What's her name?"

Faith reached down to scratch the dog's ears. "That's up to you."

The dog nuzzled Amber, licking her from her chin almost to her hairline, and then turned to Faith, who pushed it away, laughing.

Amber didn't hesitate. "Squeegee," she announced. "My dog's name is Squeegee! Because she licks everybody in sight. Thank you, Mom!"

Squeegee lunged at Amber again, trying to lick her face,

while Amber laughed and put her arms around her new pet.

Hope felt a heavy sadness steal over her. Tanner, who'd been watching her instead of Amber and the dog, noticed Hope's changed expression.

"What's wrong?" he asked.

Hope swallowed.

"The dog's probably a bad idea," she said softly, watching Faith and Amber play with Squeegee while Kenji tried to get the collar on her. "I don't even know if she'll get to keep it."

Tanner glanced at her. "Why wouldn't she be able to keep it?"

Hope shook her head. "Oh, you know. But Faith wanted to make a positive affirmation, and I decided I would try to live up to my name and be a little hopeful. Despite everything."

Tanner, looking puzzled and concerned, opened his mouth to say something. Hope took a deep breath.

"I have to go," she said, glancing at her watch. "Kenji, this was great. Thank you for everything."

"No problem," Kenji said, glancing up at her, still struggling with the collar.

"I'll go with you," Tanner said.

"You don't have to," Hope said.

"Yes, I do," Tanner said patiently. "We all do. We're helping you at the tables, remember?"

"Oh," Hope said. "Right."

The uncles nodded.

"Set a date for that helicopter ride, Amber," Marty said. "Let us know."

"The meal was delicious," Isaiah Rush said.

"Especially the potato salad," Tanner said.

"Bing, bing, bing!" Sharp Eddie said.

"Thank you for inviting us," Weary said.

"We had a great time," Pete Wysniewski said.

"Our best wishes for a felicitous day and many memorable and exuberant birthdays in your future," Jim

Thickpenny said.

"Happy birthday, Amber," Hope said, stooping to give her niece a hug.

"Thank you, Hope!" Amber said, beaming at her. "Thank you, everybody! This has been the best birthday *ever!*"

Seeing her niece's undiluted joy, Hope tried to put some energy into her smile, but she felt her sadness spread like thick, damp fog through her body. If she could just get away. Back to the tables. Anywhere.

She had to get out now. *Fast.*

Chapter 16

Hope walked down the hallway to the casino so quickly that Tanner had to make an effort to keep up.

"Hey, Hope, is everything all right?" he asked.

"Sure," she said. "I'm just ducking in here for a minute." She headed toward the women's restroom, pushed the door open, and disappeared. Tanner looked at the closed door.

The uncles ambled up.

"Where's Hope?" Sharp Eddie asked.

Tanner nodded toward the restroom. "Did she seem okay to you?" he asked. "I'm not sure she's okay."

"I'm not going in there again," Weary said. "I went in the last time. I don't exactly mind it, but I think it's somebody else's turn."

"We'll give her a minute," Marty decided.

"What?" Tanner asked. "What's going on here?"

Marty shrugged. Looked away. Looked at Tanner. Thought about it. "Hope ain't exactly on good terms with birthdays," he finally said.

"She did pretty good with this one," Pete Wysniewski said. "That I saw."

Marty nodded. "She thinks the world of that little girl," he said. "Plus, I think she likes having us here. In spite of everything."

"Until the end there," Weary said. "The dog."

Everybody nodded.

"Will somebody tell me what the hell is going on around here?" Tanner said, exasperated.

"Hope had her heart broke on her birthday," Marty said. "A long time ago, when she was a kid. She took it real hard. And birthdays been pretty sensitive ever since."

Hope had looked very sad at the end.

"What happened?"

Marty shook his head. "If she ain't told you, I'm not sure she wants you to know," he said. "And I'm not sure you gotta know it for this gig."

"If she can't snap out of it, she could mess up her card playing," Tanner argued. "At least for today."

"Then we'll deal with it," Marty said.

Hope dried her eyes in the restroom and checked her mascara. Seventeen years later, and she could still bawl at a family birthday party. What a joke.

She'd gotten out just in time—before she embarrassed herself and ruined Amber's birthday. If she'd done that, she never would have forgiven herself.

She peered in the mirror. Her eyes were a little red, but there was nothing she could do about that. At least the tear stains were gone from her face. She was about as ready as she'd ever get.

Someone knocked on the door. Hope smiled, still feeling a little shaky. One of the uncles. They were worried about her. Well, they knew the story.

Tanner stuck his head in the door. "Everything okay in here, Hope?"

She blinked, a little surprised to see Tanner. "Just coming," she said. She stroked on a bit of lipstick, glanced at herself again in the mirror, and headed for the door.

Time to suck it up.

"Tell me something upbeat and cheerful," Hope said to

Tanner as they headed toward the casino. "Something that will make me feel strong and confident and help me win." Marty had split off, saying he had to do some "research," leaving Tanner to coordinate the poker phone bank, and the other uncles had ranged ahead and were even now leaving the Desert Dunes for other nearby casinos. Tanner would stake out the Dunes card room.

"You look fantastic," Tanner began.

No compliments. Not from Tanner. No good can come from this.

"You already said that," Hope said, realizing almost to her chagrin that she did feel more upbeat and cheerful when Tanner complimented her. "I want a confidence boost to be based on something real."

"How fantastic you look *is* real," Tanner said. "But if you don't want to hear that, then play to win. Then you *will* win. And that should give you all the confidence you could want."

He was right. She just needed to go out there and play to win.

"Which table?" she asked.

Tanner glanced around. "That one," he said, indicating with a nod.

"Why that one?"

"The guy on the end is looking at his cards too long. It means he's got a weak hand, and he doesn't know how to play it."

"I'm on it," Hope said, and went to get a seat at the table.

Tanner went back to the bar and ordered a cup of coffee from Skip.

"Watch out! We're in a danger zone here," Skip said as he brought over the pot. "Everybody stay low."

"What on earth are you talking about?" Tanner asked, looking around for Frelly. Had Skip seen the FBI agent in the house? That was all he needed.

"You're still with that blonde," Skip said, pouring the coffee. "That's gotta be uncharted territory for you. Two days running and you haven't hit any landmines yet."

Tanner rolled his eyes. "Cut me some slack here," he said. "We're not dating."

"That explains it, then," Skip said, moving off. "Still plenty of time for crashing and burning."

Tanner shook his head. When had he ever crashed and burned with a woman? Every dating relationship he'd ever had—and okay, there'd been a few, but they'd all been brief—short excursions that had ended smoothly, coasting quietly to a stop.

But Skip was right about one thing. This—whatever it was he felt for Hope. This intense awareness. Yearning. Desire. Madness, even. This *feeling*—he could see himself crashing and burning over it. That aching sadness in her eyes. He'd never seen that look in a nice woman's eyes at a kid's birthday party. He'd give a lot to know what caused it, and to make sure she never felt it again. And to punch out the lights of whoever had put it there.

He frowned, watching Hope play cards. What was she doing? She'd pursed her lips and folded, after she'd bet the first two rounds.

He watched as the guy two seats over glanced at her. So now that bozo had her figured out, did he?

Maybe it was a ploy. Maybe she'd done that to throw off the other players.

Tanner watched as Hope went down another hand. And then another. And then another.

No reason to panic. She wasn't in deep. But she wasn't playing with any spark, either. She was showing tells all over the board.

Tanner dug out his phone and called her.

"Hope, get out of the game and come over here. We have to talk."

"I'm fine," she said. "Really."

"Really, you're not. Get out now. You're wasting your time and your money. I'm telling you."

He watched as she banged the phone shut, but a second later she cashed out of the game and joined him at the bar.

"What?" she said, frowning. She sounded irritated. In that white dress sprinkled with orange butterflies she looked like a flower garden filled with crabgrass—really crabby crabgrass.

"Your heart's not in it," he said. "Time to take a break."

"I can't take a break! I need to play."

"You need to *win*. Playing like you're playing now won't get you where you need to go."

"What's wrong with my game?"

"Are you kidding? You weren't focused. Your play was sloppy. You have to be better than that at the thirty dollar tables. Those players are too good for easy mistakes."

"You call yelling at me *helping?*"

He sighed.

Hope deflated. "You're right," she said. "I was playing badly. I didn't mean to snap your head off. I'm just upset. But I can't stop now."

"There's a time to play, and there's a time to sit back and count your winnings. Take the afternoon off. You'll be better for it."

"How badly was I playing?"

He shrugged. "You've played a lot better. It's okay. We'll do something else to change the pace. Something fun."

"You want to stop coaching me so we can have fun?" Hope asked. "I'm completely anxious now. How are we supposed to have fun?"

He grinned at her as he took out his phone. "Loaded question," he said. "I'm not answering it." He called Weary to tell him that they were taking the afternoon off. When he'd finished, he looked at Hope.

"So, what should we do?"

"I don't know," Hope said. "I don't have any ideas."

"In that case, we'll go bowling," Tanner said. "I have to go home first and get my shoes."

"*Bowling?*" Hope said. "You have *shoes?*"

Tanner pulled his pickup into his driveway and parked. The house was an older, ranch-style place, nothing special, in a nothing-special, middle-class neighborhood. The only thing that set it apart was its landscaping: desert plants in graceful arrangements replaced grass, and a gently curved path of crushed stone and wood chips meandered up to the front door. The yard was pretty.

"You live *here?*"

"You don't like it?"

"I do. I just thought a professional poker player would have something...flashier. The landscaping's great."

"Thanks. I bought this house a long time ago when I could afford it, and then my dad and I fixed it up over the years. Now it suits us. You want to come in?"

Tanner had turned off the truck's engine two minutes ago and already it was sweltering inside. Hope's back and arms felt gritty with sweat, and her dress was sticking to her thighs. "Sure," Hope said, as she hopped out. As she walked down the path, she admired the cacti and other succulents. Everything was thriving.

"Does your dad live with you, then?"

"When he and my mom retired, they moved to a place about a mile from here. It's just my daughter and me in the house. She's off to college next week. UCLA. Swimming scholarship."

He walked up the path and checked the mailbox before unlocking the front door.

"Won't your daughter be upset that I'm here?"

Tanner turned in the doorway and grinned at her.

"She wants me to date," he said. "She's afraid I'll grow old alone."

Hope felt herself blush. It was irrational. She wanted no

part of Tanner, and yet, *here she was, anyway*. And here he was, talking about dating. What was she doing, going to Tanner's house and maybe meeting his daughter? Was it too late to run?

Tanner laughed as if he could read her mind and stepped inside.

"Come on in," he said. "I'll just be a minute. Take a look around."

As soon as he stepped away from the doorway, Hope gasped. Tanner hadn't just fixed up the house—he'd transformed it.

The whole back of the ranch-style house was a wall of glass. And outside, most of the back yard was a pool.

And what a pool. Long and narrow, with a ladder mounted at one end and stairs at the other, clearly it was used for lap swimming. But Hope could see a water garden at the far end. Lilies and lotus flowers floated on the surface, and behind them, water flowed straight down over a copper screen in a gentle waterfall. A vaguely Japanese-looking trellis in dark wood arched over most of the pool and part of the yard, providing dappled shade for swimmers and the plants that were grouped in earth-toned jars and bowls around the patio.

"Oh wow," Hope said, moving toward the glass.

"You like it?" Tanner said, watching her reaction.

"It's *fantastic*. You and your dad built this?"

"Yeah. Go on out and look around if you want."

Hope unlatched the patio doors and slid them open, feeling a rush of warm air. The potted grasses waved gracefully in the breeze, and some of the shaded plants had rich blooms, which cast off a heady fragrance. Sections of tiled patio were interspersed with wood chip walkways, softening the surfaces. Streets sounds were muted by the gentle trickle of the waterfall. Comfortable-looking chairs were grouped around a table. It looked like a spa. Like a resort. It was the most beautiful, relaxing backyard Hope had ever seen. She wondered how Tanner could ever tear himself away to play cards in those noisy, crowded, smoky casino card rooms.

"This is so beautiful," she said. "Did you study architecture?"

Tanner smiled, still watching her face. "I wanted a nice pool. That's how it started. I did some research. My dad helped me build it. We needed a pool company to dig the hole and line it, of course."

"Of course." Hope turned and smiled at him. "We have a hot springs above our ranch. It's nice, but it's not developed at all. It's just how the water gets trapped in the rocks. It's nothing like this. This is *incredible.*"

Tanner tilted his head toward the water. "Would you like to go for a swim?"

Hope's eyes widened before she shook her head. "Oh, no thanks. I don't have a suit."

"Well, technically you don't need a suit to swim. You just really need the suit for modesty. So if you want to swim, we could figure something out. I could find some old clothes you could wear. Or I could promise not to look."

He looked so hopeful that she had to laugh. "Get your bowling stuff together," she said. "I'll just wait here."

"Okay. Let me know if you change your mind." He turned and went back into the house. Hope walked to the edge of the pool and flipped off her sandal. She swished the water with her foot, feeling it splash up the calf of her leg. The water was cool and refreshing.

Hope rubbed her arm. Her skin felt sticky and grainy, her pretty dress was wilted and clingy. She wished she'd brought her bathing suit, or at least a change of clothes. But the water splashing against her feet and legs felt great. She closed her eyes as she stirred the water with her foot, feeling it cascade down her bare legs. *Bliss.*

Chapter 17

Tanner slid open the door that connected his room to the patio. He held a couple of towels and some folded clothing.

"Hey, Hope, I found—" he started, and then he stopped and stared.

Hope stood on the top step of the pool. She was swirling the water with her feet. Her eyes were closed. Her shoulders were relaxed. Her face—she looked so, so—happy. So *not* like earlier, at the birthday party.

"Hmmm?" she answered dreamily, not opening her eyes.

He dropped the towels and old clothes he'd found on a chair and kicked off his shoes. Then he joined her at the edge of the pool.

"You want to go in?" he asked. "I found—"

"Oh, I couldn't. Really," she said, opening her eyes.

Why couldn't she? She just wanted to get one toe wet and not get the full experience? She knew what she was missing, but she was willing to miss it anyway? He'd had enough of that.

"Try it," he said, smiling at her, putting his hand on her back. "You might like it." And with that, he pushed her gently into the water. Caught off balance, she went in with a big splash, not at all gracefully. And when she came up, outraged and sputtering, he laughed and went into the water after her.

She splashed and coughed a bit regaining her feet,

pushing her wet hair away from her face. "What did you do *that* for?" she said, outraged. "I'm *soaked.*"

"You looked like you needed to cool off and float around a little, and I wanted to help you," he said, tossing his head to get the water out of his eyes.

"I have nothing else to wear. What am I supposed to do about my clothes?"

He glanced at her dress. Now that she was standing, it floated up around her waist, making her look like a blonde lotus flower. He could see her legs. All of her long legs, which was very nice. And the wet fabric hugging her breasts was very nice, too.

"I've got a clothes dryer. And an iron. You'll be fine. How're you doing over there? Feeling cooler?"

She lowered herself in the water until it came up to her neck, gently moving her arms back and forth, letting it splash gently against her skin. She still looked disgruntled.

"I can't believe you did that," she said. "Just shoved me in." She dropped her head back, letting the water flow over her face, and then stood up to let her hair stream back over her shoulders.

Then she looked at him again. "And I don't know if this dress will ever be the same. Even on sale at the outlet mall, it cost the earth." She grinned suddenly. "It was the *premium* outlet mall."

Tanner grinned back, swimming towards her slowly. He saw her eyes darken even as she started to stroke back, away from him.

Excellent.

"If it's ruined, I could replace it for you," he said. "If you want to take it off, I could check the size."

Hope laughed as she backed away from him. "I know that offer springs only from selfless generosity, but I don't need you to check the size, thank you."

"I just want to do the right thing," Tanner said, advancing slowly through the water. "Since I got you wet."

"Well, now that I'm in here, and the dress is ruined anyway, the water does feel good. I *love* this pool."

"There's nothing better than a swim on a hot day. Nothing makes you feel more refreshed. It would be even more refreshing if we weren't dressed for a polar expedition."

"Speak for yourself. I'm dressed just fine for a nice dip in the pool."

Tanner, hampered only slightly by his jeans and shirt, now heavy with water, kept moving towards her. Hope kept backing up. The pool was long, so she had some room to maneuver. That was fine by him.

She could run, but she couldn't hide. She liked being in the pool, and she liked his being in the water with her. He'd seen her eyes darken. The eyes never lied.

"I'm not sure there's room for two fully dressed card sharks in this pool." She smiled, looking like a very naughty Venus, still facing him, still swimming backwards, a little faster.

"That's your first mistake. The only shark in this pool is the one that's out to get you," he said, and then she squeaked as he dove.

Hope heard herself shriek louder than a pre-teen girl at a boy-band concert when Tanner grabbed her ankles. *What was he doing?* And then she found out when he stood up and upended her in the pool, dumping her ignominiously back into the water.

She felt her skirt swirl around her waist, probably giving him a pretty good view of her underwear. *The rat.* Although it was white cotton today, all about coverage and nothing to get too excited about.

She dove away, skidding her palm across the top of the water as he jumped after her, but the wave she created caught him full in the face while he laughed, making him swallow a lot more water than he'd planned to. She laughed then, too, as he staggered, and she took advantage of his momentary weakness to grab his shoulders and push him down, dunking him. *Good move.*

As he went under, he grabbed her around the waist and pulled her down with him. *Not such a good move.* Because when they simultaneously came up for air, he was still holding her around the waist. He'd pulled her tight against his body, and even with the cool water streaming down their skin and off their clothes, Tanner's body was warm as he looked down at her, his smile lazy but his eyes alive with heat, his lashes beaded with droplets. Her heart hammered in her chest, and Hope felt winded, but not from exercise. Her insides were hot and liquid, melting her from her ears to her toes, and her legs weren't holding her up. Her skin tingled with his closeness.

"See?" Tanner said softly. "Isn't a swim nice?" And then he pulled her closer and leaned down to kiss her.

Her voice of caution, the one that was trying to yell *No card players! No heartbreak!* seemed to have lost its usual volume. Hope knew it was in there somewhere, trying to be heard. But it was so faint, she could easily ignore it. And so, feeling free and happy and safe, with Tanner's hands and breath and lips and tongue on her, turning the pool into a steam bath and herself as light and hot as vapor, she thought, *Yes! More!* And then she reached up to put her arms around his shoulders and kiss him back.

A half-hour later, after a very stimulating water fight, they sat across from each other at the patio table, colorful juice drinks in tall glasses before them. Hope was wearing a pair of Tanner's old shorts and a baggy tee-shirt with the arms cut out while her dress spun around in the dryer, but she'd braided and pinned back her hair. Now she sipped her drink, feeling tingly and refreshed—excited but alarmed, too. What was she thinking, kissing Tanner in the pool? But she was having a *great* time.

Tanner moved his glass around the moisture ring on the

table and then looked at her, his face gentle.

"So what's with you and birthdays, anyway?" he asked.

Cold shock rippled through her. *He sure knew how to throw all his cards right on the table.*

"What do you mean?" she asked, stalling for time.

"I mean, why did you cry in the bathroom at Amber's party? Marty said you didn't like birthdays much."

"Marty told you what happened?"

"No. He said you'd tell me if you wanted me to know. So I'm asking."

Hope swallowed, feeling the familiar pain slice through her belly, her special family birthday pain.

Tanner reached out and took her hand.

"You can tell me, Hope. Your secret's safe with me."

"It's not a secret. It's just—bad family stuff."

She hated talking about this. Her past with her father made her look like a chump and a fool—and it usually made her cry, too. No matter how old she got, the pain of her father's abandonment never went away.

But Tanner was helping her with her poker game. He wanted to know, and the uncles seemed to like him. Those were two reasons to tell him. No reason, really, *not* to tell him.

And there was that water fight in the pool. The thought of it—of Tanner's hands and shoulders and lips and tongue— made her flush. Even now he sat there so quietly, while he gently stroked his thumbs over the back of her hand.

She sighed, feeling her chest compress. She swallowed.

"My father is Derek McNaughton," she began. "You probably figured that out by now, even though I lied when you asked me."

Tanner nodded, still holding her hand.

"When I was a kid, maybe starting when I was five, he took me around to the card rooms he played in and showed me off."

"When you were *five?* How did he do that? You can't

take kids into the casino card rooms," Tanner said.

Hope nodded. "They were private games. Games where he could also cheat if he wasn't winning legitimately. At first I think I was sort of a novelty for him, but then he taught me poker and I caught on really fast. He put me in a game when I was six or seven, if you can believe that, and I won. After that, he put me in games all the time. He turned me into a—commodity, I guess."

She took a sip of her drink, wishing the cramp in her stomach would go away, knowing that it wouldn't.

"I had the best time," she said, shaking her head. "Me and my dad. Playing poker with him in those rooms seemed like such a huge adventure. I felt so special. Everybody thought I was cute. My dad bragged about me. I was on cloud nine all the time. I lived to go to the poker rooms."

"Sounds like you had fun," Tanner said. "So what happened?"

"As I got older, I won more. Derek won less. By the time I was twelve or thirteen I was winning more than he was and—"

"Did he keep your winnings?" Tanner interrupted. His voice had taken on a steely edge.

"Yes, but that wasn't it. He was welcome to the money. It was—" Hope stopped, hearing with shame the quaver in her voice. She took a deep breath, then another, getting a grip, and went on.

"After I started to win some serious money, he started to not come home sometimes," she said. "The first time he was gone for about a week, and we were all frantic. Mom was sick with worry. She called all the hospitals, the cops. And then he just turned up. Everything was fine. What were we so upset about, that's what he asked. And over the next couple of years, he'd stay away longer and longer. Months at a time. We never knew where he went."

"Couldn't Marty have helped you?"

"I think Marty did try to get Derek to come home. But—

Derek stayed away longer and longer. The more and better I played, the longer he stayed away."

"Hope, don't—" Tanner said, knowing what was coming, and not wanting her to have to say it.

"And I thought I'd done something to make him mad. Maybe I didn't win enough. Or I wasn't cute enough anymore. He didn't love me anymore. I didn't know why he stayed away, I just knew it was because of something I'd done." Hope felt her stomach contract so sharply, it was like a knife to her abdomen. She squeezed her eyes shut and pressed her lips together as she felt tears pool in her eyes, her throat thicken.

Would she never get over this? Everything had happened *seventeen years* ago. She was an adult now. She should be in better control. She took a deep, careful breath, the pain making her hiccup. She was holding Tanner's hand now, gripping so hard her fingers ached.

"I thought that if I showed him how smart I was, if I just *tried harder*, he'd love me like he used to, back when it was fun, and he'd come home and he'd love me."

She felt her face crumple at the memory. Tears streaked down her cheeks, and she brushed them away.

"I know it's stupid," she said, her voice quavering.

"It's not stupid," Tanner said, his voice tight.

"So for my fifteenth birthday—he'd been gone maybe six or seven months at that point. But he'd never missed my birthday. Ever. Mom baked a big cake and fired up the barbecue and had balloons and decorations, and I waited out at the front gate until it was dark, but he never came. And I never saw him again."

Tanner laced her fingers in his.

"Hope, he's a worthless, selfish—" he began.

"I know," Hope said, sniffing. "I've told myself that, I *know* it's true, but inside I just feel that our family fell apart because of me. That if I'd done something differently, been a better card player, or maybe just a better person, more lovable somehow—that he would have loved me more and stayed with us. I still get sick to my stomach about it."

"No kid should think they have to earn their parent's love," Tanner said, his voice harsh. "You must *know* it wasn't your fault."

"In my head, I know that, but not in my gut," she said. "In my head, I know he would have gone anyway. Maybe sooner, if I hadn't played cards and made him look good and won him some money. But I'm still a basket case about it. And then he never came back, so without the winnings he and I had brought in, we got poor, so that was my fault, too. I got a job after school to help out, and we're doing a lot better now."

"You didn't *wreck* your family at fifteen," Tanner said gently. "You've been trying to *save* your family since then."

"Well, Mom held us together, and I did what I could," Hope said. "But that's why birthdays are hard. And the *really* bad part is, there are so many of them."

She smiled, a little wanly, feeling exhausted. She slumped back in the chair and closed her eyes as tears of hurt and anger and loss trickled down her face.

Now he knew.

She heard Tanner get out of his chair. She opened her eyes as he kneeled before her. His face was just inches from hers. He cradled her head in both his hands, his eyes tender, his thumbs gently wiping the tears from her cheeks. But his voice was harsh, tight with control, when he spoke.

"I've played cards with your father a couple of times, and I've always known he's not much of a poker player," he said. And now I know he's a crappy human being, too. It's cruel and cowardly to desert a family like that."

"I know," Hope said without much energy.

"The first thing we have to do is work on that birthday problem of yours. Starting today, we're going to have lots of unbirthday parties with lots of presents. Positive reinforcement, that's the ticket."

Hope smiled, more strongly this time. "That's a nice idea, but—"

"We had a nice party atmosphere in the pool, for example," Tanner said, his eyes suddenly wicked.

Hope felt herself flush under his hands. She tried to pull back, but he didn't let her go.

"That's different," she said. "We can't—"

"I'm pretty sure we can have a party atmosphere anywhere we want," Tanner said, grinning at her. "The patio, for example." And leaning into her, he kissed her, calling her bluff.

"See?" he said, when they came up for air.

Hope smiled, feeling a lot better. "You're right," she said. "It's party time."

"My dress shrank in the dryer," Hope said, coming into the living room and tugging down on the bodice.

Tanner looked up from putting on his sandals and smiled at her, that devastating smile that made her want to kiss him in the pool or on dry land—anywhere, in fact.

"It fits perfectly," he said. "Stop pulling on it. That dress looked fantastic on you before, but it was a little big. Now it looks the way it should."

She rolled her eyes. "You're impossible," she said, but she smiled.

Tanner stood up, checking his pockets for his keys as he moved toward the door. "We should go," he said.

"I'll be late," she agreed, picking up her purse.

He stopped, his hand on the doorknob. "That's not quite what I meant," he said. "You have plans for the afternoon, and you really should play tonight. So for today, time is not on our side."

He put his hand on her hip and leaned down to kiss her on the neck, a soft kiss that sent a shiver down her spine. Then he put his lips against her ear, his voice so soft, it was a whisper against her skin.

"Just so you know, pumpkin. I'm willing to wait until we have all the time we could want. Because when we go on our first picnic, we won't want to rush it. There will be lots of things we'll want to try, and plenty of tastes we'll want to sample."

Hope leaned into him, feeling dizzy and breathless.

"Can't be rushed," she said.

"Definitely not," Tanner said softly, kissing her again, gently nipping her ear. "When we go on our first picnic, we'll need plenty of time to savor the potato salad."

Chapter 18

The next morning when Hope shuffled yawning into the kitchen, wearing her thin summer shortie pajamas and a ratty robe, she saw Amber standing on a step stool by the counter and two men in dusty overalls drinking coffee at the table. She stopped abruptly.

"Aunt Hope, can I ask you something?" Amber asked.

"Sure, honey, what is it? And who are your friends here?"

"Scuse us, ma'am," the older one said, putting down his cup. "Your sister gave us a cup of coffee. We're surveyors."

"*Surveyors?* You're surveying this property? For Big Julie Saladino?"

"That's right," the younger man said, eyeing Hope's scanty attire. "He sold it to some big developer, is what we been told."

"Not yet, he hasn't," Hope said, her voice tight. "Get out of here right now. Get out and don't come back."

The older man stood up.

"We gotta finish—"

"No, you don't," Hope said, stomping over to the back door and flinging it open. "The place isn't sold yet, and I don't want to see you around here again until it is."

"Well, excu-u-u-se me," the younger one drawled.

"We're sorry if we stepped in it," the older one said. "Your sister—"

"My sister isn't here now. I'm here. And I'm telling you

to go."

"We're going," the younger one said. "But we'll be back."

"Over my dead body!" Hope called after them as they sauntered away.

"Hell of a body," the younger one said, winking at her.

Hope flushed and slammed the screen door behind them, but it didn't catch, bouncing back open again, and Squeegee dashed into the kitchen when she saw the opportunity.

Hope sighed in exasperation.

"Some watch dog you are," she said, bending down to scratch the dog's ears. Squeegee wriggled in ecstasy and leaped up, bashing Hope's nose.

"She'd be an *excellent* watch dog if she knew she was *supposed* to watch something," Amber said defensively.

"It's okay, Sweetie," Hope said, rubbing her bruised nose. She went to pour a cup of coffee, but the pot was empty, drained by the surveyors. *Honestly!* She shook her head and refilled the pot with water, added some fresh coffee to the basket and started it again. "Next time we'll tell Squeegee to take a big bite out of their behinds."

Amber giggled.

"Not *my* behind, I trust," Kenji said, coming in from the pantry. "Hi, Hope. Amber, is okra too far out?"

Hope had jumped at the sound of Kenji's voice. "Kenji! You startled me."

"Oh, sorry." He grinned at her and then glanced down at the list in his hand. "Amber and I are working on the cookbook. Amber—what about okra?"

I'm wearing my shortie pajamas and I don't rate more attention than the okra, Hope thought, but she smiled as Amber giggled again. "No," she said firmly. "Okra is *way* too complicated. All that goopy stuff!"

Hope grinned. "Kenji, want some coffee?"

"No thanks, Hope. Amber says no okra. I have to see what else we have." He headed back into the pantry.

Hope filled her coffee cup and sat down at the table the surveyors had just vacated. "Amber, what did you want to ask me?"

Amber brightened. "I almost forgot!" she said. "I wondered—I don't really understand about the uncles. Marty and everybody? Are they related to me, too?"

Squeegee got tired of waiting for Hope to scratch her ears again, and she jumped up, bumping her arm and making her spill some coffee.

"Squeegee, *stop it*. Lie down. The uncles. You know we're not biologically related to them, right, Amber? Your mom and I call them the uncles because we've known them for a long time."

"I've known *lots* of people for a long time—like my teachers—and they're not my uncles. What makes somebody an uncle?"

Hope frowned. "I'm not sure. When I was about your age, they took care of me sometimes. They were special. They loved me. I loved them. So they became our honorary uncles. Like family we chose."

"Are your uncles my uncles, too?"

"They could be, I guess. But if you wanted an honorary uncle, you could ask someone *you* like."

Amber nodded. "That way there will be more uncles to go around. Like at my birthday parties. Your uncles *and* my uncles."

Hope grinned. "That's right. But you have to pick special people, Amber. People you would do something special for."

Kenji came back into the kitchen holding a stout fennel bulb.

"Amber, what do you think about fennel?" he said.

She nodded. "Mom makes a fennel salad I like," she said.

"Okay. We'll put fennel on the maybe list." He disappeared back into the pantry.

"People you'd do something special for," Amber said, looking thoughtful. "Like Kenji."

Hope laughed. *Kenji wouldn't know what hit him.*

"You'll have to ask him, Sweetie," she said. "And don't be too disappointed if he says no. You might want to wait a little while, until you know each other better. I mean, what if he likes snails?"

Amber shuddered. "*Gross.*"

Hope grinned. "I know. Your honorary uncles don't have to be perfect, but they do have to be special. You just want to think about it."

"Okay." Amber picked up the knife, turned back to the counter and leaned into the carrot she was trimming. "Kenji *is* special, though. I'm going to ask him."

Hope stood up to get a bowl of cereal, and Squeegee, released from her massaging fingers, bounded over to where Amber stood on the step stool and barked for a treat.

"Not now, Squeegee," Amber said. "No begging."

The dog sat, her tongue lolling, grinning at her. Then Amber moved to slice the carrot and Squeegee jumped up against her, smacking the arm that held the knife. The knife slashed across the girl's other hand, and Amber staggered, cried out, pitched off the stool, and crumpled to the floor.

Hope dropped her cereal and rushed over to her niece, pushing the eager dog out of the way. She knelt down. "Amber! Let me see."

Amber's eyes were open but she looked scared.

Blood gushed from a deep gash across the palm of her hand and across the joint of her thumb. Even without getting closer, Hope could see something white inside— tendons? Nerves? Bone? She wasn't sure. But Amber needed medical help right away.

"We'll have to go and get that stitched up," she said, trying to smile and sound reassuring as she stood. "It's pretty deep. Just lie still. Can you hold your hand up? That's the girl. Kenji!" She opened the kitchen cupboard where they kept the first aid kit and pulled out some gauze pads and bandages.

"What happened?" Kenji said, already in the kitchen.

"Amber cut herself. I think she needs stitches."

"It hurts." Amber's voice trembled.

Hope knelt beside the child. "I know, Sweetie. I'm sorry. When we get to the clinic the doctor will give you something." She pressed the pads against the cut and wrapped the bandages tightly around them, hoping to stem the flow of blood. She turned to Kenji.

"Call Faith, will you? Her number's on the pad by the fridge. Amber, I'm going to raise your hand over your head and prop it up a little bit with this towel. That will slow the bleeding. Just lie still for a minute while I get dressed." Hope tore back into her bedroom, flinging off her pajamas while she ran, as Kenji grabbed the phone and dialed Faith.

Seconds later Hope was back, stuffing her wallet into her purse. Kenji was talking into the phone.

"Faith, it's Kenji. Amber's had an accident, she cut her hand." He turned to Hope. "Does she need a hospital?"

Hope nodded. "I think so."

He turned back to the phone. "We're taking her to Las Vegas General. Meet us there when you can." He hung up.

"It's the closest, and they have a good trauma team," he explained to Hope. "I've been treated there myself. You know how to get there?"

Hope nodded. "She didn't pick up?" she asked, knowing she hadn't.

Kenji shook his head. "Let's get going. We can call again from the road."

"Is Mom going to be at the hospital?" Amber's voice wavered.

Hope dropped to her knees by the girl. "Kenji left a message for her, Sweetie, but she's already in Vegas, so she'll be able to get there fast. We have to go now. Can you walk if I help you?"

"I think so." Amber started to sit up, but Kenji went over.

"I'll carry you, Amber. Don't move one bit." And with amazing grace for a man of his size, Kenji picked up the girl and carried her out the kitchen door. Hope followed him out.

"Everything will be all right," he told Amber as Hope opened the back door of the car for him. He lifted in the child and helped her lie down on the back seat while Hope opened the trunk and pulled out her emergency blanket. She handed it to Kenji, who covered Amber with it.

"Okay," Kenji said as he carefully closed the door. "I'll put the dog in the barn and follow you in my car. You get started. I'll meet you at the hospital in a few."

Hope nodded and put the car in gear, driving carefully out of the yard, turning left onto the highway, and picking up speed as she headed toward Las Vegas.

Two hours later, Hope stood in the family room outside the surgical unit, waiting for news about Amber. She'd been pacing most of the time, but now she just stood at the window and stared unseeing at the landscape. The ER doctors had decided that Amber needed a neurosurgeon to fix her hand. The cut was deep, and the nerves and tendons needed delicate, specialized repair. In addition, Amber had lost a lot of blood and was in shock. But she was young and healthy. They were optimistic she'd make a full recovery.

Faith still hadn't arrived at the hospital, and she hadn't answered any of the calls Hope had made to her cell, either. Hope wondered where her sister could be and why she wasn't picking up. Faith would never let her daughter down. Probably her cell had lost its charge, like Hope's often did.

Hope had called Tanner to cancel their casino appointment. They'd been scheduled to start play with the uncles at eleven o'clock that morning, as always, but that game was off until Faith arrived at the hospital. Suzanne would come in the late afternoon after her shift at the diner. So until Faith came, Hope would stay with Amber. When Amber came out of surgery and woke up, at least she wouldn't be alone.

Hope suddenly became aware of a tantalizing aroma of onions, hot grease, and cooked meat. She realized that she hadn't eaten her breakfast cereal and it was way past time for lunch. Her stomach growled. She turned around to see Tanner walk into the waiting room holding a bag from a fast-food restaurant.

"How's Amber?" he asked. He put the bag on the low table by the window and then wrapped his arms around her, holding her close. He felt strong and warm and powerful, and for a moment—two moments—she relaxed against him, feeling intense relief.

"I don't know yet," she said, breathing him in.

He kissed her hair. "How are *you?*"

Scared. Lonely. Upset. Better now that you're here. Hope wanted to hand him all her problems. Right now they just seemed overwhelming.

But she couldn't. Why should Tanner help her? He barely knew her. And she couldn't afford men who lived for risk. Having Amber in the hospital reminded her that she wanted no risk at all. She took a deep breath and stepped back.

"I'm okay," she said, trying to recover her equilibrium. "Amber's in surgery. It was a little complicated. I don't know where Faith is. She's not picking up."

Tanner let her go. "Amber's young. That's in her favor. Faith's phone probably isn't charged and she hasn't noticed. She'll call you eventually, right?"

Hope nodded, eyeing the paper sack.

Tanner sat down on the couch. "I brought some food," he said, opening the bag. "I thought you might be hungry. A couple of burgers and some of those egg sandwich deals.

You want something?"

Hope sat down next to him. "It's weird to be thinking about food, but I could really use an egg sandwich," she said, digging into the bag. "Do you want one? Or do you have to go?" She unwrapped a sandwich and took out a paper cup of coffee, prying off the plastic lid to take a long swallow of the rapidly cooling drink before she tackled the food.

"Mmm, this is delicious," she said around the egg. "Thank you for bringing it. I was starving. Here, help yourself." She pushed the bag closer to him.

Tanner grinned briefly. "Don't tell Kenji. He'll lose all respect for your eating habits."

Hope swallowed some of her egg sandwich, smiling back. "He'll never know," she said conspiratorially. "He went out to make a call, and I'll be finished long before he gets back."

Tanner took the bag from her and helped himself to a burger. "Anyway, I don't have to leave. I was going to play cards with you, remember? So I don't have other plans. I'll wait with you. I like Amber. She made brownies for me."

Hope looked at him. His eyes were dark and serious. Now that he was here, she realized she felt frightened for Amber. What if her niece lost some use of her hand? Hope would never forgive herself. Tears sprang to her eyes.

"I should have realized that Squeegee was too boisterous," she said, putting her sandwich down, her voice suddenly a little shaky. "I should have shut her outside."

Tanner chewed and swallowed a mouthful of burger before replying. "You can't plan for everything," he said, his voice prosaic. "Kenji probably feels just as guilty because he gave her the knives." He handed her a napkin. "Here. Blow."

His calmness was a reality check. Her smile wavered a little, but she took the paper napkin and wiped her eyes and blew her nose. "Better," she said. "Sorry."

He shrugged. "You're upset. You'll feel better if you finish your sandwich and drink your coffee."

Hope nodded and took another bite. "It's just that—" she started, her voice muffled around the egg.

"No," Tanner said, shaking his head. "Really." He took another bit of burger. "Trust me. Eat up. You have a long day ahead of you."

Hope nodded and took another bite of her sandwich.

Just then a doctor, wearing surgical scrubs and a mask, came through the swinging double doors. Hope gulped when she saw him glance around the waiting room, looking for someone.

"Ms. McNaughton?" he asked, walking over to them. "Are you Amber's family?"

Hope stood to meet the doctor and get the news. Tanner stood, too. He was all wrong for her. But he was worried about Amber, and he'd brought her an egg sandwich. That counted for something.

"Yes," Tanner said to the doctor. "We're Amber's family."

Hope felt surprise and maybe shock ripple through her. Tanner thought Amber was *family?* She swayed a little, but Tanner reached out to steady her.

"Tell us, Doctor," he said. "How is Amber doing?"

Chapter 19

Amber wasn't happy. Her hand hurt, her head hurt, her stomach hurt, and she wanted her mom.

Tanner and Kenji stood on either side of the bed, trying to help. Hope had been there when Amber came out of surgery, but she'd been sound asleep, so Hope had gone down to the administration office to take care of Amber's insurance. Faith still hadn't arrived at the hospital.

"It *hurts*," Amber whimpered. "I want a drink of water. I want a *story*. Where's *Mom?*" She tossed her head restlessly.

"Let's ring for the nurse," Tanner said, pressing the call button. "She'll have something to make you feel better."

Kenji grabbed the glass of water and held the straw out to her. "Here's some water, Amber."

Amber took a sip of water. "I want a *story*," she said. "Tell me a story."

"I don't know any stories," Kenji said helplessly, looking at Tanner.

Amber's eyes filled with tears.

"Tell her how to make a soufflé," Tanner said. "That's a good story."

"A soufflé?" Amber said, sniffling. "Okay, tell me that one."

"How to make a soufflé?" Kenji looked flummoxed. "Like a recipe? Okay. I can tell that story." Kenji pulled the chair closer to the bed.

"Mom always gets in bed with me." Amber edged sideways to make room.

"Amber, I can't." Kenji, horrified, glanced at Tanner. "You have too many tubes and things. I'll hurt you. And the nurses will be mad at me. I'm sure they won't allow it."

Tears trickled down Amber's face. "Where's my mom? She'll do it."

"Kenji will get in bed with you. I'll make sure the tubes don't get in the way." Tanner glared at Kenji. "She just wants a story." He held the light plastic tubing aside as Kenji settled himself gingerly on the bed.

"I don't know about this," Kenji said, reclining stiffly next to Amber.

"That's good," Amber said, relief in her voice, cuddling against Kenji.

"Amber, put your hurt hand on Kenji, like this," Tanner said, gently placing her hand on a pillow against Kenji's shoulder. "That will keep it elevated. Kenji, don't move."

Kenji rolled his eyes like a trapped animal.

"Okay." Amber settled down. "I'm ready now," she said, closing her eyes. "Tell me how to make a soufflé. Please."

Kenji looked from Amber to Tanner. "You start with some eggs," he said.

Tanner shook his head in exasperation. "How many eggs?" he prompted.

"A dozen. You need a dozen eggs." Kenji relaxed a little as he felt Amber nod her head drowsily next to him.

"Do the eggs have to be at room temperature?" Tanner asked, keeping his voice low.

"You need a dozen eggs at room temperature," Kenji amended. "You need a dozen, fine fresh eggs, not too small, at room temperature." He glanced at Tanner, who nodded in encouragement.

"Do you have to separate them?" Amber asked, her voice sleepy.

"Yes, you do." Kenji smiled down in surprise at the child, and Amber opened her eyes and smiled back.

"Kenji, will you be my uncle?" she asked. "And Tanner? You, too? I want you both to be my uncles."

The men looked at each other and then at the child.

"Like Marty and everybody?" Tanner asked. "You want us to be uncles like that?"

"Yes," Amber said. "Hope said you have to like people *especially*. And I like you both especially."

Kenji looked at Tanner in panic. Tanner shrugged and nodded.

"Sure," Kenji said like a drowning man, following Tanner's lead. "I'll be your uncle."

"Me, too, Amber," Tanner said. "We're in."

"Good." Amber closed her eyes and exhaled softly. "I'd like that. I'll do stuff for you, too. Hope said that's how it works."

Just then the nurse bustled in, but she halted in midstride when she saw Kenji in bed with Amber. She glanced uncertainly from the child to the men and shook her head.

"It's okay," Tanner whispered. "We're family. Her uncles."

"Yes," Amber said. "They said okay."

"It's against the rules," the nurse said, sounding confused.

"She needs a story," Kenji said, his voice low. "Her mom's not here."

The nurse paused, looking at them. "All right," she said finally. "Is she in pain? Amber, does it hurt?"

"Yes," Amber murmured, as the men nodded.

The nurse took out a syringe and injected its contents into the bag that dripped into Amber's IV tube. "She can have something now and again in two hours," she said. She smiled at them. "Make that story a good one. Amber needs her rest."

"It is a good one," Amber said, not opening her eyes. "It's a soufflé."

The nurse, looking more confused, took Amber's pulse

and made a note in the chart, then dropped the chart back in the holder at the foot of the bed. Then she nodded at them all and left. Amber stirred, getting more comfortable. Tanner and Kenji could see her shoulders relax. The painkiller was helping already.

"Tell me more," Amber said, her voice dreamy. "Do you beat the whites *first?*"

By early afternoon it was clear that Amber would need to stay in the hospital at least for one night. The painkillers were doing their work and, off and on, she slept heavily. Kenji, gingerly avoiding the plastic tubing that ran into Amber's arm, was still cuddling her, not sure how to extricate himself without waking and upsetting her. Tanner joined Hope down in the administration office to make more calls while they waited for Faith, who still hadn't picked up. Marty, however, did.

"Marty, this afternoon's shot for sure and maybe tonight is, too," Hope said into the phone. "Kenji, Tanner, and I are with Amber now, but Kenji'll have to go to work soon. I don't know where Faith is, and Mom can't get here before six, if then. Somebody has to stay with Amber, and right now I'm it. Unless Tanner wants to stay." She looked inquiringly at him.

He shook his head no and tried to take the phone away. Hope turned her back on him. *Some help he is.*

"I don't want her here all alone," she said to Marty. "She might be scared if she wakes up without anybody here, and Tanner says she hasn't been feeling that great."

Hope paused while she listened, shrugging Tanner's hand away when he touched her arm. "I know it's going to make a mess of my play. I *know* I'll have only two nights left to make my stake. But *Amber.* I can't leave her."

Tanner grabbed her arm.

"Hey!"

Tanner plucked the phone from Hope's fingers. "I have

an idea," he told Marty. "We'll call you back." And then he hung up and handed the phone back to her.

"I was *talking* here," Hope said, annoyed.

"But not getting anywhere," Tanner said. "I could stay with Amber while you play, but my idea is better. Troy could come over and stay with Amber. My daughter. She's eighteen, she's had a lot of experience babysitting. She'd do it, if she doesn't have other plans. And—did you know Amber asked Kenji and me to be her uncles? So we could introduce Troy as her new cousin. Amber might like that."

Hope grinned a little ruefully. "You're Amber's uncles now? You said yes? I'm sorry about that. I tried to get her to wait a while before she asked you. I thought it was too much of an imposition."

"Nah, I think it's cute. And I doubt the responsibilities will be too heavy. Although I guess you never know. Kenji had to cuddle up and tell her a story, which scared him half to death. But he seems to be coping. So, how about Troy?"

Hope looked at him, uncertain. She couldn't leave Amber alone. But she couldn't really afford not to play cards tonight, either. She still had to earn more than a hundred thousand dollars just to sit in the game with Big Julie. And having Tanner spot tables for her helped her game. *Every* table spotter helped. As selfish as it sounded, she wanted him helping her at cards.

Where on earth was Faith?

"I don't know," she said.

"I'll just call Troy and see what's up." He took out his own phone and punched in a number.

"Hey, Troy. Listen, I need a favor." He listened for a second, grinning. "Okay, *fine,* you have a deal. I need you to come over to the hospital and stay with a friend of mine for a few hours." He listened and then glanced at Hope.

"No, not that friend. This friend's eleven. Her name is Amber. She cut her hand pretty bad and needed surgery. She asked me to be her uncle, and I said yes. Her aunt Hope needs to go to work tonight, and I've been helping her at the casino. So it's just till Amber's mom gets here, but we don't really know how long that will be. We don't think too long."

He listened again. He laughed. "You are grounded for six months, you know that? Okay. Thanks, kiddo. Room 410C. I'll see you soon." He hung up.

"She's coming," he said.

"Thank you," Hope said doubtfully. "If you're sure she won't mind." How would Amber respond to a strange teenager hanging out in her room? Hope wasn't sure it was a good idea. But what options did she have?

Tanner grinned at her. "They'll do great," he said, as if he could tell what she was thinking. "And if I'm Amber's uncle, I think that makes Troy your niece."

Hope rolled her eyes. Amber was right. Suddenly the world seemed to be full of relatives. It was all very confusing.

Forty minutes later, Troy, carrying a colorful canvas tote bag and wearing jeans, flip-flops, and a halter top, tiptoed into Amber's room. She blinked when she saw Kenji propped up in the bed next to a sleeping blonde girl.

"Hey, Kenji," she whispered. "Is this Amber? Is she, like, totally out? And where's my dad and everybody?"

"Amber's been sleeping for a little while. She's had some pain meds recently so maybe she'll stay out. Your dad is with Amber's aunt Hope, who is hassling the insurance. They should be back any minute. Does your dad know what you did with your hair?"

Troy's long, dark hair had been threaded into dozens of tiny, narrow braids, each of which was decorated with a handful of colorful beads. The braids swung when she moved, making the beads click together. "It's a surprise," she said.

Kenji grinned. "He'll be surprised," he said. "Rasta Girl."

Troy grinned back, putting her tote bag on the floor. "I

think Dad has a thing for somebody," Troy said. "Is it Amber's Aunt Hope?"

"You'll have to ask him," Kenji said repressively, as he started to ease himself off the bed. "Help me with this tubing, will you? I don't want to do any damage here."

Troy held the tubing while Kenji stood up. "You're no help," she said. "I can see that if I want any real information, I'll just have to ask Amber."

"I wouldn't do that," Kenji said. "Tanner would have a fit."

"Ask me what?" Amber asked drowsily, opening her eyes.

Troy went over to the edge of the bed and smiled down at the child. "Hi, Amber," she said. "My name is Troy. I think if Tanner is your new uncle, then I'm your new cousin."

Amber gazed dreamily up at the vision of teenaged splendor, her hair a fantastic arrangement of braids and beads, looking like an exotic bird from a faraway land.

"*Cool*," Amber said.

When Hope got back to the room with Tanner, Troy had braided Amber's blonde hair with beads and was working on applying a coat of "Very Cherry" polish to the girl's fingernails.

Tanner took a long look at Troy's hair, and then looked from her to Amber. Their hairstyles were brunette and blonde versions of the same look—probably a style Hope hadn't counted on.

"Troy, what did you do to your hair?" he asked, frowning at her. "And Amber's hair? Did you think about asking Hope if braiding it was okay? Your hair is one thing, but Amber's is quite another. I *really* don't like this."

"Oh, *no*," Amber said, looking distressed. "Please don't mind! We're having so much *fun*."

Hope looked from Troy's hurt face to Amber's pale one. Tanner might not like his daughter's hairstyle and Faith might not like the beads in her daughter's hair, either, but anything that Amber wanted right now was okay by her.

"Don't worry," she said, going over to the bed and kissing her niece on the forehead. "How are you feeling, Sweetie? Your hair looks fantastic, and I love that shade of polish." She grinned at the older girl. "You must be Troy. Maybe you could warn your father before you shock him with a new hairstyle."

Troy smiled back with more confidence. "I'm sorry if you don't like it, but Amber and I were having a blast," she said.

"Hope, you don't have to let her off the hook like this." Tanner shook his head.

"Well, it's really up to Amber." Hope looked at her niece from several angles, nodding seriously. "She's going to be on the cover of a best-selling cookbook, you know. She needs to experiment with her look."

Amber grinned at her.

"You're the best, Aunt Hope," she said.

"Would you like me to do your hair, too?" Troy asked, mischief dancing in her eyes. "I have enough beads. We could all match."

"You are a minx," Tanner said, resignation in his voice.

"Troy's not a minx! She's an *excellent* person," Amber said firing up in defense of her new cousin.

"You're a minx, too," Tanner said.

Amber glanced at him and grinned.

"Cool." She turned to Troy. "What's a minx?"

Hope realized she was grinning, too.

Troy gave Amber a high-five on her good hand. "It's a girl who wins an argument with her father," she said, darting a look at Tanner.

Hope laughed out loud and turned to the older girl. "You've figured out by now, of course, that I'm Amber's aunt Hope. Thank you for staying with Amber while I go to work."

"No problem," Troy said. "I wish I'd known sooner that I had a cousin in Vegas. Having a girl cousin is great. I thought the only cousins I had were two boring boy cousins back in Detroit."

"My brother's kids," Tanner said.

"So," Troy said, turning bright eyes on Hope, beads clicking as she moved her head. "You have to get to the casino, right? You're a card player like my dad."

Hope shook her head. "I'm not a pro. I'm actually on vacation from my real job, just trying to earn a big chunk of money in a short amount of time. Which is maybe doable if I keep at it and my luck holds."

Troy nodded, looking from Hope to Tanner and back. "My dad is the best, so if you stick with him, you have a good chance."

Tanner sighed. "There's a future for you in marketing, kid. Think about it when you get to UCLA."

Troy grinned at him. "So go, you guys. Burn up those tables. We'll be fine here."

"Yes," Amber said, admiring her nail polish. "After this, Troy promised she'd tell me stories about high school."

Tanner groaned.

"Lord help us," he said.

Chapter 20

Big Julie Saladino stepped out of the shower, wrapping himself in the monogrammed blue-on-white, long-staple Egyptian cotton bath sheet the casino provided its guests, and stepped barefoot up to the sink. Except for Drake, he was alone in the suite. He'd spent last night with Marilyn, who'd gone to the gym to meet her trainer. Big Julie had taken the opportunity to have an in-room massage.

The truth was, Big Julie was tired. Remembering which suite he was supposed to be in every day and keeping two women happy—or at least quiet—took more strength than a circus elephant and better timing than an air traffic controller. So far Marilyn had spotted Baby just that one time, and although she'd gotten real cheesed about it, her screechfest had had an upside for him. But how long before Baby figured everything out? And then what? Baby had options.

So that was the first thing.

He heard the doorbell ring as he lathered his face with the casino's triple-milled, vanilla-scented English soap. Drake's raised voice. Then he heard a series of bumps and bangs as something crashed against the door. That was room service with the breakfast he'd ordered, on time for once. The food could wait for three minutes while he shaved.

He was still shaving when the bathroom door burst open

and two big thugs rushed in.

That was the second thing.

The doorbell had not brought room service, but the Russians. They'd learned on arrival that Mrs. Marilyn Saladino and spouse were staying in suite fifteen-oh-one of the Desert Dunes Casino and Resort—just two floors down from themselves—and they had formulated a plan.

The plan started out great. Armed and dangerous—all except for Alexei, whose future, as their prospective attorney, could not be risked by a felony conviction—they stole an empty laundry cart from the hallway and the maid that came with it, pushing the tiny terrified woman and the giant cart before them down to fifteen-oh-one.

The door to the suite, concealed in a tiny alcove, was entirely filled by the cart and the maid. The Russians hid along the hallway, out of sight from the suite's security view of the door.

"Ring the bell," Johnny Red hissed to the maid.

The maid turned, stark terror in her eyes. Johnny Red turned to the triplet closest to the door.

"Markov, ring the bell," he said.

"Why can't I ring the bell?" asked Yakov.

"Just somebody ring the bell, dammit!" Johnny Red snarled.

Yakov squeezed past the frozen maid and rang the bell. Then he jumped back out of sight.

When Drake looked through the keyhole, he saw only a small, dark, nervous woman. Made lax by insufficient danger, he fell for the oldest trick in the world and opened the door.

"Yeah?" he asked. "What—" But before he could formulate the question, the five Russians jumped into the alcove, pushing the maid and the cart before them, rushed into the suite's foyer, and tackled him.

"Hey!" Drake shouted, struggling against the maid, the

cart, and the Russians. "Who—?" He shoved the cart against Alexei and two of the triplets, dodging the maid and taking a calculated swing at Johnny Red, which fell short.

"I'm gonna kill you!" snarled Yakov, who had been struck by the cart in a tender area.

"*Alto!*" squeaked the maid in horror. "*En nombre de Dios!*"

The struggle was violent but brief. Even facing five-to-one odds, Drake might have come out the victor, since two of the five Russians had little training and less practice in overcoming a strapping personal bodyguard with many years of experience in the Special Forces.

But Johnny Red had come prepared. While Yakov, Markov, and Igor grappled with Drake's arms and legs and tried to take away his gun and Alexei watched to make sure the maid didn't make a break for the phone, Johnny Red calmly uncapped a small vial. Holding it far away from his body, he dumped the contents into a paper towel he'd brought just for this purpose and held it over the struggling Drake's face.

In a matter of seconds, Drake slumped to the floor.

"Presto, sleepo," Markov said with satisfaction.

"Let's move," Johnny Red said.

Yakov and Markov each picked up one of Drake's arms and legs and started to drag him into a closet.

"*Dios!*" groaned the maid, making the sign of the cross. "*Mi loca vida!*"

"So, how do you like Las Vegas?" Alexei asked her in a futile attempt to distract her.

Yakov and Markov shoved Drake's feet after the rest of him and slammed the closet door, blocking it with a chair they propped under the doorknob.

"We're good," Markov said, dusting his hands.

"*Hombres horribles,*" the maid wept.

"The Desert Dunes is a fantastic facility," Alexei told her. "You do a great job here."

Meanwhile, Johnny Red and Igor went looking for Big Julie. They crept through the huge apartment until they got to the master bedroom. Gluing their ears to the bathroom door, they heard the little sounds of shaving—the water gurgling in the sink, the knock of a razor against the porcelain, the soft grunts of Big Julie as he scraped his skin.

They crouched outside the door. Surprise was everything. Johnny Red held up his fist and put one finger in the air. Igor nodded. One. Then two. Then three.

They burst through the bathroom door.

When Johnny Red and Igor crashed through the solid oak bathroom door, Big Julie couldn't have been more surprised than if Lenin himself were leading the charge.

"What the—?" he started as he staggered back from the sink, but he had grasped the situation in a heartbeat. He tried to fend off the attack, but there was nowhere to run, nowhere to hide.

"Get outta here! Drake!" he roared, to no results.

And that was the third thing, because Johnny Red, the putz who wanted Big Julie's Jersey territory, wouldn't have gotten this far if Drake were still in the picture. And of course Big Julie knew who his attackers were. Johnny Red had swaggered around the streets of Jersey often enough, even though Big Julie himself had never had the pleasure of socking the newcomer upstart in the jaw, him or his Mob soldier, neither. The Russian goons had come out here to Vegas to get done on neutral ground what they couldn't get done on their home turf, where Big Julie had plenty of friends and well-wishers who just happened to know a few things about firearms.

"*Go back to Moscow, you stupid Russian!*" yelled Big Julie. "You're not getting New Jersey—and you're not getting me, neither!" He tried to shake free from Johnny Red's grip even as Igor grabbed him from behind. Big Julie's large, wet torso and unsecured towel gave the Russians little purchase, but the two-against-one odds were poor and the towel hampered his best moves. Big Julie lost the towel within minutes and found himself inexorably dragged out of the bathroom toward the suite's entryway.

Not good. If the Russians got him out of the suite, he didn't think he'd ever see the inside of it again. Not in one piece, anyway. Maybe in several smaller pieces, tucked inside a suitcase. Just not, he hoped, the genuine Louis Vuitton matched luggage set that Marilyn had bought to the tune of five grand just two days ago. She'd *never* get the blood out of that.

Speaking of Marilyn, where the hell was she? Or Baby? *Somebody* had to be up here *somewhere* who could get some help.

"Help!" Big Julie shouted. "Fire! Help!"

"Shaddup!" Johnny Red yelled, trying to slug Big Julie in the mouth. Big Julie dodged, and the blow glanced off his lower jaw as he ducked. Big Julie didn't worry about being slugged. He hadn't risen to the top of the Jersey organization without taking a few hits. He thrashed against his captors as they hauled him out to the entryway, bucking and yelling the whole way.

"Yakov, get the chloroform!" yelled Johnny Red, trying to hang on to Big Julie as Markov leaped to his aid.

Yakov stared at Johnny Red. "But boss, you used it all up on the other guy."

"Holy Mother of Russia!" boomed Johnny Red.

By the time Johnny Red and Igor had muscled Big Julie into the entryway and the door where the laundry cart was jammed, Johnny Red saw the first flaw in his plan. He'd meant to kill his arch-rival here in the foyer, dump him in the laundry cart, take him out to the loading dock behind the casino, stash him in the getaway car, drive him out to the helicopter pad, give him a nice ride, and then drop him into Lake Mead, right behind Hoover Dam.

The trip seemed like it would be fun. Big Julie would

fall out of the sky into the water, which would make a nice, big splash, and the pilot had promised to pack a picnic lunch and fly over the Grand Canyon, too, as long as they were out there.

The problem with this program leaped to Johnny Red's consciousness when the maid took one look at Big Julie, buck naked, kicking and flailing, dripping water, half his face still covered in shaving soap, and screamed in a pitch that could break glass.

"Eiyeeeeeee!" she wailed. The scream and its echo seemed to reverberate around the suite and down the hallway—and for all Johnny Red knew, down the elevator shaft to the security office. Alexei, who'd been trying to engage her in small talk with poor results, jumped up and clamped his hand over her mouth.

Johnny Red pondered his problem. The maid, so handy when they stole the laundry cart, now was a hindrance. What to do about her? He couldn't shoot Big Julie right here with her watching. He couldn't leave an eyewitness to murder, and killing her, too, was out of the question. He couldn't even really push her out of the suite and shoot him behind closed doors, because she'd seen the weapons, she'd hear the shot, and either way, she'd *know.* And if she knew, she'd scream. Johnny Red would swear to that on a stack of *Das Kapital*s.

He wasn't the only one who'd seen the problem.

"Uncle," Alexei said in desperation, holding his hand over the maid's mouth while she struggled to break free. "What are we going to do?" He flinched when the maid bit him.

"Let me think a minute," Johnny Red said.

"Hurry," Alexei urged, trying to stay away from the maid's teeth.

Johnny Red thought while Yakov, Markov, and Igor held the still bucking and thrashing Big Julie, and Alexei kept his hold on the biting, kicking maid. *Leave no witnesses*. That was the first rule. And the second rule was, *kill no innocent bystanders*. So he had to try to reconcile these opposing forces. The dialectic was always difficult, even for Lenin. And for Stalin—well, forget it. The man couldn't find a dialectic with a divining rod. Bottom line: Johnny Red couldn't kill Big Julie and the maid, too. Big Julie, as a parasitic member of the decadent bourgeoisie— yes. The maid, as a conscientious member of the working proletariat—*nyet*!

"Change of plans." Johnny Red announced. "We don't kill Big Julie now. We do it in the helicopter. Then he goes into Lake Mead, just like we planned, and we still get our picnic."

"That works," Alexei said, "but what do we do about her?" The maid, exhausted from her exertions, slumped against Alexei. He gestured toward the maid, whose arm he still gripped.

Johnny Red shook his head impatiently. "We keep her with us till we get to the car. By the time she calls for help, we're on our way." The only question was, how were they going to get a naked and struggling Big Julie down to the getaway car?

Johnny Red paused for a second, giving Big Julie an opportunity to jerk a hand free. He used it to punch Igor in the jaw.

"Ow!" Igor said, letting go to punch Big Julie back.

Igor's swing missed. Big Julie yanked upwards against Yakov and Markov. Caught unaware, they lost their grip. Big Julie, now unleashed, found that his way to freedom was still obstructed. The laundry cart blocked the front door, and he couldn't retreat because Yakov and Markov were right behind him.

"Help!" Big Julie yelled as he jumped around, avoiding the Russians and looking for a way out. "Help! Murder! Fire! Help!"

"Ei-yeeeeee!" the maid screamed, Big Julie's nakedness

jumping in the hallway proving too much for her sensibilities. Alexei, who thought she'd pierced his eardrums, finally remembered his belt. He ripped it out of his pants, grabbed the maid's wrists, and tied them behind her. Then he picked up Big Julie's discarded towel and stuffed a corner of it, as gently as he could under the circumstances, into her mouth. When the maid was secure, he turned back and assessed their circumstances.

The situation did not look good. Big Julie was not subdued. The maid could not be counted on. The triplets were ineffective. And if the bodyguard woke up in the closet—well, he couldn't think about that. And he wouldn't need to think about it if he could get things under control.

First, he needed a weapon. Everybody else had one, but no one was using it effectively. Surely the Jersey Mob boss had a little something handy—something not too incriminating —squirreled away somewhere in this suite. He dashed off to the bedroom.

Big Julie lunged for the doorway, trying to squeeze past the laundry cart, and the triplets rushed after him before he could get away. Johnny Red lunged for the limp paper towel lying on the floor. Grabbing it, he, too rushed Big Julie. The avalanche of Russians squeezed Big Julie, forcing him in a tight space between the wall and the cart. Thus immobilized, Johnny Red was able to press the paper towel over Big Julie's nose and mouth.

"What the—?" Big Julie asked, swinging his arms and kicking, trying to break free.

Johnny Red hung onto Big Julie and the paper towel as Big Julie thrashed around, not getting noticeably weaker. Seconds later, Alexei returned waving a giant pink leather dildo.

"Look at this!" he said, swinging it at Big Julie's head and connecting solidly. Stunned by the unexpected blow, Big Julie swayed on his feet. Johnny Red took advantage of the moment and dumped Big Julie unceremoniously into the laundry cart.

"Nice work," Johnny Red said to Alexei, dusting off his hands. "Who knew we'd find a blackjack in here? Except it's—you know. Pink." He looked at it more carefully. "And not a blackjack. It's—a symbol of a corrupt capitalist regime. Could be useful, though. Bring it." He turned to the maid, who, tied and gagged, was cowering in the corner.

"Don't you worry none," Johnny Red said, not unkindly, to her as he released her from her bonds. "We're all gonna go now, out the door and downstairs through the casino to the loading dock. You're gonna push the laundry cart. You do what we say, you forget our faces, nobody's gonna get hurt. But you gotta shut up. You make any noise, you're gonna do laundry for the angels. You *capiche*?"

The maid bobbed her head, looking terrified.

"You'll be fine if you don't scream no more," he reiterated, not reassured by her frantic nodding. "We just gotta get through the casino, and you gotta have a short memory. That's it. Okay, let's roll."

Johnny Red arranged the Egyptian cotton bath sheet, now slightly the worse for wear, over the unconscious Big Julie. Then Yakov, Markov, and Igor pushed the laundry cart out of the apartment and over to the elevator and punched the call button. Alexei, holding the pink dildo in one hand and the maid's elbow in the other, carefully locked and closed the door after them.

The elevator car arrived, the doors opened, and the triplets pushed the laundry cart into the empty carriage.

"Okay, Comrade, take over." Johnny Red pushed the maid behind the laundry cart. She took hold of it gingerly.

Johnny Red sighed. "Just act normal," he told her. "Just go like you always go."

They descended a few floors in silence.

"I don't ride the guest elevators," the maid ventured. "Ever. Always the service elevator. Otherwise, we are fired."

Johnny Red rolled his eyes. Obviously there was more

to being a proletariat than he'd realized.

"You see your boss, you tell him that you are bringing us more towels," he said. "The guest is always right."

"We don't get the towels from this elevator," the maid said. "Or put them in this kind of cart."

Johnny Red hissed.

"Did I not just tell you the guest is always right?" he asked. "*I am a guest. I am right.* If anybody asks, you are getting us towels. And then shut up. Do you understand?"

"*Si*," the maid said. "Only—"

"And now *shut up!*"

The car opened on the eighth floor, where a large group of happy vacationers was waiting to go down. Johnny Red moved to the middle of the opening, where he reached out his arms, resting his hands on either side of the doors, blocking the entrance.

"This one is full," he said. "Take the next one."

The happy vacationers took one look at Johnny Red standing in the way, Alexei holding the pink leather dildo, the triplets, and the terrified maid with the laundry cart, and they backed off. Just then Big Julie groaned and stretched, recovering consciousness, which caused the laundry cart to twitch. The vacationers gasped.

"Alexei," Johnny Red said.

Alexei stepped forward and swung the pink dildo into the cart at Big Julie's head. Big Julie went quiet.

The elevator doors closed.

Johnny Red turned to the maid. "See? Not hard at all."

"*Si*," she said, very pale.

At the ground floor, the Russians got off first, and Johnny Red courteously held the doors open while the maid struggled to get the cart off the elevator. The flimsy wheels got trapped in the track for the door, and finally Johnny Red reached in, grabbed the cart, and yanked it out.

"Come on," he said, leading the way down the shopping atrium.

"*Senor!*" the maid said, momentarily abandoning the cart and trotting after him. "It is forbidden! The cameras! We will be stopped! I will lose my job and be sent back to Mexico! My children. *Please,* Senor."

Of that plea, Johnny Red had heard only one—the most important—word.

"Cameras?" he asked.

She pointed to the chandelier. To the light sconce on the wall. To the molding above the doorway.

"*Si*," she said. "Everywhere."

Damn. He should have remembered that about these big, corporate casinos. The guest bedrooms weren't bugged and miked and watched 24/7, but the hallways, elevators, restaurants, and gaming rooms were. You couldn't pick a booger around here without every slick guy in a suit knowing about it.

Now what? It might be too late—but it might not.

"Heads down," he ordered. "Keep 'em down. Alexei, go get us some disguises. Right now."

"Here?" Alexei said, looking around. "*Now?*"

"You can find us something. *Go!*"

Alexei patted the maid on the shoulder and took off. The others stood in the opening of the shopping atrium, staring at the floor.

Five minutes later, he was back with a small bag. "These were all I could get on short notice," he said. He opened the bag and pulled out six pairs of Groucho Marx glasses, with the big plastic noses and heavy eyebrows attached.

Johnny Red scowled. "These don't hide our looks none!"

Alexei grabbed a pair and put them on. "No," he said, "but think about it. What will somebody say when they ask who pushed the laundry cart through the casino? They'll say, five guys and a maid wearing Groucho Marx glasses. They won't remember what else we looked like."

Johnny Red put on his glasses. The others followed suit.

Alexei handed the last pair to the maid. She looked confused, but put hers on, too.

"Okay," Johnny Red said. "Igor, you got the parking stub? Get the car now. Meet us out at the loading dock where we said. Space number eighteen, the one behind the kitchen."

Igor nodded, and wearing his Groucho Marx glasses, dashed off to validate the parking stub and retrieve the car. The others set off through the shopping atrium, heading for the exit, clearly marked, that would lead to the service entrance and loading dock. They soon discovered that the cart, with Big Julie's two-hundred-fifty pound body at dead weight and sprawled at odd angles, was too heavy and clumsy for the maid to steer by herself. She kept driving it into tourists and sometimes the blackjack tables. Alexei helped her push it. Johnny Red lead the way, and Yakov and Markov brought up the rear. The cavalcade moved forward, and the crowds of tourists, gamblers, and employees flowed around them like water.

"See?" Alexei said reassuringly to the maid. "You're fine. Nobody is paying any attention to us."

Upstairs in a small, windowless room filled with banks of monitors, a small table, and a couple of orange plastic office chairs, FBI Agent Roy Frelly played gin with casino guard Mavis O'Toole. She was up by fifteen dollars so far, and at this rate she'd be able to get herself a very nice lunch, courtesy of the federal government.

Her partner, Justin Trinkler, the junior member of the team, worked the flat gray and white surveillance monitors, his eyes darting from scene to scene across the casino. The walls were bare, but taped to the console were wanted posters with grainy photos of Johnny Red and six other gambling miscreants the casino wanted to keep off its floors and away from its machines and tables.

From his vantage point across the room, Trinkler started

to laugh.

"You should see this," he said.

"Gin," Mavis said.

"Dammit!" Frelly said. "I thought I had something going there. Let's see."

Mavis put her cards down.

"Crap," Frelly said, looking at her winning hand.

"No, really," Trinkler said. "You guys should look at this."

"What?" Mavis asked, marking the scorecard.

"Just come over here. You won't believe it."

Mavis sighed, but she got up and went to look over Trinkler's shoulder. She could afford to give up the game. With this most recent hand, her triumph over Frelly—the worst card player in Las Vegas—was complete. She now had earned enough for the steak sandwich special at the grill. In Mavis's opinion, the steak sandwich special, when offered, was not to be missed.

"What?" she asked again.

"Take a look." Trinkler pointed out the screen.

Then Mavis laughed, too.

"Roy, get your butt over here and take a look," she said. "You'll like this."

Frelly rose reluctantly and went to stand with the two casino security guards.

"What?"

"There." Trinkler pointed.

Frelly blinked. Four men and a uniformed maid pushing a laundry cart, all of them wearing Groucho Marx glasses, lurched down the casino aisles, heading, presumably, for the exit he could see at the top of the screen.

He laughed too. Then the seriousness of the situation struck him.

"They're stealing a laundry cart!" he said, straightening up.

"A heavy laundry cart," Trinkler agreed.

"Something's in it," Mavis said.

"Probably a TV set!" Trinkler said.

"Probably more than one," Mavis, the more experienced guard, said, looking at the cart.

"And the maid's in on it!" Frelly said.

Mavis straightened. "Let's just go get these guys."

Grabbing their jackets, the three of them rushed out of the security office, leaving the wanted posters fluttering in their wake.

Chapter 21

Faith pulled into the service driveway of the Desert Dunes casino, did a three-point turn in the empty lot, and backed her refrigerated van into loading dock number eighteen, which led into the Ginger Palace restaurant. Today she was delivering vegetables to Kenji while Kenji was out at the ranch, working with Amber on their cookbook. It was funny how things happened.

She grabbed her orders clipboard, jumped out of the cab, swung the back doors open, and hopped into the cargo area. The boxes of produce had been labeled for each destination and loaded in the order that they'd be delivered. Faith checked off the boxes for the Ginger Palace, hung the clipboard on the hook by the door, and muscled the first four crates onto the dolly.

Farming, she'd come to realize, was not for lightweights. The hours were brutal and the work never-ending. On the other hand, she was her own boss. She was growing good food. And she never had to go to the gym.

With the crates piled four deep on the dolly, she dropped the bridge plate that let her roll her vegetables from the truck to the concrete loading platform. Glancing from side to side to make sure she hit the swinging doors squarely, she headed toward the kitchen.

With the unerring cunning of a wild forest creature,

Johnny Red realized that he and his entourage were the object of pursuit long before they reached the exit sign at the end of the casino hallway. He turned his head to glance back at Alexei and the triplets.

"Run!" he shouted, breaking into a sprint.

Alexei turned to see what Johnny Red was so worked up about. And then he saw it, too.

Two security guards—a young man with spiked hair and a middle-aged woman in glasses—followed by a gasping geezer in a sport coat, trotted after them. Johnny Red had been made, and no surprises there. The noose around their operations had been growing steadily tighter. They'd had trouble in Jersey—with the feds, the cops, and Big Julie Saladino's unexpectedly loyal crew. Now here.

But, Alexei thought, he'd never expected that they'd be dodging the law while wearing Groucho glasses and pushing a laundry cart filled with a naked Jersey mobster across a Vegas casino floor.

They'd thought they could take over the east-coast protection rackets by taking out Big Julie here in Vegas. That was turning out to be a bigger challenge than they'd expected. Now instead of Big Julie dead and the Jersey rackets secured, they had Big Julie naked and unconscious in a laundry cart. This did not look like a step in the right direction to Alexei. If the cops out here knew Big Julie, then one call to the feds would tell them that his abductor was probably Johnny Red.

This attempted kidnapping and potential murder could not turn out well for a person who intended one day to practice the noble profession of law. If they were caught, Alexei didn't see how he could explain it.

So Alexei's bottom line was that they couldn't get caught. He turned back to the cart and, leaning into it, broke into a sprint. "Run!" he yelped to the maid.

The maid turned, too, and when she saw the security guards in swift pursuit, she gasped in fright. She knew what they were after.

Her.

"*La migra!*" she shouted to the other workers in the casino. "Immigration!" She leaned into the cart next to Alexei and gasped with the effort to push it faster.

Yakov also turned to see what threatened him, and in the determined crew running after them, he saw a one-way ticket back to the old country. Reaching out, he grabbed the cart on the other side of the maid and helped them push.

"Faster!" he shouted as they ran down the hallway with the cart, scattering tourists like bowling pins, bumping into casino workers fleeing the immigration threat. "We'll be okay. Igor's bringing the car around."

Igor, in fact, had not brought the car around. He had not counted on the Dobbs-Wilkinson wedding and the many attendants, friends, and family members who'd driven to the Desert Dunes to attend the sumptuous ceremony in the casino's Hearts Afire chapel. Igor's getaway vehicle was just one in an excruciatingly long line of cars in the wedding party that were waiting to exit the parking garage. The drivers were in a party mood, honking their horns, revving their engines, blasting their radios, and driving erratically while catcalling each other through open windows, enjoying the echoes that bounced off the concrete walls.

Come on, Igor swore, honking his horn to no effect whatsoever. He glanced at his watch. Surely by now Johnny Red and the others would be through the casino and waiting for him at the loading dock. The success of their venture was, literally, riding with him. He *had* to get out of the parking structure and back into the loading area. He was the *getaway car*. Getaway cars did not get stuck in *parking garages*.

Igor honked his horn in fury.

Pushing her dolly loaded with vegetable crates, Faith

had just reached the swinging doors to the back entrance of the restaurant when three people pushing a laundry cart burst out of the Ginger Palace kitchen and smashed into her. Momentum was on their side. The force of their combined pushing, their speed, and Big Julie's weight in the cart were too much for Faith to withstand. Unbalanced by the heavy vegetable boxes, she lost her footing and staggered back, feeling the dolly start to tip.

Johnny Red and Markov crashed through the door after Alexei, the maid, and Yakov pushing the cart. They rammed into the cart and their companions, creating a stew of bodies, speed, and confusion. The anarchy of shoving forces pushed Faith back another step. The dolly keeled over.

She made a grab to save the vegetables and took one step too many, realizing her mistake too late. With a startled cry, she fell off the dock, letting go of the dolly as she went over. The boxes toppled off the dolly onto the dock and fell open. Cabbages, rutabagas, beets, and carrots spilled out onto the platform and over the edge to the pavement below, where Faith lay motionless in the hot morning sun.

The Russians and the maid were instantly stilled. They all rushed to the end of the loading dock and peered over the edge to the motionless woman sprawled among the root vegetables on the pavement four feet below.

The maid made the sign of the cross and wrung her hands. "*La pobrecita*," she moaned. "*Madre de dios, la pobrecita.*"

"Shit," said Markov.

"Did we kill her?" asked Yakov.

"I hope not," Alexei said grimly. "We better not have."

Johnny Red, looking like thunder, scanned the service area.

"Where in the name of Trotsky's assassin is the getaway car?" he asked.

The car wasn't there.

While Johnny Red swore on the names of dead and discredited Bolshevik revolutionaries, Alexei surveyed the scene and saw a solution.

He jumped down to the pavement and dashed to the cab of Faith's truck and leaned in, checking the ignition. *Bingo*. Keys.

"Come on!" he yelled to Johnny Red, waving his arm and getting into the cab. "We'll take the truck!"

Johnny Red instantly shouted his thanks to the rehabilitated revolutionary heroes and leaped down onto the pavement.

"Bring the cart!" he yelled to Markov and Yakov, and yanking open the passenger door, hopped into the cab. Markov and Yakov muscled the heavy cart full of Big Julie Saladino across the bridge plate and into the back of the truck, jumped in after it, and kicked the plate to the ground. The maid crossed herself and fled back into the kitchen.

Alexei turned the key and revved the engine just as FBI Agent Roy Frelly, Mavis O'Toole, and Justin Trinkler burst out of the kitchen in hot pursuit. Seeing the vegetable truck heading out of the loading dock confused them for an instant. But then they saw the laundry cart and their quarry through the open rear doors as the van pulled away.

"Stop!" Frelly yelled. "FBI!"

Alexei stamped on the accelerator and the truck screamed out of the space, heading for the driveway and the open road. Frelly pulled out his service revolver and, taking careful aim, shot at the truck and missed.

He was aiming to shoot again when a heavy projectile came from nowhere and hit him just above his left eyebrow, momentarily blurring his vision and stunning him. Markov— the 1988 all-Soviet representative to the European Games in the shot put—had hurled a beet with unerring accuracy and hit the agent in the head. The beet dribbled away across the loading dock and dropped onto the pavement below.

"Hey!" Mavis O'Toole yelled, grabbing Frelly's arm. "What are you doing? No shooting!"

A second beet sailed over her head and smashed into the wall behind her.

"Hey!" she yelled again, this time at the truck.

A fusillade of beets followed. She and Justin ducked and bobbed to avoid the missiles. Frelly was hit several times.

The truck barreled out of beet firing range, heading for the driveway.

"They can't shoot us now," Alexei shouted confidently to Johnny Red. He glanced over. "We're almost at the boulevard. Five more seconds—three more seconds!—and we're safe."

"Come on!" Mavis O'Toole yelled, grabbing Justin's arm. "They're getting away! We gotta call the cops! Call the FBI! Put out an APB! *Move!*" And with that the two security guards grabbed Frelly, still stunned from the beet attack, and rushed back into the casino to call for help.

Igor, driving the getaway car, finally got clear of the parking garage. He gunned the motor as he downshifted, burning rubber as he peeled out of the garage's driveway. He threw the change the attendant had given him into the back seat of the car. Now was not the time to play neat with quarters. He glanced at his watch. *Shit.* Too much time had gone by. By now Johnny Red would be pacing on the dock, ready to kill him. By the time they got up in the helicopter over Lake Mead, Johnny Red would be throwing two bodies out of the open doors—Big Julie Saladino's and his own.

But maybe not. Maybe not if he drove like the wind.

He ground the accelerator to the floor, rounding the corner that led to the back of the casino. Ahead of him was the service driveway. In a crowded, public space like a casino with cameras everywhere, every second counted when you were staging a getaway.

Igor took the service driveway on two wheels traveling at sixty miles per hour. Before he could see what was coming, and well before he realized he'd have to slam on the brakes, he smashed head-on into the Happy Valley Farmer vegetable truck driven by Alexei.

Metal screeched on metal. Glass crunched. Airbags popped. Steam hissed.

Flung against the shoulder harness, his head bouncing against the steering wheel and now stunned by the impact, Igor slumped over the steering wheel of the smashed-up getaway car. His head ached. He tasted blood, and realized his mouth was full of shattered teeth. His nose felt broken, swollen and numb. His ribs were bruised, and his ankle screeched in pain. In misery, he rested his head against the steering wheel.

In the truck, Alexei and Johnny Red were cut and bruised, but as passengers in the larger, heavier vehicle, they'd fared better. Neither had broken bones.

Markov and Yakov were merely bruised. The momentum of the crash had propelled them into the boxes of produce, and the reaction had tossed them against the wall of the truck. They'd fallen heavily to the floor, but they hadn't fallen out of the van.

Which was more than could be said for the laundry cart. The cart, too, had bounced wildly during the collision, but its tiny wheels gave it more mobility on the metal truck bed than it had had on the casino's carpets. The cart had rolled into the vegetable boxes going forward, then bounced off and skidded across the length of the truck and shot out the open doors, where it landed heavily on the pavement, tipping over and spilling Big Julie, still naked and unconscious, onto the concrete.

The carnage was complete.

The noise of the crash roused Faith, who sat up groggily and looked around. It took a few seconds before she realized that there'd been an accident, that her truck was involved, that it had been stolen, and that the thieves were still in it.

She had to call for help. She got to her knees and then

stood, holding onto the edge of the loading dock for support, feeling shaky and nauseated. Her vision was blurred. Her hands and arms were scraped raw from the fall. One wrist throbbed with a sharp, painful ache. She didn't have her phone. It was in her purse, in the truck. And no way was she going over there to retrieve it. Either the thieves were alive, or they were dead. And she didn't want her phone bad enough to find out which.

She raised one leg, swinging it onto the loading dock, and hauled the rest of herself after it. She lay still for a moment to recover from the effort. The rough cement dug into her raw palms. Her arms ached. Her head swam. Her wrist screamed in pain. But she was on the dock.

Standing carefully, she staggered toward the kitchen doors. Just as she entered, she looked back out to the driveway again. Now she saw that there was a big, naked guy lying on the pavement next to a laundry cart. Faith squinted, her head throbbing. There couldn't be a naked guy. It must be a—what? Sea lion? A pink sea lion?

Faith realized she'd probably taken a pretty good bump on the head. She fell through the swinging doors into the cool, dark kitchen, looking for a phone she could use to call the cops. And then an ambulance. Because she was pretty sure she was seeing things that weren't there.

Several minutes later, Alexei lifted his head. He looked around. Next to him, Johnny Red groaned.

"Hey," Alexei said, stretching his arms to see if anything was broken. "You all right?"

Johnny Red sat up and slowly rolled his head. "I think so," he said.

Alexei opened the door of the cab and stepped carefully down to survey the damage. The front of the truck was smashed. The headlights were gone, and the grill would never be the same. Maybe the radiator was cracked, too. No getaway here.

He leaned into Johnny Red's window.

"Come on," Alexei said. "We've got to get out of here. We don't want to be around when the cops get here."

"We gotta take Big Julie, too," Johnny Red complained, easing out of the truck. "He's over there."

Alexei looked at the big man lying naked on the pavement.

"No," he said, going to the back of the truck. "We have to leave him. We can't take the cart, and he's still out cold. We can make another grab for him later. The plan's still good. Get Igor out of the getaway car. We have to move."

Johnny Red limped over to the sedan. The rental car was a total loss. The front was accordioned to half its normal size. The hood had sprung open. The bumper was half torn off and dragged on the ground. Inside, Igor still sat dazed, leaning into the exploded airbag. Pale powder drifted in the air.

"Come on, you son of a procrastinating anarcho-syndicalist," Johnny Red said to Igor, who became a little more alert with the abuse.

Johnny Red pulled open the car door and grabbed Igor's arm. Igor wobbled on his broken ankle, but he got out of the car.

"Everybody okay?" Alexei asked as he came up with a shaky Markov and Yakov. "Let's go, then."

The five men limped slowly the fifteen feet out to the boulevard. Traffic was heavy. Alexei stuck his hand in the air, but three cabs passed them by. Then he realized what was wrong.

"Lose the Groucho glasses," he said, and everybody did. Alexei raised his hand again, and a passing cab shrieked to a halt in front of them.

They staggered after it and dropped gratefully into its air-conditioned interior.

"Where to, fellas?" the cabbie asked. He looked closer. "Jesus. It looks like you guys got yourselves in an accident. Or a fight."

Nobody spoke.

"I guess you're right," Alexei finally said. "We should go to the hospital."

"Las Vegas General's the closest," the cabbie said. "And they got a good trauma center. Been there myself."

He gunned the motor and sped away.

Chapter 22

Twenty minutes later the service driveway was crowded with police and emergency vehicles, security personnel, FBI agents, cops, and EMTs. Two young, handsome paramedics from the fire department checked out Faith. Behind them, a police photographer took pictures of smashed beets that had left brilliant purple stains on the casino walls where they'd hit, random rutabagas and stray carrots rolling around on the ground, and a large, pink dildo lying on the loading dock.

Faith felt woozy, disoriented, and flustered from the male attention. One of the EMTs flashed a light in her eyes, and one examined her aching wrist.

"I don't think it's broken," the tall blond one said as he wrapped an elastic bandage around her wrist, smiling at her. "But you'll need to go to the hospital and get an X-ray just to be sure."

"I don't think you have a concussion," the one with the smoldering eyes said. "But they can check you out there. Will your insurance cover Las Vegas General? They've got a good emergency room there."

"That's fine," Faith said.

The naked man who'd been lying on the pavement— Faith had been right about that—was now lying on a gurney with an IV running in his arm, where another set of paramedics worked on him.

"Is he going to be all right?" Faith asked as the EMTs

packed up their gear. "What was he doing in my truck?"

"We think it was some kind of religious cult that worships vegetables as sexual symbols," Smoldering Eyes said.

"Really? Well, I'm all for that," Faith said.

"Our other patient doesn't have anything life-threatening," Blondie said, nodding at Big Julie. "He should be all right."

"Wait right here for a minute," Smoldering Eyes said. "The police want to ask you a few questions before we take off."

Faith sat in the open doorway of the ambulance, feeling the heat beat down on her bare head. Where was her hat? Her arm throbbed. She should call Hope. She *would* call Hope when she got her phone back.

A uniformed cop about a size too large for his uniform came over with a notebook.

"I understand that's your van," he said.

"Yes," Faith said for what seemed like the hundredth time. "I was unloading crates of vegetables. Some guys burst out of the kitchen, pushed me back, I fell off the dock, knocked myself out. They stole the van, but they didn't get very far. Just across the parking lot. As you can see. Before they got into an accident. Can I go to the hospital now? I don't feel very well."

"We're going to have to confiscate the load for evidence," the cop said.

"Confiscate the load? You mean the vegetables?" Faith asked, not understanding. The cop nodded.

"You can't," Faith said, puzzled. "The Ginger Palace paid for those vegetables. They're *fresh*. The chef—Kenji Hasegawa —he needs them. For the customers."

"They're evidence in a criminal proceeding," the cop said. "They're the weapons."

"They're not weapons!" Faith said. "They're *beets!* They're *dinner!*"

"And we're taking your truck, too," the cop said.

"You *can't!*" Faith said, feeling hot, wounded, angry, and abandoned. Her wrist hurt, her head throbbed, she felt dizzy, and she wanted to go to the hospital. "I need the truck to work!"

"You'll get it back," the cop said. "Here's a receipt." He handed her a pink slip of paper.

"When? Next month, when it's too late?" she said, kicking the ambulance, hurting her toe.

"When we're done with it," the cop said, closing the notebook.

"Where were you when the van got stolen, that's what I want to know," Faith said. "Some cop you are."

"Miss? We'll take you to the hospital now," Blondie said.

"Sure," Faith said, climbing into the ambulance, taking care that she didn't hurt the hand that was screaming in pain. "You men are all alike. You take me for a ride and then dump me. What do you care?"

Blondie looked startled and then glanced at his partner.

"We can give you something for the pain," Smoldering Eyes said.

"Nothing's going to fix this," Faith sniffed, but she let him stick the needle into her arm anyway.

When they got to the emergency room, the paramedics helped her to the desk where a clerk was typing and then left her, as Faith knew they would.

"I was in an accident," Faith said to the clerk. "I need to see a doctor. For my wrist and head."

"Name?" the clerk said, typing.

"Faith McNaughton." Faith rested her hand gingerly on the edge of the desk. It felt better to keep it elevated.

The clerk typed in Faith's name, but then frowned at the screen.

"You're here for yourself? You mean you're here for *Amber*, right?" she asked. "You're her mother?"

"Yes," Faith said, confused. "What about Amber?"

"We've been trying to reach you," the clerk said. "We need some information from you about Amber's health insurance. Your sister—Hope, is that right?—couldn't supply it all."

"Amber's *here,* in the *hospital?*" Faith said, suddenly focused.

"She's doing fine," the clerk said. "She's out of surgery."

"*Surgery?*" Faith asked, her voice rising.

"Whoa," the clerk said. "I've got your sister's contact information right here. I'll call her. She might still be in the hospital."

"*What kind of surgery?*" Faith asked, her voice escalating. "And what do you mean, Hope might still be in the hospital? Hope's in the hospital, too?"

"I'll call Amber's doctor; he can fill you in," the clerk said, punching in some numbers. "And maybe we can get you something for the pain." She ripped a form out of the printer. "And while we're waiting, can I get your group number?"

Hope and Tanner had just reached the hospital parking garage when Hope's phone rang for what seemed like the umpteenth time. The hospital's number came up on the display—probably more insurance problems, Hope thought, annoyed. But she picked up anyway.

"Your sister is here," the clerk said. "Faith?"

"Faith got here? Oh, good," Hope said, relieved. "She can finish the insurance forms, then."

"She's doing that now," the clerk said. "While she waits for X-ray."

"What? Why is she waiting for X-ray? What happened to Amber?"

Tanner stopped, alert.

"Not Amber, Faith," the clerk said.

"*Faith* needs an X-ray?"

"Yes," the clerk said. "And an MRI. But the nurse doesn't think her injuries are too serious."

"Faith has *injuries?*"

"Possible broken wrist and concussion."

"*What?* What happened?" Hope almost didn't notice when Tanner put his hand on her elbow and started to steer her back to the emergency room.

"She was in some kind of accident," the clerk said. "I need her group number."

"I'll be right there," Hope said, closing the phone. She turned to Tanner. Her face was pale.

"No wonder Faith didn't pick up. She had an accident. She's waiting for an X-ray and MRI now."

"Good thing we're already here, then." Tanner put his arm around her.

"Fifty percent of the McNaughton family today has had an accident bad enough that they had to come to the hospital. The *same* hospital. What are the odds?"

"I don't think Jimmy the Greek is taking bets on it," Tanner said, as the emergency room doors whooshed open and greeted them with a blast of cool air.

Faith was sitting in a hard plastic chair in the emergency room, waiting her turn, holding a lightly bandaged hand gingerly in her lap, and looking wan and disheveled. When Hope saw her sister looking so forlorn, she rushed over and put her arms around her.

"What happened, Sweetie?" she asked Faith. "How are you?"

"What happened to Amber?" Faith asked, clinging to her sister. "Nobody can find the doctor, and all they would tell me was that it was a hand injury. And they won't let me go up there to see her until I've been checked out."

"She was slicing vegetables, and she cut herself. She had surgery to repair nerve damage, but the doctors think everything went okay. She had specialists. We called you a zillion times. I guess we know why you didn't answer. What happened to *you?*"

Faith shook her head. "An accident. It was weird. There was a naked guy. I feel awful, but I don't think I'm hurt real bad. And the cops took my truck! They think beets are *weapons!*"

"Cops are dopes," Tanner said, sitting down next to Hope. "Everybody knows only *frozen* beets can be weapons."

Hope choked back a laugh as she sat down and even Faith chuckled, a watery sound. Tanner handed Faith the box of tissues that sat on the table next to him.

"We'll get you in to see Amber," Hope said, feeling determined. "I bet you have plenty of time before the X-ray. But you don't have to worry about her. Troy's staying with her. They're having a lot of fun up there."

"Troy?" Faith looked confused.

Tanner nodded. "My kid. She's on a beading rampage. She and Amber are doing girl stuff, so they're fine for a while, although you might not like Amber's new hairstyle."

"New hairstyle?" Faith asked, but Hope stood up.

"I'll just go ask about your X-ray. Then you can go see Amber. She was asking for you." Hope went over to the desk and leaned in. Tanner watched her walk away, the sway of her hips, the slope of her back and the curve of her neck as she leaned over the desk. She was utterly beautiful, and never more so than when she was kicking butt for her family.

"What happened to your truck?" he asked, still watching Hope as she argued with the clerk. Faith told him, sniffling, and by the time she was done, Tanner saw that Hope had achieved victory. She walked back to them, just in time to hear the end of the story.

"She says you can go up," she said. "The cops have your truck?"

"And the vegetables. I didn't make the deliveries! Not even to the Ginger Palace. So what is Kenji going to do for tonight? And if I don't fulfill my contract, he won't order from me again. I was so counting on this, Hope! My first commercial customer, and Kenji is so nice, and I know he'd recommend me to other restaurants, and now it's all over because the cops took everything!"

"Faith, it's all right," Hope started, putting her arm around her sister.

"No, it's not! It's *ruined*, Hope. And I've let you down *again*." Faith started to cry in earnest.

Hope pulled her sister into a hug. "You haven't let me down, Faith! Nothing's ruined. You were in an *accident*. We'll call the customers and explain. They'll understand. It's all right."

Tanner watched them for a moment.

"Faith," he started.

Faith looked up and sniffed.

"I know somebody who could maybe get your truck back from the cops. But what about the deliveries? You can't do them if your arm is broken, and Hope really has to get to the casino."

Faith brightened. "If we could just get the truck to the Ginger Palace, Kenji and the sous chefs could unload the crates this one time. Like Hope said, everybody else can wait a couple of days."

"Okay, let me see if I can find my guy." Tanner took out his phone and pressed the speed dial for Jack Sievers, his childhood friend and lawyer extraordinaire.

As the phone rang, Tanner looked at the sisters—two faces so similar, and yet so different, and only one that made his heart leap—and wanted to wipe the worry from Hope's eyes.

She shouldn't have to solve all the McNaughton problems by herself.

"Jack? Listen, can you shake yourself free this afternoon, right now? I have a problem."

"Tanner, I can always count on you when I'm getting bored. Did the feds toss you in the slammer again? I am ready to go mano-a-mano with that hopeless Frelly."

"No, it's not about me. I have some friends here. One of them was in an accident with her vegetable delivery truck, and the cops have confiscated everything as evidence. But her business will take a hit if she can't make her delivery to the Desert Dunes today. I'm hoping that you can ransom the truck and get it over here."

"Oh, great, Wingate, another prestigious job. And—not that it's the main thing, but can they pay me? Or am I doing it for a lifetime supply of carrots?"

"If they can't, I can," Tanner said.

"If they can't, I want UNLV basketball tickets," Jack said. "Put them on."

"I should buy stock in that stadium," Tanner said. "Thanks, Jack. The business owner is Faith McNaughton. Here she is." Tanner handed the phone to Faith.

Faith looked at him, a question in her eyes, as she took the phone.

"This is Jack Sievers," Tanner said. "He's a lawyer. He's been relying on me for friendship since grade school. I thought I'd give him a chance to do something for me for a change."

Tanner grinned as he heard Jack yell "I heard that!" And then he turned away to let Faith talk to Jack and was rewarded when Hope gave him a shaky smile.

Hope looked at Tanner handing the phone to Faith and almost burst into tears of relief herself. *Maybe this horrible day would turn out okay after all.* She smiled at Tanner but felt it crack a little around the edges. He put his arm around her.

"What?" he said.

She felt herself relax into him. She didn't want to—she could stand up for herself *and* her family. She'd been doing it for a long time. But he'd brought hamburgers and waited with her for Amber and got Troy to come over and called the lawyer and now he had his arm around her and she didn't feel quite so alone anymore.

Long-term, card players were not for her. But for right now—she wanted to lean a little.

"That was nice, what you did," she said. "Thank you."

He rested his cheek against her hair and she felt herself melt.

"Don't thank me until Jack gets that truck back by dinner time."

"Whatever he can do is great. Have him send us the bill."

"He said he'd settle for carrots."

Hope smiled into Tanner's shoulder. "No, he didn't. I really am grateful, Tanner."

Tanner rubbed his cheek against her hair. "Grateful enough to go for a swim at my place?"

Hope leaned away from him and looked into his eyes. He smiled, a slow and wicked smile, a smile of promise. His eyes held heat, too, and mischief. But his jaw was determined. Hope felt a shiver run down her spine. He was flirting, but he had Intentions. She knew it.

Would she be willing to go swimming? The idea was attractive, but she feared the waters might be too deep.

Faith closed the phone and turned back to them. She looked happier.

"Jack said he'd try, but no promises," she said. "He said he'd call me. It sounds like he knows what he's doing."

Tanner nodded. "He does. He will."

Faith nodded. "Okay. I'm heading upstairs to see Amber. I know you guys need to get back to the casino. I'll be fine. Thanks, you guys." She gave them each a hug, taking care not to jar her injured arm.

"Watch your hairdo when you get up there," Tanner warned her as she released him. "Trust me, it's at risk." He left to retrieve the car from the parking garage while Hope walked Faith to the elevator.

"Mom will get here as soon as she can," she told Faith. "She was coming to see Amber anyway, and now she can help with the vegetable delivery, too."

As soon as the elevator doors closed behind her sister, Hope headed for the emergency room's side exit, where Tanner would be waiting with the car. She was shocked as she walked down the hallway to see Big Julie Saladino lying on a gurney.

Was everybody she knew in the hospital today?

"Mr. Saladino! Is that you?"

Big Julie opened his eyes, cut and swollen with purple bruises. His shoulders were bare underneath the thin blanket that covered him, and Hope thought he probably wasn't wearing anything at all underneath it. Why was he naked?

"What happened?" she asked.

"Fell," he said through a cut lip. "Who're you? Oh, wait. You're the broad wants to play cards on Saturday. You're lookin' better than when we met." He gave Hope a slow appraisal that made her blush.

"Um, yes, thank you. Baby's been taking me shopping. I do want to play on Saturday if the game's still on. How badly are you hurt?"

"Game's on. This is nothin'. You should have seen me the time after—well, never mind. This ain't nothin', that's all."

"I'm glad to hear that. Can I get you anything?"

"Nah. Thanks, though. They're gonna take me for an MRI pretty soon. It's backed up. How do you figure that? Don't we pay taxes? That's what I want to know."

"I'll call Baby for you, how about that? Take care of yourself. I'll see you Saturday," Hope said, taking out her phone. She gave him a little wave as she pushed her way out of the side door.

"Baby?" she asked when she connected. "Did you know that Big Julie is in the hospital? I just ran into him at Las Vegas General."

Baby gasped. "Really? And he didn't call me?"

Hope paused, thinking about the naked gangster lying on the gurney. "I don't think he has his phone with him. He's all cut and bruised. He said he'd been in a fall."

"Is he hurt bad?"

Hope saw Tanner drive out of the parking garage and head her way.

"He *looks* bad, but he says it's nothing. I didn't talk to a doctor."

"I gotta get right over there! Thanks, Hope. I owe you!" Baby hung up, and Hope ran to meet Tanner waiting in the car.

A nurse came over to check on Big Julie while he waited for the MRI. They really had to find him something to wear. Having this man lying naked in the hallway, even if he was covered by a blanket, was not appropriate.

The patient seemed to be asleep, so the nurse decided not to wake him. Sleep could be the best healer, and she'd called his wife. She said she was coming over right away. Lots of times family members could perk up a patient when they needed it most.

Entering the hospital, Marilyn saw a young, vampy-looking blond running towards her. With a shock, she realized that the tramp was the same one she'd followed in the casino a few days before.

Big Julie's slut. She was *here*. Marilyn felt her teeth grind together. She'd thought after that fight—well, she'd thought wrong. The slut was still here. The nerve of Big Julie. When she thought about everything she'd done for him, and this was the thanks she got. Well, she'd show him, and that cheap bottle blond, too.

Hurrying now, she went up to the receptionist and asked for Big Julie's room.

"415C," the receptionist said.

Turning, Marilyn saw that her rival had heard this, too. Snarling, she stormed for the elevator, the tramp in hot pursuit.

Baby realized in shock that the woman asking for Big Julie's room must be Marilyn. After all this time, she finally was meeting the wife, if you wanted to call this "meeting." Marilyn was just about what Baby expected—way older than herself, overweight, her hair dyed a flat reddish brown. Baby couldn't see what Big Julie still saw in Marilyn, but obviously the big dope was afraid of her or lazy or something, because here she was and she sure wasn't looking like she was going upstairs to ask Big Julie for a divorce.

But Baby knew what Big Julie wanted. Big Julie wanted to divorce Marilyn to be with her. And if Marilyn thought she could just kick her out of the hospital when Big Julie needed her the most, Baby would just have to show Marilyn how wrong she was.

They rode the elevator in silence to the fourth floor. When the doors opened, Baby sped down the hallway toward Big Julie's room. Marilyn was surprisingly fit for a woman of her size and age, and Baby could hear her pounding footsteps behind her as they rushed down the corridor. And then there was the room, and Baby burst in, Marilyn right behind her.

Big Julie, bloody and broken, but unbowed, lay supine on a white hospital bed. A nurse leaned over him, gently adjusting a pillow.

"Well, isn't this cozy," Marilyn said from behind her.

Big Julie looked toward the doorway. "I was wondering how long it would be before youse found me," he said.

"How are you feeling?" Baby asked, rushing in and leaning over Big Julie from the other side of the bed.

"Just fine," Big Julie said, glancing warily at Marilyn.

"Back off, girls," Marilyn said, coming in and dropping her handbag on one of the visitors' chairs. "You too, honey," she said to the nurse.

The nurse rolled her eyes and marked Big Julie's chart.

"Enjoy your visitors," she said with the barest hint of sarcasm. She went out, closing the door behind her.

Baby picked up Big Julie's hand and stroked it. She'd show Marilyn.

"Julie, I been so *worried,*" she said. "You gotta let me take care of you." She kept her eyes riveted to Big Julie's face. She'd show him how much she cared. And that Marilyn, too.

"Won't happen," Marilyn said, sitting down on the chair.

"Big Julie, tell her." Baby said. "About us."

Big Julie closed his eyes.

Marilyn laughed. "You mean, how he told you he'd divorce me to marry you?"

Don't lose it, Baby thought. *Big Julie wants you.*

"Honey, he won't do that," Marilyn said, smiling knowingly. "He'll never divorce me. He can't afford to."

"Money! Is that all you can think about?" Baby asked, her voice rising.

"It isn't about money. It's about who he is. You think he's the boss of Jersey, don't you? Well, he isn't. My father is the boss. Big Julie is the second boss."

Big Julie groaned. "Marilyn—" he began.

"You rest now," Marilyn said to him. "Let the girls talk. Your tootsie here should know how things stand."

"I got a name!" Baby said. "Use it!"

"Baby, sugar—" Big Julie said.

"Quaint," Marilyn said. "So, like I was saying, Baby-Sugar, my husband is the second boss. If he doesn't screw up, he'll be boss one day. What do you think his chances of promotion are if he divorces the boss's daughter?"

"He don't care about promotion!" Baby said firmly. "He

cares about me!"

"He cares about promotion," Marilyn said. "But even if he didn't, let's say he divorces the boss's daughter, knowing the boss's secrets. How long do you think it would be before the boss decides Big Julie's a threat to the organization?"

Baby paled. "Julie! Is that true? You would be in *danger? You?*"

Big Julie shrugged.

"I know it's hard to take in," Marilyn said, almost kindly. "Why don't you think it over somewhere else?"

"I don't believe you!" Baby said, her heart sinking. "You'd say anything to make me go away! Well, I'm not leaving." She sat down on the other visitors' chair.

"Don't you worry none," she said to Big Julie. "I'll stay as long as you need me."

Big Julie groaned.

The door opened and a doctor walked in.

"Well, isn't this nice!" he said, smiling at the group. "Your wife and daughter are here to visit."

"Oh, shut up," Marilyn and Baby said together.

Chapter 23

Hope sat at the poker table, perfectly still. Her new hat and sunglasses covered her eyes and most of her face. She'd been playing for an hour, and already she was in deep. The minimum bet was eight hundred dollars. She had one hundred ten thousand dollars of chips in front of her, but she'd started the game with the hundred thousand, so she was ten thousand ahead. She needed to make twenty thousand more today before she faced Big Julie's game tonight.

She could do it, if her luck and her nerve held. And good cards wouldn't hurt, either.

Only one player was still in the game. They were in a faceoff, waiting for the other to fold first. It was noon Saturday. If she were Gary Cooper, it would be high noon, and she would be the lawman facing the gunslinger out in the dusty street, each waiting for the other to shoot first.

Tanner had picked the table, and he'd made a good choice. The other players had lost their chips quickly and dropped out. The last player was a soft guy with a moustache. Moustache Man was good, but not as good as he thought he was. He had about two hundred thousand in chips, but he'd had most of those when Hope joined the game.

Hope felt the familiar hum in her head and the tingle in her fingers as her nerves tightened. She was hyperaware of Moustache Man's every movement, his every tick and tell. After an hour playing with him, she *knew* this guy. Knew what moves he'd make, how he'd bet, when he'd fold. And if she stayed steady and had a little luck, she could win everything right now.

They both had a good chip stack. They both had depth and could play for a while. But Hope felt the killer instinct. She could take Moustache Man. She was sure of it.

Her hole cards weren't much, but Hope was in the big blind and Moustache Man called. Hope watched the dealer burn one card, then turn the three cards for the flop. No help there for her: Ace of clubs, four of clubs, ten of hearts.

Hope felt her breath come and go out of her lungs, nice and easy. She kept her face relaxed. She didn't move a muscle, didn't move her head, her hands, her feet. To her left she felt the tension scream from Moustache Man. She sensed him twitching without even looking at him.

Moustache Man checked. Hope checked.

The dealer burned a card and turned over the fourth card. The nine of diamonds. Moustache Man leaned in and bet twenty thousand dollars.

So Moustache Man was holding *something* good. What? Two pair? A pair of nines and what else?

Hope thought, letting chips flow through her fingers. She thought about what the uncles and Tanner had talked about all week. She could call, or she could raise. Be aggressive. Play hard. Play to win.

She raised forty thousand dollars.

Moustache Man's eyes flashed across the table at Hope. He called. So he was prepared to go that far. He thought his cards were good enough to beat whatever she had. Well, time would tell.

The river card was a jack.

Hope watched while Moustache Man jammed his thumbs into his waistband.

Yes, Hope thought, focusing on Moustache Man. *There it was. The low-confidence tell.*

Moustache Man checked.

Yes.

Hope bet everything she had left, pushing all her chips into the center of the table. She heard a gasp from the spectators. She felt the adrenaline rush, a sweet, hot flood of confidence.

And waited to meet her fate.

Moustache Man's eyes widened in shock for an instant. And then he slumped, resigned, as he tossed his cards back to the dealer. He didn't want to risk sixty or seventy thousand dollars more to see what cards Hope held.

The pot was Hope's. And she was up eighty thousand dollars.

She felt a deep, peaceful satisfaction, knowing she'd played well.

She glanced to where Tanner was watching. He shook his head, grinning at her, and gestured to see her cards. She held them up so he could see.

King, seven.

Hope watched as Tanner's jaw dropped. She smiled, tossing the cards back to the dealer. She'd had a nothing hand. A hand most people would never have bet into the flop. But Hope had read her opponent correctly and knew that her bluff—her huge, over-the-top, game-ending, all-in bluff—would scare off his winning hand. And it had.

And now she was done. She'd made the two hundred thousand dollars she needed to play Big Julie, with fifty thousand to spare. It was Saturday noon on a dusty street, and she, Gary Cooper, had won.

The dealer scooped the chips over to Hope, and she picked them up, shaking hands with Moustache Man.

"Thanks for the game," she said. "I enjoyed it."

"You had amazing cards," he said.

"I was lucky," she said, although of course neither amazing cards nor luck had had anything to do with her win.

Marty picked up his coffee cup and held it aloft. "To Hope."

"To Hope!" Tanner lifted his glass of orange juice, and the uncles lifted their cups or glasses of coffee, juice, water, or in Jim Thickpenny's case, champagne. A large and festive lunch covered the big, round table at the Golden Palace all-you-can-eat four-ninety-five dim sum buffet.

"You should have seen her play that last hand," Tanner told the uncles. "You would not have believed it. She didn't turn a hair. She went all-in on the worst cards I've ever seen. Unbelievably gutsy."

"I'd have believed it," Marty said, nodding. "She could play the pants off just about anybody when she was *twelve*."

"I was channeling Gary Cooper," Hope said. She looked, Tanner thought, adorably pink and pleased with herself. "You know, in *High Noon*. Facing the gunman at the end of the street. Although Gary Cooper was facing a whole gang in that one, and all I had was Mr. Moustache."

"You like old movies?" Tanner asked. *That was another thing they had in common.*

Hope nodded, helping herself to pot stickers. "Late night TV, my secret vice," she said.

Tanner could think of other late-night vices he'd like to tempt her with.

"She's a natural card player," Pete Wysniewski said. "You see them every so often. Stu Ungar. Like that."

Weary nodded. "You played some remarkable poker this week," he said to Hope. "Truly remarkable."

"Bing, bing, bing!" Sharp Eddie said, finishing the Mongolian beef.

"Unbelievable streak," Isaiah Rush said. "You were fantastic all week."

Hope blushed furiously.

"Thanks to you all," she said. She took a deep breath. "I'll never be able to repay you guys for coming out here and getting me this far."

"Hey," Marty said. "Stop. No more of that. We always felt we shoulda done more for you back then. What we did this week is nothing. We're square."

"And we had fun," Sharp Eddie said, laying aside his napkin and sitting back with a sigh of satisfaction.

Jim Thickpenny nodded. "We were delighted to accommodate your unexpected and fascinating request for assistance."

"We're just glad to see you again, Hope," Weary said.

Tanner watched Hope smile with her lips pursed together. She was trying not to cry. What had these people—such unlikely friends—meant to each other years ago? He'd give a lot to know. Someday, he hoped—and if he had anything to say about it—she'd trust him enough to tell him.

As they started to file out of the restaurant, Marty held Hope back.

"Got something for you here," he said. He pulled some sheets of paper from inside his coat pocket. "Did some research. Thought you might need it."

Hope took the papers and looked at them. "What's this?"

"These are most of the players you'll likely meet tonight at Big Julie's," Marty said. "Big Julie tends to play with a bunch of guys regular, and another two or three that rotate, depending on who's flush or who's in town. Like that."

Hope nodded, reading more carefully. "This is fantastic, Marty! This will really help. How did you get this?"

"I asked around. The six regulars is there, plus Big Julie. Then you, that's eight. Maybe one other. Last week one guy went to the hospital with a peanut allergy, might be him. If not—sorry, kiddo. It was the best I could do on such short notice."

Hope looked at him with shining eyes. "You've got everything here! Names, style of play, tells, winnings, even photos! Everything!"

"Everything I could find, anyways. You can't have us spotting tables for you up there. You'll be on your own, and you're coming in cold. They know each other, and how everybody plays, so you got it tougher than the other players. I thought this could even your odds a little bit."

"Marty, I love you. You think of everything." Hope put her arms around him and held him close.

"Jeez, Hope, stop that. It's nothing," Marty blustered, and Hope took pity and let him go.

"It's everything, Marty. I won't forget what you did for me this week. Let me know if I can repay the favor. I mean it."

Marty patted her awkwardly on the shoulder. "You're a good kid," he said. "If I had a kid, I wouldn't mind if she turned out like you."

Hope felt herself beaming at him.

"I'd have been proud to be your kid," she said.

Tanner watched Hope and Marty from a distance and wondered what the Jersey card player was saying that made her smile at him like that and wondered what Marty had given her. His last will and testament? A treasure map? It wasn't any of his business. But whatever it was, it had sure made Hope happy.

Well, he had an afternoon to make Hope happy, too. He was free until this evening, when he had to play in Big Julie Saladino's weekly card game. And he'd make sure that Big Julie won, too, whatever it took, because otherwise he'd be violating the terms of his probation. He had a lot of reasons to stay out of jail now, starting with the one that was standing over there talking to Marty the Sneak.

Hope waved goodbye to Marty, and then, there she was. Coming toward him, a big smile on her face.

"You picked a good table for me this morning," Hope said, as she joined Tanner, beaming. "Thank you." He looked lazy, strong but relaxed, where he leaned against the wall waiting for her. He had that quirky smile on his lips and a glint in his eye, and although she knew that he was a card shark and could pounce at a moment's notice, she had to admit that he'd really come through for her when the chips were down. She'd made her stake. Tonight she'd play Big Julie! She felt as light as meringue.

"All part of the service," Tanner said. "Do you have plans for the afternoon? It's a nice day to go to Mount Charleston for a walk."

Hope glanced at him, surprised. Was he asking her on a *date?*

"I don't have *plans*," she said. I was thinking I'd go home for a horseback ride."

"Isn't Saturday the traditional day of rest for horses?"

Hope grinned. "Urban myth. Typical. I don't know how these things get started. You know, if you wanted to learn to ride, you could take Blondie. A blind, one-legged goat could stay on Blondie."

"Oh, good. I've finally been compared to a blind, one-legged goat. Another thing I can cross off my bucket list."

Hope laughed and glanced up at him. "What else is on your bucket list?" she asked. *What was she doing?* She was *flirting* with Tanner. That was bad. Her voice yelled at her. *No flirting! No heartbreak!*

"I'll tell you if you take the walk with me."

Hope ignored the voice. She felt light and carefree, reckless and on top of the world. She could conquer anything. Overcome all obstacles. They would have a good time this afternoon, that was all. Tanner would not break her heart.

She wanted to go on a hike with Tanner. She wanted a date. *She wanted him to kiss her again.*

"I can't hike in these clothes," she said, glancing down at her linen cropped pants and high-heeled sandals.

"We can buy you something," Tanner said. "You've earned it."

"I sure did." Hope turned and they started to walk toward the shopping arcade. She felt the bounce in her step as they passed the shops. "I just need shorts. I've got boots in my car."

It didn't take Hope long to find a pair of poppy-pink nylon hiking shorts. Then she went to meet Tanner, who had bought bottled water for the hike.

"All set," she said.

Tanner looked at her long legs, tanned under the bright pink shorts. "My day's already improved," he said.

"Wait until you see me in my hiking boots," she said. "That'll really float your boat."

They took Tanner's truck to Mount Charleston, about thirty-five miles away, which promised good hiking, higher elevations, and cooler temperatures. As Hope climbed out of the truck at the park's trailhead, Tanner grabbed a knapsack from behind the seat.

"That's the water?" she asked.

Tanner locked the truck. "Water, snacks, nylon blanket," he said. "A few basics."

"Good thinking," Hope said. "In case we can't find the restaurant."

Tanner grinned. "Exactly."

They struck out on a hard-packed dry trail that led upwards between groves of ponderosa pine and white fir. Hope breathed in the sharp pine scent in the clear, thin air.

"I don't get out here enough," she said. "Usually I get home from work and go for a ride. I love that. But—"

"Variety is the spice of life," Tanner agreed.

They left the pine grove behind, heading steadily uphill, and entered a stand of aspen. In late summer, the trees were just starting to turn color, but wildflowers still bloomed. Hope could see a few butterflies clinging to the purple petals. Overhead the sky was a thin, high blue, sprinkled with white cumulus clouds.

"Let's stop for a minute," she said.

Tanner opened the knapsack and handed her a bottle of water. Hope cracked the top and took a swallow, taking in the color and light. She smiled at Tanner.

"This is beautiful," she said.

Tanner smiled at the happiness in her face. "Yes, it is," he said. "Never more than now."

Hope's smile widened. "It's a good time of year."

"It is in my calendar."

They walked on, meeting no one. About an hour later, Tanner stopped.

"There's a waterfall just up that branch trail," he said. "It's probably mostly dry by now, but it would be cool. Want to check it out or go on to the top?"

"Let's check it out," Hope decided. They followed an abandoned road for a few minutes, which narrowed to a path and then barely a track.

"Are you sure this is the right way?" Hope asked, following Tanner through what looked like unmarked trees and scrubby brush.

"Trust me." They rounded an embankment and Hope gasped.

"Like it?"

"*Like* it? This is *amazing*." The waterfall—probably about eighty feet tall—started more than forty feet above them and disappeared into the rocks below. Now in late summer, the flow had slowed to a thin ribbon, but drops still bounced over the rocks and splashed onto the surrounding ground. The air was much cooler in this area, and grass, jimson weed, and black-eyed Susans flourished near the falls. The area was cool and vibrant with color—a magical spot of oasis on the warm, dry trail.

"How did you know this was here?" She mopped her face.

"It's marked on the trail maps. It's just that not many people come this far. Here, drink some more water. I've got another one if we need it." Tanner handed her a bottle.

"Can we sit here awhile?" she said. "I'm warmer than I thought."

"Me, too. Wait before you sit," he said. "I'll put the

blanket down."

He pulled the ground cloth out of the knapsack and spread it out over the grass near the waterfall.

"This is *heaven.*" Hope dropped to the ground with her water bottle and gazed at the falls. "I bet this is something in the spring." She tilted her head back and drank the entire bottle, wiping her mouth when she was finished.

"That hit the spot," she said, putting the empty back in the knapsack. "I didn't know I was so thirsty."

Tanner watched Hope drink her water, drink it so fast that some of it escaped the edges of the bottle and trickled down the sides of her mouth and dripped onto her tee-shirt. He watched her throat move as she swallowed the water, at her flushed and moist face, at her tee-shirt as it absorbed the spilled water. He watched her soft mouth as she wiped it afterwards.

He felt an irresistible urge to lay Hope back and to kiss her senseless. *Heaven help me,* he thought, knowing that heaven didn't have anything to do with what he was thinking.

"I'm glad we did this," Hope said. She unlaced her boots, kicking them off, and lay back on the blanket, closing her eyes and stretching. "I feel great. I won today, I had lunch with the uncles, I'm in a beautiful place in the mountains, what more could anybody want?"

I know what more I want, Tanner thought, as he gave in to his impulses. He leaned over and kissed her.

Hope's eyes flew open in shock. She'd been taken completely unawares by Tanner's kiss. Not *unwelcome* unawares. But a person might want to be *ready.*

"Whapf?" she asked, her lips compressed by Tanner's.

Tanner raised his head an inch. "Shhh," he said. "I'm kissing you. Show the respect that deserves."

Hope grinned, her nose so close to his they almost touched.

"You surprised me," she said. "What was I supposed to do?"

Tanner rolled his eyes. "Pucker up. Say, 'oh, Tanner.' You can say that a couple of times, as needed. Kiss me back. Sheesh. Even a junior high school student knows the basic routines."

Hope laughed. "You know, if I'd been standing up and holding, oh, say, a Ming vase, and you came up behind and surprised me like that, I'd have dropped it, and then the world would have lost a priceless artifact. Just think how sorry you'd be."

Tanner twisted his head around, checking out the small clearing. His face was so close to hers that his hair brushed her cheek. "Yeah, Ming vase. I'm seeing that."

"I'm just saying. So, okay, I fluffed it. Should we try again?" *I want to try again.*

"You want to try again?"

Hope felt a second of insecurity, wondering if she truly had fluffed her romantic moment, and then she saw the devil dancing in his chocolate-brown eyes. She felt herself grin.

"Well, we could go look at Ming vases instead. There's an exhibit—"

She didn't finish the sentence before Tanner leaned over and kissed her again. This time Hope was more prepared, and she still felt shocked. Tanner's lips were soft but demanding and electric and molten, and Hope felt herself fall into kiss. Then Tanner raised himself until his face was a few inches from hers and looked into her eyes with such intensity that Hope felt the earth slip away and the stars rush forward. And then he kissed her again, with such heat that Hope thought her blood was on fire. After a few minutes, Tanner stopped again and smiled at her.

"Exhibit?" he asked. His voice held laughter, but his eyes held only heat.

"Shhh," Hope said, feeling a little dazed. "Show some

respect." She put her arms around his shoulders, felt the warmth of his body through his clothes.

"I can do that." Tanner kissed her again, settling down next to her, sliding his arm under her neck, cradling her. The breeze, cooled by the waterfall, tickled her bare skin, and Tanner let his mouth trail over her cheek, his fingers tracing her ear, his lips and tongue tasting her skin. Hope felt a languid heat build in her core and head south.

"You look good enough to eat," he said. "Like an ice cream cone. Lickable."

Go ahead. Lick me. "What's with the food all the time?" she asked. "First it's pumpkin. Then it's potato salad. Now it's ice cream. What's with that?"

Tanner leaned down and kissed her mouth. "I guess since I met you, I've been hungry all the time," he said, kissing her neck. "And all I can do is think about eating." He kissed her collarbone. "You."

Hope caught her breath. *Excellent idea!*

Tanner grinned. "What a good idea," he said. He kissed her mouth again, then lifted her tee-shirt a few inches and reached down and kissed her bare stomach.

The languid heat stoked into a raging fire. He had to stop now, or stopping would become impossible. But she didn't want him to stop, now or ever. They were outside. People could see. But she didn't care who saw.

"Hope," he said, licking into her belly button, nudging the waistband of her shorts.

Hope felt her hands go to his hair.

"Stop it," she said, even as her hands ran through his hair. Her voice sounded desperate in her own ears. "People will come. Rangers."

"We haven't seen anyone all day." Tanner's fingers were tracing lazy patterns on her stomach, pushing her tee-shirt higher, as he kissed his way up her rib cage. Hope wanted more, a *lot* more. Except he had to stop. Before the Rangers came with the Ming vase.

"We're outside." Hope moaned, felt her breathing quicken.
"We're in heaven," Tanner said. "Or about to be."

Chapter 24

"Heaven," Hope said. She stirred against him, feeling the warmth and solidity of his chest.

"Heaven," Tanner repeated. He nudged her tee-shirt still higher. Tanned skin showed through the white lace of her bra. Tanner's heart lurched.

"Sometime," he whispered as he kissed her through the lace, "you're going to tell me how you got that all-over tan."

"Rock pools. Outside. Our place. Told you?" Hope said breathlessly.

Tanner brushed her breasts with his fingers, drawing patterns over the wispy lace, watching her flesh tighten against his touch. *Responsive.* He smiled. And she liked what he was doing. She seemed to have forgotten the Rangers and Ming vases already.

Cooperatively, the bra had a front closure, and Tanner unhooked it.

"Wait! *Outside!*" Hope gasped and arched her back against him.

"We're alone," Tanner said, licking her shoulder, feeling himself go a little dizzy at all the smooth pink and tan skin, the full breasts, Hope's glowing face. He put his head down and kissed her.

When Tanner unhooked her bra and kissed her, Hope thought her body flew off the ground, her heart leaped so hard. Her mouth went dry, her breath quickened, and a jolt of scorching heat seared her from head to toe, settling below her belly as a hot, insistent throb. Even as a tiny atom of rational thought tried to cry out that she was outdoors and exposed and anyone could see, her arms acted on their own. Reaching up for him, she slid her fingers in his hair and held on while his teeth, tongue, and lips, pulled, licked, and nibbled on her sensitive skin, both relieving her aching flesh and creating new spots that demanded his attention.

"Wait," she whispered, moving restlessly against him.

"Can't," he said, flicking his tongue against her skin. "Delicious."

He slid his hand down her belly and down, under the waistband of her shorts. Faint from heat and desire, her mind screamed, *Yes, yes, yes!* shutting down the cautionary voice that said *Slower, later, not here, not now!* She wanted *more*. She wanted *Tanner*. She wanted *all* of him, and she wanted him *now*.

She might have said something. Had she said something? Maybe she didn't need to say anything. He didn't seem to need directions. Tanner's hand slid inside her shorts, eased under the elastic of her panties—and, oh no, oh no, oh no— oh. Oh yes. Oh good.

He was sliding her shorts and panties down over her hips, down her legs.

"Ah," Hope said, her mind shorting out under the delightful things his fingers were doing. "Um." They shouldn't be doing this. She shouldn't be—naked! Practically. She was practically *naked*. She couldn't think. Had she heard something? "What?"

"Tell me when I do something you like." Tanner slid down her body, away from her. He kissed her stomach, her hip, her thigh, as he stroked down her calf, past the inside of her knee, back up. He settled down between her legs, holding her hips. He nuzzled her heat.

"Oh!" Hope said, shocked and thrilled at having him *there*.

That was—unbelievable. He was—incredible. Whatever he wanted, he could have. As long as he—. Her mind went blank.

Her breathing quickened. His soft hair, brushing her belly, was tantalizing. Her skin felt bright with tingling. She arched against his hands, clutching his hair. She was on a roller coaster, climbing.

Tanner's tongue flicked out, finding her most sensitive spot, teasing her.

"*Oh*," Hope moaned. *Higher.*

Tanner slid two fingers into her, stroking her, fueling her fire.

Hope inhaled. *Almost there! Almost—there! There, there, there!*

Tanner's fingers probed, his tongue teased, his mouth— his mouth—. Hope panted, needing more air, more room, more of everything. *More, more, more!*

His mouth pulled.

"*Ohhhhhhh. Oh, yes!*" Hope said. She felt the whoosh from her lungs as she collapsed. "Oh. Oh."

She lay on the blanket, limp with fatigue and content to her bones. She inhaled in contentment, smelling the pines and Tanner's special musky odor. The water trickled down the rocks, occasionally splashing a droplet over them, cooling their skin. The soft breeze rustled the trees and grasses around them. The sun was warm on her legs. A bird cackled from an aspen. She felt utterly part of her surroundings—a wood nymph, who'd spent a sunny afternoon cavorting with a handsome, devilish satyr.

Tanner moved his hands to her hips.

"You okay?" he asked. "You can stop pulling my hair now."

Hope smiled, her eyes closed. She was too relaxed to open them. "It's nice hair," she said. "I like it."

"You can pull it again, later." Tanner came up to lie alongside Hope, reaching for his wallet.

Hope turned into him, draped her arm over his chest,

and kissed him. She opened her eyes, realizing with shock that although she was nearly naked, he was still fully clothed. She slipped her hand under his tee-shirt. His skin was warm and firm.

"Aren't you going to take off your shirt?" she said.

"Should I?" he asked, his voice lazy as he took out a condom.

"I think so."

"Okay." But he didn't take off his shirt.

Hope started to feel uncomfortable. She pulled her shirt down over her still open bra. She was still much more undressed than he was. *Much* more. It was one thing for him to say the Rangers weren't coming. He still had his clothes on. He wouldn't be arrested for public indecency.

"Hand me my shorts," she said.

"What?" Tanner said. He turned his head to look at her. Just inches from his chocolate-brown eyes, Hope watched them go from inquisitive to tender. He sat up and pulled off his shirt. Then he unbuttoned his jeans and pulled them off, too.

"Now we're even," he said. "Except I'm totally naked."

Hope gazed at his chest. He was broad and strong, with muscles rippling across his shoulders. His arms were powerful, ropey with muscle and tendon. His skin was tanned. His waist was trim, his hips narrow. He was perfect.

"Ah," she said, gazing at him, her mind gone blank.

She felt that tingle begin again, that tingle that let her know her nerve endings were doing a happy dance. Tanner looked like he could devour her on the spot. And she'd hand him the fork and spoon.

"Do you want to know my fantasy?" he asked, his voice very soft.

"What fantasy?" She swallowed.

Tanner braced himself on one arm and whispered softly in her ear, his breath warm.

"I have this thing going where you're the fair but naughty queen of all peoples from the planet whatever, and you have legions of men to do your sexual bidding but I'm your favorite, so you took me on this picnic and you're naked and dancing in the sun but I have to worship you from afar until you are ready for me. And you have me do many, many very naughty things to you hour after hour until I am weak with exhaustion and enslaved to you forever."

Hope turned into him. "Really? That's your fantasy? Dancing in the sun like a wood nymph?"

"Yes. Dancing and doing naughty things. Except that you're more a queen than a nymph. Same principle, though." Tanner nuzzled her neck.

Hope reached for his shoulder and kissed him, tasting salt on his skin.

"So now I've danced and made you do naughty things, and then I bid you take off your shirt." Hope turned her head and bit him gently on the arm, then kissed the tender spot.

Tanner inhaled. "The fantasy lives."

"And I'm still your queen." She licked his ear.

"You are."

Hope smiled, tightening her hold on his shoulders. "And you have to serve me."

"I do. Until I am exhausted."

"Then it's time you got busy."

Hope leaned away to pull off her own shirt, but Tanner took her hands away. He put his hands on her waist and catching the shirt, started to draw it up slowly over her body. When the shirt was over her head and her breasts exposed, he leaned down and kissed her soft skin, licking her, brushing his thumbs against their fullness. Hope's breath hitched in her throat.

Yes! Her wood nymph queen sang. *Yes, yes, yes!*

"Um?" Hope said, feeling dizzy. She leaned into him, resting her head against his shoulder. "Can you…"

Her bra followed. He looked at her, letting his hand drift from her face down her breasts to her stomach, up her arm.

Hope felt her breath catch in her throat.

"You are the most beautiful woman I have ever seen," he whispered. He held her so close, she could hear his heart pound.

"Mmm," she said. She nipped him again on the shoulder. "Are you ready for your nymph queen of all the peoples now?"

Tanner grinned. "Observe your humble servant."

"Ah," Hope said, gazing at him. All of him. He was magnificent. Strong. Big. Powerful. Dark. Beautiful.

And best of all, ready.

"I live to serve," Tanner said, following her gaze.

"The words every woman longs to hear," Hope said.

Tanner reached for her, leaning into her as he stroked her face, her shoulders, her breasts, teasing and tasting her flesh, nibbling her ears and licking her sensitive places. And then, reaching down, he gently parted her legs and touched her with both hands, sliding fingers into her and massaging her.

Hope heard herself whimper.

"How's that?" he whispered. His fingers had found a magic place.

More, more, more!

"More?" he applied pressure, a little here, a little there.

Faster, harder! To the left!

"Ah," Hope said. Her breath came in little panting gasps.

"Like that?"

"Ah!" Hope said, tossing her head. Tanner tore open the foil covering the condom, fumbling a little in his haste, and put it on. And then he kneeled between her thighs.

"Whatever you want, Hope," he whispered. And then he was inside her.

Hope moaned. The pressure mounted as he thrust, and the wave he created inside her gathered strength and power.

Yes, yes, yes!

"Ah!" Hope said. "Ah! Ah!"

"Tell me," Tanner said, surging inside her. He held her

face with his hands, covering her body with his.

Faster, harder. The wave built, the tension trembled—and then—the wave burst, sending showers of sparks over her eyes, flooding her skin with sensation.

"Ahhhhhh," Hope said. She felt bathed in bliss. Tanner thrust into her again, one last hard slide. She heard his breath catch and then he edged to her side and tucked his arm under her shoulder and held her close.

Hope breathed him in. Her body slowed, and she felt limp with pleasure and contentment. She heard all her cells applauding.

She relaxed against him, feeling languid. In a few minutes, she heard the birds again, the trickling water, the light breeze.

"That was good," she said. "I enjoyed that."

She felt Tanner smile against her hair. "That was the plan," he said.

"I'm going to take a little nap now." *Because wood nymph queens could lie naked outside with their favorites. That's what they did.*

"Right behind you," Tanner said.

And nestled against each other, they slept.

When the sun shifted behind the trees, Tanner woke. Trying not to dislodge Hope, who was sprawled across his chest, he reached for his watch.

Time to go.

He looked down at Hope, her face flushed in sleep. She'd surprised him a little today. He thought he'd meet more resistance to being out here in the open. And to being his woodland queen. But she'd gotten into it. And she'd liked being with him. He knew it. She was hooked, just like he was. He'd watched her face, her eyes, her expressions. He *knew*.

Reaching over, he gently brushed her hair away from her face.

"Hope," he said.

She blinked, coming awake, not moving, still holding

him. She yawned.

"How long did we sleep?" she asked.

"About an hour."

She nodded. She lay still for a minute.

"I'm lying on a rock," she said finally. "It's jabbing me in the hip."

Tanner grinned. "Thank you."

Hope laughed. "I mean, a *real* rock."

"Stop with the compliments. My ego doesn't need it."

Still grinning, Hope pushed herself up, sitting next to him. The light through the trees dappled against her skin. She looked breathtaking—every bit the queen of planet whatever that he'd imagined her to be. But she was more than beautiful. She was radiant with happiness, and Tanner knew that he was part of the reason. He smiled.

Hope hadn't let herself feel much joy over the years, that much was clear. Tanner wanted to make sure that nothing got in the way of her joy again.

Tanner felt his heart expand in a way it hadn't done since—well, maybe since never. Since Troy was born. He picked up Hope's hand, stroked her palm with his thumb.

"I'm busy for the next few days," he said. "I have something to do tonight, and Troy and I are spending tomorrow with my folks before she goes to college, and Monday I'm driving her to LA. I'll be back Wednesday. Are you busy Wednesday night?"

"No," Hope said, looking at him massaging her hand.

"Then I'll see you Wednesday night, all right?" he said. "We can have dinner. And I'll call you from the road."

"Wednesday," Hope said. "That'll be fun."

Yes, it would. Tanner tilted up her face and looked at her eyes. Unguarded, they were a perfect shade of blue.

"Okay," Tanner said. "I'll see you Wednesday, then. That's a promise."

Chapter 25

Hope sang along with the radio the whole way home. She belted out rock and roll tunes, harmonizing with the melodies and pounding out the beat on the steering wheel. She felt high with adrenaline. She couldn't help it and didn't want to stop it. She felt great.

When she walked into the kitchen, Faith knew that something had happened.

"Have a good day?" she asked, smiling at her sister.

Hope felt her face stretch from her smile.

"I'm on a winning streak," she said.

They ate dinner and Hope sang to the radio while she washed the dishes, her hips swinging to the music. Suzanne two-stepped around her as she dried and put away, and Squeegee howled, making Amber and Faith laugh. Then before she drove back to Vegas to play in Big Julie's nine o'clock card game, Hope lay on her bed and studied the crib sheets Marty had given her. The players' bios were remarkably thorough, describing each poker player she'd be most likely to meet in tonight's game.

But her mind wandered to Tanner. What he'd said, what he'd looked like. How he'd made her feel.

Well exercised, for one thing.

Stop that! That part had been good, no, okay, great, in fact, *wonderful*, but sex wasn't everything.

He'd paid attention—to what she said, what she wanted.

What she liked.

And he'd helped her. With her game. The hat. Bringing Troy to the hospital for Amber. Calling his friend Jack Sievers for Faith.

Not to mention, making her feel really, really—

Stop that! She was worse than a kid with her first crush. She needed to *focus.* Everything she'd done all week was for *nothing* if she didn't win tonight. And winning meant not just defeating Big Julie, but all the other players who'd be there. None of them probably were top-notch players, but they'd all be able to beat her if she didn't pay attention.

She rustled the papers, trying to put Tanner out of her mind. All right. Bucky Newsom. According to Marty, Bucky played conservatively. His face sweated under pressure. When he was confident, he pushed up his glasses. Hope looked at his picture. His face was fleshy and red. He looked like he needed to get his blood pressure checked.

Hope turned to the next page. Alejandro Vargas. Very cool player, Marty said, until he started to lose. Then he played every hand fast and recklessly. *Alejandro and Derek, two of a kind*, Hope thought.

She went through the pages of all the known players, memorizing them until she could remember them flawlessly.

And then it was time to go.

Hope stood up, leaving the pages on her bed, tucking her keys, wallet, and sunglasses into her purse, and picking up her hat. Just one more thing to do.

"Wish me luck," she said to her family as they lounged in the den watching a movie. She watched them from the doorway. *If I win*—when *I win tonight*—*I'll be able to watch movies on Saturday night, too,* she promised herself. *Then everything will be worth it.*

Faith stood up and went to give her sister a hug.

"Good luck," she said. "You look fantastic. You'll kill them."

"Thanks," Hope said. She glanced down at her new red

halter dress, clingy and slinky. If it distracted the men tonight, so much the better. "I don't need to kill them, though, except metaphorically."

"That works." Faith grinned and plopped back down on the sofa.

"You look slammin', Aunt Hope!" Amber said. "Say hi to Tanner."

Hope blushed. "Slammin'? Ah, thank you, Sweetie, but I won't be seeing Tanner tonight," she said.

"Break a leg," Suzanne said, grinning. "And have fun."

"Don't wait up," Hope said. "I'll be late." She didn't think she could have fun tonight. This afternoon with Tanner—that had been fun. But tonight was about work. Tonight if she wanted to win the ranch back from Big Julie, she had to play her best game.

Tanner whistled as he finished dressing, tucking his wallet into his pocket and putting on his watch. He glanced in the mirror over his dresser to see Troy watching him from the doorway.

"Off again?" she asked, digging her toe into the carpet and sighing.

Tanner grinned. He'd miss Troy when she went off to UCLA next week, no question. But he'd be glad when she was gone, too, for several reasons, one of which was her over-the-top Abandoned Child gambit when she wanted something.

"The FBI set me up in a game tonight at the Desert Dunes," he said. "Remember? I told you. They want me to help nab a Mob boss."

Troy nodded, straightening up and looking troubled. "Will there be guns?"

"No way," Tanner said, giving his daughter a hug. "The Mob boss certainly won't want any. The FBI says we'll all be frisked on the way in. They're taking precautions. Don't worry."

"Be careful, Daddy, okay?" Troy looked like a kid again, a little unsure. Tanner watched her. Sometimes she was anxious about him, afraid that he, like her mother, would disappear without warning. Troy didn't like it when he consulted for the FBI. She was afraid the agency would get him killed. And this time—Tanner had to agree—the agency might. But he had to cooperate with Frelly whenever the agent demanded. If he refused, he'd go to prison.

Nineteen years and four months into his servitude to the FBI, and now it was almost over. Only eight more months, and then he'd be done. His probation would be over, and he'd be free of the FBI and Agent Roy Frelly forever.

"I'm always careful, Sweetheart. I probably won't be home till very late, though. Do you want to invite Lizbeth to come over?"

Troy brightened. "Could we order out for pizza?"

"Sure. But no boys. Not unless Lizbeth's parents come over for pizza, too."

"Oh, *Daddy*. As if I don't know the rules by now. You know, I'm going to college in *two days*." Troy turned and flounced down the hallway.

"And no boys then, either, unless a parent is present," Tanner called after her. He grinned as he watched her go. Then she turned around.

"So where were you this afternoon? You didn't call. Have you been out yet with that woman you like? Hope? She seems nice."

Tanner's mind boggled. Why couldn't Troy have gone to college *yesterday?* How did women figure this stuff out? It was like they had some kind of secret code.

"As a matter of fact, we went for a hike this afternoon," he said.

"Ha! I *knew* it," Troy said, grinning broadly. "Whistling, a dead giveaway. You must have had fun. I liked her at the hospital."

"I'm officially uncomfortable now," Tanner said.

Troy laughed. "I'm ordering the vegetarian special, extra large. I'll leave you a slice."

Tanner picked up his keys, shaking his head. *Women*. He'd never figure them out.

But it sure was fun to try.

When he got to the casino, he went straight to the security office, where he met Lee Gauger and the lovely Darla. Agent Roy Frelly was absent.

"Where's Frelly?" Tanner asked.

"He went to get some aspirin," Gauger told him. "He's been on light duty since he was attacked and injured during an apprehension attempt here at the casino."

"Right, I heard about that," Tanner said. "He got bopped by a beet, right? How's he doing?"

Gauger shrugged. "He'll be fine."

"The crooks got away, didn't they?" Tanner asked. "Did you ever figure out who that was?"

"I can't comment on an ongoing investigation," Gauger said stiffly.

"Gotcha," Tanner said. "Well, you can't be too careful out there. If someone isn't slinging beets at you, they're slinging rutabagas. It gets dangerous."

"Shall we get down to business?" Darla asked. Her voice was frosty.

"By all means," Tanner said. "What have you got for me?"

The agents showed him the small camera installed in the pen they wanted him to use.

"It's got a mike *and* a camera," Gauger said. "So you gotta keep this piece exposed."

"It clips to your pocket," Darla said, showing him. When she had the pen securely fastened, she patted his chest.

"There you go," she said.

"Sorry, Darla, really," Tanner said, removing her hand. "I'm involved."

"Since when?" Darla asked.

"Since you asked. Now—what if they take this pen away from me at the door? I assume I'll be frisked."

"We're prepared for that." The frost was back in Darla's voice.

"Don't be mad," Tanner said. "There was never a way we were going to work. I don't date law enforcement. It's my only rule."

"Card players have no rules."

"We do," Tanner said. "You'd be surprised."

"As far as we know, you'll be frisked," Gauger said, raising his voice and glaring at Darla. "Don't worry. We got lots of options here." He handed Tanner a briefcase.

"Camera in there," he said. "See? Here's the eye. Put the briefcase facing this way out. It'll pick up everything."

"What if they open it?"

"They won't see anything." Gauger opened the briefcase to show him. The case looked empty except for a cell phone.

"Here." Gauger handed it to him. "Camera in here, too."

Tanner pocketed the phone. "You guys think of everything."

"We got a baggie full of button models taped to the toilet tank cover," Gauger said. "You take a leak when you get there. Then you try to stash the cameras around the apartment. If you can. They're teeny, but don't get caught. The manager says there's plants all over the place. Stick some in those."

"It's more important that you stay in the game than get all these cameras to work," Frelly said, coming through the door and holding a small paper bag. "One or two should be enough." He had a big, purple bruise on his forehead as well as a black eye. The beet brigade had done a good job.

"Okay," Tanner said, when he understood how to operate all the models. "You're monitoring these from someplace, right?"

"Right. Us and the state guys and the IRS. We got

maybe thirty, forty guys on the detail."

Tanner's jaw dropped. "You have all those cops *here, tonight?* Tell me again why you need me?"

Frelly sighed. "You're the only guy we know who plays poker good enough to play in Big Julie's league. So just remember to do what you can to keep the pots high, because that adds to what he ain't paying to the IRS."

"That's an important point," Gauger said. "We can't make a case if we don't show that Big Julie is playing for huge dollar sums. So if those guys want to bet their Rolexes or boats or girlfriends—whatever they want to put in the pot—you up the ante. We got you covered."

Felly nodded. "When the state guys and the IRS says we got enough, we come through the door. And then Big Julie goes to the big house for a long, long time."

"Fine," Tanner said, feeling almost sorry for Big Julie. He picked up the briefcase and headed for the door. "Let's play poker."

Hope got to the Desert Dunes just before nine o'clock, right on time. Her hands were damp and her arms had goose bumps as she punched the elevator button for the sixteenth floor at the Desert Dunes. *Adrenalin, okay—fear, not okay,* she reminded herself for the millionth time as the elevator ascended and glided silently to a stop in the empty hallway.

She took a deep breath and knocked on the door of suite sixteen-oh-one, which Drake opened immediately.

"If it isn't the shopper," he said, grinning appreciatively at the red halter dress. "And look if all that spending hasn't paid off. Sorry, Sweetheart, but I gotta search you."

"For what?" Hope asked, annoyed. "What do you think I could possibly hide in this dress?"

"Something good, that's for sure," Drake said. He swiftly disarmed her of her purse, and opening it, checked its contents, divesting her of her two hundred thousand dollar stake. Then he patted her down.

"These games became a lot more fun since Big Julie started inviting women," Drake told her, brushing down her skirt after he'd felt between her legs.

"Don't count on seeing me again," Hope said, flustered and irritated.

"Damn," Drake said. "And I was just thinking about asking you out."

Hope entered the suite she already knew well from her visits with Baby. Big Julie was at the kitchen counter, mixing himself a drink, and she went over to say hello.

"So you won your stake," the mobster said as she approached him. "All's I was hearing in the casino this week was about a lucky streak this dame was on. Her and Marty the Sneak, burning up the tables."

"That was us," Hope smiled back, "but it wasn't all luck. And now I plan to win that ranch back from you."

Big Julie laughed. "We'll see. Meet Bucky here."

Hope had already recognized Bucky Newsom, the conservative player with high blood pressure. They shook hands.

"Help yourself to a drink, something to eat," Big Julie said, waving his hand expansively to the buffet table. "Everybody else is in the living room. We're just waiting for one more. New guy."

Hope nodded, poured herself a mineral water, and headed into the living room to meet the other players and see how Marty's bios matched the real characters. Fifteen minutes later she'd been introduced to everyone. In the middle of a conversation with Richard Stackhouse (weak player, bluffs too much), she heard a slight commotion at the door.

The last player. The unknown one.

She turned back to Stackhouse to finish the conversation, when she heard a rumble of voices coming toward the living room. Big Julie led the way in.

"Everybody," he said. "Meet our new player this week.

Make him welcome, because we don't want him to feel bad when we fleece him."

The other players laughed and waved. Hope glanced toward the door.

"Tanner Wingate," Big Julie said.

From across the room, Tanner's stomach pitched to the floor. He couldn't believe what he saw. What the hell was Hope doing here? Hope, in a drop-dead red dress, as pale as a sheet, staring at him with dark, horrified eyes. *This* is why she wanted that big stake? To play *Big Julie Saladino?*

His shock and dismay were tinged with fury, but he smiled as the other players stepped forward to shake hands. He'd spent a week refining this woman's card game so she could play with a *mobster?* Was she Mob, too? Or Mob wannabe? She and Baby were going to become Big Julie's top lieutenants now? What the hell was wrong with her? Didn't she realize how much trouble she could get into? She could get caught up in the FBI sweep tonight.

Why the hell was she here?

One by one, the other players stepped up. Bucky Newsom, Alejandro Vargas, Sandy Schraf, Peter Wong, Mark Ladick—he remembered that one, the peanut allergy. Then the one who'd been talking to Hope—Richard Stackhouse. Then finally, Hope stepped forward.

"We've met," he said to Big Julie when he started the introduction. "What brings you to the game tonight, Hope?"

"Necessity," she said. Her voice sounded calm, but she was still pale. "You?"

"The same."

"Yeah, yeah, everybody's gotta play cards. Come on, let's sit down, get the game going," Big Julie said, urging them both toward the table.

"Excuse me, Julie, I gotta use the head first," Tanner said. *I have to get those cameras in the toilet tank. And think for a minute.*

"Sure, sure," Big Julie said. "Down the hall."

"I'll go with you," Hope said.

"What?" Big Julie asked just as Tanner said "Good."

"I need the restroom, too," Hope said, steel in her voice.

"It's a one-holer," Big Julie said. "You can use the can in the bedroom."

"I'll just wait for Tanner," Hope said.

"Suit yourself." Big Julie turned and joined the other players at the table. Hope and Tanner walked down the hallway.

"What the *hell* are you doing here?" he whispered, trying not to sound as angry as he felt.

"I'm trying to win the ranch back." She sounded as angry as he felt. "Derek lost it to Big Julie in a card game. Big Julie said he'd let me try to win it tonight before he sells it. That's why the uncles came out here. To improve my game. I *told* you. What are *you* doing here?"

Tanner stopped in the hallway and ran his hand through his hair in frustration.

"The ranch is at stake? You're getting kicked off the ranch? You *didn't* tell me. *Nobody* told me. Jesus, are you kidding?"

Hope's eyes snapped. "Do I *look* like I'm kidding? Why else would I be here? I met with Big Julie last week, and he said if I earned the stake, he'd put the ranch on the table. Why are you here? Do you *always* play with gangsters?"

"Not usually," Tanner said. "Tonight's a big deal. I—"

"Everything all right down there?" Big Julie called out. "You two can't find the can, or what?"

"We're good, Julie," Tanner called back. "I'm just trying to persuade Hope here that ladies always go first."

"The cards is getting cold out here."

"Be right with you." Tanner opened the bathroom door and motioned Hope inside.

"Listen," Hope said when Tanner had shut the door behind them. Her voice sounded desperate. "I have a decent shot at winning this if you're not at the table. Can't you play Big Julie next week? I have to win the ranch *tonight*. Big Julie already has a buyer. They offered *two million*. The money's in escrow. The title's being transferred. The buyers are putting a destination resort on our land. We'll lose *everything*. I have *one* chance to get the ranch back, Tanner, and it's *tonight*."

Tanner felt numb.

"Hope, I can't," he said. Hope stared at him, and he watched as the light dimmed in her eyes. "I have to play so that the winnings—"

"I don't care about the winnings," she said. "You can have everything else. Just let me win the ranch."

"I *can't*," he repeated. "I have to—"

"Just the ranch," she pleaded. "Then I'll leave the game, and you can clean up the cash. You don't want the ranch, either."

"I can't let you win," Tanner said, not wanting to look at her eyes anymore. "If I could swing the ranch to you, Hope, I would, but I can't. Everything is set up so that—"

Hope turned her head. "That's why you were practicing that card trick that day at the bar," she said. Her voice sounded harsh and bitter. "I should have known then that no good would come from playing with you."

"Hope, I'm sorry. I'll make it up to you. I'll—"

"You *can't* make it up to me, Tanner. If I don't win tonight, the ranch is sold. Then everything is gone." She shook her head, anger and resignation in the gesture. "If I had a buck for every time a card player ripped me off and said he was sorry, I'd own that damn ranch by now. I *knew* you were bad news, just like Derek. *Card players*. I can't believe I let myself fall for your line."

"*Hey*," Tanner said, startled at her vehemence. "I didn't rip you off. If you'd told me—"

"If I'd told you, everything would still be the same. You'd still be in this game, telling me that you can't let me win the ranch and you can't play Big Julie next week instead. If you think you didn't rip me off, come out next week when we're packing up, and ask Faith and Amber and my mom how they feel. See what they say."

She flung open the door and went back to the living room.

Tanner stared after her, feeling angry, but sick, too. *She was wrong.* He hadn't ripped her off. He just hadn't known. His anger simmered with the false accusations she'd thrown at his head.

But she was right about one thing. She *would* lose the ranch tonight.

She had to, or he'd go to prison. And he wasn't going to prison.

He'd make it up to her later. Somehow. But in the meantime, he still had work to do.

He lifted off the toilet tank cover, ripped off the baggie taped there, and stuffed the contents into his pocket. Then, he too, rejoined the players in the living room.

"Jesus, took you long enough," Big Julie said. "I coulda lent you some Metamucil, you need that crap."

Tanner, his heart pounding, tried to act natural as he refilled his glass and then stopped at the ficus plant, pretending to feel its leaves while he attached a button model camera to a branch, before he returned to the table.

"I'm fine, Julie," Tanner said as he sat down. "Sorry. Hope and I were catching up on old times." He glanced at Hope, but she kept her eyes on the table. *Fine.* She could be that way.

"Let's go, then. I start the deal," Big Julie said.

Hope jerked her head up at Big Julie's words.

"There's no dealer?" she asked. Card games without dealers were more susceptible to cheats. She didn't want to suspect Tanner before the game had even begun, but she had seen him practicing card tricks almost a week ago. And he was so *positive* that she'd lose.

"Who needs a dealer? It's just a little card game among friends," Big Julie said. He sat down and picked up a pack of new cards, broke the seal, and started to shuffle. Drake passed out equal chip stacks to all the players.

Big Julie slapped the deck down on the table in front of Sandy Schraf, who sat on his right.

"Cut," he said.

The game started.

Hope kept her eyes glued to the table as she watched the deal go around and tried to control her emotions. Anger, disappointment, helplessness, and fear—none of it would do her any good right now. All those feelings would just cloud her judgment in the game. If she was to have a prayer of winning against Tanner, she had to keep a clear head.

Maybe her situation wasn't hopeless. Just because Tanner knew how to cheat didn't mean that he would. He might play an honest game tonight because otherwise she might give him up to the other players. Big Julie was no wimp. He'd throw Tanner out of the game—or worse—if he caught him cheating.

And even if Tanner did cheat, she was prepared. She could play to counteract it.

Tanner was no doubt a far more experienced player than she was, but she still had a chance. Skilled players won, but even skilled players got bad cards and bad breaks. Books were written about excellent players who had losing sessions, losing streaks. Players who lost their nerve.

She glanced Tanner. He didn't look like he'd lose his nerve.

She'd have to play her very best—better than she'd played all week—and she'd have to have luck, too, if she was to win. If she waited for the right cards and played them aggressively, like Marty—and Tanner—had told her all week, she could win.

Tanner was a professional poker player and a known card cheat, but she'd won two hundred fifty thousand dollars in one week. And even professional poker players and known card cheats had to respect that.

Chapter 26

Tanner was cheating.

Hope thought she'd been prepared for the possibility, but the blind rage that swept over her when she saw him do it stole her breath and left her shaking. She wanted to lunge across the table and strangle him with her bare hands.

Just like Derek. He was *just like Derek.* A laughing, charming, handsome *devil* who'd run over your heart and steal your purse, and then leave you, bleeding and wounded, wondering what you'd done wrong when he got what he wanted and walked away.

How could she have been so stupid? Why did she fall for it? She'd *known* what would happen if she got mixed up with Tanner.

If she let him get away with it, he'd take the ranch—her life—from her. *Just like Derek.*

She didn't know how to tell the other players. And she wasn't sure that she should. No one else had noticed, so it would be her word against Tanner's. And she didn't want Big Julie to shut down the game, which he might do if he thought his "friendly" get-together had been infiltrated by a pro—a *cheating* pro. Shutting down the game was the last thing she wanted.

But she wanted Tanner to stop cheating. Before he stole her home out from under her.

The trick he was using wasn't complicated. Derek had

used the same technique—had *taught* her the same technique. When it was his turn to deal, Tanner gathered the cards, talking the whole time, flattering the winners and inflating their egos. But instead of bunching the cards into the deck randomly, he arranged them the way he wanted them—high cards at the bottom of the deck. That part was easy to spot.

The cheating riffle shuffle was easy to spot, too, if you were looking for it. Tanner held half the deck in each hand and caught the cards at their corners before pushing them together. Riffle shuffles, if done right, kept cards in the deck where the cheating dealer wanted them. Tanner left the face cards on the bottom of the deck. Just like Derek used to do.

Then came the hard part—at least it had been hard for her when Derek taught her the trick. When Tanner cut the cards, he had to palm the high cards from the bottom of the deck. She'd never been able to manage it, but Tanner's hands were large, with broad palms and long, flexible fingers. Just as Derek had done, Tanner easily concealed the cards in his hand.

After the cut, he put the face cards at the bottom again. He dealt the pocket cards to all the other players legally, from the top, but he dealt the aces and kings to Big Julie from the bottom of the deck.

Simple to spot, if your father had shown you from childhood how to cheat at cards. Simple, if you knew what you were looking for.

There was only one thing that Hope hadn't figured out. Derek had used this trick to augment his own game, increase his own winnings. Tanner used it to augment Big Julie's.

Why would Tanner do that?

It was a mystery. Still, whether Tanner wanted to benefit himself or Big Julie didn't matter. He was cheating. Either way, if he didn't stop, she'd lose the ranch.

The first time she saw it, in the first round, on Tanner's first deal, she was so outraged she hardly knew what to say. "Use a riffle shuffle much, Tanner?" she'd asked, raising her eyebrows pointedly at him. "You don't see that very often anymore. Among pros. *Honest* pros, anyway."

Tanner had laughed, glancing at her. "Well, *I'm not a pro*," he'd emphasized. "So I don't know much about fancy shuffles."

Which made Tanner an habitual liar—also just like Derek.

She'd boiled as Big Julie had taken the pot with his pocket aces and the trip ace on the turn. Luck, everyone had called it, but she knew better. Tanner had *handed* Big Julie that pot. Twenty minutes later, when Tanner was dealing on the second round, she said something again. How else could she make Tanner stop? Only by letting him know that she saw what he was doing. That she *knew*. He'd been culling the cards after the last showdown, gathering the high cards together unobtrusively while he talked, diverting everyone's attention.

"You must play a lot of cards," she said, trying to sound admiring. "You've got the patter of a con artist."

She'd gone a little too far. The other players stilled at her words—her fighting words.

"Well, listen to the little lady," Richard Stackhouse said finally into the silence. "You looking for a way to explain your losses to your boyfriend, Sweetheart?"

Everybody laughed except Hope, who gritted her teeth over the insult. As if she had to explain her losses to anyone! As if she weren't beating Stackhouse by a margin of three to one.

"She probably just hasn't lost much before," Tanner said, putting the face cards on the bottom of the deck while everyone looked at her. "She's so pretty, all the men probably let her win."

Everyone laughed again, harder this time. So now

Tanner wasn't only cheating on her, he was *laughing* at her, too? No, she definitely didn't want Tanner to get into trouble with these players. She wanted him drawn, quartered, and hung out to dry, and she wanted to do it *herself*. She'd like to stuff those planted trip aces down his throat, right now, while she showed these braggarts what a *real* riffle shuffle looked like.

But after that attempt to make him stop, she'd shut up. She'd told Tanner as directly as she could what she'd seen. He'd gotten the message—she knew he had because he'd glanced at her, his own eyebrows raised—but he hadn't stopped palming the cards.

Trying to circumvent the cheating was exhausting. She couldn't think only about how to play her best game. She had to think how Tanner was skewing the cards for Big Julie, and how he might skew them because he knew her style of play. She had to shift her strategies constantly, trying new things to keep him off balance. Because although Tanner had helped her get to Big Julie's table, now that she was sitting here, he was doing his best to wipe her out. He *wanted* her to lose.

She would *not* give up without a fight. She would not give in to his sleazy, dirty, underhanded—not to mention illegal—tactics.

Because if she lost, everything she'd worked for—not just this last week, but for the last ten years—would be for nothing. She would lose the ranch. Her family would have to start over. And that would be Tanner's fault. Because he cheated her out of it.

How could he do this to her? Had this afternoon meant *nothing* to him? Did *she* mean nothing to him?

Evidently not. And if she meant nothing to him, he had to mean nothing to her, too.

All she could do—and that was quite a lot—was play her best. If she could push Tanner out of the game, it would be just her and Big Julie, playing for the ranch. Playing honestly, if Tanner were out of the picture.

A big *if.* But not impossible. Even the best card players—even pros—had bad days, bad hands, and bad deals. She had to play her best so she could stay in the game and hope that she would have the skill or the luck to beat him or that Tanner would have a bad break and go down.

The game went on. One by one the other players lost their stakes and dropped out. Four hours into the game, when Hope's back ached and her eyes burned with fatigue, only she, Tanner, and Big Julie were left.

"You play a hell of a game," Big Julie said to Hope as he got up and stretched. "They told me you did, and they was right."

"Thank you," Hope said as she stifled a yawn, thinking, *you have no idea.* She was playing *brilliantly.* If Tanner weren't cheating, she might have won by now.

"Yes, you're playing very well." Tanner glanced at her, his eyes unreadable. She felt a new surge of anger—she was running out of steam but she didn't seem to be running out of fury—and she glared back, her eyes narrowing, even as she watched him gather the cards from the last hand, putting all the high cards on the bottom. It was Tanner's deal. *Another hand about to go to Big Julie.* Well, at least Tanner did have a real idea of how well she was playing.

"You play very *creatively,*" she said, looking at him deliberately and then at his hands. "You intend to play this hand with as much—gusto—as you've played all the others?"

Tanner frowned at her quickly. "I just play the cards I'm dealt, like everybody else." His voice had a sharper edge than usual.

"Hey, no need to get testy," Big Julie said. "We're just playing a friendly game here. I want something to drink, do you guys want something? Drake!"

Drake appeared silently in the doorway. "Bring us some drinks," Big Julie said. "Coffee for the lady, right,

Sweetheart? And bring us some a them little cocktail wienies!"

"Better make it mineral water," Hope said. "I've had so much coffee, any more would make my hands shake."

"Can't have that, now, can we?" Big Julie asked jovially, helping himself to a sandwich.

"It would be especially bad if the *dealer's* hands shook," Hope said pointedly, looking at Tanner. "That might *reveal* something." Tanner never glanced up as he shuffled, that deceptive riffle shuffle, and put the deck down in front of Big Julie.

Big Julie took a huge bite out of his sandwich and cut the cards, slamming the cut down on the table, winking at her as he did so.

Hope watched in exhausted anger as Tanner palmed the cards during the cut. *He is stealing the ranch from me,* she thought. *Right now, this minute, he's stealing it from Faith, from Mom, from Amber. Hand by hand in this crooked card game, he is stealing our home and our livelihood. We'll never get it back, everything we have will be gone forever, because of what he's doing right now.*

She wondered if Tanner's cheating was more elaborate than she guessed—if Tanner was dealing not just ace pairs to Big Julie, but had dealt all the cards he wanted to the other players. She knew there were card mechanics—cons, grifters, magicians—who could do this. Derek had not been that skilled, although he'd taught her what to watch for. She hadn't spotted Tanner doing it, however.

She was a little further behind now. Big Julie had eight hundred thousand dollars in chips, Tanner had seven hundred thousand, and she had five hundred thousand. Not bad, all things considered. But players with poor chip counts had less flexibility to bet, less room to maneuver. She either had to win big and win *soon,* or she'd be out. If nothing changed, her chip count would just be whittled away slowly over time. Tanner would see to that.

Tanner dealt the cards, top-of-the-deck cards to himself

and her, bottom-of-the-deck cards to Big Julie. Hope watched her opponents as they picked up their hands. Big Julie's eyes opened a little wider, so he had a good hand. Tanner's face, as always, remained impassive.

Hope glanced at her own cards. Ace, jack. Not bad, but it wasn't the best hand, and she wasn't in the best betting position. She called.

"Let's make it interesting," Big Julie said. And he dropped the deed to the ranch on the table.

Hope's heart lurched in her chest. *Sure*—now, when she had the least maneuverability, the ranch came up.

Still, there it was. Her home. Lying there on the table. Hers for the winning. She could feel herself staring at it. It was so close. So tantalizingly close.

This is why she'd come. This is why she'd played for four hours, against these terrible odds and Tanner's cheating. All her play for the last week had come down to this one hand. It was now or never.

Could she rake it in? Could she win it—and her family's security, Faith's business, all of it—could she get it for them? Could she outwit Tanner at his own game and win it?

Tanner folded.

Why did he do that? He really didn't have the cards? Or did he want the showdown over the ranch to be just between her and Big Julie? Hope glanced at Tanner quickly, but his eyes were focused on the table.

Hope considered her options. She needed to play smart, but if ever there was a time to take a risk, this was it. This was the hand she had to win.

How could she do it?

Tanner had dealt the hand, so Big Julie had good cards. The question was, *how good?*

Should she tell Big Julie that Tanner was cheating? If she wanted Tanner out of the game for good, now would be the moment to expose him. If Big Julie threw Tanner out of the game, at least the game would be fair. She couldn't let

Tanner just steal it from her without a fight. *And now was the time*. Now when the ranch was on the table. Now or never.

She'd be taking a big risk. Big Julie might just end the game entirely, and she'd lose any chance of winning the ranch back, ever.

Tanner, of course, would be furious. Not that she cared. Cheaters deserved no one's mercy.

She'd do it. She'd tell Big Julie that Tanner was cheating. She took a deep breath.

"Big Julie, I have to tell you something," she said. *The cheating must stop. I can't let Tanner take the ranch away from me. And this is the only way I can stop him.*

Tanner glanced up. His eyes flared, but Hope was too tired—and too angry—to care what he thought. She looked away as Drake came into the room carrying a tray of full glasses.

"You may not realize this," she began, as Drake served her a mineral water with lime. When the bodyguard stretched over the table to serve Big Julie, his coat parted, revealing a gun in the waistband of his slacks.

Hope swallowed. *A gun*. At this "friendly" poker game.

She hadn't thought about guns. If she ratted out Tanner to Big Julie, what would happen to him? Big Julie was in the *Mafia*. They thought nothing of killing their enemies.

She didn't want the Mafia to kill Tanner. Not until she could kill him herself.

Because—*Tanner*.

Her mind flooded with images of the afternoon. The hot, sweet, afternoon. She looked across the table at him, at the hands that had just tossed in his cards. She thought about how graceful and compelling his hands could be, how they could entice. They were helpful hands, too. He'd brought hamburgers to the hospital and called Troy to bead Amber's hair and got Faith's truck back.

Hope felt poised at the brink of a precipice. She was so angry at Tanner that she wasn't sure she could think straight.

She never wanted to see him again. She never wanted to talk to him or go out with him or have anything to do with him. He was too slick, too glib, too polished, and too charming. He could con the diamonds off a red ace.

But she didn't want him to be killed, either. Nobody should be killed for a piece of property, not even the ranch. Not even Tanner, the *rat*. The lying, cheating, scum-sucking, *card-playing rat bastard*.

No matter how angry she was. No matter how devastated. Not even when everything she had was at stake. Not even when he'd put her in this terrible situation.

He'd left her with impossible choices. Lose-lose choices. Either she ratted Tanner out to Big Julie, which could result in the end of the game or the end of Tanner's life. Or she could stay silent, which would result in the loss of the ranch, the failure of Faith's farm, and the sale of her horses.

"What?" Big Julie demanded impatiently. "What don't I realize?"

Hope hesitated.

"Just how tired I am of mineral water," she said finally, trying to sound normal. "Drake, could I please get a glass of wine instead? You can water that ficus with the mineral water."

"*Not* the ficus," Tanner said urgently, and all heads turned to him.

"Not the ficus," he said again firmly. "Water something else. Ficus trees are too sensitive for fizzy water."

"I think there's a service that comes in to water the plants," Drake said, shaking his head as he picked up Hope's mineral water and left the room.

"Who cares about the damn bushes in here?" Big Julie said. "Play cards."

It was Hope's play, and it was now or never for the ranch.

She pushed all her chips in to the center of the table. A half-million dollars' worth.

"All in," she said.

Five hundred thousand dollars, and I'm playing like it's chump change, Hope thought. Well, she might as well treat her chips like chump change. She'd either lose it all slowly, or she'd lose it fast, in this one hand.

Or—just possibly—she'd win the ranch.

In her peripheral vision, she saw Tanner watch her, but she kept her eyes on the table.

"Pretty confident," Big Julie said.

"All or nothing, that's me," Hope said.

With the betting concluded, Hope and Big Julie turned their cards over. Hope showed her ace, jack. Big Julie showed his ace, nine.

Shocked, Hope stared at the cards. *Big Julie bet a two-million-dollar ranch on an ace, nine pair?* What was the *matter* with him? That hand *sucked.*

A small wave of optimism rushed through her. Her pocket cards were stronger. So far she was ahead. Tanner might have tried to give Big Julie two aces, but he'd only managed one, paired with a nine. Was that a mistake?

Tanner, out of the game but still acting as dealer, turned over the flop. It was ace, six, eight. Now Hope had a pair of aces with a jack kicker. Big Julie had a pair of aces with a nine kicker. Hope's hand was still stronger. Her breathing quickened as she realized that the ranch was within her grasp. She could *win* this hand. She could win it *all. On a hand that Tanner dealt.*

The turn brought up another six. So now Hope had two pair: aces and the sixes on the board. Big Julie had two pair, as well, the aces with the sixes, but Hope still held the jack, and Big Julie had only the nine. Hope still held the winning hand.

She heard her heart pound. She was almost there! Only one more card to play. One more card and the ranch could be hers. She could do this! *She could win the ranch from Big Julie!*

What were the odds?

There was a chance—an almost nonexistent chance—that Big Julie could win the pot on the river. Only one card could give him a win. He'd need a nine, which would give him two pair—aces and nines. That would beat Hope's aces and sixes. What were the odds? Very slim. Almost impossible.

Another possibility, still slim, was that if the river was higher than her jack—a queen or king—she and Big Julie would have to split the pot. She didn't know how they'd do that.

If the card was anything else, the ranch could be hers. *Would* be hers. A rush of certainty, of optimism, swept through her. *She could win.* She felt it in her bones, down to her toes. *This hand was hers.*

Tanner turned over the river.

It was a nine.

Big Julie won the hand.

Hope felt a heavy punch to her chest, a blow so heavy that couldn't breathe. She felt dizzy, and her ears hummed.

She'd lost the ranch.

The ranch was gone.

Forever.

She'd lost.

She'd let her family down. She'd lost everything her family loved in life. On that one turn of the card.

She'd lost five hundred thousand dollars in one hand in a private card party. Just like Derek used to do. Thinking she'd win, just like Derek used to do.

Her stomach heaved, clenching so tight that she thought that she'd throw up right there. Or that the wave of fierce contractions in her belly would force out the tears from her eyes.

She couldn't—she *wouldn't*—cry in front of these men. She bit her lip, struggling for control.

She felt bitter and angry and very, very tired. She might have lost to Big Julie in a fair game, she'd never know now. But she'd had no chance at all in a stacked game with

Tanner at the table. It was over.

Everything was over.

If she could move. Her legs felt as heavy as concrete pillars.

"Sorry, little miss all-or-nothing," Big Julie chortled as he raked in the chips and took back the deed to the ranch. "What you got is a whole lotta nothing."

And it's always fun to play with a generous winner, too.

Hope focused her mind, willing herself to stand, and pushed herself to her feet. She felt defeated. Lost.

"Thanks for the game, Mr. Saladino," she said, picking up her purse. "I appreciate the opportunity."

"Why you rushin' off so fast?" Big Julie asked expansively. "Stick around. Finish your drink."

"Thanks, but it's late and I have to go."

She left the table, holding herself stiffly, keeping herself in check. Tears blurred her vision as she headed for the front door. She had to get out of here.

"She shouldn't play if she can't lose," she heard Big Julie say behind her, and then she heard footsteps coming after her.

"Hope!" Tanner called, but his voice gave her the impetus to quicken her pace, heading toward the foyer, fleeing from him and the game and the ruins of her life. Flinging open the door of the suite, she stepped out into the hallway and fled to the elevator, stabbing the call button repeatedly.

The elevator took too long, and Hope's heart pounded as Tanner came out of the suite and strode toward her. *What did he want?* He hadn't done enough, now he wanted something *more?*

"Hope," he said. "I'm sorry."

She turned her back on him and punched the elevator button again.

He came up behind her and reached for her arm.

"Don't *touch* me," she hissed, jerking her arm away. "Get away from me."

Tanner stepped back as though he'd been slapped. "Hope, honey, I'm sorry, you got a bad beat just now, but you weren't going to win tonight."

She looked at him, feeling all the weight of her anger and loss. The ranch, yes. That was gone forever. But Tanner, too. She couldn't afford to love another selfish, lying, cheating, cardplayer. She couldn't afford to live with that much uncertainty and pain.

She'd known better, too. She just hadn't listened to her own instincts.

"*Was* it a bad beat?" she asked, her face impassive, wondering if he'd lie and if she'd know if he were. "Or did you bring up that river card on purpose?"

Tanner glanced away. For a second he said nothing, and Hope had her answer.

Where was that elevator? Any time now would be good.

"I had to," he said finally. He looked around to make sure Drake or Big Julie weren't listening. "And—by the way—thank you for not saying anything. Listen—"

"No, *you* listen." Hope held up a hand to stop him. "Go away, Tanner. Go back to the card game. Go get what you came for. Just—go away."

"Hope, I meant what I said, we can figure something out. I'll call you tomorrow."

Finally the elevator, and not a minute too soon. Hope stepped into it and hit the button for the lobby.

"There is nothing to figure out," she said as the doors closed. "Didn't you hear me? The ranch is gone, Tanner. The game's over. Don't call me tomorrow. Don't call me ever again."

Chapter 27

The gray, early morning light that filtered in around the edges of Hope's curtains brought a new day but only fresh heaviness to her heart. She rolled away from the window, staring into the blackness of her room, not wanting to get up, not wanting to get out of bed at all.

She knew she should try to get up and appreciate the day. It would be one of the few mornings she had left at the ranch.

No one else knew yet. No one knew that she'd lost everything last night—the ranch, Faith's business, their home. When she got back to the house, everyone had been asleep. She hadn't wanted to wake them with bad news. It was too late to call Marty.

She didn't remember getting home. The only thing she remembered was that when she got to the top of the long driveway and saw the full moon glowing silver in the indigo sky, casting a glittery sheen over the house and barn, she put her head down on the steering wheel and wept. How long she'd stayed out there, she had no idea.

Now it was dawn. Hope buried her head in the pillows, trying to bury her thoughts, as well. She'd have been better off if she hadn't played poker at all. She should have just taken a week's vacation and enjoyed her last moments at the only place she'd ever called home. Or packed and looked for an apartment. Instead, she had wasted a week playing cards. She'd earned a quarter million dollars, and then lost most of it in one evening. That had to be a record of some kind.

And worse, playing cards had proved how much like Derek she was. How callous she'd become about huge sums of money. She'd bet a half-million dollars on one hand, and she hadn't thought twice about it, just like Derek.

And she'd lost.

Just like Derek.

And then there was Tanner. The man who'd stolen her heart and then the game.

Leaving her with nothing. Less than nothing.

Just like Derek.

She'd thought that she'd learned not to love handsome, charming, fun-loving men who cheated at cards and made you feel special only as long as it was convenient for them. But evidently, being scarred by heartbreak once was not enough.

She had to forget Tanner *fast* and move on. Before he could do anything more to her—anything worse.

Hope eased out of bed, her limbs aching and her throat thick and dry, and pulled on her jeans and boots, kicking the red halter dress to the back of the closet. That one was going to the thrift store before they moved. She never wanted to see that dress again.

The house was still silent. Normally Faith got up early to weed and water the vegetables, but since she'd sprained her wrist, she couldn't do much. And now, of course, they could leave the vegetables in the ground to rot.

The horses were different. Hope had to take care of them until she found a buyer. *If* she found a buyer. Hope's face twisted when she realized what would happen if she couldn't find someone to take the animals—if she couldn't even give them away. She had only two weeks to find them good homes. It wasn't much time.

Hope moved through the quiet house, heading toward

the kitchen to pick up an apple for herself and some carrots for the horses. When she got to the kitchen, though, she saw Faith was up. Remorse swept over her again.

"Hope?" Faith whispered. Her bright, eager eyes focused on her sister. "How did it go last night?"

Sorrow, regret, bitterness, and loss flooded through her, and Hope felt her expression crumple. Sobs rose from deep within her and caught in her throat.

"I—I lost, Faith. I lost the ranch. I'm so, so sorry."

Faith's face sagged as she stared at her sister. "You lost?"

Hope nodded as tears poured down her cheeks. She lifted her head and bit her lip.

"I was never going to win. Tanner told me. He cheated to make sure. The ranch stays with Big Julie."

"Tanner *played?* And he *cheated?* Are you positive?" Faith dropped into a chair.

"Yes. I saw it. I'm positive." Hope dashed the tears away, reaching for a tissue.

Faith looked lost. "What can we do now?"

"We don't really have any options. I tried, I did my best. I'm just—so sorry I couldn't save the ranch for us. I guess it was a bad idea for me to get everybody's hopes up."

"If Tanner cheated, there was nothing you could do. We know how that goes." Faith tried a small smile, but her voice wavered.

Hope watched her helplessly, her own face wet with tears. She wanted to hug Faith, comfort her, but she felt so bruised and beaten herself, she had nothing left to give her sister.

I shouldn't have let them think I could win, Hope thought as she left the kitchen and stumbled out to the barn. *Now two card players have crushed this family.*

Banjo tossed his head when he saw her, whinnying a hello.

"Hey, there, handsome," Hope crooned, feeling a rush

of love for her horse. *Banjo's loyal*, she thought. *He doesn't cheat at cards*.

She gave him the carrot, patting him, rubbing her hands over his chest and body, feeling his heavy muscles under the warm hide. Banjo turned his head, snuffling her pockets, nudging her gently.

"I've missed you," she murmured to the horse. "Should we go for a run?" *Before it's too late. Before we can never go out together again.*

Banjo nickered, tossing his head.

Hope wiped her eyes with the heels of her hands. She pulled the heavy wool blanket and worn Western saddle onto the horse's back, cinching the saddle snugly, then slipped on the bridle. When she led Banjo out of the barn into the cool dawn, he pranced in anticipation.

"We don't have much time together anymore," she told him as she mounted. "Let's make every minute count." She turned the horse down the road toward the mountains and gave him his head. Banjo broke into a canter and then, feeling frisky, stretched out to run.

The cool morning breeze stung her face, and Banjo's hooves churned up dust and grit that brought tears to her eyes. Hope leaned low over the horse's neck, urging him to run faster. Her hair streamed out, blending with Banjo's mane, as the horse pounded down the track.

Running wouldn't solve anything, she knew that. She couldn't run away from her problems or her memories.

But for a little while, just a little while, as Banjo's strong legs thundered over the ground and carried her higher into the mountains, she could forget that it wasn't the wind or the grit that made her cry. And she could pretend that the male animal she loved most in the world was a horse, not a man.

After her ride, Hope rubbed down Banjo and cleaned all the horses' stalls, turning them out to the pasture. Then she went into the house, dreading what she'd find there.

Since both Faith and Amber were out of commission for many household tasks because of their hurt hands, Suzanne was putting out cold cereal before she went to work at the diner, which opened later on Sunday. All heads turned to Hope when she entered the kitchen.

"I'm sorry, Mom," she said again, hating that she was the person who let them all down. "I really tried."

"We know you did, honey." Suzanne put the cereal and milk on the table and wrapped her arms around her daughter. "Nobody blames you. You did the best you could."

My best. Not nearly good enough.

"Now you can stay home at night with us," Amber said, her bandaged hand propped on a pillow on the table.

Hope gave her niece a watery smile as Faith gave Hope a hug, too, and they clung to each other for a minute.

"Even you can't fix everything," Faith whispered. "We were wrong to put all the burden on you."

"I thought I had a decent shot," Hope said. "And I think I did until Tanner came along."

"Will I get to keep Squeegee?" Amber asked anxiously.

"We'll do our best, sweetie." Hope let go of Faith and poured herself some coffee. "We'll look for a place that allows dogs."

"Squeegee's a *good* dog." Amber still looked worried. "Can Kenji and I still work on the cookbook?"

As Faith reassured her daughter, Hope thought about what she'd have to do this morning. Call the uncles. Try to find someone to take the horses. Find a new place to live. Every call taking away one more piece of the life she'd known. How could she do it? Just end her old life like that?

It happened. Suck it up.

The voice in her head was so loud that for a second Hope thought someone had spoken aloud. But then she realized— that voice was her old friend. The voice that was born the day her father never came home. The voice of determination.

You had to try, the voice said now. *You failed. So what. There's no shame in failure. Only in not trying.*

She sniffed and reached for a tissue. She'd tried to save the ranch, and she'd failed. But she still had fifty thousand dollars from the week's play that she hadn't had to stake in Big Julie's game. Maybe they could afford to buy a house. It wouldn't be a ranch, but Amber could keep her dog. That at least would be something.

They all ate breakfast together and then Hope took a shower, put on clean jeans, and drove into the city. She wanted to say goodbye to the uncles. They'd all be leaving today, and she wanted to thank them again in person. Telling them on the phone about her loss—and Tanner's betrayal— didn't seem right. Marty would still be at the Golden Palace, probably playing one last hand and enjoying the four-ninety-five all-you-can-eat dim sum buffet. She found him at a cashier's window, converting his chips to currency.

When she saw him, all her resolve and determination deserted her.

"Marty," she said, and when he turned, his face bright and expectant, her face crumpled again. "I couldn't do it." Her voice caught on a sob. "I lost everything."

Marty's face fell. "Oh, no, Hope, honey, that's too bad." He patted her awkwardly on the shoulder, sounding like he'd rather be anywhere else. "Don't cry, Little Hope. It's all right. It's not the end of the world. Come on, let's get a drink. It'll buck you up."

"It's not even *noon!*" Hope said, sniffing, wiping her tears away. "I just ate Cheerios!"

"There's nothing like a stiff belt with an old friend to get you over hard times," Marty said firmly, leading her toward the VIP bar.

In ten minutes, Hope was sitting in a deep leather lounge chair, a huge snifter of very old brandy in her hand. She tasted it. *Very* smooth.

"Now tell me," Marty said. "Who played?"

"Everybody you said," Hope said, "and one you didn't guess. Tanner."

Marty choked on his brandy. "*Tanner* played? *He* was the unknown?"

Hope nodded, feeling a little better. Marty was right. A stiff belt with an indignant old friend *was* picking her up.

"And I asked him to let me win the ranch," she said, taking another sip of the brandy. "And he said no."

"He said *no?*"

Hope nodded again, leaning forward a little and lowering her voice. "But the worst thing was, Marty, he cheated."

Marty leaned back, putting his brandy snifter down carefully on the mahogany table next to his chair.

"I'm going to kill him," he said.

Hope beamed at him. "Marty, I love you for that, I really do," she said, taking another sip of the brandy. "But I don't want you to get into trouble."

Marty looked at Hope with sadness. "You like him, don't you, Little Hope. I was afraid of that."

Hope swallowed, feeling the wattage of her smile dimming. "Well—he helped last week. And—" she took a deep breath, "I guess I did like him. Until, you know. Last night."

Like him. *That* was an understatement. But whatever they'd had was over, and he was gone, out of her life, gone, gone, gone. Over and out.

"Hope, honey—" Marty swallowed helplessly and looked away.

Hope shrugged, taking another sip of her drink. "It's okay, Marty," she lied. "It's nothing I won't recover from. I know better than to get involved with someone like that. Someone like Derek."

"That low-down, lying, stealing, son of a—" Marty caught Hope's glance.

"Snake," he finished. "You're *sure* you don't want me to kill him?"

Hope grinned weakly. "He's got a kid," she said, "so, no. The weird thing is, Marty—"

"What?"

"I don't know. I've been thinking about it. Tanner cheated, I saw him. How he picked up the discards and culled the high cards and then did that riffle shuffle, when he palmed the cards—everything. But he wasn't benefiting from the cheats. Or not by much. He *was* ahead of me in the chip count, but mostly Big Julie benefited."

"Big Julie benefited? You're *sure*?"

"I know what to look for, Marty. I know what I saw."

Marty crossed his legs and took another sip of brandy.

"*Big Julie* was the chip leader."

"Yes." Hope wondered what Marty was thinking.

"Huh," Marty said.

"What?" Hope asked, finishing her brandy.

"Nothing," Marty said. "I don't know. You're right, it's strange."

After three brandies in the VIP lounge, Hope was feeling quite a bit better, and by the time Marty called the other uncles in to share a lunch of beer with potstickers, Mongolian beef, garlic spinach, and long-bean prawns, she was feeling almost optimistic.

"Next time you'll take Tanner," Marty said confidently, when the story of Hope's loss and Tanner's cheating had been told again to the shock and disgust of the rest of the uncles. "You're plenty good enough."

"Bing-bing-bing!" Sharp Eddie said, spearing his fifth potsticker.

"You had a hell of a week," Isaiah Rush said. "One for the books."

"Truly brave and brilliant play," Weary Blastell said, pouring beer for everyone.

"I've never seen anything like it," Pete Wisniewski said.

"Your tremendous aptitude for the more esoteric points

of play are indicative of a truly strategic style," Jim Thickpenny said. "Should you ever contemplate undertaking a career in professional gaming, we have more than creditable evidence that you will find optimal success."

"Thanks, you guys," Hope said, draining her glass and setting it down with a thump. "I appreciate everything you've done for me all week, more than you know. Coming out here—everything." She beamed fuzzily at the uncles.

"To Hope!" Weary said. All the uncles raised their glasses, while Hope, humbled and grateful, felt tears spring from her eyes.

"Come on, now," Marty said, handing her a clean paper napkin. "Don't get weepy. I'll drive you home. You're *skunked*."

The uncles had made her feel a lot better, so after Marty and Weary took her home, Hope decided she could start her most difficult moving task. She had to find a place for the horses. She sat down and picked up the phone.

Hope sold Banjo with her first call to the riding stable down the road. Banjo would hate all the amateur riders sawing at his mouth and kicking him in the ribs, but his new owners were decent people and knowledgeable about horses. And she could still go out and ride him sometimes.

After promising to deliver him in two weeks, she hung up and cried.

But Blondie and Ralph were much harder to find homes for. Blondie was gentle and good with children, but she was old and needed frequent veterinary care. Ralph didn't have a mean bone in his body, but his bouncy gait made him almost impossible to ride. Who but the McNaughtons would want a horse no one could ride? Hope spent three fruitless hours calling ranches, stables, and riding clubs. No one would take the horses.

She buried her head in her arms and cried again, defeated. These animals were like family to her. Blondie and Ralph looked to her for comfort and attention, and she was betraying them. She was terrified to think about what might happen to them if she couldn't find homes for them.

Faith set a sandwich on the table next to her. "I'm sorry about the horses," she said.

Hope nodded and sniffed, wiping her eyes with the back of her hand. "I'm sorry about the farm."

They were silent a moment, thinking about their losses.

"Your cell phone's been ringing all afternoon," Faith said finally. "Want me to get it for you?"

"Sorry," Hope said. "I thought I'd turned it off. It's probably Tanner."

"He sure wants to talk to you."

"And I sure don't want to talk to him."

Faith eyed her sister. "You know, he might have had a reason for cheating in that game."

"Maybe he did. Derek always did."

"Hope—"

"I can't talk to him, Faith. The ranch is gone. Whatever he wants to say, the ranch is still gone. Anyway, he's Derek all over again. A slick card player. I just can't."

"You like Marty. And the rest of the uncles. They're card players."

"But the uncles are all business. They're stand-up guys. They're *pros*."

"Tanner's a pro."

"Tanner's more of a professional con artist. And—" Hope couldn't bring herself to say the words. She stared blindly at the red and yellow flowered oilcloth that covered the table. Faith pulled out a chair and wrapped her arms around Hope's shoulders, and Hope crumpled under the weight of her sister's sympathy.

"I like him," Hope said, her voice breaking. "Tanner, I mean. *Really* like him. He's sparkles and chocolate. For a little while, I just—I thought—I just wanted—" She reached blindly for a tissue and Faith pushed the box closer.

"I *knew* it was a bad idea," Hope said, wiping her eyes. "I just couldn't seem to stop myself."

"Oh, Hope, I'm so sorry," Faith said as Hope trembled with loss.

"I've known him for a *week*," Hope hiccupped. "And since then, between him and Derek, we've lost the ranch, the vegetable farm, the horses, and we don't have a place to live. Imagine if I'd known him a *year*."

"We're not doing real good right now," Faith agreed. "It's not all Tanner's fault, though."

"It's not just that Tanner lied and cheated," Hope sniffled. "That was bad. Really bad. But it's not just Tanner."

She blew her nose. "It's me."

Her head felt thick and heavy. "I bet a half-million dollars on a throw of the card. A half-million dollars, Faith! On one hand. Think what we could have done with a half-million dollars."

"You didn't steal the rent," Faith said. "Anyway, Big Julie wouldn't have let you cash out of that game. He wouldn't have let you come home with the half-million. And Hope—" She stroked her sister's hair until Hope met her eyes.

"The ranch is gone," Faith said. "But if you wanted to earn more money for yourself—for us—you could keep playing cards. Turn pro. You burned up the tables this week."

Hope sniffed back tears, squaring her shoulders, facing facts.

"Tanner's not the only one who's just like Derek," she said. "I am, too. I liked it, playing like that. I liked it too much. I don't want to be like that. I don't want to be addicted to cards or casinos or anything like that. And Tanner brings that out in me."

Faith looked doubtful. "Well, it seems a shame to give up the sparkles and chocolate and whatever made you sing during the dishes on Saturday night. Are you sure there's not some way you could—work it out with him somehow?"

Hope sighed, wiping away the last of her tears.

"I don't see how. We're oil and water. Card players and chief financial officers. They don't mix."

Faith stood up. "Well, let's think about it," she said optimistically. "Even if we've lost the ranch, I'm not sure you should have to sacrifice Tanner, too."

"It's not a sacrifice," Hope said, trying not to sound woebe-gone. "It's self-preservation."

Faith looked at her sister with sympathy. "Speaking of self-preservation, you look beat. You got in so late and got up so early. Why don't you take a nap until supper time?"

She *was* beat, Hope realized, and a nap sounded like a good idea. She'd need her rest for the changes—the downsizing—that was still to come.

Chapter 28

While Hope spent her Sunday mourning her losses, Tanner spent most of his Sunday in the beige conference room of Las Vegas's FBI bureau. He had never gone to bed after the card game, and he was now officially too tired to move. His eyes felt full of sand, and his muscles weighed too much to move. In an effort to stay awake, he'd checked out the vending machine down the hall and tried the vile swill they called coffee. The foul brew, which had to have been boiling in that vending machine for at least two years, had tasted bitter when he swallowed it and sat like a furious porcupine in his belly ever since, stabbing his guts with bilious darts.

Or maybe that was just the fear he'd tasted.

Jack Sievers sat next to him, looking dapper and cranky. Jack had put on a suit and tie for the occasion, which Tanner had to appreciate since Jack had dressed at six in the morning. The two of them had been sitting there for hours—ever since the Saturday night game had broken up at Big Julie's and the feds had swooped in and arrested the mobster. Tanner had called Jack as they'd headed to the federal office building, and they'd chatted quickly before the agents debriefed Tanner on the game. At dawn, when the rest of the IRS agents and state police involved in the sting had gone home for some sleep, Jack, on Tanner's behalf, demanded a meeting with the FBI's Special Agent in Charge for Las Vegas. And now they were waiting.

"Aren't they ever coming back?" Jack complained now. He looked up at the surveillance camera tucked into the ceiling tile.

"Hey!" he yelled at the camera. "Hurry up! What's taking so long?"

"Maybe they're trying to find someone who knows how to type," Tanner said.

Jack sighed. "I'd go out and pick us up some food and decent coffee, but I'm afraid I'd miss the excitement," he said.

They looked around the empty conference room.

"Right," Tanner said. "Excitement." He paused. "I hope I'm not wasting your time here."

Jack glanced at Tanner with a thin smile. "This will work out," he said. "You'll see. I didn't go to that fancy Ivy League law school for nothing."

"I know," Tanner said, watching his friend turn into a shark of a lawyer. He tried to smile except his face felt too stiff and his stomach felt too cramped. "That's what I'm counting on."

The night had been the worst of Tanner's life. He'd won the game—or rather he'd thrown the game so that Big Julie had won it—which kept the FBI off his back and his butt out of prison. But he was terrified that in the process of winning the game, he'd lost Hope. He'd never seen her so angry. She'd thrown those poisonous barbs at him all night. But in the end when she'd walked out it was the resignation he'd seen on her face that had really crushed him. She *knew* he'd betrayed her. How could he come back from that?

But she must feel *something* for him. Something besides rage. Because if she didn't, she'd have told Big Julie last night that he'd been cheating, and he'd be out in the middle of the Mojave desert somewhere pushing up cacti by now instead of sitting here in the FBI conference room with Jack. But she hadn't told Big Julie.

He was trying to hold onto that thought.

Still, he'd taken the ranch from her. He'd told her he would, and he had. He'd told her they could work something out. She hadn't believed him. And then she'd walked away. Said she never wanted to see him again.

In fact, he didn't know if he could get the ranch back. He was trying. If he failed, he'd lost more than a card game. He'd lost any chance he'd had to share something with Hope.

He didn't know if he could repair the damage he'd done to her, even if he did get the ranch back. Hers wasn't the kind of anger that could be melted with candy and flowers. He would never forget the way she'd looked when she'd walked away. Maybe his betrayal had been one too many. Maybe she'd never forgive him.

Jack perked up and sat up a little straighter.

"Here they come," he said.

The door opened and Special Agent Roy Frelly and Lee Gauger came into the conference room with someone Tanner had never met. They all held paper cups of a beverage that smelled like coffee, so Tanner knew they hadn't gotten it from the vending machine. He felt a surge of annoyance. Just how bad could this day get? He'd played cards with a gangster, he'd betrayed Hope, she'd dumped him, and the *stupid FBI couldn't even offer him a decent cup of coffee*. After all he'd done for them.

"You guys are getting the red carpet treatment," Frelly said. "This is Special Agent in Charge William Andrews."

"Is that red carpet over here, too? Because I don't see anyone bringing us coffee," Tanner said. "Pleased to meet you."

"This whole evening has been highly irregular," Andrews said, pulling out a chair and sitting down. "There's no precedent for what you're proposing."

"I guess that's why you're called Special Agent in Charge," Tanner said, still annoyed about the coffee. "You get to make the decisions."

"Tanner," Jack said.

"I also called the district attorney," Andrews said.

"I hope you gave Brent my regards," Tanner said. "Do you have our agreement?"

"Tanner," Jack said. "I'm the lawyer. I get to ask all the offensive questions."

"Oh. Right. Okay."

"So, Mr. Andrews," Jack said, "Do you have our agreement?"

Andrews dropped a file folder on the conference table. "Let's go over it one more time, with everybody at the table. Just to make sure there are no misunderstandings of what happened and what *will* happen as part of this agreement."

"As long as you make it fast," Tanner said, glancing at his watch. "I still have a lot to do today."

"*Tanner*," Jack said. "Gentlemen. Let me read the agreement while you're talking. That will save a lot of time."

Andrews opened the file, sliding a stapled document across the table. Jack took a pen out of his breast pocket and, holding it over the document, started to read.

The Special Agent in Charge cleared his throat.

"Mr. Wingate, you played cards last night with known Mafia don Guilio Saladino, also known as Big Julie Saladino, to meet the terms of your probation, is that correct? Our directive was that you would play with him at his regularly scheduled game—a game in his suite that meets the Nevada state legal definition of an unlicensed gambling establishment. In the course of that game, you guaranteed that Big Julie would win a sizable amount of money—even if it meant that you cheated in the game—with the expected outcome that Big Julie would not register his winnings for the IRS as is required. Is that correct?"

"You know it is," Tanner said.

"And partway through the game, did you really leave Big Julie's suite and threaten Special Agent Gauger?"

"Don't answer that, Tanner," Jack said, looking up sharply.

"I would *never* threaten anyone," Tanner said.

"You sure as hell did," Gauger objected. "I still think we should throw you behind bars for that."

Tanner shook his head. "I merely explained the relationship of cause and effect. And I suggested Special Agent Gauger contact his superior officer for advice."

Jack grunted and turned a page.

"You did too threaten me," Gauger said. "When you left the suite and chased after that woman—" Gauger consulted his notes, "—Hope McNaughton. One of the rotating players. We've got it all on tape. She went all-in on the hand that had the ranch in the pot, but she lost the hand and then she was out. Wingate here pursued her down the hallway before the game was over. He could have ruined the entire operation right there."

"But I didn't," Tanner said.

Gauger scowled. "So after the McNaughton woman gets in the elevator, Wingate here speaks into his pen microphone, calls me out of surveillance, says that if the FBI doesn't give the ranch property back to the *original* owner—"

"That being Derek McNaughton, not Big Julie Saladino," Tanner interrupted.

Jack looked up from the document. "Since Big Julie won it from Derek under circumstances that would substantially and materially call into question the legality of the gambling transaction," he said.

"Yeah, yeah," Gauger said. "So we're all standing out there in the hallway by Big Julie's suite, and Wingate here threatens that if we don't give the ranch back to Derek McNaughton instead of seizing it like is our legal right—not to mention responsibility—to do, that he, Wingate, would let Big Julie know that we was staking him out. Thus for sure blowing our entire operation."

"Wasting thousands of taxpayer dollars," Frelly chimed in.

Tanner sighed. "As if you care about taxpayer dollars, Frelly."

Frelly looked injured. "Of course I care about taxpayer dollars. I'm expecting to get a bunch of them in my pension. If you don't do nothing to screw it up."

William Andrews broke in, staring at Tanner.

"It is almost inconceivable to me that you threatened to reveal our stakeout to Saladino. You had to have understood the consequences. You could have gone to prison for *twenty years*—your full term—for failing to cooperate with last night's operation." Andrews looked incredulous.

"Would never happen," Jack Sievers said, glancing up.

"Ha," Andrews said, not laughing. "We could ask a jury to decide."

"A *Vegas* jury," Sievers said, returning to the document.

"Believe it," Tanner said. "I was perfectly willing to accept the consequences of not cooperating with you."

"It would have screwed up your whole life," Andrews said in disbelief.

"So would not getting the ranch back to the rightful owner," Tanner said.

"Still—"

"I took a calculated risk," Tanner said. "You guys have demanded a lot more from me over the years than my probation required. Nothing in the original agreement says I have to go undercover. It doesn't say I have to enter into arrangements that threaten my safety. Last night I did both."

"Big Julie's bodyguard always carries a gun," Jack said, not looking up from what he was reading. "Maybe Big Julie, too. Surely there are other weapons in the suite." He turned a page. "Putting himself in harm's way—possibly getting shot—*that's* the 'grievous bodily harm' that's *prohibited* in my client's probation agreement. That's what *you're* supposed to prevent happening to *him*."

"Right," Tanner said. "Grievous bodily harm, no have to do. And in return for not suing you for violating the terms of my probation and requiring me to do things I'm not trained for and thus in doing them might die, all I asked you for—through Special Agents Gauger and Frelly here—was that you choose to enforce the law in one way rather than another. Give the ranch back to Derek McNaughton—"

"Which is entirely within your purview to do," Jack interrupted.

"—instead of keeping it for yourself," Tanner finished. "Besides, what do you want with a ranch?"

"It's all crap," Frelly said morosely. He took a little amber bottle of pills from his pocket, pried off the lid, and shook two into his hand. Popping them into his mouth, he gulped some coffee, swished it around in his mouth, and swallowed with a grimace.

"Agent Frelly," Tanner said. "I see you're not yet recovered from the attack of the killer beets. How are you feeling?"

"My head feels like a watermelon thrown off a ten-story building," Frelly said. "Thanks for asking."

Jack looked up from the papers. "This is acceptable," he said to Tanner. "Sign here." He handed Tanner a pen and Tanner signed the document, promising that he would not sue the agents, and in exchange, the FBI agreed not to retain the deed of the ranch they'd seized according to federal property forfeiture laws in the arrest of Big Julie Saladino. Instead, they would revert the deed to Derek McNaughton, the original owner of the property.

"See? We do know how to type," Andrews said, as he countersigned.

"I never doubted it," Tanner said.

After they left the federal building, Tanner treated Jack to a cup of real coffee from a real coffee shop. "What now?" Jack asked, as he took a long swallow and sighed in satisfaction. "Or are we done with this?"

"We're done with the feds," Tanner said, drinking some of his own coffee. "Now, all I have to do is find Derek McNaughton and persuade him to do the right thing."

"Sounds like fun," Jack said with a grin. "You need me for that part, too?"

"Are you kidding? You and everybody else. Here's my plan." Tanner lowered his voice and started to talk.

By the time Tanner had filled Jack in, they'd had something to eat, and they'd gone to Jack's office where he'd filed one set of papers and created another set, Tanner was starting to feel more optimistic than he'd felt since he first spotted Hope at Big Julie's card game. He'd been calling Hope all afternoon to no avail, but with this progress, he at least had something positive to report. *Now I can explain everything*, he thought as he called her again in midafternoon and listened to her cell phone ring. She didn't answer—*again*—so he left a message and then called the house. Faith picked up.

"Faith, it's Tanner," he said.

"Tanner, how *could* you?" Faith asked, her voice charged with anger and reproach. "You played against Hope, and you *cheated?*"

"There were extenuating circumstances," he said. "Is Hope there? I'd like to explain."

"She's here, but she went to say goodbye to the uncles and then she sold Banjo and now she's sleeping, so I'm not going to wake her. She's had a long week and she's really upset. We all are. You know, Tanner, in the old days they used to *kill* card cheats."

Tanner exhaled on a sigh. "I'll explain everything as soon as I can. But right now I'm in Jack Sievers's office, and he needs to talk to your mom."

"What about?"

"He's going to explain that to your mom, okay?"

"We don't need a lawyer," Faith said.

"Faith, cut me some slack here," Tanner said, losing patience. "I've been up all night and I'm tired and upset, too. Put your mother on the phone. Please."

Faith sniffed. "All right," she said. "I'll get her. Just so you know that we are very disappointed in you, Tanner. *Very* disappointed."

Disappointed, hell. That was the least of it. Tanner rubbed his gritty eyes. He was now officially heading toward thirty hours with no sleep, and he was exhausted, annoyed, and terrified. What if this didn't work and Hope never spoke to him again? What if it *did* work and Hope refused to see him anyway? What then?

"Yes?" said Suzanne. "Tanner?"

"Suzanne," Tanner said. "Listen. I'm with Jack Sievers. He's a lawyer, an old friend of mine. He got Faith's truck back when the cops took it."

"Oh, yes," Suzanne said. "She mentioned that."

"Okay, good," Tanner said. "He needs to represent you. Officially, I mean. There has to be paperwork. I'm going to put him on the phone now, and he'll tell you what you have to do."

"Okay," Suzanne said. "Paperwork? Represent me for what?"

"Jack will explain everything," Tanner said, handing the phone to his friend.

A short time later, Marty was in his room packing. The clock radio, tuned to an opera station, had Tosca on the air, with Maria Callas singing the lead. Now *that* gal had a set of pipes. Marty hummed along as he emptied drawers and hangers.

Just when Maria hit her high C in the Act Three, Presto! Su, Mario! section, his phone rang.

"Yeah," he said when he picked up the phone.

"Marty, it's Tanner Wingate. I need—"

Marty hung up. The aria built to a powerful crescendo as Marty jammed his socks into the pockets of his wheeled carry-on and grabbed his shirts off their hangers. The clanking hangers chimed in with the orchestral cymbals.

The phone rang again.

"Yeah," Marty said, folding the shirts.

"Don't hang up," Tanner said.

Marty hung up. He took his extra pants out of the room's dresser and folded them, putting them on top of the shirts. Callas's voice rose above the thundering timpani as Marty jammed down the lid of the carry-on and zipped it shut.

The phone rang again. This time Marty checked the caller ID. *Him again.*

"Hope's in trouble!" Tanner yelled just before Marty yelled "Get lost!"

There was an instant of silence.

"You *caused* the trouble, you jackass," Marty said. "I'm not talking to you."

"I can fix it," Tanner said fast, before Marty could hang up.

There was another instant of silence.

"You got a plan?" Marty said finally.

"Yes," said Tanner. "But I need your help."

"I'm listening," Marty said.

Thirty minutes later, Marty had unpacked his suitcase and was out at the curb of the Golden Palace. A new, black SUV rolled up to the red velvet rope, the back window purred down, and Tanner stuck his head out.

"Marty, there's room up front," he said.

Marty opened the front door and got in. He glanced with no apparent nervousness at Kenji, a two-hundred-fifty-pound mountain behind the wheel. Then he turned around to talk to Tanner, who sat in the back with Jack Sievers.

"These aren't your wheels," he said. "This ride's too nice for you. You carjack this vehicle?"

"I couldn't fit everybody in my truck," Tanner said. "Kenji Hasegawa is your driver. And Jack Sievers here is an attorney. Kenji, Jack, this is Marty."

The men all nodded, sizing each other up.

"You're the muscle?" Marty asked, looking at Kenji with interest.

"No, *you're* the muscle," Tanner said. "You're the one supplying all the gravitas."

"Gravitas?" Marty asked. "I thought that was a smoked fish."

Kenji smiled. "A smoked fish," he said. "Good one."

"Hey," Jack said. "I thought *I* was gravitas. I'm the lawyer."

"I'm biggest," Kenji said. "I'm gravitas. The smoked fish."

"You can all be gravitas," Tanner said. "Mainly I need Kenji to *look* threatening, Marty to *be* threatening, and Jack to do the paperwork."

"What will you be doing while we're all being gravitas?" Jack asked.

"I will be restraining myself from killing the bastard," Tanner said.

Everyone observed a moment of silence.

"Will there be weapons?" Marty asked, clinically disinterested.

Kenji glanced at Tanner in the rearview mirror. "Weapons? Nobody said anything about weapons. Should I have brought my knives?"

Marty sized up Kenji again. "You're a knife man?"

"Well—I'm a chef. The knives are incidental."

Marty laughed. "This will be fun."

"That's what I think, too," Tanner said, not smiling at all.

Kenji, following the instructions of the SUV's GPS system, got them to Derek McNaughton's place without mishap. He pulled up to the curb, parked, turned off the engine. They all looked at the house.

"I'm feeling a lot better about this now," Kenji said.

Tanner glanced at him, surprised. "What do you mean?"

Kenji shrugged. "Well. you're my friend and I'd help you regardless, but—" He looked out at Derek McNaughton's place.

"Derek McNaughton's got money," Kenji finished.

"Hell, yes," Marty said. "That's an effing mansion."

"Well, a small mansion," Jack corrected.

"Okay," Marty agreed. "A *small* effing mansion. Who would have guessed he had any money? He's not much of a card player."

"Looks like he's got a *lot* of money," Jack said.

"Some of it was Hope's money," Tanner said, feeling a spurt of rage for Derek McNaughton's theft. "Let's go in and get it back." He got out of the car, slamming the door with more force than was necessary, and strode to the front door.

Marty stepped in front of him and rang the bell while Jack detoured over to the garage. He put his hands against a glass window and leaned in to see.

"Car's here," he said, coming back and dusting off his hands. "Nice Mercedes E-Series. I looked at one of those when I was trading up."

"He's here, then," Tanner said, hearing how grim he sounded.

Marty rang again, and then they heard footsteps approach and the door swung open. Derek was tall, and his posture was straight and relaxed. His light hair had gone mostly gray and his freckled face was weathered from the sun, but his light blue eyes were clear.

Hope's got good genes, Tanner realized. He didn't like him any better because of it.

"Marty!" Derek said, looking surprised. "And Tanner? Tanner Wingate? Who are the rest of your friends? And what are you doing here?"

"Long story," Marty said. "Can we come in?"

"I'm not sure—" Derek said, but Marty had already

pushed his way past the front door.

Tanner followed Marty into the house. "We're the guys who're helping Hope," he said. "Remember her? She's your daughter."

A half-hour later, Tanner lost his temper.

"The ranch is mine," Derek said. "You said so yourself. You got it back from the feds. I appreciate that. Thank you."

"We didn't get it back for you, you son-of-a—"

"Tanner." Marty raised his hand and turned to Derek. "You're the middleman here, Derek. The feds can take back the ranch, or you can sell it to Suzanne for a reasonable amount. Either way, you won't keep it. And why let the feds have it?"

"I don't see why I shouldn't keep it. It's mine now. Are you sure you won't have any of this melon? It's delicious."

Kenji reached out for the melon plate and picked it up.

"We're not here for melon," he said, and carried it into the kitchen.

"Big guy," Derek said, as he watched Kenji disappear down the hallway.

"And he knows how to use knives," Jack said.

"Like a *pro*," Tanner said.

"*So like I said*." Marty glared at all of them. "That ranch is going to Suzanne."

"The hell it is," Derek said.

Feeling crowded by anger and inaction, Tanner jumped to his feet. All eyes swiveled to him.

"Derek, let me spell it out for you," he said. "You're going to sell the ranch to Suzanne for a fair price."

A smile creased Derek's face. "Fair market value is two million dollars."

"Not even close," Tanner snorted. "One dollar. Jack has the paperwork right here."

Derek laughed. "You're crazy." He started to get up just as Kenji came back from the kitchen. "Excuse me, boys,

I've got to—"

Tanner put his hands on Derek's shoulders and shoved him down so hard the chair rocked back. Derek's eyes opened in shock.

"Sit down, Derek, while I explain why one dollar is a fair market price. Seventeen years ago when you abandoned your family, you had two minor children and a wife who was unemployable."

"She was a showgirl," Derek said. "She made good money."

"Not two kids later, she didn't. Or couldn't, with limited education and no other skills," Tanner said.

"We split the assets in the divorce," Derek said.

"She kept the cash, you kept the ranch," Tanner nodded. "She used the thirty thousand to support them all while she looked for a job because you didn't pay alimony or child support. When the cash ran out, your older daughter, Hope—remember her?—she was fifteen. She got a job off the books after school to help meet expenses, because *you*, Derek, charged them rent."

"Suzanne never complained," Derek said.

"When did Suzanne ever complain?" Marty asked. "That's why you married her. Now shut up, Derek, because if you don't, I can make you."

"You wouldn't," Derek said, but he glanced at Marty's fists.

"Any of us would," Marty said, unclenching his hands and rubbing them down the legs of his pants.

"*So*," Tanner said, "because Suzanne wouldn't ask a herd of stampeding buffalo to stop trampling her, you never paid child support and you never paid alimony. You charged them rent. You didn't maintain your property. You didn't contribute to your kids' college educations—"

"I don't have to do that!" Derek said. "They're eighteen, they're adults. They don't have to go to college."

"You are pathetic," Kenji said, shaking his head. "I wish

I had my knives. My *dull* knives."

"I never liked you," Marty said to Derek. "In all those years, we only tolerated you because we loved Little Hope and we worried about how you dragged her all over. We thought if you were taking her into card rooms when she should have been home in bed, we should be there, too. At least, that way we knew nothing really terrible would happen to her. But you were a pathetic excuse for a father."

"Marty!" Derek said, sounding wounded.

"*Here's how I figure it*," Tanner said, getting their attention back. "If Suzanne had gone to court, she'd have been entitled to a share of your earnings. The child support you never paid, that would have been about one-fifty, two hundred G's. Based on your earnings. Maybe more, now that I see this house."

"Never!" said Derek.

"The alimony you never paid for seventeen years, that would have been about six hundred thousand," Tanner said.

Derek sounded strangled.

Tanner grinned, a feral grin. "Should have stayed married, huh? The health insurance the court would have ordered for your kids and Suzanne over the years, about one-fifty, two hundred more. That takes me to just under a million. Add in a few trips to Disneyland, a couple of prom dresses, some college expenses, and what-have-you, and I make it something over a million."

"Sounds about right," Jack said, nodding.

"Plus the alimony you're *still* not paying Suzanne," Tanner said. "And, worst of all, the winnings you stole from Hope when she was a minor and still trying to earn your affection, you miserable creep."

"He did *that?*" Marty asked. "I never knew that."

"He did," Tanner said. "I'd like to know how much it was."

"I have a pretty good idea." Marty settled back, his eyes hooded. He looked at Derek like he was a dead, smelly thing he'd found in a sewer. "It's a good thing I didn't know that then," he said.

"It's not too late to do something about it now," Kenji said, sounding hopeful.

"Add it all up, you owe them big time," Tanner said, turning back to Derek. "And that's why you'll be transferring the ranch to Suzanne for a dollar."

"No," Derek said.

"Yes," Tanner said. "And here's the part you'll never get. They are a terrific family. Suzanne has worked her butt off at a diner all this time to make ends meet. Hope got an MBA with no help from anybody, and now she's a chief financial officer at a software company."

Kenji nodded. "Faith has her own business. She grows organic vegetables. Beautiful produce. And your grand-daughter. Little Amber—"

"I have a granddaughter?" Derek asked.

Kenji frowned. "How could you not know you have a granddaughter? She's *eleven*. You haven't even talked to them in eleven years? Amber likes to cook. She and I are writing a cook-book together."

"And you *dumped* them," Tanner said, feeling his anger start to boil over. "You ran out on them. And for what? They weren't *good enough* for you?"

"It wasn't like that—" Derek said.

"It was *exactly* like that," Tanner said. "Jack, give him the papers."

"Sign here," Jack said, pushing the papers and a pen across the coffee table.

"You don't understand!" Derek said, his voice rising. "I *can't*!"

"You can, and you will," Tanner said, fury making his voice cold.

"No. I mean it. I really can't." Derek dropped his head into his hands. "I'm broke," he said, his voice muffled.

Tanner rolled his eyes. "Oh, right, I'm seeing that," he

said. "*Shut up and sign the papers.*"

"It's true," Derek said, his head still bowed. "I'm washed up. Penniless. The ranch is all I've got. Julie Saladino's buyer is still interested. I'm selling it to him."

"No, you're not," Tanner said, clenching his fists. "You're selling it to *Suzanne*. You don't seem to understand your situation here, Derek. We're here to make sure you do sign these papers. Using whatever means we have to."

Derek lifted his head and looked at Tanner's face. He swallowed.

"Look. I got no income," Derek said, looking at them with eyes full of helplessness. "I—I can't play cards anymore."

"What do you mean?" Marty asked. "You in a twelve-step program or something?"

"No," Derek said. He sat silent.

"*Talk*," Tanner snarled.

Derek exhaled. "Well. I'd been doing good. When I was on my own. Got lucky enough to buy this house, some other stuff."

Tanner grabbed the front of Derek's shirt, yanking him out of the chair. "You think leaving your kids was *lucky?* You won a lot of money but gave them *nothing?* Because it was *lucky?*"

Marty stood up and put his hand on Tanner's arm. "Let him say what he has to say."

Tanner let go of Derek's shirt. Derek bounced back down into the chair, looking relieved.

"So I was doing okay, and then, after a while, I wasn't. Had a spell of bad cards. And I…"

"*What?*" Tanner barked.

"I made a deal. At the casino. With a dealer," Derek said.

Tanner shook his head with contempt.

"You are an idiot," he said. "You conspired with a card room employee to rip off the casino?"

Derek looked embarrassed. "Something like that," he said.

"He dealt you high cards and when you won, you gave him a kickback?"

"Something like that," Derek said again.

"So the casino found out, the employee was fired, and you're banned from the casinos for life," Marty said.

Derek looked at the floor.

Tanner scowled at the washed-up gambler. Hope—the whole family—was better off without this loser.

"That doesn't change anything," he said. "Suzanne still gets the ranch. You weren't charged with a crime. You can get a job and earn money that way. Millions of people do it."

"I don't know anything but cards!" Derek protested.

"Actually, Derek, you don't know cards all that well, either," Marty said.

"No kidding," Jack said. "So has anything changed here, or are we going ahead?"

"Nothing's changed," Tanner said. "Derek will sign the papers selling the ranch for one dollar to Suzanne. If he doesn't, we hurt him."

"Or worse," Marty said.

"Hurt you can't imagine," Jack said. "IRS hurt."

Tanner frowned. "I was thinking I'd just beat him to a bloody pulp."

Derek flinched.

"I can't advise your doing that," Jack said. "It would not look good on your resume, and Mr. McNaughton's having to get a job for the rest of his life will be punishment enough."

"But what can I do?" Derek said. "I'm not qualified for anything!"

Tanner smiled, an evil smile.

"I have an idea," he said.

Chapter 29

"Where to now?" Kenji asked as, business concluded, the men piled into the SUV parked in front of Derek's house.

"Home," Tanner said. "I've got dinner with my folks and Troy in about an hour and I'm driving her to LA tomorrow. Jack, are we square with the paperwork?"

Jack patted his briefcase. "For now. I still have to get the mandatory survey and inspections completed, stuff like that. Just dotting the i's and crossing the t's. That will take me a couple of days. For all intents and purposes, Suzanne McNaughton owns the ranch. I'll call her and tell her tomorrow once I have everything lined up."

"I appreciate this, Jack."

"Crap, Wingate. I wouldn't have any fun at all if I didn't have you for a client. Anyway, I'm sending you a bill."

Tanner felt euphoric as he entered the house, but cold fear caught up with him as the evening wore on. He tried to reach Hope before and after his dinner and before he fell into bed, but she never picked up.

The next morning, Tanner sat shotgun in Troy's only slightly used Miata as she peeled down Interstate 15 on their way to Los Angeles. She looked like she was having a great time, singing and tapping her fingers on the steering wheel in time to the music. And why wouldn't she be having a good time? She was driving a blue convertible.

She was going to college. She was on her way.

Tanner slumped against the side of the car, trying to get in the mood of the road trip, trying catch Troy's enthusiasm. But instead he felt—unsettled.

Hope was not answering her phone. There could be a million reasons for that. It was turned off. The battery had died. She'd lost the damn thing. She was at work. She was out riding. She'd gone deaf. She'd joined the French Foreign Legion and was hunting bandits in the Sahara on a camel.

He stared out at the desert landscape—the hot brown hills, the scrubby plants, the rocky terrain—wanting to see, *somehow*, Hope on a horse or a camel or even in a car. Nothing.

Where was she? It was almost two full days since she'd lost that damn stupid card game. She should know by now that the ranch was Suzanne's. Hope couldn't still be mad at him, could she? By now the McNaughtons should be partying.

So why wasn't she talking to him? He didn't want to think what it might mean that Hope wouldn't talk to him.

Tanner reached down to his knapsack at his feet and took out his phone.

"Daddy, who are you trying to call? Is it Hope? Are you having relationship problems *already?*"

"I'm not having relationship problems," Tanner said.

"Who are you calling then?"

Tanner sighed. "Hope," he said. He dialed. Listened to her voice mail kick in. He hung up. He'd already left a bunch of messages, and he didn't need to leave another one.

Troy leaned over and patted his arm in sympathy. "If she's mad at you, no wonder you're grouchy."

"It's nice that you care, sweetheart, but fathers don't get grouchy, they take away the car keys if their daughters don't watch the road."

Troy laughed and put her hand back on the steering wheel. "And you think you're not grouchy!"

"Absolutely not," Tanner said. "You're going to college,

we're taking a road trip, and we're having a great time."

Troy glanced at him thoughtfully. "You still look tired. Why don't you take a nap? We're a long way from LA, and when the phone rings, you'll hear it."

Tanner nodded, hunching down on the seat and closing his eyes. But what if the phone never rang?

Monday morning, when Hope went into the kitchen for breakfast, she saw two men wearing work coveralls, masks, and gloves scraping paint from the kitchen windows.

"Who are you, and what are you doing here?" she asked, not even really trying to control her anger. They didn't have to leave the ranch for two more weeks. Big Julie or his buyers didn't need to have workmen in their kitchen *yet*.

One of the men straightened up, pulling off his mask. "Bob" was stitched over his pocket.

"Sorry to bother you," Bob said. "We're here for the lead abatement survey. You know, it's mandatory now after a place has been sold."

"Can't you do this later?" Hope asked, her voice tight. "Like in about three weeks?"

Bob looked doubtful. "I don't think so. The lawyer said we had to get this done as soon as possible. Acted like it was a big rush."

Hope sighed. There was nothing she could say about it, really. The place wasn't theirs. It just seemed so—*rude*.

"What else do you have to do?" she asked.

"Just the lead," Bob said cheerfully. "Some samples from the windows, walls, anywhere we see paint, and we're out of your hair. Shouldn't be too long."

"Fine," Hope said. "I have some calls to make, so if you can be as quiet as possible, I would appreciate that."

"You won't even know we're here," Bob promised.

Fat chance of that, Hope thought, pouring herself some coffee.

"That sure smells good," Bob said wistfully.

It's not his fault that Big Julie sold our place.

"Help yourself," Hope sighed. "Cups are in the second cupboard by the door."

As the workmen poured themselves some coffee, Hope settled down with the day-old Sunday paper. She read all the real estate ads carefully, circling the best options and calling to make appointments for viewings. None of her possibilities were good ones. She'd just do the best she could—and hope she was luckier at finding housing than she was at clutch poker games.

By Wednesday morning, Tanner was back in Las Vegas, feeling something approaching terror. Why hadn't Hope called him? He'd survived LA traffic, settled Troy in her dorm room, taken her and her new roommate out for pizza, done some shopping, attended a parents-of-new-students briefing, and deflected with as much grace and tact as he could the interest of several single moms also visiting the campus.

He'd also called Hope several times each day. He'd never reached her.

Then he'd flown home, checked his answering machine for messages, and called Hope a couple more times. Nothing.

Hadn't Hope forgiven him yet for that lousy card game? Wasn't she happy now that her family had the ranch back? In frustration, he called Jack.

"So what's going on with the McNaughtons?" he asked when his friend picked up.

"Well, hello to you, too," Jack said. "When did you get home?"

"An hour ago," Tanner said. "Haven't you called Suzanne yet?"

"The paperwork's almost done," Jack said. "Everything should be filed and finished by tomorrow. Suzanne, however, is a hard woman to reach. I called all day Monday and never got her, so I sent her a letter. She should get that today. Tomorrow at the outside."

"You just stopped calling? So they don't know they own the ranch yet?"

"They do not," Jack said.

"That's great!" Tanner said. "Well, not great, but a load off my mind."

"And yet, you're a wreck," Jack said. "I take it your girlfriend's still not speaking to you."

"Not yet," Tanner said. "But she will. I'm driving out to her place right now, and I plan to charm the daylights out of her."

"There's a plan," Jack said. "But you want to make sure that she's home first. I'm not kidding, those people never answer their phone."

On Wednesday morning Hope got ready to look at houses and interview real estate agents.

"I'm optimistic," she told Faith as she tossed the newspaper and her notebook into her bag. "These places can't *all* suck. We've *seen* all the sucky ones already."

Faith grinned. "That's being optimistic?"

"Absolutely. I fully believe that there's an overpriced, badly maintained house we can afford to buy. Want to come along?"

Faith laughed outright. "Sounds like fun, but I can't. The uncles are taking Amber and me for her birthday helicopter ride over the Grand Canyon."

Hope smiled. "I forgot about that! Well, maybe after I look at the sucky places to live I'll go shopping with Baby."

"From what you've said, it seems like all Baby ever does is shop."

Hope grinned. "She needs an outfit. She thinks that Big Julie is planning to say goodbye, and she wants to wear something that will make him realize what he'll be missing."

"What kind of outfit is that?"

"I'm not sure. With Baby, it wouldn't take much. A nice burlap sack should do it. We probably have one in the barn

I could give her. So—can I drop you off at the airport, or wherever, and pick you up afterwards?"

"That'd be nice. Call Baby and make your plans and I'll get Amber."

They shut Squeegee in the barn again, and the dog whined and jumped against the door when she realized she wasn't going along with them.

"First thing we do when we get settled, Amber, is send Squeegee to obedience school. No more surgery for cut hands," said Hope, as she and Faith climbed into the front seat of the car and Amber settled into the back, her arm propped on a pillow.

"She didn't *mean* to," Amber said earnestly. "She just likes to play."

"I know, she's a happy dog, that's the good part. If we'd given you a vicious, knife-wielding killer dog for your birthday, I think your mom would be *really* upset."

Amber giggled. But as she looked out the window, she got quiet. "Do we really have to move?" she asked. "I was thinking about my old school. I might miss it. You know. A little bit."

A blinding rush of rage ripped so unexpectedly through Hope's chest that she lost her breath. She'd like to strangle Derek with her bare hands. He was like poison dropped from the sky, killing everything in his path. And Tanner would be next. If she ever had the chance—

She felt Faith's hand on her shoulder, patting her gently. She took a deep, shaky breath, trying to get her equilibrium back.

"Hope's just looking at places today," Faith said. "We won't make any decisions until we see it, too. And then we'll invite all your old friends over to see you, you can have overnights and Saturdays with them, that will be fun, and you'll make a lot of new friends at your new school. And it'll be a lot bigger. I bet you'll have a lot of really cool classes. They might even have a computer lab."

"I know," Amber said, her voice very small.

"You'll be able to see Kenji and Tanner more often, too," Hope said, trying to get on Faith's everything-will-be-great bandwagon.

"Next week your hand will be a lot better, sweetie," Faith said. "You and Kenji will be cooking up a storm and having loads of fun. And we will, too, while we sample it. Hope, let's stop for the mail while we're here."

Hope pulled up to the mailbox at the end of their long driveway, seeing the little red flag pushed up, signaling delivery. She leaned out of the window and, opening the box, pulled out a handful of envelopes and catalogs.

"Here's some stuff about vegetable boxes for you," she said, handing business letters to Faith. "Catalogs for you, Amber." She smiled at the girl as she handed the slick glossies back to her.

"I haven't had the heart to tell the customers that the business is over," Faith said, flipping through her envelopes. "I haven't even told Kenji. I've got to do that soon."

Hope didn't reply. She was staring at a slim, cream-colored embossed envelope that lay on top of the stack. She glanced at the return address. A law firm. Mecklenburg and Sievers. Addressed to their mother.

More letters from law firms. More bad news. It never rained but it poured at the McNaughton place.

"I'll take Mom's mail," she said, stuffing it, along with her own bills, into her bag. "Do you want me to take yours? What if the breeze from the helicopter blows everything away?"

"Would hate to lose those bills," Faith agreed, smiling, as she handed Hope her mail. "Oh, no."

Hope laughed as she stuffed the mail into her bag and tossed the bag into the back seat. "We're off," she said as she closed the mailbox door and turned left onto the highway.

When Tanner failed to reach anyone at the McNaughton ranch, failed to reach Hope on her cell phone, and failed to reach Faith, he called Baby. Desperate times called for desperate measures.

"Sure, I know where Hope is," Baby said. "What's the problem? She's coming over here. We're going shopping."

Tanner held the phone out away from his ear and stared at it in astonishment. He'd been trying to talk to Hope for *four days*. Now he finds out she's talking to *Baby?* All this time *Baby* knew where Hope was?

"I need a very *particular* kind of outfit," Baby said now. "And I think she needs one, too. You know, Tanner, you've been really mean to Hope. She told me what happened at that card game. And now Big Julie is in really big trouble, and Hope is upset, and *I'm* upset, and it's all your fault. Everybody is really, really mad at you."

"I know," Tanner said. "I'm trying to fix it, but honestly, Baby, I can't fix anything with Big Julie. He's in trouble, no lie. But maybe I can fix everything with Hope. I really need to see her. How about if I come over now?"

"No," Baby said. "Then she'd be really mad at *me*."

"Hope doesn't need an outfit," Tanner said. "She looks great no matter what she wears. Please?"

"Aw, that's sweet," Baby said. "Why couldn't Big Julie ever say nothing like that to me? No."

"Baby, I am a desperate man here. I can't fix things with Hope if you don't let me see her. *Please.*"

Baby sighed. "All right. But you better make it good, or she'll be mad *and* I'll be mad. Come over when we get back. Around three-thirty."

"Thank you," Tanner said, feeling a rush of relief. "I'll be there. And—Baby. I'm sorry about Big Julie. Although I think you can find somebody better."

"I think I'm going to have to," Baby said, sounding a little bit sad.

"We must find him!" Johnny Red shouted to his colleagues. "We must make our move! It is now or never!"

"What do you want us to do?" Markov asked. He was eating a club sandwich that room service had delivered. Markov loved room service. You just called, and twenty minutes later, the food arrived, hot and delicious, at your door. Of course, Johnny Red had taught him to realize that the food was brought by a member of the oppressed working class who would never own a share in the means of production. But after Markov signed the slip and saw what the waiter earned with the mandatory tip, he wasn't convinced that the waiter was truly oppressed. He wondered what the waiter's base salary was. Perhaps, in fact, the waiter *could* afford to own a tiny portion of the means of production. Because look at their own line of work. It wasn't all gravy. Johnny Red tended to be a capricious employer. Danger lurked in every operation. The competition was fierce. And considering how much Markov had to pay his lieutenants, and how nice it was in Vegas, maybe he could become a waiter himself and—

"We must try again!" Johnny Red said, pounding on the table, causing Markov to jump to attention and making his sandwich bounce on its plate. "We must storm the Winter Palace! We must overtake the guards!"

"You wand uth do gidnap Big Chulie again?" Igor asked, horrified. He had temporary caps on the six teeth he'd smashed when he'd crashed the getaway car into the getaway truck Alexei had stolen. His broken nose was swollen, making breathing difficult, and he couldn't sleep from the pain of his bruised ribs and broken ankle. He still walked with crutches. He didn't feel up to pushing Big Julie into a laundry cart and running through the casino with him again.

"That didn't work out so good last time," Yakov agreed. Although Yakov had bounced around some in the vegetable truck and had bruises to prove it, he hadn't been seriously injured. Still, he didn't relish repeating the experience.

"Comrades, have courage!" Johnny Red bellowed. And then, in a severe lapse of his Communist training added,

"To the victors belong the spoils!"

"Well, we ain't exactly victors here," Markov said, working on his last bite of ham and turkey on toasted focaccia with a swirl of garlic aioli.

Johnny Red whirled on him.

"*Yet!*" Markov added quickly.

"We must act quickly and with precision!" Johnny Red said. "We must be as sharp as the Bolsheviks' bayonets, and we must be as courageous as the Stalingrad defenders. My friends, we will win, or we will die trying!"

"*Die?*" Yakov repeated, hoping that Johnny Red was speaking in metaphors.

"Could dying be worthan thith?" Igor said, who felt pretty close to dying right now.

"You really should try these curly fries," Markov said, generously pushing the plate into the center of the table for all to reach.

"Bah!" Johnny Red said, but he took one of the spiral french fries, dipped it in the sauce, and popped it in his mouth.

"Food for the petty bourgeois," he said with contempt as he chewed. Then he looked up in surprise. "But it's good. What's that white stuff?"

"Garlic aioli," Markov said. "Smooth yet tangy."

Johnny Red took another curly fry and swabbed it in the garlic aioli as the others gathered around the table. Then he leaned forward conspiratorially, waving the curly fry.

"All right," he said. "Here's my plan."

Tanner entered the Desert Dunes Resort and Casino at three o'clock and realized he was a half-hour too early to meet Baby and Hope. To kill some time, he opened his phone and checked his messages. One from Amber, telling him about the helicopter ride, which he returned, telling her what he was doing; one from Troy, which had to wait; and one from Jack. Nothing from Hope. He strolled through the resort, stopping briefly to stare at a black sequined dress in the window of an expensive shop. He briefly imagined Hope in it, although she didn't need sequins to sparkle.

At three-twenty he headed for the elevators that led to the suites. As he walked down the hallway, he saw a group of five men step into a waiting car. They looked like tough guys fallen on hard times—they were all big, but they all moved slowly because two of them limped and the third was on crutches. Tanner picked up his pace, trying to catch them, but even so, by the time he got to the elevator bank, the doors had closed and the elevator had ascended.

He watched the lit numbers above the doors increase as the elevator rose. Fourteen, fifteen, sixteen. Sixteen stayed hot. The men were getting off on the sixteenth floor. The floor of Baby's and Big Julie's suite.

What were five men, one on crutches, doing on Baby's floor? Of course, there was another suite on the floor. They didn't *have* to be going to see Baby and Hope. Still.

Tanner was curious. And a little uneasy.

He punched the call button and waited impatiently for a car to descend, watching the numbers over the elevator doors as the cars rose or descended toward the lobby. Behind him he barely noticed the dinging of the games, the whooping of the winners, the conversations of the tourists, and the piped-in music.

"Wingate!"

Tanner turned and saw FBI Special Agent Roy Frelly puffing slightly as he strode toward the elevators. "Where the hell do you think you're going?"

Tanner sighed and glanced at the elevator display. The closest car had paused at five on its downward trajectory. Eight more months to deal with Las Vegas's idea of federal law enforcement. It seemed like a lifetime.

"Agent Frelly, what a surprise," Tanner said. "Are you following me?"

"Heck no," Frelly said. "Why bother? We got your phone number. No. I got other fish to fry, and I saw Johnny Red come in here and go up these elevators."

"Who?"

"Johnny Red. I showed you a picture the other day, remember? The Russian mob guy. He just went up to Big Julie's suite. Him and his henchmen. Sixteen-oh-one. At least we assume that's where he's headed, since he wants to kill Big Julie and all. Not that he'll find him there." Frelly scowled briefly. "His lawyers sprung Big Julie today. We put him on a plane back to Jersey."

Tanner felt the floor open up and swallow him. He didn't know much about the Russian mob, but he knew they were ruthless. They wouldn't let anyone get in their way. *And they were headed for Big Julie's suite.*

And in Big Julie's suite, Hope would definitely be in their way.

"The Russian mob is upstairs in Big Julie's suite?" he demanded. "Hope—my—my—fiancee's up there! And Baby! They could get hurt!"

"Jesus, Wingate! You know that for sure? Why do you always hold out on me?" Frelly's red face turned six shades darker. "We got SWAT in position! Now you're telling me there's civilians in Big Julie's suite? A baby? Listen! You stay here, understand? Don't do nothing stupid! Don't go nowhere! I gotta let the SWAT team know! I gotta call backup!"

Frelly pulled out his phone and punched a number into it as he churned down the hallway. "Hold your positions!" Tanner heard him yell into the phone. "We got civilians in the suite, and the Russians are coming!"

Tanner watched as Frelly steamed into the security office. Russian mobsters had headed upstairs to take out Big Julie, the FBI was on it, and that could mean gunfire, with Hope and Baby in the middle of it. Minutes counted here. Anything could happen while Frelly was doing whatever he was doing. And a SWAT team—Tanner shuddered to think of a SWAT team managed by Frelly.

Behind him, the elevator dinged and the doors opened. Without a second thought, Tanner stepped inside the car and punched the button for sixteen.

Chapter 30

Hope had laid her new outfit out on Baby's bed to look it over when the suite's doorbell rang. The dress was elegant, deep blue in a gauzy fabric with a cinched waist and tiny rhinestone buttons down the front. Hope had no idea where she could wear it, but Baby had said, if the dress was right, you would find the occasion.

She had put out the earrings and shoes to go with it when Baby called her from the dining room.

"Hope, honey? Can you come in here a minute?"

Baby's voice sounded funny, but Hope didn't think a thing of it until she entered the room and saw Baby sitting on one side of the big table with five burly men sitting at the other.

"What's going on?" Hope asked.

"Have a seat," the oldest man said to Hope.

"Is we going to have varenikis again?" one of the big ones said, looking eagerly at Baby.

"No!" Baby squeaked.

"*Have a seat*," the oldest one said again.

That's when Hope noticed that he was pointing a gun at her.

Hope looked at the business end of the weapon and, in a second, thought of all the time she'd wasted being furious and hurt at Tanner, of how much she loved her sister and mother. How she'd never see Amber grow up. How she'd never again feel the sun on her face or the cool softness of the water in Tanner's swimming pool or the hot roughness of his hands on her skin. Or hear Tanner's heart beating against hers as she slept next to him.

How she'd be killed in this suite in the Desert Dunes. By mobsters.

This is what comes of playing cards with Big Julie, she thought. Not that she'd have a chance to do *that* again.

Hot dizziness swept over her and she had to grab the edge of the table for support. Panic and loss filled her throat as she stared at the ugly weapon that would end her life.

She and Baby would die here. Nobody would know. Nobody could stop it.

And then her little voice spoke to her. Her old impatient friend, the one who made her think hard and make tough choices.

Don't die. Live.

Hope gasped, clutching the table until her fingers cramped.

Suck it up. Figure something out.

She sat down abruptly, even as dark pinpoints started to sprinkle behind her eyes.

If I get out of here, I'll tell Tanner—

What would she tell Tanner? What could she say that she hadn't already revealed?

I'll ask him—why did he do it? Why did he lie, cheat, and steal? Why did he let me down? Because I wanted to risk it. I wanted to take a risk with him.

She took a deep breath, shocked to realize what she'd just thought. *She'd wanted to take a risk with Tanner. A card player.* But then there was the game. That had changed everything. And now—now she wouldn't be able to ask him why he'd hurt her, unless she could figure out a way to get out of this mess.

She took another deep breath, and the dizziness passed. The dark prickles behind her eyelids cleared up. She breathed again and looked at the five gunmen. Well—four big, pasty-looking gunmen and one really handsome, nervous-looking kid.

"That's right," Johnny Red said, waving his weapon at her. "Now, let's get acquainted."

Tanner stepped off the elevator at the sixteenth floor and instantly realized the flaw in his plan.

How could he get into the suite?

He decided the direct route was his best choice. He tried the door. It was locked, of course. That would have been too easy. He knocked on the door. He could see movement through the security fisheye in the door, but no one answered.

Tanner stepped back and looked around. He didn't see the SWAT team, although he supposed the purpose of SWAT was to stay hidden until needed. He hoped that they weren't somehow focused on the windows, ready to shoot anything that moved.

He thought about calling out to Hope, but that might put her in danger.

As he stood in the hallway thinking about his options, he heard a whirring clank followed by several thuds and a pneumatic wheeze. Elevator doors—service elevator doors—opened, and then the protesting wheels of a burdened laundry cart squeaked down the hallway.

Tanner smiled.

The maid came around the corner and skidded to a stop when she saw Tanner. Tanner put out his hand and stopped the momentum of the heavy laundry cart.

"*No! No! Por favor!*" she exclaimed. "*No me tome!*"

Don't take me. Where on earth did the maid think he'd take her?

"Hi." Tanner beamed his I'm-completely-safe smile at the diminutive maid who trembled before him, clutching the laundry cart in self-defense.

"I locked myself out," Tanner said, shrugging his shoulders as if to say, *I'm so silly*. "Could you please let me in?"

The maid relaxed. "*Toallas?*" she asked hopefully. *Towels.*

"No *toallas*," Tanner said firmly. He struggled in vain to remember his high school Spanish and then gave it up in frustration. "*Keys*," he said, pointing to the door. "I can't get in."

The maid's eyes clouded. "*Los gángsteres viven allí*," she said. *Gangsters live here.*

"*Sí*," he said, beaming at the maid. "*Soy la policía.*" *I'm the police.*

"No," the maid said, patting her hip. "No gun."

Everybody's suspicious these days, Tanner thought. *Too much television.*

Tanner shook his head and held his finger to his lips, pointing down the hallway. "*SWAT. Por todas partes.*" He made a circle in the air. Would that mean "everywhere" to the maid? He doubted that Frelly's SWAT teams were anywhere, much less everywhere, but maybe he could fool the maid. *Maybe.* If she could understand him. He probably should be jailed for murdering the Spanish language.

But the maid seemed to get it. She opened her eyes wide and glanced down the corridor.

"*Entiendo*," she whispered. "*Sí.*" She silently handed him a stack of clean towels. "*Use este disfraz*," she said.

Tanner grinned at her. She thought that the towels would be a disguise. And maybe they could. And if they didn't, maybe he could smother the Russians with them. He took the towels and then nodded at the locked door.

"*Por favor*," he said.

The maid unlocked the door and pushed it open for him.

"*Muchas gracias*," Tanner said.

He was in.

When Tanner came into the suite's dining room carrying an armful of clean towels, Hope's heart turned a summersault. She was never so glad to see anyone in her life.

But what was he doing here? He wasn't here to see Baby, was he? She felt a pang and quickly smothered it.

Whatever Tanner was here for, he'd walked right into a trap. These guys had *guns*. Didn't the dummy know he could get hurt?

And what was with the towels?

Despite her annoyance, she felt a smile of relief light her face. Towels or no towels, she was happy he'd come. Maybe he could think of a way to get them out of this.

"Who are you?" Johnny Red asked, as Yakov and Markov stood up, brandishing their weapons.

"I brought towels," Tanner said, beaming at the Russians. "I'm her boyfriend." He nodded at Hope, smiling confidently at her.

Boyfriend? Hope thought, shocked. He thinks he's my *boyfriend?* We aren't even *speaking!*

"Then you don't want her to get hurt," Johnny Red said ominously.

"No, I don't. Here's your laundry." Tanner handed Yakov the towels and sat down in the Russian's chair. Yakov looked nonplussed and then headed toward the bathroom with the stack of folded towels, putting his gun on top to weigh them down.

"So, what's going on here?" Tanner asked.

"These are our hostages," Johnny Red said.

"They want to exchange us for Big Julie!" Hope said.

"I already said how that won't work," Baby said. "Big Julie and I are through. I went to see him. He fit me in because Marilyn was getting her hair done! Can you believe that? To *me*, he says that. And then he says he's gotta let me go! He don't care now if I'm a hostage."

"By all the Russian saints and martyrs, he *must* care!" Johnny Red exclaimed in shock. "You are divine! The varenikis!"

Baby turned sad eyes on him. "He don't. I swear. Didn't I give him everything? The best years of my life. And then he picks Marilyn! Although," she added judiciously, "I got a nice severance package."

Tanner nodded. "Big Julie has other plans," he agreed. "He got released on his own recognizance and is making a deal with the feds."

"Released? He got released from *where?* Made a deal with the *feds?*" Alexei asked. He glanced at Johnny Red. "Uncle, maybe—"

"Released on his own recognizance?" Johnny Red asked. "This cannot be! We got a tip! He is here!"

"No," Tanner said. "He was arrested for income tax evasion. I was there. And now he's making a deal. He's not coming back."

"Arrested? *Income tax evasion?*" Johnny Red shouted, jumping up.

Yakov, back from his towel errand, slipped into Johnny Red's chair.

"So can we go now?" Tanner asked. "We're sorry and all that, but—"

"No!" Johnny Red said. "He'll come back for her." He nodded at Baby. "He likes her. He won't want us to hurt her."

"*Hurt* me?" Baby wailed. "Why hurt *me?* Anyway, he won't—"

"I don't think so," Tanner interrupted. "I just ran into the FBI downstairs. They've got a SWAT team positioned, backup on the way. Your tip was a lure to get you here."

"You will be our human shield," Johnny Red said. "All of you. You will get us out."

"I don't think I have the outfit for that," Baby said.

All eyes turned to Baby, wondering what kind of outfit she'd need to be a human shield.

"Your outfit will work fine to shield us," Johnny Red said.

Out of the corner of her eye, Hope saw the Grand Canyon tourist helicopter fly up to their window and hover.

"I think that's the FBI black ops helicopter out there, waiting to shoot you through the windows," she said tentatively. "You better run now. While you still can."

Igor looked through the dining room window at the helicopter that said "Grand Canyon Tours" in huge purple and orange letters.

"Thadth a douritht helicopder," he said. "Idth nod for black opth."

"That's how the FBI paints *all* its black ops helicopters," Hope said firmly. "You think they actually paint them *black*?"

The helicopter flew closer to the Desert Dunes, and Tanner, repressing a grin, turned and squinted through the window. Amber waved energetically at him through the window. He waved back.

"He'th thignalling," Igor said.

Amber leaned back reaching for something and then Marty leaned forward past her and squinted toward the windows.

"Let's see!" Johnny the Red said, leaping toward the windows.

"Do you recognize Marty the Sneak?" Tanner asked, as he waved to Marty. "He's with the Jersey mob. He's identifying you for the agents right now."

Johnny Red gazed out the window, saw Marty, and then with a horrified oath, dropped to the floor. The crash jarred the mobster's weapon, and the gun went off. The blast ricocheted through the suite, and across the room from them, the huge ceramic pot holding the ficus plant splintered into a thousand colorful pieces. The ficus slowly toppled to the floor in a mess of dirt and shattered leaves.

"You shot the ficus!" Tanner yelled. "Be careful with that thing! You could hurt somebody!"

"Stalin's ghosts!" Johnny Red gasped. "We never counted on the FBI! And the Jersey mob is informing! To get us out of the way! They are nothing but the lap dogs of imperialism!"

"I don't know where the SWAT team is," Tanner said,

telling the truth for the first time in the last twenty minutes. "But I think you should get out of here while you still have a chance. We'll stand in the windows so you can get away. They won't shoot us."

Johnny Red pointed the gun up at Hope from his position on the floor.

"Where's Big Julie now?" he asked Tanner. "The truth, or she dies!"

"He's on his way back to FBI headquarters," Tanner lied. "He's meeting with the FBI at—" Tanner glanced at his watch. It was four o'clock. "Four-thirty. You could intercept him if you hurried."

"You could even make a deal with the FBI," Hope said. "Your *own* deal. A *better* deal."

"Yes!" Johnny Red shouted. "Let's go!"

"Uncle, I'm not sure—" Alexei started, but Johnny Red had jumped to his feet and, bending low at the waist to stay clear of the windows and the black ops helicopter outside, tore from the room. The other four men rushed after him. Tanner heard the outer door slam shut behind them. The helicopter peeled away from the window and headed toward the Grand Canyon, two hundred fifty miles away.

Silence filled the room.

"Tanner—" Hope said.

"Just a minute, Pumpkin," Tanner said. He took out his phone and dialed a number.

"Agent Frelly? Tanner Wingate. Listen. Johnny Red and his four associates are heading over to FBI head-quarters right now. If you hurry, you can intercept them."

There was a pause. Hope could hear squawking on the other end of the line.

"Well, it's a long story. They think they're going to intercept Big Julie. Yes, I know he's not there. But if you hurry, you can arrest these guys right now at the elevator. Don't thank me. I'm always happy to help." He closed his phone.

"Tanner—" Hope tried again.

"I'll be right with you, Sweetie," Tanner said. He opened his phone and hit a number on speed dial.

"Jack? Tanner. Listen."

Hope watched him grin and felt a sharp pain shooting through her jaw. She realized she was grinding her teeth.

"I have a new customer for you," Tanner said. "You have to get down to the FBI office right away. The clients have deep but shady pockets. Five Russians who are allegedly mobsters but are probably innocent businessmen just engaging in legitimate trucking and associated commerce."

Tanner looked over at Baby. "Baby, how good is your Russian?"

Baby looked indignant. "As fluent as my grandmother's, born in Minsk," she said, sparks shooting from her eyes.

Tanner smiled. "What's your real name?"

"Real name? Baby," Baby said, confused.

"I mean on your birth certificate. What did you mother name you?"

Baby looked down. "Angela," she said, sounding apologetic.

"That's a pretty name."

Tanner turned back to the phone and Hope felt a throbbing pulse in her temple. She'd been *glad* to see Tanner? She'd been *worried* when he walked into a room full of Russian gangsters? Now it was all, *just a minute, Pumpkin,* and *I'll be right with you, Sweetie*, like she was one of her mother's regulars at the Bluebell Café. And *Baby!* Was Tanner forever planning to flirt with her friend? She was *so done* with this. Him and his lying, cheating ways.

Tanner had turned back to the phone. "Jack? About the Russian mobsters. Their English is pretty good, but I'm sending you a translator, just in case they need help with procedure." He paused for a second while Jack talked.

"No, trust me. This translator is good. Her name is Angela. You'll like her."

Tanner paused. Then he grinned.

"Don't thank me. I'm always happy to help." He folded up the phone and dropped it in his pocket.

"Baby, I just got you a paying gig translating Russian for my friend, Jack Sievers. You'll need to get over to the FBI building right away. Look for the guy with the briefcase."

"You got me a job? *Really?* I've never had a job," Baby said.

"It's a week for firsts," Tanner said. "The job's not much, but I think you might have fun with it. Jack sure will, and he's a guy who needs more fun."

"Well, Big Julie's gone, so I gotta do something," Baby said and picked up her purse. "And now's as good a time as any to figure it out." She grinned at them as she headed for the door.

Chapter 31

Tanner watched Hope while Baby's heels clacked against the tile floor and the outer door opened and then clicked shut. Hope was scowling at him, her eyebrows furrowed across her forehead, her blue eyes, the color of ice, narrowed to slits. She crossed her arms over her chest.

Not good.

"Alone at last," he tried.

Her mouth thinned.

"I missed you," he tried again. "While I was gone."

She crossed her legs.

"We have a date tonight, don't we? I've been looking forward to seeing you. Is something wrong?"

She uncoiled from the chair, uncrossing her legs and unfolding her arms, and paced to the other end of the room.

"Is something wrong? Is something *wrong?* What *isn't* wrong?" She put her hands on her hips and glared at him.

Tanner decided to go for innocence. "You mean the card game? Pumpkin—"

"Yes, the card game! The *cheating,* Tanner! And losing the ranch! Everything I worked for! Our lives are wrapped up in that ranch. And knowing that, even though I asked you not to, you stole it anyway!"

"You didn't lose the ranch," Tanner said. "You got the ranch back. I'm sorry I had to play like that. The FBI made me. It was that or twenty years in prison."

Hope rolled her eyes. "The FBI made you? Well, that's an original excuse, at least."

"Even better, it's true." Tanner frowned. Didn't she hear what he'd just said?

"You *cheated*, Tanner! I was there, remember? We played Big Julie, you cheated, what a surprise, poof! Ranch is gone." She paused. "What do you mean, it was that or twenty years in prison? What *about* the FBI?"

"What do you mean, 'I cheated, what a surprise?'" He felt a spurt of anger.

Hope backed down, resignation replacing most of the fury in her voice.

"You're a con artist, Tanner. I googled you. You cheated twenty years ago, and you cheated last Saturday in the game with Big Julie. I don't know who you hurt twenty years ago, but last Saturday you hurt me and my family, and we're not coming back from that too well."

Tanner shook his head in frustration. "I got twenty years' probation for conning that million when I was a stupid kid," he said, raking his hands through his hair. "That's how you knew my name when we were introduced, right? It was big news at the time."

Hope nodded.

"I'm *still* on probation for that stupid crime," Tanner said. "I've got eight more months to go. I have to help the FBI with whatever gambling sting they put me on, and they put me on Big Julie. They're trying to get him on a tax racket. I had to make sure he won, and then they arrested him. If I hadn't helped them, I would have gone to prison for twenty years."

Hope eyed him with hostility. "Poor Big Julie. Isn't that entrapment, or something?"

"Poor *Big Julie?* What about me? Anyway, I'm sure Big Julie's got good lawyers. Of course, I do, too, that's why I'm not in jail, either."

He watched with cautious optimism as Hope dropped into

the sofa and put her head back against the cushions.

"Well. I guess that explains why you stole the ranch. You did what you had to do. But now the ranch is gone. My family's uprooted. And—well, I haven't changed my mind. I'm not seeing you anymore."

Tanner's heart plummeted. She understood about the probation, but she wouldn't see him anyway? She didn't love him at all? She didn't even like him? Everything was truly over?

He couldn't accept that. He didn't believe for a minute that Hope didn't feel something for him.

If she didn't, she'd have ratted him out to Big Julie.

"Why won't you see me? You have to know that I haven't cheated in a card game in twenty years, until the game with Big Julie. Ask anybody. Ask Troy if I've let her down—well, except about the terrarium. Don't ask her about the terrarium. I did let her down a little bit about that. But that's the only thing."

"What?" Hope asked, looking confused.

Tanner plunged on. He had to make her understand. "And your family isn't uprooted, Hope. That's what I'm trying to tell you. Suzanne owns the ranch now."

Hope frowned. "What are you talking about? I was there, remember? *Big Julie* owns it."

"Big Julie *doesn't* own it. I've been trying to tell you. Your mom owns it. Jack sent her a letter telling her. You didn't get the letter?"

Hope remembered the letter from Mecklenburg and Sievers addressed to her mother that even now was lying in her bag. She picked up her bag and pulled out the letter, scrutinizing the return address.

She looked up. "This is just another of your tricks."

"I don't have any tricks. Call Jack if you don't believe me."

She fished her cell phone out of her bag, dialed, and was put through to Jack.

"Hope, you are a difficult person to reach," he said. "Did you get my letter?"

"I have a letter from Mecklenburg and Sievers, but it's addressed to my mom and she's not here. I want to confirm what's in it. Can you tell me?"

"I don't see why not. Your mother owns the ranch free and clear. Derek sold it to her for a dollar. I'm—"

Hope blinked. "Wait a second. *Derek* sold it to my mom for a dollar? That's not possible."

"Sure it is. I've got the paperwork right here. And believe me, a lawyer is never wrong about paperwork."

"How did Derek get the ranch? Just two days ago it was Big Julie's."

"Well, after that it was Derek's," Jack said firmly. "The lead abatement report isn't in yet, and we have some other conveyances to file, but I think everything should be wrapped up by tomorrow."

"Lead abatement," Hope said, remembering Bob. "Were those the guys who came out on Monday?"

"They were."

"I'm glad I gave them coffee, then."

Jack laughed. "Do you have any other questions?"

"Well, of course I do, Jack. How did Derek get the ranch?"

"It reverted to the original owner, according to federal forfeiture law, after Big Julie was arrested during the card game. That was Derek McNaughton. And Derek sold it to Suzanne, through me, for a dollar."

"Why did he do that?"

"He realized that he hasn't treated your family fairly for the last seventeen years, and to make up for not paying alimony, child support, and other court-ordered expenses, he decided to sell you the ranch. He's doing the right thing here."

"And yet, everything sounds so wrong. When did Mom give you a dollar?"

"Actually, she gave me two dollars. One dollar went to

Derek for the ranch and one went to me, to retain my services."

Hope paused to think. Jack's story was too glib and his voice was too smooth. She knew she was missing something. She just didn't see what.

"So Jack, tell me. How did you get mixed up in this?"

Jack cleared his throat. "Maybe you want to talk to Tanner about that."

"Maybe I want to talk to you. Are you the family lawyer, or not? We can fire you, you know."

"Oh, no, don't do that. You're my most lucrative clients."

Hope laughed. "Oh, good, we've retained a snotty lawyer. Send us a bill. If we have a two-million dollar ranch now, we can afford to pay it. I just want to know how we got here."

Jack voice sounded amused. "Give it up, Hope. You want to find out what happened, talk to Tanner. I'm his lawyer, too. I can't reveal any confidences."

"I knew it! You guys did something."

"The dollar that your mother gave me three days ago for legal fees is now earning me about ten cents an hour. Gotta go, Hope. My *pro bono* cases make me richer than you guys."

"But Jack—"

"The letter says that Suzanne owns the ranch. Talk to Tanner. Heaven knows he's been trying to talk to you."

Hope closed the phone and dropped it into her purse before she turned back to Tanner, a puzzled look on her face.

"Mom owns the ranch," she said, sounding stunned. "Evidently, we don't have to move after all."

"Told you," he said, stepping closer. "Hope—"

"Stop right there," she said, cutting him off. "Thank you for getting the ranch back. I don't know how you did it, but I appreciate it. Very much. Don't think that I don't. But that doesn't change anything, Tanner. You're still who you are and I'm who I am and that's oil and water. And I'm still mad at you."

"You're *still* mad?" Tanner looked incredulous. "What

about?"

"Well, there's the ranch. Okay, we got it back, but you *stole* it! By *cheating!* And you've always been a cheater. And cheaters never change. I learned that from the best. Look at Derek! You're just like him. You take risks. You court danger. You come strolling in here, looking to get killed! Those Russians had *guns!* What were you *thinking?*"

Tanner started to feel optimistic again, even though Hope seemed to be just getting warmed up.

"And all that *just-a-minute-Pumpkin,* and the *I'll-be-right-with-you-Sweetie* garbage!" Hope said, sounding exasperated. "Who do you think you're talking to? You think I'm a *toy* for your convenience and I just keep smiling while you pull all the strings? You're manipulative and a con artist and a crook and you don't fool me for one minute! You'll never stop flirting with Baby, and yes, I'm still mad at you!"

She did look really upset. Her eyes glistened and her chin trembled and he thought she was the bravest, smartest, most wonderful person he'd ever met.

He took a step closer and felt his heart swell and grow tender as he looked at her. He was helpless with desire and need and he realized as surely as he stood there in the suite that he felt something for Hope that he'd never felt for any other woman.

"Hope," he said. "I love you."

The churning anxiety, fear, rage, and hurt that Hope had been feeling for four long days and especially the last hour all shrieked to a halt, poised quivering to resume their mad rush through her heart but waiting for a signal to go.

"What?" Hope asked, wondering if she'd heard him right.

Tanner took another step closer.

"I love you. I know we haven't known each other very long, but I can't help it. I want to be with you, I want to marry you. I'll wait if you're not sure. But I'm sure."

Hope's emotions still quivered on the brink. *What?* He *loved* her? He wanted to *marry* her? She wasn't sure she could even *speak* to him again, and he was talking about *marriage?* This conversation was moving *way* too fast, and in a direction she hadn't anticipated.

"I'm so sorry about the ranch, I'm sorry about everything. You've had a really rough couple of weeks, but I'll make it up to you."

Hope watched him take another step closer. *One more step and he'll kiss you, and then you'll forget everything that made you mad.*

Suddenly that didn't seem like such a bad thing.

Tanner stepped closer and picked up her hand, lacing his fingers between hers. Her heart kicked up a notch.

"Are we square, Hope? Can I do something else to make everything right? Because this really is all for nothing if I'm not square with you."

Hope rubbed her forehead. She felt unstrung. All her life—or at least since Derek left them—she'd made plans. She thought things through, made plans, and carried them out. She knew what she thought about things. Knew what would happen if she broke her rules.

Chaos. Heartbreak.

That's what would happen if she lost her discipline.

Now, it turned out, she hadn't known anything after all. She'd lost control of events, and yet the worst *hadn't* happened. She'd gotten involved with a card player, and she was still in one piece. Tanner hadn't ripped her off. Somehow, the ranch was theirs. Tanner had made that happen. She didn't know how, but he had.

She felt her defenses crumbling. She remembered how just a few minutes ago she thought that if she survived being held hostage by the Russians she'd tell Tanner she wanted to take a risk with him.

What kind of risk was it? Getting involved with a card

player seemed like a huge leap of faith to her, but Tanner hadn't let his daughter down. Except evidently, about the terrarium—whatever that was about. But he'd raised Troy by himself and done a great job from what she could tell.

"We're *not* square," she said, but with less energy, her heart thundering in her chest. "I don't know anything! About you, or what happened, or *anything.*"

"You're unsure, I understand that," Tanner said. "And I upset your world view. But you can count on me. I'll never let you down. I'll tell you everything you want to know. Ask me anything you want. We have all the time in the world. We can go slow."

He raised her hand, his fingers still interlaced with hers, and kissed her palm. The gesture, so gentle, so tentative, made Hope's heart lurch and her breath catch in her throat.

"Well, okay," she said, "but we don't have to go *that* slow."

Special Agent Roy Frelly of the FBI was standing near the elevators that led to the suites, doing his job, when Tanner Wingate and that blonde stepped out of the elevator. They looked as happy as pigs at a corn roast. Wingate's arm was around the blonde's shoulders, and they were gazing at each other with goofy smiles on their faces as they headed for the exit.

Special Agent Frelly was a little disappointed that in the last week before his well-earned retirement, he'd been unable to command the SWAT troops to bring down the Russian mobsters. Still, they'd made a routine arrest, which should earn him a bonus or at least a citation, and that alone could command very high fees in private security work if he chose to pursue that post-retirement option.

He turned in satisfaction to the new guy he was showing around, another troublemaker, who would replace Wingate as a security advisor when they cut Wingate loose. The new guy was staring after the couple with a look of yearning on his face.

"She's just as beautiful as her mother was at that age," Derek McNaughton said.

"You each get a phone call," the FBI clerk said to the five alleged Russian mobsters. The Russians, Jack Sievers, and Baby all gathered in the federal detention center for the Russians' processing.

"I want to call my wife," Johnny Red said.

"I want to call my lawyer," Yakov said.

"I want to call my broker," Markov said.

"You have a *broker?*" Johnny Red asked.

"I wand do gall by docdor," Igor said through his broken teeth.

"I want to call Esperanza," Alexei said.

Four sets of eyes swiveled to look at him.

"The maid." Alexei blushed. "Remember? The one who helped us with Big Julie. We have a date tonight. I'll have to cancel."

"I might be able to get you out of here in time," Jack said.

"Angela—" Jack said. "Can you work late tonight?" He stuffed a sheaf of papers into his briefcase and glanced up at the distracting blonde vision who sat next to him on the plastic chairs in the FBI building. Every time he looked at her, he felt dizzy.

"Call me Baby," Baby said. "Everybody does."

"Baby." Jack tested the name. "How about if I just call you that in private?"

Baby tilted her head at him, speculating. "In private?"

Jack nodded. "Over dinner? To discuss the case."

Baby smiled fondly at the lawyer next to her. Tanner was right. Jack Sievers did need to have more fun.

"A girl has to eat," she agreed. "Do we have to discuss the case?"

Big Julie asked for a second brandy Manhattan from the

flight attendant, and when she brought it, he tasted it with deep satisfaction. Everything was gonna turn out all right. The only bad thing was that he'd had to cut Baby loose. He'd miss her, but Marilyn put her foot down, and with her father's health still good, well—. If Big Julie knew anything, it was when to fold a hand that couldn't win.

On the upside, the Russians had been arrested, so that was the first thing. He and Marilyn were flying first class back to New Jersey where, Big Julie was confident, his lawyers could straighten everything out. They were already working on it. His people were talking to their people, and of course, he'd have to pay off some people. But the lawyers said that if he just paid the back taxes and the fines—and maybe some rather large *gratuities*—he could stay out of the slammer. So that was the second thing.

But that led to the third thing.

"This is gonna tie up our cash for a while," he told Marilyn, who sat on the window side.

"I know," Marilyn said. She turned from the window and smiled at him serenely.

"That means we're gonna hafta tighten the belt," Big Julie said. "I'm sorry, honey, but—"

"It's all right," Marilyn said, patting his knee. "I'll give up the gym membership. I know other—*better*—ways to exercise."

The next day Hope and Faith threw a lunch party at the ranch. Kenji cooked, with help from Faith, Suzanne, who'd taken the day off from the Bluebell Café, and a one-handed Amber. Hope showed Tanner, Jack, and Baby around the ranch while the others fixed lunch, and by the time the uncles drove up in a shiny rental minivan, everyone was hungry.

They sat outdoors on picnic tables stretched end to end across the shaded patio. Marty focused on smothering his chili with cheese, chopped onions, and sour cream before he turned to Suzanne.

"Now that you own the ranch free and clear," he asked,

"what are you planning to do?"

"Do?" Suzanne asked, puzzled. She spread some butter on her cornbread muffin and took a satisfied bite.

"You could retire," he said. "For example."

"Enjoy the fruits of your labors," Weary Blastell said, helping himself to salad.

"Play a little poker," Pete Wysniewski said, tasting his beer.

"Go out line dancing," Isaiah Rush said.

"Bing, bing, bing!" Sharp Eddie said.

"Pursue the leisured pastimes to which you are entitled and have long necessarily denied yourself," Jim Thickpenny said.

"I couldn't retire," she said, shaking her head. "We still need income. I still have expenses."

"You could make plans," Jack said.

"What kind of plans?" Suzanne asked.

Jack shrugged. "Big Julie's buyer wanted to put a destination resort on your property. If they could do it, you could do it. If you wanted to."

There was a moment of stunned silence.

"Oh, I don't see how we could," Suzanne said.

"It would take capital investment," Hope said thoughtfully.

"Could we have an organic restaurant?" Faith asked Kenji.

"It would be fun!" Amber said.

"We know some investors," Marty said.

Hope turned to him doubtfully.

"*Legitimate* investors," Marty said, without heat.

"On that note, I have something for Suzanne," Jack said. He opened his briefcase and took out a large, fat, cream-colored envelope with an embossed return address.

"A copy of the deed," Jack said. "For your files."

A letter from a law firm, Hope thought. *A good one.*

"Oh, thank you," Suzanne said. "Everybody. Really. I never thought—everybody did so much. We can never repay you."

"You call us when you're in trouble," Marty said. "That's

what family is for."

"You always got our markers," Sharp Eddie agreed.

Shortly after that, the party broke up. Kenji drove back to work. The uncles left in their minivan to go to the airport, promising to come back to Vegas for next month's big Hold 'em tournament. Amber, Faith, and Suzanne went inside to research desert resorts with organic restaurants on the Internet.

"I brought you a present from LA," Tanner said to Hope when everyone had disappeared. "In all the excitement yesterday, I forgot to give it to you."

"A present?" Hope asked. "What is it?"

Tanner sat down on the porch swing and, reaching for her hand, tugged her down with him. He took a long, narrow box from his pocket and handed it to her.

Hope opened it. A chunky silver charm bracelet lay on a bed of white cotton.

"Oh," she breathed. "It's beautiful." She took it out to look at it more closely.

"It's personalized," Tanner said. "For when you play cards."

Hope dropped her hands in her lap and turned to him, resolution in her eyes.

"I can't play cards anymore," she said. "I realized—"

"What?" Tanner asked, confused. "Why not?"

"I was turning into Derek," Hope said. "And I won't be like him."

Tanner stared at her in astonishment.

"How are you like Derek?" he asked. "You're not like Derek. What do you want to do right this minute?"

"Right now?" Hope asked, her turn to feel confused. "Sit here. Talk to you. Watch the sun go down. Maybe go for a ride. What do you mean?"

"Do you want to go to a casino and play cards?"

"Well, not right now. But—"

"So you're not addicted to playing cards, like Derek. Do you feel like abandoning your family?"

Hope rolled her eyes. "Well, no, but—"

"Stealing Amber's share of the cookbook advance?"

Hope looked shocked. "Of course not!"

"Okay. You're not like Derek, and you won't turn into Derek if you enjoy playing cards, Hope. You could be professional, if you want to. You're good enough. You're better than I am probably, although it kills me to say so. Playing cards well doesn't turn you into Derek. Lots of card players are honest, upright, fun-loving people." He pointed his finger to his chest.

Hope laughed. "Well, I'm not sure—"

"I am," Tanner interrupted. "Trust me. You can have fun in a card room and not be a jerk or an addict. And—*when* you decide to play cards again—the bracelet might help keep you focused on the game."

Hope looked into his eyes, warm with love and confidence. She felt something in her heart soften and melt. When she looked in his eyes, she felt his confidence reflected back in her. Felt her old fears dissipate.

"I won't let you down," Tanner said softly, tucking a strand of her hair behind her ear. "I'd never let you turn into Derek. I mean, *eeeew*."

Hope laughed, a deep, full-throated laugh, letting her head drop back on his shoulder.

Tanner put his arm around her and pulled her tight.

"So, look at your bracelet. For when you play cards, or even when we go out on a date."

Hope turned and kissed him lightly on the cheek.

"Thank you for a beautiful bracelet," she said. Then she held it up to look at it more closely.

"What—that's a pumpkin!" She fingered the small charm. "Tanner! What if someone figures out—" She looked at him, laughing but pleased and a little embarrassed, too. "But it's *fantastic*. So much detail."

"I thought it was you." Tanner grinned at her.

"Who ever thought I'd be a pumpkin?" Hope asked, as she examined the next charm. "What's this one? It looks like a potato."

"It *is* a potato. I couldn't get a bowl of potato salad. Of course you don't need fake potato salad, because you have me. This is just a reminder."

Hope felt herself turn pink, but she shook her head in mock resignation. "You are very bad," she said.

"What? I make *great* potato salad," Tanner said.

"It's not polite to brag about your potato salad," Hope said primly, but she was laughing again. "And this is a vase. Don't tell me. A Ming vase."

Tanner grinned. "They didn't have a Park Ranger, either," he said. "Crummy jewelry stores."

"And this last one is—a pair of handcuffs?" Hope blushed even pinker.

Tanner leaned over and kissed her.

"So that when I'm bad you can punish me," he said.

"You seem to be bad most of the time," she said, trying to keep her voice stern, but that was hard when someone had their arms around you and was nibbling your ear in a most distracting way.

Tanner leaned back and stroked her face, his hand so gentle on her cheek that she shivered, his eyes so alive with love and heat and pride that she thought she'd fall into them just to steady herself.

"If anyone can reform me, I bet you can," he said. "But it's a big project. What are the odds?"

"Not good." She shook her head in mock resignation. "It would take a long time. Maybe a lifetime. And we'd have to get started right away."

"A lifetime," Tanner said, pretending to think about it. He nodded. "Well, I'll take that risk. I'll go all in. If you will."

Hope smiled, her heart full. "You bet I will."

ABOUT THE AUTHOR

Kay Keppler was born and raised in Wisconsin and now makes her home in northern California, where she lives in a drafty old house with a wonderful fireplace. In addition to fiction, she writes regularly for the *Writers Fun Zone* web site and other popular and scholarly publications.